C000163204

HECTOR DRUMMOND

The Biscuit Factory Vol I: Days Of Wine And Cheese

CantusHead Books

Published by CantusHead Books

ISBN: 978-1-9999907-2-5

Cover design by Caradoc Moore

hectordrummond.com

2000-01
Semester 1

2000-01
Semester 1
Week 3
Tuesday

Ren Christopher, a new member of the Philosophy department at Grayvington University, gradually becomes aware of the glare directed at him by Millicent Bartonella, herself a new member of the English department. He glares back at her, as if to say, 'I am aware of your glare. Your glare has been noted. It has also been assessed, and found wanting.'

Millicent turns her glare instead to Miles Honeywell, Ren's new buddy from Psychology, who returns fire, so Millicent looks down her long nose at him. Millicent's new colleague Lenora Helminth, whose mouth corners haven't turned upwards in a long time, decides to help her out with a disapproving look at Ren and Miles. Lenora is good at disapproving looks because as a budding sociologist she does them a lot. After she passed her PhD *viva voce* examination at Lancaster her external examiner remarked to the internal examiner on the quality of her facial expressions, which had succeeded in making him feel that the questions he was asking her were the very essence of stupidity. (Which they were, although not for the reasons Lenora thought.)

Ren, however, is not fazed by Lenora's attempt at browbeating by eyebrow. Glare at me all you like, he thinks, I'm not backing down. Didn't anyone tell you that disapproving scowls don't work on philosophers? Try some arguments instead.

Lily Richmond from Economics, a resolute young women who isn't going to let two creeps from English and Sociology stare down her fellow group members, curls her lip at Lenora and her group. Adrian Vespula from Law, a more conciliatory character who is already attempting to establish himself as a well-known wit, tries to smile back and twinkle his eyes, as if that produces magic dust that floats him up above the fray. Which, despite his rat-like features, it does, and so Lily's lip-curl passes instead to Malcom Ascaris from Politics, the fourth member of the other group.

Ascaris, a bearded and bespectacled man with a facial expression of eternal righteous fury, is sure his group, The Panopticon, is in the right, but is somewhat less confident of the arguments being produced by his fellow group members in the face of the onslaught produced by The Fabulous Lorenzos, and so he chooses to look sternly instead at the baby-faced physicist, Douglas Oram, who seems a less belligerent character than the other three.

The course director, Creighton Balderstone, a largish red-haired man with fleshy lips, like L. Ron Hubbard with a beard, pitches in, to Ascaris' relief, because Balderstone is of course on their side. Although Ascaris can't help noticing that Balderstone, who initially struck him in their first class last week as intelligent and knowledgeable, comes across as rather more foolish today when up against The Fabulous Lorenzo's assailment.

The Lorenzos are exasperated with the bear-like course director, who seems to them an unhappy, overweight blusterer with a barely disguised fear that his course and his career are about to come rightfully crashing down around his ears. (Ren can't help picturing him with a Navy cap, like Hubbard used to wear. Perhaps he'll mail him one.) Balderstone had instructed the groups to do a project each, from a list of topics concerning teaching that he had put together. Each group was to choose one of the topics and gather together some relevant data by either collecting some data themselves, or finding some previous research. The Lorenzos had chosen the topic 'Gender discrimination in teaching' – the other topics were no better – and had presented some thorough studies of UK high school teaching which showed that modern high school teachers were spending more time paying attention to the girls in their class than the boys. Miles, who as a psychologist knows a lot about real research into educational practises, knew where to find this material. They had expected that this research would merely be the starting-point for some healthy debate; it's not supposed to be the final word on anything. But Balderstone and the four Panopticon clowns have been outraged far beyond what the Lorenzos had expected.

What they are outraged about, it turns out, isn't just that this research supports conclusions that the Panopticons think just have to be lies. They are also angry that the Lorenzos have resorted to using empirical evidence. Empirical evidence, according to Millicent Bartonella, is a grand narrative, and like all grand narratives it exits to promote a point of view, which is not necessarily more valid than other points of view. Empirical evidence, according to Malcom Ascaris, who Ren has dubbed 'Voroshilov', is a tool of oppression, being used in this case to suppress women. Lenora Helminth said that all scientific data is just a construct of its cultural context and should be treated like any other cultural pronouncement. Adrian Vespula, who considers his views more nuanced and less nakedly relativistic than his dogmatic colleagues, said that the underlying power structures at work here should make us sceptical of any such research.

Vespula is definitely Beria, Ren thought. He even looks like Beria. The same rodent-type features. And, unlike the other three, he's not a true believer. He's spouting the official jargon in order to look after number one, much like the NKVD man had.

The argument has at this point turned back onto the presentation the Panopticons made earlier. Ren is already struggling to remember what exactly it was that the Panops had said. That lot had also chosen 'Gender discrimination in teaching' as their topic, but their presentation definitely veered more towards the jumbled-stream-of-consciousness-using-plenty-of-the-latest-Sociology-buzzwords side of things. Clear presentation of real data: not so much. The Panopticons' idea of gathering relevant 'data' was just to write what they felt, in the latest postmodern style, with the occasional handwaving quote from a Continental luminary as a supposed back-up. But this did seem to be what the course director meant by gathering data. Everything seemed to come back to what he called 'critical reflection', which so far had involved plenty of reflection, in the sense of reflecting back Balderstone's own views, but not much in the way of criticism.

The Panopticons had talked about 'hegemonic practises' (a term not clearly explained), and 'normative culture' (also not clearly explained) and 'exclusive cleavances' (not explained even one little bit). Academics and teachers operate uncritically from within ideological frameworks, and these must be constantly challenged with reference to equality and disability issues. At least, that is the best Ren can come up with a translation of what the Panops said. A less charitable interpretation might read, 'Translation unavailable'. Or 'Input empty of coherent content'. Lenora had gone on about 'othering' and 'normatising' – or is it 'normalizing'? – and sometimes even 'alienation', though Ren got the sense that that word had to be carefully handled now that it's getting a bit out of date.

Ren is acquainted with this sort of stuff from his days as a Philosophy graduate student. The others in his group have had much less experience of it, and are shell-shocked. Especially Douglas, the physicist, who is completely gobsmacked. A young man greatly sympathetic to the arts, he had assumed that the attacks that had been made on the Humanities and Social Sciences in recent years had been greatly overblown and exaggerated. Now he is seeing first-hand that those attacks had, if anything, understated the situation. Here's the latest generation of English, Law, Social

Science and Politics academics, and they're repeating almost meaningless catechisms, and refusing to engage in anything that could be called critical discussion.

'What exactly are "inclusive practises"?' Ren had asked at one point.

'Creating neutral spaces where students can interact with diversity', says Lenora Helminth, or, to give her her Ren-name, 'Vyshinsky'.

'What does "interact with diversity" mean?' says Miles.

'We acknowledge difference,' says Millicent. 'We accept difference.'

Ren hadn't been sure who to name Millicent after, but he had eventually decided on Krylenko.

'We avoid otherness to create agencies of interactions that transcend normative culture,' says Lenora.

'What does that mean in practise?' asks Lily.

'I think it means they put playpens in the classroom,' Ren says.

At this Balderstone, as course director, interjects. 'This is the sort of thing that is being critiqued,' he says. 'You need to change your attitude if you want to pass this course.' Balderstone looks daggers at Ren. 'And if you don't pass this course then you don't get through your probation.'

Ren knows what that means. Probation is the initial three-year period that all new lecturers have to navigate before their positions are made permanent. If you don't get through that then you're out. And the University of Grayvington had recently made it a condition of probation that all new lecturers complete the new Teaching in Tertiary Education (TITE) course that has been developed at Grayvington, and which according to rumour the University is hoping will be exported to other Universities, although clearly that isn't going to happen, because why would any other University bother to buy in a load of old cobblers when it's so easy to make your own?

Ren decides to shut up for a while, but Miles persists. 'Are you telling me, as an empirical scientist who is familiar with the latest research in teaching practise, and who will be telling his students how to do and apply empirical research, some of it in this very area, that I'm supposed to learn how best to teach my subject by ignoring, by actively rejecting, that empirical research?'

'We can't tell you what content you can teach in your lectures,' says Balderstone. 'They're your lectures, so that's your business. But these are our lectures, and this is our business. You have to do what's required here just as your students will have to do what you require of them.'

'So I've been hired by this University as a psychologist, and they're requiring me to undertake training which goes completely against what they've hired me to teach and research?'

Ren can see that Balderstone, under his tone of attempted reasonableness, is pretty pissed off. The Lorenzos are directly challenging his whole course, and undermining his credibility, but if he backs down too much his authority will be shot.

'If you can approach this course in the right spirit you will learn something, and improve your teaching,' he says through gritted teeth, like a PE teacher talking to a rebellious student who doesn't want to do the cross-country running, but who can't be punched in the stomach. 'If you can't approach it in the right spirit you will be deemed to have failed the Critical Reflection component of the course, and if you fail that section you cannot pass overall.'

'How are we supposed to pass this course then?' asks Lily. 'I mean, what do you expect us to do? We took the topic, and gave it some critical reflection. Quality critical reflection,' she said, eyeing the Panopticons defiantly.

'That's not the sort of critical reflection we're looking for,' says Balderstone.

'So what are you looking for?' says Douglas. 'Because I have no idea.'

'He wants the sort of thing that that lot produced,' says Ren sourly, nodding towards the Panopticons. 'Correct?'

'More or less, yes.'

'So you need to be a Continentalist, or a postmodernist, to pass this course,' says Ren, making a statement rather than a question.

Balderstone glares at him, trying to think of a reply that neither confirms nor denies this. But Douglas, who isn't spoiling for a fight like Ren is, just wants to get this course over and done with, so he asks, 'Could you perhaps recommend some readings we could do to help us get an idea of what you're looking for? I notice you haven't set any readings for this course, and that makes it a bit difficult for those us from a non-Humanities background.'

'Well, I was expecting you, as academics, to be able to cope with this section of the course without needing readings, but perhaps in view of the difficulties you're having I'll get some recommended readings set for you.'

Ren reads this as, 'Seeing as you're making so much trouble for me I'd better throw you a bone.

'That would be most useful, thanks,' beams Douglas.

Ren groans. He knows the sort of thing Balderstone will set. Foucault. Derrida. Judith Butler. And worse.

Before they can get out of the class they are forced to listen to another group, who have christened themselves 'Wetlands', a name which pretty much sums them up. Ren had noticed how quiet they had stayed during the previous discussions. They are led by a nervous, milky geographer called Desmond Sproule, who is already growing a beard, a botanist who is growing an even worse beard, and two others whose department Ren doesn't know. Their topic is 'Diversity Issues in Higher Education' – all the topics are the same, really – and they say (or rather the geographer says; the others are virtually mute) much the same as the Panopticons, only with less assurance, and with more obvious crawling to Balderstone.

Ren concentrates on comparing the two bewhiskered Wetlanders. The geographer's beard disconcerts him, as it is clearly growing into the standard issue geography teacher beard. He had assumed that regulation false beards were issued to all geographers upon graduation, to be firmly attached as soon as a Geography-related position was obtained, but here is Sproule, clearly halfway through the growing of such a beard, and it's one hundred per cent non-artificial. Ren's thesis has been shot down like an intelligent design advocate who holds that there can be no halfway house with the eye, but who's just been presented with a primitive eye, lacking the refinements of the modern eye, but which clearly functions as a rudimentary but effective light-detecting organ. Ren starts to compose in his head a suitable letter to *Nature* announcing his discoveries within the beard-Geography nexus.

The botanist's mycoid undertaking, on the other hand, looks like a fungal growth of a type which could probably be found on the cover of one of his own textbooks. Are academics starting to look like their books, like dog owners are reputed to look like their dogs? Perhaps this fungus is one that the botanist himself has discovered and written about in his PhD thesis, and his beard is a celebration of his discovery. That made sense, in so far as it isn't much of a celebration of the art of beard-growing.

Finally one of the other members of the Wetlands, a woman who looks like she's angry about not being able to grow a beard, and not just in the abstract sense, says something, although it seems to be the same as what Sproule has just said, only with the words re-arranged. But then that could also be said of the Wetlands' whole talk vis-a-vis the Panopticon's talk.

Ren looks at his watch, and sighs. It isn't just this class, as bad as it is. He just doesn't like sitting in lectures any more in general. He's had years and years of sitting in lectures, listening away until his ears bled, and he's had enough. Maybe in ten years time he'll enjoy it again, but dammit, he's got his PhD, and one of the rewards of that is supposed to be that he doesn't have to go to lectures or sit exams any more, especially ones that involve so many lanuginous lefties. It should be inscribed on PhD testamurs in gold: 'Excused from having to go lectures for all eternity.' Well, except for departmental seminars, conferences, and talks he wants to go, obviously. But no more classes. He feels cheated. He can't even pass the time looking at the hot women and fantasising about them, because there are none, apart from the beautiful economist Lily who is unfortunately out of sight behind him. The only useful thing about this class is that it's giving him an insight, albeit a depressing one, into the tactics the Continentalist left are currently using.

The length of the previous discussions means that there's no time for discussion after the Wetlands' presentation, to everyone's relief, except for Lenora the sociologist and Malcom from Politics, who give the impression that they're still itching to play Thor and slam down their hammers.

'The start of my career and I'm already just ticking boxes and trying not to make waves,' mutters Ren as everyone troupes out.

'The sea around you looks pretty choppy to me,' says Lily.

2000-01
Semester 1
Week 3
Friday

The Lorenzos stumble out of the Psychology building in the late afternoon, after finishing a fairly fruitless session trying to work on their TITE group project, due at the end of the semester. They blink in the bright sun, which has just come out, and Ren suggests they go to the student bar.

'We need a drink after that session,' he says, although mainly he just wants to gaze at Lily some more. We are privileged to have such a prominent member of the gourgeoisie in our ranks, he thinks, although he uneasily notes that many females would also consider Miles to be a member as well.

They sit on the lawn in front of the bar. This is one of the few bits of grass left on Greenwood Glade (which is what the main campus is called). Sitting out here is vastly preferable to sitting inside the bar, which is a windowless, airless, black-painted dungeon, full of undergraduates, and inevitably fogged with smoke. Even the smoke can't quite disguise the smell of mould that inheres in the walls.

The Lorenzos are feeling good because it's sunny, and it's the end of the week, although it's not the end of the week really, as they'll all be working over the weekend, but it feels like the end of the week. They're all still getting used to this concept of the 'working week' after their years as grad students. Especially Ren, who used to get drunk on any night of the week he felt like, who'd sleep in for as long as he wanted, and who sometimes lost track of what day it was. Life as a grad student is a privileged one, he thinks. At least it is if you're smart and in the Humanities. It's not so

12

good if you're a plodder in the Sciences.

The other three are happy to have put their grad student days behind them, to be on the next rung of their academic ascent, and to have some money and respectability and kudos. They gladly accept the loss of freedom, and the shouldering of responsibilities, that goes with all that. Ren doesn't. He doesn't really want to be an academic. It's just that he'd rather die than get a normal job. He has plenty of philosophical ideas, though, and he wants to get them out of his system. He plans to do that, and in the meantime line up something more interesting and glamorous. He doesn't have much of an idea of what, but he's sure something better will turn up.

They're all feeling relaxed, when Lily takes her top off, and she's just wearing a singlet, not too tight, but tight enough, and then it's like they all get tractor-beamed up by this fabulous sun to some empyrean realm. Then she rubs it in further by letting her hair down. It's not so much that she's more beautiful doing that than she was before, it's just that the sense of her loosening up draws them further into her aura. She holds up her glass of white wine and it's like it has waterproof LEDs inside it, and the glow reflects onto her lovely, amused face. The boys, the overgrown boys who all fancy her, are sucked in by the vacuum cleaner of love, suddenly yanked over the threshold that separates fancying and love. Or perhaps it's just the line between fancying and infatuation. They're grabbed by giants from behind and thrown through the air so that their stomachs feel funny. Do I know any giants, Ren thinks? Well, there are the giants of my field, Plato, Locke, Kant... no, more likely to be a modern giant. Rudolph Carnap perhaps. Rudolph Carnap is throwing him around, like a dwarf he has torn off his shoulders. 'You feel dis in groinal tubes, ja, shortzen stuff?'

Ren knows what the others are feeling. He can sense the sap rising all around. He can think of nothing worthwhile to say. Not that that ever stopped him before. But now it does. At least don't say anything stupid. They're all just sitting there, sitting slack-jawed, staring at the smiling Lily. Ren's tongue dries up, literally. He's got the Saharas in advance of his hangover. Going through the hangover process in reverse would be interesting, he thinks. You'd feel a bit shagged out two days before your binge is due. Then the next day you'd start out pretty tired and listless, and you'd feel worse and worse as the day wears on. You'd maybe start vomiting, if you're the vomity type, and a mega-headache would increasingly impose itself upon you until you can take no more and you have to go bed and sleep it off. You can at least sleep; in fact, you're incapable of being awoken during the night, until you suddenly wake up next morning completely crazy. You jump out of bed, stumble downstairs dangerously, and then you start weaving all over the kitchen, knocking things over while you stuff yourself with snacks while singing away to yourself, and then you can't wait to meet up with your friends who are also off their nuts, so you all get taxis to meet together and laugh hysterically over stupid things, while you knock back whiskies, which makes you less crazy. Then you all have a few more hours of drinking beer and wine, which knocks the edge off the mania, but still leaves you feeling happy and sparky, until you're feeling normal again, at which point you have to go off to do some work. You're feeling somewhat flat by that point, and a bit stressed.

It doesn't sound that appealing, so he takes a sip of his beer to irrigate the Sahara. Miles and Douglas do the same. Douglas is looking at Ren and Miles like he doesn't think he can compete with them.

'You seem to have an extra big smile, Lily. Are you extra happy for some reason?' says Miles. Ren can tell that Miles is cursing himself for saying something so dim-witted, although it's better than anything he could have come up with at that moment.

'Yes, I'm happy because my boyfriend has been promoted. He's going to be a Professor.'

Down, down, down they tumble from their empyrean

realm high above the Earth, down through the various levels of reality, down through Plato's world of the Forms, down through the realm where everything exists in twelve dimensions, down through Cockaigne, or cloud-cuckoo land, down past the castles in the air, down through the realm where everyone is a cartoon drawing, down through the level where angels sit upon clouds, and back down to Earth, with a bump. The sun has gone behind a cloud. It's not the same Earth as before, is it, thinks Ren. This is a different place. Evil Twin Earth. Like Earth, but everything is corrupted and foul and depressing. Douglas looks like he's going to cry. As well he might, he probably now has a meth lab hidden at the back of the Physics laboratory area, and he sells meth to the students. No, that's not evil enough. He sucks off tramps for sips of Special Brew. No, too much, dial it back, the meth lab it is. Miles will be a gigolo on this planet. I wonder what I do now? Do I sell essays to students to fund a drug habit? Perhaps I do moral philosophy now. God... a shudder goes down his spine. *Maybe I'm in Theology in this world*. He drinks some more beer to get a grip. Douglas looks miserable, but Miles looks like he's already convinced himself that it was no big deal, just a passing fancy, the next honey will be along soon enough.

'Well, this calls for a celebration then,' says Ren. 'Champagne?' At least he's got his voice back again.

'I wouldn't trust any champagne you get from the student bar,' says Miles. 'They'll probably just give you white wine with lemonade added to it.'

'White wine with lemonade's a bit fancy for a northerner like me,' says Douglas.

After Ren has been to get them all another drink, Lily tells them about her boyfriend. He's a forty-two-year-old Senior Lecturer – soon to be Professor – at the LSE.

'Forty-two? Forty-two?' says Ren. 'That's positively mummified, Dr Burkenhare. Are you getting him a pair of slippers as a present? Or an iron, to iron his skin?'

'Yes, Ren, he's all wrinkly,' says Lily. 'And he smokes a

pipe.'

'Well, good timing, you bagged him just as he's about to retire. Just in time for a round-the-world cruise.'

'I think Lily has a Daddy complex,' says Miles. And immediately regrets it, because Lily goes a bit red at this.

'Just because your Daddy was your granddad, Miles,' says Ren chivalrously, trying to take the attention away from Lily's embarrassment.

'And my great-granddad,' says Miles. 'Give the man the credit he's due, thank you very much.'

'And your uncle?' says Douglas.

'Goodness me, we're a respectable family. I don't know what sort of things go on in your family, but we have some morals.'

'He was also his aunt,' says Ren to Douglas in a stage-whisper. 'Miles is a bit sensitive about that.'

'What's your boyfriend's name?' asks Douglas.

'Jason.'

'Econ?' asks Miles.

'Yes.'

'A conference affair, I expect?' asks Ren. 'They're so romantic, after all.'

'Yes.'

'Whoa, those Econ conferences,' says Miles in a Californian accent. 'I hear they're, like, totally crazy, dudetta.'

'What field is he in?' asks Ren.

'Oh various things, industrial structure, economics of climate change, labour economics...'

'You'd better get that ring as soon as you can, girl, he sounds quite a catch,' says Miles. 'You must be dizzy with excitement.'

'Ha! Like your stuff is excitement personified!' says Lily.

'Miles tried to tell me what he does last week,' says Ren, 'but I fell asleep within seconds. But climate change? Labour economics? Not a teensy bit lefty, is he?'

'Well, a little bit, yes. But he's gradually been coming to

his senses. He started off very left-wing.'

'The one field where you might meet some non-lefties, and you bag yourself a lefty.'

'But he's a sweetie. And it's not like I'm right-wing myself, you know. Just because I don't like the radical left, or Continentalism, doesn't mean I'm Milton Friedman. Or that I want to marry him.'

'Same here, 'says Douglas. 'I wouldn't have voted for Michael Foot, but you won't catch me ever voting for the Conservatives.'

'I voted for Blair,' says Miles. 'As did anyone with any sense.'

'Indeedly-doodly,' says Douglas. 'I certainly don't want to marry Milton Friedman. Keynes, maybe.'

'Do you want to marry Milton Friedman, Ren?' asks Miles.

'Of course I do, you fucking fools. Milt's the one man I'd go gay for.'

'Really? There goes my theory about how you got your job,' says Miles.

'That was pure expediency. I just closed my eyes and thought of the pension. And the super-fast internet speed we academics get. Anyway, I'm going to get a T-shirt made up saying "Cum Dumpster for Milt".'

'You could borrow Miles' shirt,' says Douglas, 'the one that says "Cum dumpster for Dad", and cross out the "Dad" and write "Milt" instead.'

'Well, well, well,' says Miles, 'Our northern chemist proves himself an impudent scoundrel.'

'Impotent?' says Ren.

'When I come to your office, Dougy-boy,' says Miles, 'and find Beresford Sadler up to his balls in your sigmoid then don't expect me to keep quiet.'

'That's right Douglas, you can expect him to join in,' says Ren.

'No prizes for guessing you're all single,' says Lily.

'Well, we lack Jason's refinement and erudition,' says

Ren. 'That is to be admitted. Miles, in addition, lacks Douglas' work ethic, which he has in place of talent, and Douglas lacks the confidence Miles has in asking for sex five minutes into a date.'

'While Ren lacks Douglas's tender touch with a vagina,' says Miles.

'Plus he has the disadvantage that his chosen field is about two thousand years out of date?' says Lily.

'Touche, fair lady,' says Ren. 'And touche, cheeky cunt.'

'Well, those are my middle names,' says Miles. 'At least Cunt is. I'm having the Cheeky added by deed poll.'

'Well, yes, we are all single,' says Ren. 'At least, I know I am, and simple induction tells me these two are as well. Pray tell, where does Jason hail from?'

'Undergrad, Oxford. Postgrad, LSE.'

'But where does he actually come from? Was he created in a lab?'

'Surrey. In quite a good five-star lab.'

'You are a bibacious lot,' says Ren, noting the near-empty glasses. Time for another round.

'It's my shout,' says Douglas. 'Allow me. Plus I need a piss.'

When Douglas comes back with the drinks the sun comes back out. They're all getting slightly crazed by the booze, banter and general merriment, and the heady but possibly unwarranted feelings of optimism about what lies ahead. They clink glasses in a toast.

'Hear, hear for Grayvington,' says Ren. 'The only place stupid enough to employ us.'

'Speak for yourself,' says Douglas. 'I had offers from Leeds, Glasgow and Durham.'

'And you chose here? Are you insane? Why?'

'I come from Leeds, and I want to feel like I've escaped it. Glasgow and Durham are too far away. I wanted to live in the south, where London's not an age away. And Grayvington has a good physics department. And Garrett Slade is here, and I want to work with him.'

'Economics is good here too,' says Lily. 'Is Philosophy not so good?'

'Well, it's okay as far as the analytic people go. The big problem with it is that it's a split department. Lots of Continentalists. And they're all shitheads. Plus there are some other shitheads as well, like the Head of Department. And Derek The Frog. So the shithead quotient is quite high.'

'How's Psychology?' says Douglas.

'It's all right,' says Miles. 'Good cognitive people here for me to work with.'

'I see you also have Lucius Birch,' says Ren.

'Who's he?' says Douglas.

'I think I've heard of him,' says Lily.

'Big social psych guy. Flavour of the month amongst the *New Statesman* types. Gets his work into the newspapers.'

'He's a bit of an arsehole in person, though,' says Miles.

'A left-wing darling who's an arsehole?' says Ren. 'That's unheard of.'

'He's left-wing all right. That surprised me. I wasn't expecting him to be so left-wing in person.'

'Really?' says Ren. 'But all his research somehow, magically, supports left-wing conclusions?'

'That just the way the research turned out.'

'Is that so? So he's Mr. Objective, and the world just happened to turn out to be left-wing?'

'Well, yes. I don't think he's fiddling his data, if that's what you're implying.'

'Who knows what's he's up to. But I would trust him about as far as Balderstone would be displaced by a kick up the bum from me. I mean, do you trust Balderstone? The Panopticons? Wetlands? Would you swear an oath that they're objective and trustworthy?'

'I guess not.'

'Hell no,' says Lily.

'Hell no squared,' says Douglas.

'But they're in bullshit fields, where you can say any old rubbish,' says Miles. 'I'm in Psychology. You can't fiddle

19

things there. Anything you put out has to go through peer review, where serious people check over your work.'

'Well...' says Lily.

'What?' says Miles.

'It has to be said that most people in social psych are left-wing themselves.'

'But...' says Miles, trailing off.

'Ren has a point,' says Douglas. 'It's hard for a referee to sniff out fiddling data unless they start with an attitude of scepticism.'

'Which they won't have,' says Ren. 'He's publishing what they want to hear. There's no-one in that field who has any scepticism at all about that sort of research, so they just wave it on through.'

'And it's not necessarily even about fiddling data,' says Lily. 'It's also about how you set things up, the assumptions you have, which may not get properly challenged when all your referees have the same mindset. That's something we're reasonably good at in Economics. It's more mixed politically so there isn't as much groupthink going on.'

'No way,' says Miles. 'Lucius may be an arse, but he's not crooked.'

'Let's hope for the sake of your department's reputation that he's not,' says Lily.

Miles spots something which allows him to change the subject. 'Fuck, look who it is.'

They all look around.

'Who?' says Douglas.

'The tooth fairy?' says Ren.

'Your secret Latvian wife and three kids?' says Lily.

'No, they're all safely stored away in organ banks,' says Miles.

'Including the tooth fairy?' says Ren.

'Look over there,' says Miles, indicating with his head.

'Jesus,' says Ren, hastily looking away. 'You could have warned us. I almost made eye contact. Could have been blinded.'

'Oh,' says Douglas. 'What a pleasant surprise. The cream of our fellow Class of 2000 compatriots.'

Malcom Ascaris and Lenora Helminth are walking out of the bar with some other people, with drinks. They are about to sit down on the grass near the Lorenzos, when they see their TITE rivals out of the corner of their eyes just in time for them all to move on a safer distance away.

'Who are they with?' asks Douglas. 'They all look the same as Malcom and Lenora, only a bit younger.'

'Judging by the serious but self-satisfied looks they all have on such a lovely Friday afternoon I'd say that probably they're postgrads from Politics and/or Sociology,' says Lily.

'I think the red Marx T-shirt that Mr. Groovy Stubble is wearing would confirm that deduction,' says Miles.

'It was an induction, not a deduction,' says Ren.

'And to think some people say philosophers are pedants,' says Miles. 'How unfair of them.'

'Do you like it when non-psychologists get psychological terms wrong?' says Ren, who doesn't wait for an answer. 'They are a tomentose lot. Especially the women.'

'Comatose? Already?' says Douglas.

'Tomentose. Hairy,' says Ren.

At this point a mustachioed man in his early-mid thirties, wearing camouflage trousers and a 'Smash the State' shirt, joins Malcom and Lenora's group.

'Fucking hell, it's Tony fucking Shaver,' says Ren.

'Who's he when he's at home?' says Miles. 'I mean, apart from being the obvious saviour of society.'

'When he's not being the people's poet, he's a lecturer in my department. One of the delightful departmental adornments I was telling you about earlier.'

'So if he wants to smash the state what would he do if someone goes over and punches him in the snozz?' says Miles. 'Call the police?'

'Oh, he's no anarchist,' says Ren. 'He's just another hard leftist. They all pretend to be anarchists, because that seems cooler than saying that really you're a big-state socialist conformist, who'll ruthlessly prosecute his endless rules using a violent, knock-on-the-door-at-3am enforcement machine. That doesn't pull as many chicks as saying you're an "anarchist". Except for the fat, hairy, angry ones, who want that sort of society too.'

'People like him sometimes really do act like they want anarchy, though,' says Lily.

'Well, they do want temporary anarchy,' says Ren. 'That's an old leftist tactic. And a fascist one too. Temporary anarchy provides them with the opportunity to take over, and then enforce their iron fist. Believe me, any such anarchy will be most fugacious. Look at how Soviet Russia got created. Jesus, I can't even glare at the fucker, because I have to work with him. Time for more drinks, I think. Miles, will you do the honours this time?'

Miles comes back with drinks, crisps and peanuts. 'Best to have some food with all this alcohol,' he says.

'A packet of crisps isn't going to do much,' says Lily.

'I've still got some food in my backpack,' says Douglas, who rummages around in it, before pulling out a banana.

'The drunken monkey,' says Ren.

'Anyone want a bite?' asks Douglas, to headshakes.

'Drunken monkey indeed,' says Miles. 'I met a guy at a conference who was telling me about some new theory called the drunken monkey hypothesis.'

'A theory about Douglas? How very prescient,' says Lily.

'It's the theory that we primates developed a smell, and a taste, for alcohol because alcohol is a pretty reliable indicator of the presence of ripe fruit, because ripe fruit starts to ferment after a while.'

'That's true of the student bar,' says Ren. 'The young men have noticed the link between the alcohol and the presence of plenty of ripe fruit.'

'You're a ripe old fruit yourself,' says Douglas.

'Anyway, this theory may not be true,' says Miles, 'but it may be worth a grant application. Get funded to investigate why we like alcohol. Ren can be my first test subject.'

'I'll volunteer,' says Lily. 'if you can get a grant to test taste discrimination in alcohol imbibers.'

'Sure,' says Miles, 'you can be at one end of the discrimination spectrum with your fine wines. Ren can be at the other end with his lager, and his vodka and lemonades.'

'Let's just get the University to let us set up our own Institute. The Institute for Advanced Alcohol Research,' says Lily.

'We've all had that idea,' says Douglas.

'I'll be Professor of Beer Goggles,' says Ren. 'Miles can be Reader in Special Brew Studies. Lily can be Professor of Pencil Shavings and Hints of Chocolate. Douglas, Professor of Meths. Professor Douglas Oram, the distinguished creator of a whole new field, Methematics.'

'Or should it be Methemetics?' says Douglas.

'Up to you old boy, it's your field,' says Miles.

'Great. How do we put this plan into action?' says Lily.

'We leave the campus soon, for precautionary reasons,' says Ren, 'and then we drink copious amounts of alcohol in various hostelries around the city, repeating this procedure on numerous occasions, thus acquiring skills, knowledge and talents that the University and various grant-dispensing bodies will eventually be unable to ignore.'

'A capital idea,' says Miles. 'As long as we can write the application on the back of a beer coaster.'

2000-01
Semester 1
Week 4
Wednesday

Ren approaches the bar at the staff club. The weekly departmental seminar, where visiting guest speakers come to give a talk, has just finished, and as seminar organiser he's glad to see the back of it. He needs to be poisoned, and the quickest way at present to get the requisite dose into his veins is to dilute the stuff and ingest it orally.

Today's speaker has been a distinguished philosopher of science called Hedley Beagle from the University of Longford who spoke on the unreality of time, a topic which makes Ren rueful because the problem he currently has with time is its scarcity, not its non-existence. Not that he said anything like this in public, that's the sort of ho-ho-ho joke you'd expect Beresford Sadler, the boorish Physics Head of Department who turned up to the talk with Douglas and his distinguished colleague Garrett Slade, to make. This sort of joke had almost certainly made the rounds nearly a century ago, Ren thought; no doubt Bertrand Russell himself made a similar joke to McTaggart. Probably around the time Dirty Bertie discovered that he had a knob and started boffing various horse-faced goers, while writing peace-bollocks pamphlets encouraging us to surrender to the Commies (which he was still doing half a century later). 'If time is an illusion, dear Taggie, then I need to imagine myself up some more, I can't commit intercourse and advance the cause of international socialism at the same time, can I? Not when I've also got to dismantle your damnable British idealism, ho-ho-ho.' Beresford Sadler actually makes jokes like this at philosophy talks, imagining that it causes the philosophers to think of him an astute observer of philosophical history.

The Head of Physics thinks of himself as Hemingwayesque, both physically, and in terms of his forceful, yet (so he imagines) charismatic personality, but his habit of angrily throwing his ample weight around has resulted in his colleagues calling him 'Norman Mailer' behind his back. (Later on the nickname will be changed to 'Russell Crowe', once Crowe tubs up and starts throwing telephones at people.) Beresford always turns up, in a bit of a mood, to any Philosophy talk that seems in any way related to physics. He's well known for his temper, and his general intolerance, but he seems to have a particular chip on his shoulder about philosophers discussing physics. The reason Garrett often comes with him is to try to keep him under control.

Beresford always misunderstands what is being said at these talks, and today was a doozy. The Beagle is an upper-class smoothie, an assured, although sometimes contumelious, Cantabridgian, and Beresford, always sensitive about what he (but no-one else) sees as his humble origins, took an instant dislike to him, which may have injected a little more vapour into the cloud chamber that Beresford thinks of as the philosophical part of his mind.

The Beagle was not, despite the title of his talk, arguing the unreality of time, but was arguing against the existence of what is usually called 'the moving present'. He was in fact arguing for the 'spacelike conception' of time (sometimes called the 'four-dimensional' theory of spacetime), a view that is popular with many physicists, and which seems to be what Sadler himself believes, as far as anyone can tell, but Beresford in his usual temerarious fashion decided early on that the Beagle was arguing for a position that everyone else, including Garrett and Douglas, could tell he wasn't arguing for. So bullfighting Beresford was going to step up and take the Beagle – a mere theoretician, and of the wrong field at that – to task over the Beagle's presumption to discuss matters that he was manifestly unqualified to discuss. An embarrassed Garrett, no fan of the Beagle himself, tried to steer Beresford off his hapless course, but failed.

The misunderstanding was partly the Beagle's fault, though, because Hedley, assuming that everyone present was both a philosopher and well-schooled in J. M. E. McTaggart's original arguments against the reality of time, as well as the subsequent well-known developments in the field (well-known to metaphysicians, that is) had said very little in the way of introductory or scene-setting remarks. Or perhaps the Beagle just assumed that anyone who didn't have this background knowledge would have the decency to keep their mouth shut. Either way, he was mistaken. A philosopher as experienced as he should not have made such a mistake, for rogue audience members can turn up at any Philosophy talk, not just in the provinces and the wilder extremities of the country, but even at the top places, and these philosophists are hardly ever deterred by a lack of knowledge of the topic under discussion. The more they misunderstand, the more chaotic their intervention will be, so visiting speakers who jump right into the guts of their talk are taking a risk. Not a running-into-a-burning-building-type of risk, of course, but no-one wants to travel hundreds of miles to give a talk on their research and then have fifteen minutes of the discussion wasted by a strange man wearing green glasses.

In Hedley's defence it could be pointed out that dozens of peripatetic philosophers make such a mistake every week across the country. There are possibly three, maybe even four or five, Travelling Wilburforces, as Ren calls them, making the same mistake this very afternoon, possibly even at Oxford or Cambridge where visiting speakers can be lulled into a false sense of security, thinking that here, surely, in these blessed groves there cannot be any Alan Pettigrews present, but sometimes there are, even in such hallowed halls.

These three, or four, or five, philosophers, it should be noted, will not frame this thought using the term 'Alan

Pettigrews'. Only Grayvington philosophers invoke the Pettigrew name, as we shall discover. (Alan, mercifully, was not present today for the Beagle's talk.) One such philosopher, Toby Smalls, is at this very moment at UCL, about to give an evening talk, thinking – despite his many years of experience which, were he to examine that resource, would reveal the weakness of such an optimistic conjecture – that surely there cannot be any Maurice Dabneys present here. This belief is situated in what philosophers call an opaque linguistic context, meaning that one cannot replace the term 'Maurice Dabneys' with a co-referential term such as 'Alan Pettigrews', because while Smalls believes that there cannot be any Maurice Dabneys here, he does not believe that there cannot be any Alan Pettigrews here. Nevertheless, both terms, 'Maurice Dabneys' and 'Alan Pettigrews', refer to the same thing, namely the class of time-wasters who have acquired the delusive belief that they are philosophically adroit, and who turn up regularly to advanced academic philosophy talks and engage the speaker and various unfortunate audience members in confusing and unhelpful dialogue. (It should be noted that our genarch of Physics, Beresford Sadler, does not qualify as an Alan Pettigrew, at least not a full-blown Pettigrew; perhaps we should call his type a 'Beresford Sadler')

There is one Grayvington philosopher who never makes this sort of mistake about his audience, and that is Tristram York, who, incidentally, made rather a good comment today in the Beagle's talk. But he is unusually sensitive to the presence of Pettigrews, and has been known, at his own talks, to ask the chairperson, at the point that the chairperson brings in his carafe of water and empty glass (just before people start drifting in and generally milling about), whether any such audience members can be expected at his talk. Such a question is considered to be slightly bad form, but understandable, and usually raises some shared, guilty, laughter of recognition.

The time-waster who will shortly be getting on Toby

Smalls' wick has no name that anybody in the London audience knows – generally people avoid socialising with Alan Pettigrews, and so the name of any particular Alan Pettigrew will only become known should that Pettigrew be the type to volunteer it – but this particular London-based Pettigrew is generally referred to in the common room after talks as 'the eccentric chap with the green glasses' by the more polite academics, and 'the loony with green glasses' by the more blunt.

Anyway, all this, or rather none of it, is going through Ren's head as he approaches the staff club bar. What's in his head is the intent to purchase a beer. Which beer he should get is a complex decision which involves weighing up various factors, such as the beer's alcoholic strength, its price, the awfulness of the taste – most beers taste bad to Ren, but especially ales, bitters and wheat beers – and the embarrassment quotient of buying a lager, whose blander taste he can more easily tolerate, but which will elicit scorn and mockery from those of his colleagues who hold that the only beers worth drinking are obscure ones which have sticks and ambergris and bits of beak floating in them, and which smell to him like they contain a mould that has evolved to be resistant to alcohol. Also to be factored in are how many of his lager-deriding colleagues are here tonight, and what mood they are in. And also how much of a shit he currently gives about the venting of their opinions on lager drinking.

He eventually decides that tonight his preference is to avoid another tedious round of lager-bashing, because he wants to get the conversation quickly onto TITE before Hedley drags everyone into a conversation about his views, so he orders a pint of something awful called – as far as he can remember three seconds later – Mildewmarch, an ale which the beardies from the Campaign for Right Proper Gravy, Whippets and Brews have given the seal of approval to. And, of course, a packet of pork scratchings.

He notices even before the barlady returns that something isn't right. The delicious home-made pork scratchings in a clear packet that the staff club used to serve have been replaced by a commercial variety in a brightly-covered tinfoil pack, bearing the name 'Oinkers', which he knows from previous empirical research to be an inferior product in every way, unless you prefer your scratchings to taste and feel like popcorn mixed with puffed-up honeycomb. Ren reflects that if the bearded campaigners were really serious about keeping British pubs the way they should be then they should be complaining loudly about the replacement of wholesome, nutritious dead pig skin and fat with this tasteless cavity insulation. Perhaps he would write to them. But he would have to resist the temptation to start the letter, 'Dear beardies...', otherwise they wouldn't take him seriously, and that would take all the fun out of it.

'I've only been at this University for a few months and already it's going to the dogs,' Ren says, indicating the Oinkers, as he avoids sitting next to Hedley and Sadler and instead pulls up a chair to sit next to his friend and fellow Philosophy lecturer Compton Hart, a smartly-dressed thirty-something with curly, sandy-coloured hair, and a liking for cigarettes, which are becoming forbidden fruit at Universities. 'The fatty esculants are not what they were.'

'I think you're the only person who comes here who eats pork scratchings,' says Compton. 'Those ones you've been eating recently had been on the shelves for ten years before you turned up and started eating them. Now you've eaten them all the manager finally had to buy some new ones.'

'Not true,' says Ren. 'I've seen no less a personage than the Professor and Head of the Art History Department, Harold Furter, eating packeted pork rind.'

'You mean old Frank?' says Compton. 'You're really going to use him as an example?'

'What, just because he's the fattest man in Western academia?'

'He's the fattest man in the whole galaxy. He was eating

deep-fried bits of Jabba the Hut, not pork scratchings. Why do you think they have a double door here for an entrance? That was put in a couple of years ago just so Frank could fit through. He got a grant for it. They'll be rolling him around on his sides soon. Harold the Barrel.'

'I expect he has a glandular imbalance. Or he's big-boned.'

'He has big dinosaur bones stuck in his throat if that's what you mean,' says Compton. 'They keep his oesophagus wide so he can pour down beer direct from the barrel.'

'No, no, no', interrupts Derek Lucas. 'Frank considers himself a cultured man. He might drink from the barrel, but it's always good wine. He only eats pork scratchings when he thinks no-one's looking.'

'Why must my brethren be so ashamed of themselves?' says Ren.

'Are you not aware', says Derek, 'that pork scratchings were developed in the thirteenth century by medieval monks as a way to prevent young men from masturbating? That's why masturbating really took off in the seventies, when the salt levels were changed.'

'Never change the salt levels, I say,' says Ren. 'That's like my motto for life. Never change the salt levels.'

'Someone's changed the salt levels for this department recently,' says Compton.

'A more pertinent fact,' says Ren, 'which you gentlemen may be unaware of, is that pork scratchings have more vitamin K in them than the equivalent number of melons in the University's girls' volleyball team.'

'That one's definitely a lie,' says Compton.

'Made-up, yes,' says Ren, 'but not a lie, because I don't know it to be false. And it's not obviously false. It could possibly be true, if melons have no vitamin K whatsoever, and the scratchings have a trace amount. And my knowledge of the vitamin K levels in melons is, shall we say... scratchy?'

'Do pork scratchings have any vitamins whatsoever in

them?' says Derek. 'That seems doubtful.'

'How do I know, I'm a philosopher,' says Ren. 'Ask a biochemist. Bound to be one in here somewhere. Ask the bar to page a biochemist.'

'A biochemist wouldn't necessarily know anyway,' says Derek. 'The vitamin levels of assorted bar snacks and citrus fruits might not be the sort of information they make sure to always have at their command. It may be information they have, in fact, never possessed, it being of no earthly use to their more specialised alchemical pursuits.'

'Well, perhaps they know the core bar snacks and popular fruits,' says Ren. 'Peanuts and oranges. But I agree. They may rely, for the more obscure comestibles, on nipping over to the science library when the topic comes up in conversation.'

'As I'm sure it would if the VC walked in and was pelted with so many tomatoes that the issue of tomato poisoning came up,' says Compton.

Compton was someone that Ren had been immediately drawn to when he arrived at Grayvington, not only because he is, in Ren's view, if no-one else's, good company, and not only because he is even more down on Continentalism and postmodernism than Ren, but also because he is the only person Ren has ever met in academia who is a conservative, and isn't afraid to admit it (although he only admitted it once he had got his permanent appointment). That was something that Ren, who had only started recovering a couple of years ago from a standard dose of leftica idiotica acquired in his teens, admired.

Ren decides that this is a suitable time to talk about the TITE because none of the Department's Continentalists are here (they are, of course, staying away because today's talk has been an analytic talk). He's wondering how best to bring up the topic up, when Compton says, 'So you were going to tell me what happened yesterday at the titty.'

'Yes, I'm afraid it's all become very titty-politti,' Ren says, sounding a bit too pleased with his prepared line. He starts to fill Compton in on what happened in the TITE yesterday. Some of the other philosophers present – Walter Clutterbuck, Tristram York, Martha Gelber, George Bagnall, Bill Porterfield, and Derek – keep half an ear on what he is saying, as much as they can with Hedley and Beresford bashing away at their other ear. They're mostly sympathetic to what Ren is saying about the TITE. Derek is as hard left as they come, but he has no truck with Continentalism. The rest are analytic soft leftists, and regard Continentalism, in their understated way, as 'unfortunate'. But it's hard for Ren to be heard as the visiting speaker and his antagonist are continuing their pointless and loud argument at the other end of the group. Ren can see Douglas, who is stuck next to them, looking over at Ren's end of the group wondering whether he could politely move away, now that Beresford and Hedley are fully preoccupied with demonstrating how ignorant the other is.

'Oh dear,' says Martha to Ren. 'I was afraid something like that might happen with that course, but I didn't think it would get as bad as that.'

'It's that Balderstone chap,' says Bill. 'No wonder it's like that with him in charge.'

'It's not just him, though,' says Compton. 'This is what the people behind it wanted. The whole of SADE are like that.'

SADE, which stands for the Staff and Development Unit, is the department that runs the TITE and other staff development courses.

'This is the beginning of there being no escape from the left,' continues Compton. 'You will be forced to be a leftist if you want to be an academic. Eventually it will become law that you have to be a leftist, not just in academia, but in the wider world.'

'You always exaggerate these things,' says Derek. 'And I'd rather you didn't call them leftists. The real problem with the SADE lot is that they're foisting mumbo-jumbo on intelligent people who have previously been trained to think well. What we need is to make academic people teach what they know better, not to cloud their minds up with poison gas.'

'From what I've heard none of the SADE people know anything about teaching academics to be better teachers, it's not just Balderstone,' says Ren. 'They're terrible teachers themselves.'

'Yes they are,' says Martha. 'I went on one of their short courses a few years ago, it was a disgrace.'

'Not a surprise,' says Walter. 'You know they're all just rejects from other departments?'

'Are they? What do you mean?' says Ren.

'I mean that most of them have not been hired in as teaching specialists. Most of them don't have a background in education at all. They're people who their original departments wanted to get rid of, because they were no good at research or teaching, or both, but as it's hard to sack an academic, they got shunted off instead to SADE.'

'Great, so we're being taught by third-raters who couldn't hack it as proper academics themselves,' says Ren. 'So where does Balderstone come from?'

'He's one they did bring in from outside. But I don't know what his background is,' says Walter. 'Do you?'

'He conveniently doesn't have a staff webpage,' says Ren, 'so I don't know what he has. But he appears to have never seen anything so outlandish as an educational research finding, so I doubt he would come from Education.'

'Well, you say that,' says Compton, 'but a lot of Education departments have been colonised by the left, and their training is now worthless.'

'You mean colonised by the Continentalists,' corrects Derek.

'Education departments were colonised by the left a long time ago,' says Compton. 'That opened the opportunity for them to be further colonised by Continentalists, which has now happened. And now they're got their foot through the door into the rest of the University system.'

'Well, I'm going to ask Grant, as Head of Department, to write a letter of complaint on behalf of the department,' says Ren. 'My other issue with the course is the inordinate amount of time it takes up. The whole thing needs to be completely overhauled, or dumped.'

'They won't dump the general idea of having training courses for new lecturers, that's here to stay,' said Compton. 'So the line has to be that it should be taken over by empiricists. It should be shorn of the politics, and it should be reduced in the time it takes up.'

'You know we're only doing one afternoon of video work?' says Ren.

'One afternoon a week?' says Walter.

'No, one afternoon in total,' says Ren.

'You mean where they video you giving a mock lecture?' said Bill.

'Yes, apparently four of you get to do it in a group, which means you get about half an hour spent on you for filming and analysis. This course goes for two whole years, and we get half an hour of video work. Half. An. Hour. Out of two years. That sort of thing should be the basis for the whole course. Regular filming of yourself and analysis of how you're doing, are you speaking too fast, too slowly, are you being too boring, how comprehensible are you for the level you're teaching at, are you getting better at this as you go along, and so on. That's the sort of thing that's needed. A proper nuts and bolts servicing of your teaching over a couple of years. Not half an hour of it, and then five hundred hours of postmodernist propaganda, which you must parrot back, or pack your bags. You know, I might just not go any more.'

'But don't you have to pass the course, otherwise you don't pass probation?' says Walter.

'Yes, but probation is three years long. My contract doesn't say that I have to start it in my first year. I could re-enrol next year, when it might have improved.'

'Or got worse,' says Compton.

'Well, I'm going to get Grant to do something. I'm also getting some of the other people on the course to get their Heads to do something too.'

'Another drink for anyone?' says Walter.

'Another pint of Mildewmelter, please,' says Ren.

'Mildewmelter?'

'Or whatever it's called. Mildewmouse? Something like that.'

'Would our guest...' begins Walter, before raising his voice, 'Would our guest like something as well?'

'Yes thank you,' says Beresford, looking up from the argument. 'Another red please.'

Walter looks embarrassed. 'I, er, meant our guest speaker, but of course I will get you a red, Beresford. Hedley, would you like a drink?'

'I'll have red too, please.'

'Medium or large?'

'Oh, large I should think. Thank you.'

'Large for me too, thanks,' says Beresford, who isn't going to let Hedley outdrink him.

Half an hour later taxis arrive, drinks are hastily finished, and they head off to a Chinese restaurant called Taste of Dragon. This isn't a place they've ever been to before, but the Beagle had said he wanted Chinese when he'd been asked a few days ago. Everyone was hoping that Beresford wouldn't come, because his argument with the Beagle has become tedious (so much so that Douglas and Garret had declined the offer to come taste some dragon), but Ren is glad Beresford is coming because it means that they aren't all obliged to feign interest to the Beagle about his talk, and he can talk to the others about the TITE and whatever else they feel like talking about.

Ren notices that Compton avoids sitting near Derek at the restaurant. Although the two have quite a lot of in common, and can sometimes engage in witty conversation together in a public setting, privately they hate each other, and each greatly disapproves of the other's political beliefs and moral character. Also, Derek has a tendency after a few drinks to start going on about his pet interest, French political rebels, and they've all heard what he to say on this topic eight-hundred and seventy-three times, except for the new boy Ren, who has only heard it five times. It's this Francophile tendency that has earned Derek his long-established nickname, 'The Frog', although the recent students assume it's because of his looks, which are becoming more amphibian as he ages. Previous generations of students, in the days when Derek was not so jowly and squat, assumed it was because of the shaggy old green fisherman's jumper he would always wear. Other students swear that it's because he's always wanting student princesses to kiss him, although if he's still doing that now, in his fifties, it's doubtful he's having much luck.

Beresford and Hedley have simmered down for now, and are talking to George Bagnall, who has managed to get in between them, but Ren notices with suspicion that Derek is making extra sure that they both get plenty to drink.

Compton and Ren are sitting next to Walter Clutterbuck, a trim, neat little departmental veteran, and a former Head of Department. They are talking about their current Head of Department, a late middle-aged man of Hungarian-descent called Professor Grant Kapshar, who came into the department a few years ago. Kapshar, it is rumoured, has been instructed by senior management to improve the department, shaking it up if need be. Walter and Compton are speculating that this suits the desperation he has to feel important, something which he isn't getting adequately from his publishing, which is mostly quantity over quality.

Kapshar is chiefly distinguished by three things: his platinum-blonde hair, his proficiency at getting funding, and his inability to feel human emotion. Or at least to display it. Hence his nickname, Robot, bestowed on him by Compton. (He had other nicknames before, like Warhol and Dracu, but now it's mainly Robot. This nickname has not yet been drawn to his attention.)

'How to explain Robot?' says Compton. 'What is the point of Robot? Answer: He is a machine for getting grants.' Compton is enjoying being able to trot out some of his best lines again for Ren's sake. 'That is his purpose. That is what he excels at. What's more, he is the most efficient grant-getting machine in the world, because he manages to extract great wads of grant money with the most meagre material ever submitted to a grant panel. Somehow the thinnest gruel, with hamster-powered intellectual content, that varies only slightly from what he has submitted the previous five times, convinces the people who are supposed to know who to shower with moolah to shower it over him. He's like a fifties B-movie hypnotist, holding up a telephone book and they throw money at him, stuffing it into his shirt and his socks.'

'At least each grant gets credited as another departmental success,' says Walter. 'We're not complaining too much.'

'Maximum monetary output for minimal intellectual input,' says Compton, who hadn't finished.

'So how does he do it?' asked Ren.

'For one thing, he knows how to write grants,' says Walter. 'I've had to look over quite a few of his before they're sent off, and he writes in precisely the way you have to with a grant application.'

'That's because he's on so many grant panels himself, making decisions on who to give grants to,' says Compton. 'He's learned how to do it. That's his real area of specialisation.'

'Yes, all the main grant players are on these panels,' says Walter. 'They're the ones who know how to write them, because they know what grant panels are looking for. He'll tell you himself – if you want to learn how to write grants, get yourself on a panel. Good advice.'

Their conversation stops as some food is placed on the table, and Derek pours more wine for everyone around him, making especially sure to fill Beresford and Hedley's glasses. George keeps trying to change the subject, but Beresford especially is itching to get the conversation back to the topic of time. It appears now that they have genuine areas of disagreement.

'It's a big job, putting in a grant bid,' says Compton. 'There aren't as many grant bids put in as you'd think.'

'The sheer amount of numb-numbing work involved in submitting even one puts most people off,' says Walter. 'And most people haven't a clue how to do an effective one.'

'Yes, why put so much work into something you think you have little chance of getting anyway?' says Compton. 'And for most philosophers there isn't really any need to have a grant anyway. For now, at least.'

'Another problem,' says Walter, 'is that many of those that are submitted have something not quite right somewhere in them. Ticked the wrong box, submitted the wrong figures, written outside the box. Grant is good at getting it all right. Ticking all the right boxes, literally and metaphorically'.

'It's the perfect job for someone who is at heart a bureaucrat,' says Compton. 'If his grandparents hadn't left Hungary he would have made an ideal Communist functionary. When the robots have put the rest of us out of work he'll still be there.'

'The robots will be programmed to copy him?' says Ren.

'To a tee.'

'The other thing,' Walter says, 'is that he has no qualms about writing the sort of inflated puffery you have to write about your research to be in with a chance of getting a grant, because he believes it. You have to big your research up. Make it sound grander than it really is. Most of us old-fashioned British academics are much more modest about our work, at least in public, and we're not used to talking about our work as though we're writing about someone else.'

'He will attempt to re-program you, you know,' says Compton. 'Soon you'll be pressured to write a grant with him. He will induct you into the dark arts of grant-writing. He'll be doing it for himself, and the department's sake, but he'll also think he's doing you a favour. Which he is, if you want grants.'

'And as a young person, you should do,' says Walter. 'That's the way the Humanities are going to go, grants and funding will matter more and more over the next few decades. Glad I'll be retiring before all that comes. So if you can stand it, let him teach you.'

'I get the impression Ren isn't the type,' says Compton. 'You're lucky you had that postdoc position so you could get those papers published, I think if you hadn't the department would have hired someone with a more modern attitude.'

'More modern?'

'More compliant. More timid. A team worker, i.e. do what the Head tells you. Your sarcastic attitude has been noticed. They don't like academics having their own personalities any more. I've found this out myself. Why do you think Derek's never been promoted?'

Compton lowers his voice so he can't be heard, not that there is much danger of this, as Beresford and Hedley are starting to argue more loudly again.

'He may be a left-wing arsehole,' says Compton, looking carefully at Derek, 'but that's not why. It's because he's too fond of his status as an iconoclast.'

'I thought it was because he never publishes?'

'Well, that too. But he'd still have trouble getting promoted, because he says, shall we say, unhelpful things, especially to the higher-ups.'

'Like what?'

Compton glances at Derek again. 'Let's just say he considers them sell-outs. Traitors to the cause.'

'He's got a point.'

'Indeed. Robot wanted him to apply for a grant recently, but he just said no. Didn't go down too well.'

'You never just say an outright "No" when the Head asks

you something like that,' says Walter. 'If you don't want to do it you've got to be more subtle than that.'

'What would you say?'

'You'd say something like, I've love to, but I have X, Y and Z on my plate at the moment. Or you suggest a future project instead when you have more time. You've got to find something that makes it reasonable of you to say no. Or gives the appearance of being reasonable.'

'Robot is pushing things back again to the old style of department where there was a big Professor who rules the roost and he just tells everyone what to do, based on whatever he thinks is right,' says Compton.

'Or in his case, whatever the higher-ups approve of,' says Walter. 'All he cares about is looking good on the metrics so he can get promoted to senior management.'

'Why would anyone want to go into senior management?' says Ren, who's still young and naive enough to be enjoying his research.

'As you get older some people lose interest in their research, and money becomes more important,' says Compton. 'Senior management is where the really big salaries are. And the bigger your final salary, the bigger your pension. You no longer have to slave away at your research, or waste your time taking seminars full of undergraduate dimwits. You get to make the decisions, and you're pretty insulated from their consequences. You swan about with the great and the good at fancy restaurants. And you get a secretary who does a lot of the drudge work for you.'

'It won't ever happen for Grant, though,' says Walter. 'He's uncomfortable to be around. Being a bastard is no impediment, not that he's really that much of a bastard compared to some of that lot, but you've got to have a bit of charm, which he doesn't.'

'Yes, he's about as much fun as flat lemonade,' agrees Ren. 'The permanent frown, the weary impatience with human frailty... I can see why the higher-ups might want him running a department, but you wouldn't want to have to deal with him all the time yourself.'

'He's valuable to them where he is, doing what he's good at,' says Compton. 'So although he doesn't realise it, he's never going to get to that level.'

'But how does he manage to make any friends? How does he get on with people in his field, and on grant panels?'

'You haven't met those people. A lot of them are like him,' says Walter.

'They're not exactly his friends,' says Compton. 'More like fellow droids with the same batch number, who have mutual interests.'

'He's not really that bad when you get to know him,' says Walter, who sees the good in everyone.

Robot's colleagues have noticed that recently he's started showing an interest in human emotion. At least, an interest in simulating it. One of the most frightening things anyone's ever seen is Robot's attempt to replicate the human smile. It's an awful thing to witness, which leaves anyone unfortunate enough to be in the firing line feeling like they've seen things humans aren't supposed to see. A glimpse through a crack in the tent into the workings of the human mind, enough to give them the sense of how deflatingly gimcrack the whole thing is.

You can see it happening in slow motion. First there's the opportunity for a smile which Grant fails to immediately register. Seconds pass. Then the realisation dawns on him that this is when he should be smiling. Maybe the worst part is that you can almost see the old-style Soviet-era tape decks in his head shifting around as a new spool is loaded, and cranes are brought into position ready for cranking up the mouth corners.

Then it comes. The ersatz, non-Duchenne smile. For most observers this is the worst part. The corners of the mouth go up, but it's like a corpse having its features adjusted by the undertaker, an impression which is highlighted by the red lines Robot has coming down on both sides of his mouth to the bottom of his face, which stand out conspicuously against the almost albino whiteness of the rest of his skin, making it look like he has the hinged mouth of a venquilitrist's dummy.

As the corners of his mouth are hauled upwards, the rest of his face stays exactly the same. Robot doesn't understand that you smile with your orbicularis oculi – the eyelid – muscle as much as with your zygomatic major muscle. Some swear that his eyes become even angrier as his mouth is tormented into position, as though the eyes are registering his real feelings at the imposture he is being forced to adopt in order to deal with these erratic and untrustworthy flesh-based creatures. Robot is perhaps guided by knowing that meat-machine detection systems are often jury-rigged and are thus manipulable – the robin red breast, for instance, can be fooled into attacking a piece of red cloth if it's on its territory. But Robot leaves his red cloth in place for the wrong amount of time, and then the cranes let go too quickly.

'Can we kindly not talk about Robot's smile when we're eating, please?' says Bill.

It's getting hard to talk about anything now, as the two time lords have had a little too much Tardis fuel to drink. They've resumed battle, and are getting louder and louder, each denouncing the other's field, much to everyone else's embarrassment. George especially is looking red in the face, and looks to be about to faint from shame. The whole restaurant is being forced to listen, and the waiters are nervously hovering, waiting for their moment to rush in and politely ask them to be quiet. Compton, Ren and Walter start chatting again in an attempt to disassociate themselves, and to provide some auditory cover, but their efforts are futile.

Beresford is accusing Hedley of sticking his philosophical oar into areas he doesn't understand.

'Leave physics to the physicists,' Beresford says. 'You don't even understand the basics of what's going on, so your theories have no relevance to anything. You're embarrassing yourself.'

The audience tenses at this. The argument has left the arena of specifics, and looks like heading into general drunken abuse territory.

Hedley is not fazed. A confident and polished Oxbridge product, he has dealt with plenty of this sort of attitude before from better physicists than Beresford. But he is getting fed up with the man and wishes he would go away. He is also drunker than he realises.

'What are you playing at, buster?' he drawls, with effortless contempt. He is winding Sadler up like a master. 'You come along to another department's dinner, and insult their profession? Who asked you to come?'

'It's not a departmental dinner, it's the dinner for your talk which was open to all.'

'The talk was open to all. The dinner wasn't. It's a private dinner and you've gate-crashed it. I never heard anyone invite you. Do you think a philosopher would dream of inviting himself to a Physics dinner and then spend the dinner insulting the field of Physics?'

'Wouldn't worry us,' shouts Sadler. 'We could handle him. We'd squash him like a bug!' Sadler bangs his fist into his palm, perhaps unnecessarily, to illustrate said squashing manoeuvres. 'I'd tell him to bring it on! Say what you want!'

'Do you know anything about philosophy of physics? Or even philosophy of science?' says Hedley. 'Have you ever read anything in the field, you ignoramus?'

'Do you know anything about physics?'

'I have a fucking Physics degree,' says Hedley.

'Undergraduate degree. Means nothing. You have a superficial and screwed-up understanding of everything.'

'I doubt it, I read Physics at Cambridge, not at your department. Whereas you know less about the Philosophy of Physics than my third-year undergraduates. You haven't even read any David Lewis. But then, my students don't have the disadvantage you have of being at a second-rate

University. I suggest you acquaint yourself with the literature before you go shooting your mouth off.'

'Please,' gasps George, who is holding his chest. Ren wonders whether he is going to complain about Hedley's general insult to Grayvington, an insult which Hedley appears to be unaware he has made. 'Please could we keep it down and not make it so personal?'

'You wouldn't know a fucking Boltzmann equation if I etched into your forehead with a fucking chisel,' shouts Sadler.

So this is the famous Sadler temper, Ren thinks, that Douglas, via Garrett, has told him about. The two antagonists did not appear to be personally acquainted before today, but Ren wonders whether there is something in Hedley's past that has made Beresford so hostile. Did he once insult Beresford's sister? Did Hedley ever stop him getting a grant?

'Do they let you play with chisels, then?' says Hedley. 'Is that what you try to split atoms with here?'

George has his head down on the table; he seems to be having a serious panic attack. The waiters are dumbfounded. They've never seen anything like this before. Everyone, the waiters, the cooks, the other customers, even the academics themselves, are now weirdly fascinated by the question that is hovering in front of their mind – what happens when academics lose it with each other? What exactly do they do? Do they just ramp up the academic references? Challenge each other to a fencing duel? Face off on a special edition of University Challenge? Hit each other with theses?

'What does a philosopher split an atom with?' yells Beresford, who makes the ominous transition from sitting to standing. 'A piece of chalk?'

'Sit down,' says Hedley, who knows Beresford is close to losing it now.

'A piece of fucking chalk?' Beresford bends over to talk more directly to Hedley's face. 'You fucking chalky cunt.'

'Sit down, you great gas giant.'

Beresford picks up a bowl of sweet-and-sour chicken and rice and shoves it across the prone body of George, who appears to be hyperventilating, into Hedley's face. There are horrified-but-delighted gasps from the whole restaurant. It's not like a fight in a restaurant never happens, but it's not supposed to happen between academics. Ren can almost hear the other customers telling their friends tomorrow, 'No better than animals, they were, those supposed eggheads.' Which is pretty much what he'll be telling people too.

Hedley grabs a fistful of prawn crackers and scrunches them on Beresford's face. Beresford just stands there and takes it, as if to say 'I'm Hemingway, that all you got?' Then he quickly and, he hopes, expertly, jabs Hedley in the stomach. He expects this to knock Hedley down and finish the job, but although Hedley is winded, he still manages to walk around the table to pick up a plate of ribs, which he throws at Beresford. He clearly means for the ribs to go all over the larger physicist, but most of them scatter and miss the target. The greasy plate, meanwhile, has slipped out of Hedley's hand by accident and it cracks Beresford on the forehead, and breaks in two, one half falling onto George, who has deciding that feigning complete unconsciousness is the best policy. Beresford's head has been sliced, and blood starts seeping out of the wound. Hedley looks annoyed with himself for losing his cool.

'Well, you brought that on yourself,' Hedley says. Then, as though realising that a witty retort is what will tip the scales back in his favour, he adds, 'Physics in action.' The restaurant is silent. He realises that his line hasn't quite done the job, so he says, 'If that's how you're going to treat a visiting speaker, I'm off,' and he stalks out of the restaurant unhindered. The waiters part to let him through.

As he slams the door behind him the restaurant erupts with excitement, anger, and outrage. Ren notices that George is making strange-sounding moans, and it's him that some of the others are attending to, rather than the gash-headed Beresford, who is in disgrace. Then Ren realises that Hedley has left something important behind.

'His briefcase,' he shouts over the tumult. 'Hedley's left his briefcase behind.'

Hedley's train tickets are probably in there, so Ren picks it up and runs out of the restaurant, his unconscious registering some surprise that George has been placed on the floor. He looks around for Hedley, and sees him a long way further off than he expected. Hedley is stalking off determinedly, looking like he is trying to get as far away from the damage as quickly as he can. Ren eventually catches up with him.

'Hedley,' he shouts. Hedley ignores him, hoping that he has misheard and that wasn't his named being called.

'Hedley. Hedley, you left your briefcase behind,' Ren says. Once Hedley realises he's not being chased by the manager, he turns around.

'Ah, my dear boy, thank you so much. I'd completely forgotten about that in all that commotion with your oaf of a colleague.'

'I'm sorry about that guy, Hedley. Like you said, he wasn't one of us, so I wouldn't call him my colleague. I'm new here, but I've already heard stories about him from people I know in Physics. Apparently he does shit like that a lot.'

'Quite all right, no need to apologise, young man. Are you rushing back to the scene of devastation now at Chase the Dragon? I'm not sure that's wise, there may be police arriving soon.'

Ren doubts that, but he can't say he's very keen to rush back to the restaurant. As organiser, his meal is free, so there's no need to pay a share of the bill. (Whoever pays for it tonight will be reimbursed by the department.)

'I need a drink after all that,' says Hedley. 'How about we jump in a taxi and go somewhere more salubrious?'

'Well...' Ren looks doubtful. Not going back to the restaurant is one thing, but just going off drinking with

Hedley seems a bit much. And what was up with George?

'The drinks will all be on me. As long as you take me somewhere chic.'

'Well, I can't really say no to that. C'mon, there's a taxi rank around the corner from here, I think.'

Ren knows nowhere chic in Grayvington. He's not sure there is anywhere chic in Grayvington, but then he's only been here a few months. He tells the taxi to take them to the Cock Up, a fairly pricey cocktail bar.

At the bar Ren, who is a cocktail fan (or, as Miles says, a girl), sets about ordering the most exotic and expensive cocktails he can. An amused Hedley follows suit. Hedley is clearly keen not to talk about time or the philosophy of physics any more, which suits Ren, but then he starts going on about how right-wing Tony Blair is. Why, Ren thinks, are the Cambridge smoothies always so left-wing? Does the ghost of Philby still haunt the place? Ren nods and murmurs, bored, wondering how many Eastern European agents Beagle would happily condemn to death, like Philby did. Perhaps we'd better talk about time after all, he thinks, and gets Beagle talking about temporal parts.

'The trouble I have with the idea of temporal parts,' said Ren, 'is what's the relationship between them? What connects temporal parts, and makes them add up to a physical object?'

'The relationship between them is a causal connection,' said Hedley.

'How is there any causal connection? Does the earlier time-slice of the object, call it X, cause the later one, Y, to come into existence? They're numerically distinct things. How does X cause Y to come into existence?'

'Well, Y arises out of X.'

'What does that mean, though? On your theory there's just one thing at t1, and another similar but numerically distinct thing at t2. And how can X causally affect Y anyway, if X exists at t1 but not t2 which is the only time Y exists?'

'But how do you overcome the problem of temporal intrinsics? I was sober earlier in the day, now I'm drunk. Two incompatible properties. How can I have both properties? Is it that the properties I actually have are really being-drunk-in-the-afternoon and sober-in-the-evening?'

'You mean the other way around.'

'Do I? Oh yes, the other way around. Hic. But those don't seem like the actual properties I have. I'm drunk simpliciter, not drunk-in-the-evening. And being sober and drunk don't seem to be relational properties either, so don't say what I have is the relational property of being drunk in relation to this Wednesday evening.'

'I wasn't going to say any of those. I agree they're not satisfactory. You four-dimensionalists always bring up the problem of temporal intrinsics, and it's not something I claim to know how to deal with. But I'm interested in what a prominent four-dimensionalist says about the relation between temporal parts. I can never get a straight answer to that issue.'

Ren had asked for it. A straight answer was definitely not what he got; Hedley rabbited on for half an hour with his views on this issue, until Ren managed to change the subject again. Ren wasn't sure Hedley's answer made much sense, but it was hard to tell as they'd been drinking so many cocktails. It was even harder to tell the next day, when Ren could remember little of it.

Last orders are called. 'Are you not gedding a train then?' said Ren. 'Where you stayin?'

'I was gedding a train. I've forgotten all about thad. Fug. Fug. Fug. I'll have to gedza hotel room for the night. Shid. Hope I can still ged one at this late stage.'

'You can crashz at my place if you wan.'

'Is it fid for human habidation?'

'Give it three more monthz and it won't be, but I haven't been here long enough to completely bacherlorise it yed.'

'Do you have anything do drink there?'

'Juss some beer and a bol o' whikky.'

'Will I have to drink out of a doothbrush cub?'

'I'm not a complee animal. A number of glazzes exist, and some of 'em may even be washed and located in clean cuberdz.' Ren quickly corrects himself. 'Relatively clean cubberds.'

'Hokay, lead da way.'

The two ramsquaddled academicians stumble out of the cocktail bar and find a taxi, which takes them to Ren's place. They are supposed to be men of wisdom, and sagacity would firmly suggest to them that they call it quits at this point, but they left her in their dust a while ago, so instead Ren opens the whisky and pours them two large glasses full.

They carry on like this until 2am, when Ren pulls out his spare mattress and duvet for Hedley to sleep on, and stumbles off to bed. His head has not been on the pillow for very long, and he is about to fall off a sheer sleep-cliff, when the door opens. Hedley enters, swaying. It's hard to see what's up because Ren only has the hallway light to see by, but something about Hedley doesn't look quite right. What's different? Ah, it's because he has an erect penis sticking out of the middle of his boxer shorts.

'Ren, loog at dis.'

'Have you god an SDD? Better gedda doctor to loog at it tomorrow. I can't diagnose id.'

'It needs your addenshun.'

'There's some coddon buds in the bathroom cabinet, ged some out and tage a swab for the doctor. Nuttin I can do, I'm not qualified.'

'No, I wan you to put it in your mouth.'

'Cud it out, dude. That's nod hygienic. Go way.'

'Just give it a rub.'

'You dirdy old basdard. Jesus Crize, stob wanging in fronta me. Fug ov.'

'Ren, but you don' uddersdan. I haven't had a proba sdiffy for over a year. A year. God one now. Don wanna waste it. Wanna share it. Wid you. It's my gift. For all the whiggy. And your marvellous companee.'

'The neighbourz godda dog, go and fug that if you're horny. I think ids a boy.'

'He'z come to life cossa you, you should celebrade wid me.'

'You're ov ya fuggin head, just go away and led me sleep. Bazad.'

Without realising it Ren goes off the cliff, into a deep, deep sleep. Later on he is disturbed by dreams of the Beagle trying to bugger next door's dog, which in his dream is a Beagle, though in real life there is no neighbour's dog. Which is good, because he would struggle to look it in the eye again if there was. The dream goes on for an uncomfortably long time, as Hedley stumbles around in pursuit of the unwilling dog, his anniversary boner sticking out of his boxers which he tugs with one hand while he tries to catch the dog with the other. Thankfully he doesn't ever succeed in having his way with the dog, but his pursuit is relentless, and Ren is fearful that at some point Hedley will become enraged and suddenly clamp his hand with frightening ferocity around the dog's neck and insert himself into the dog's behind.

2000-01
Semester 1
Week 4
Thursday

Mountain ranges form and disintegrate while Ren sleeps. Finally he opens his eyes a fraction. His vision is tenebrous, obscured by non-philosophical gunk, while his brain is quietly telling him, 'You're not going to like today. That's no fucking joke. You're really not going to like today.' But he thinks that maybe today can just be avoided altogether by going back to sleep, until he catches a glimpse of the clock just as he closes his eyes. 13:25. 1:25 in the afternoon. Oh God. He has three classes starting at 2pm. He hadn't set the alarm because, well, a bit squiffy last night, dear boy, and also, not even he needs to set an alarm for a 2pm class. Or so he thought.

He jumps out of bed and immediately keels over onto his knees with agonising head pain. Even if he can make it in time is he in any fit state to be able to teach? They're only seminars, where the students discuss the lecture content with the 'seminar leader', but seminars can be even harder to teach than lectures, and his brain feels like it has been drained of fluid, dried out for a while, and then topped back up with a solution of liquid bleach. But better he's there in a bad state than not there at all. He goes to the kitchen cupboard. He thinks, or rather prays, that he has some prescription-level codeine tablets left from a pack given to him by a biochemist friend. There's only two left. But two will do. He washes them, and two paracetamol tablets, down with a glass of water. Of Hedley there is no sign. He has vacated the premises.

There's no time to change out of the clothes he was

wearing last night. He rushes out of the door and gets in the old bomb he bought when he arrived in Grayvington. It was the cheapest car in the local classifieds section, which he bought to tide him over until he could afford to get a better one. Perhaps that was a mistake, he thinks. It's from the eighties, and it's already had to go into the local garage for repairs. Right now he needs a car he can trust, and this one isn't it.

He wishes he could just call in sick. But you can't just call in sick because you have a hangover, or even because you're, well, sick. Unless it's tuberculosis you turn up and teach. Of course there are high-flyers who'll miss classes because they're jetting off to a conference in New York that week, but even then they would give plenty of notice, and usually they would have arranged cover. You never just blow off a class, especially a lecture. You can't have forty-five, or one hundred and twenty, or one hundred and eighty, or three hundred and fifty students turning up to discover a notice on the lecture room door saying today's lecture is cancelled. Unless you currently have a steering wheel column where your chest should be.

And if you did miss a lecture that would usually be a disaster in terms of the course structure. It's almost impossible to reschedule a lecture, unless you have a tiny class, and if you can't reschedule it that puts you a week behind, and that screws up the essays, because that's one less essay topic for the essay due in two weeks, and some students had already planned to write on the content of the missed lecture, and the seminars after that lecture were all going to be on that material, but now none of them know that material. And it's hard to fit in an extra lecture at the end of term, which means that however you rejig things you're going to lose some material, which will make the exam more difficult to set. If you try to incorporate the content of the missing lecture into the remaining lectures that will take weeks of rewriting – rewriting lectures for that sort of purpose always takes vastly longer than you'd think

– and it will make all the remaining lectures unsatisfactory, as you try to cover too much material in too little time. So although it may seem an unnecessary hardship to give your lecture when you're practically on your death bed, not doing so is worse than actually dying.

Admittedly he is more macho about all this than some of the more delicate members of his department, notably Adalia Greenflower. But she just teaches the same postmodern make-believe every week. She could give one lecture, or thirty-seven, and it wouldn't make any difference. But really, though, you have to do your teaching, regardless of your condition. Not only can you not let students down, but there's also the fact that, financially speaking, Universities rely on teaching. Governments might still fund some Physics departments if they didn't teach, but they aren't going to fund Philosophy departments if they don't teach, or if they mess up their teaching.

And teaching undergraduates is the public face of Philosophy, seeing as no-one outside Philosophy ever reads what philosophers write any more. (This is in fact true of most University disciplines.) If philosophers started teaching only when they felt like it, that was going to get out. Hundreds of undergraduates would tell their friends and families, newspaper headlines would ensue, investigations would be called, and unless there was a swift about-turn that would be the end of academic philosophy. So even though it's just some seminars, and for his own course at that, he's going to do them, hangover or not. If the old-school Mummers could carouse all night and still turn up to rehearsals the next morning, then he could at least make a 2pm class. If you can't do the time, don't do the crime.

As he drives he is jolted out of his thoughts by his brain detecting a smell that shouldn't be there. It's faint, but it's unmistakable. Semen. Nothing else smells like it. Why does his car smell of semen? It certainly isn't his own. But how could somebody else have spunked in his car? He's heard of vandals pissing in your car, but ejaculating? He sometimes leaves his windows a little bit open, but how could anyone... Maybe it's old semen from the previous owner encrusted in his seat that is being brought out again because of his movements in the seat over the last few weeks. He tries to sit as still as possible, which is a good idea anyway because he feels like he has a psychotic imp inside his skull who is applying and tightening a clamp around the front left part of his brain. Tightening it beyond any level that even an imp could think reasonable. The ejaculate smell is so faint that he thinks he must be imagining it. A phantosmia. Probably caused by olfactory bulb damage, hopefully temporary, brought about by an excessive alcohol intake.

Whether or not the car is tainted by semen, it at least provides him with a breakdown-free ride to the University today. When he gets onto the campus, at 1:45, he has to be careful, because clueless students with their heads in the clouds often drift across the roads in front of the cars, oblivious to the presence of the metallic death machines in their midst, and his reflexes are going to be slower today. So many students wander around the campus in a daze, their heads full of philosophy, science, history, romance, current politics and the self-importance of youth, talking excitedly to the other idiots they've made friends with, that the idea that a car might, in this very oasis of learning, mangle their fresh body or throw it thirty yards up into the air and then back down onto the hard road, breaking their neck, seems very remote to them, despite the fact that cars are passing them by the whole time.

Can he find a parking spot? Some people should have fucked off for lunch, but possibly those spots have been filled by people coming in at lunchtime, or coming back from lunch. He drives around the Terminal building where Philosophy is located, but there's nothing. He feels the pain in his head acutely. He goes over to the car park near Psychology. Nothing. His brain increases its throbbing. Did someone add some pesticide to the bleach solution sloshing about in his skull? Chemistry building? Yes, a spot. Yes, they added pesticide. He parks, but now he'll have to run to get to the Terminal Building on time.

It's a horrible run, if one could even call it a run. For some reason he is favouring the right side of his body, like he has hemiparesis. The way his brain feels, he may have had a stroke and just not noticed it over the headache. And he's barely even noticing the headache right now over the screaming of his body to stop running and lie down on the footpath for a half hour's rest. Never has bitumen looked so comfortable and inviting; he just wants to snuggle up into it. But he pushes on like a marathoner completing the last few dozen yards, dragging the left side of his body behind him, like that marathon runner everyone saw a few years ago who had something go very wrong with their body just before the finish line, but who was determined to get over the line regardless. If you've run almost twenty-six miles, you've got to do the last few yards to get over the line, whatever the physical cost. Stopping now is not an option.

He reaches the front door of the Terminal building, and shifts down a gear, from a semi-run to a brisk walk, trying to hide his horror-film gasping, trying to appear normal. It's 1:55: he's going to make it. But he still needs to take the stairs rather than the lift, because that will be quicker. His mind is, at least, distracted from the awfulness of climbing the stairs in his condition by blurry and disjointed memories of last night which have started to seep, unbidden and unwanted, into his consciousness. A paralytic, backlit Hedley, stroking himself while framed by the bedroom door. Oh fuck me. He remembers now Hedley's membership offer. No wonder the greasy fucker scarpered this morning.

He gets to his office at 1:57. Thank God none of his colleagues are in the corridor at the same time to see him, he must look a mess, but there's no time to sort himself out. He gets his attendance sheets and a pen. The first room he's teaching in isn't far away. I'm going to make it, he thinks, although I'm not sure my body is.

As Ren briskly walks to the teaching room, he can feel himself covered in sweat, which is starting to go unpleasantly cold. The sweat is probably itself highly alcoholic. His hair is soaked. He enters the room to some odd looks, and sits down. 'I've just had a game of squash', he says, to explain his sweat-soaked state. That was probably a mistake, he thinks. They'll smell the booze, they'll see my state, they'll know I'm lying. I might as well be a wino from the park who's just wandered in. He attempts a smile to reassure them that all is well. That was also probably unwise. He doesn't think it came out very well. Probably even worse than one of Robot's smiles, and it doing it has hurt his head some more.

As he takes the register he surreptitiously sniffs the air to see if he can smell alcohol. He can't, but what he can smell shocks him. It's faint, but not as faint as it was in the car. Semen. Sea. Men. He has a horrible realisation. It wasn't in the car. It's... on him. Hedley. That limaceous bastard Hedley must die. Horribly. Where is it? It's hard to tell, but he thinks the smell emanates from above his nose line. His head. His hair. Hedley must have spunked onto his hair. You fucking dirty cunt, Hedley. I'm ruined, he thinks. I've walked into my own personal Gallipoli. Dozens of rifles are drawing a bead on me now, about to blow my career, and my life, away.

After the pause brought about by this train of thought, he resumes his attendance check, calling out some more names. He realises why the smell is now less faint than before. Hedley spoofed into his hair, and it dried overnight. But when he ran from the car park his hair got soaked in sweat, and now the dehydrated semen has been reconstituted, the liquid gel regenerated like fruit juice from concentrate. Jesus, has it been recreated in all its thick white odiferous glory? Is it now slowly sliding off his hair, about to fall in mucus-like globs onto the attendance sheet in front of him? He has finished the attendance register, but he's frozen in place. He desperately wants to run out to the nearest toilet to check himself in the mirror, but he is unable to move or talk. Maybe he should pretend to smooth his hair down with his hand to get rid of it, but he cannot bear the thought that he would bring his hand down to eye level and see it covered in cum.

Get a hold of yourself, he thinks. The semen isn't going to reconstitute itself back to how it was. Not after all this time. That couldn't happen, right? It's all broken down now, surely. Has to be. But there's still the smell. He prays that the smell (or the booze smell, for that matter) won't carry far. There are no students sitting in the front two rows, as usual. Normally he'd get some of them to come and sit closer, but not today. Just stay away from the students, and keep them away from you. Would all the girls recognise the smell anyway? Even if they have had experience of the stuff, they may not have the familiarity with it that the boys have. But then they are third-years. So maybe... no, this speculation isn't helpful. Concentrate on the seminar.

The students in this class are normally chatty, and get on with the discussion without too much prompting, but perhaps sensing something today, they don't say much. He forces himself to grit his teeth and ignore the pain. It takes a superhuman effort not only to talk, but to stop himself holding his head and squeezing it. When is the fucking codeine going to kick in? He's trying very hard to get things going, even though in his head he's really thinking of ways he can kill Hedley at the next conference they're both at, and gradually the students warm up and eventually the conversation starts to flow. He's not doing a bad job, but all that's keeping him going is the expectation that the codeine will kick in any moment now, and the desperate hope that what is coating his hair can't be seen or smelt. The fact that the students are acting fairly normally gives him hope about his hair.

The class draws to an end, still without any codeine rush.

He starts to get nervous. The class has been fine, but in a minute he is going to have to go and examine himself in a mirror, and he's afraid of what he might see. The students file out. He avoids rushing out, trying to act normal, but what if one of the students wants to come and talk to him? None do, though. That's good, as long as it's not because no-one wants to talk to a man with hair covered in penis snot. As soon as he can he leaves the room. He avoids the toilet across the corridor in case any of the students have gone into it. He goes the other way to the students, wandering around the building in search of another male toilet, but is unable to find one. He's starting to panic because he has to be in another building in a few minutes for the next seminar. Somewhere in this building there must be another male toilet, but a lengthy peregrination is not something he has time for. He's forced to go back to the toilet outside the teaching room, which should at least be free of any students from his class by now.

He closes the door and looks in the mirror. There's no visible sign of cum on his hair. Relief floods through him like the codeine should be doing. Perhaps it is the codeine, released now by the disappearance of the tension that was preventing it from working. He looks rough, and his hair looks dishevelled, but nothing too out of the ordinary for a philosopher. His head still throbs, but that no longer seems to matter. He sticks his head under the tap and soaks his hair, and then gives it a quick blast under the hand dryer.

He's a bit late for the next class, but not so late that it matters. As he takes the register, he feels the codeine wash trickle into his consciousness, and his headache starts to recede. Everything is all right after all. He even starts to see the funny side of Hedley's behaviour. Silly old bugger. He suppresses a hysterical chuckle. Maybe he won't kill him after all.

Ren goes back to his office after his classes. He had intended to go home afterwards, but he's feeling a lot better now, and he needs to get some work done. But Compton spots him going in, and comes to see him.

Compton looks bemused at the state of Ren, not that he looks that good himself. 'Well, that was an interesting night, wouldn't you say?'

'Indubitably so,' says Ren.

'What happened when you ran after Hedley?'

'I found him. Then we went and had a few drinks somewhere away from Beresford. What happened at the restaurant?'

'I don't suppose you know what happened. George collapsed with a suspected heart attack, and we had to call an ambulance.'

'Fucking hell.'

'The staff wanted to kick us all out because of the fight, but they could hardly do so with George in such a bad way, waiting for an ambulance. So Beresford alone was given his marching orders, which he took with bad grace. He didn't even pay for his meal, insisting that it should come out of the department's visiting speaker fund. He said Hedley had forfeited his right to the free meal.'

'Arsehole. So what's the situation with George? I assume from your light tone that he isn't dead. Or isn't dead yet.'

'He's okay. Turns out it wasn't a heart attack. They think it's something to do with his oesophagus. They let him out of hospital this morning. He's okay, but a little weak. But then he's not the strongest person to start with.'

This is an understatement. George is, in Ren and Compton's view, the most deliberately unfit person the Western world had seen for around two hundred and fifty years, since, in their estimation, Lord Melbury of Chichester, who had himself carried everywhere by his servants, and who once went eleven years without ever standing up. The last time George did any physical exercise was in a school PE class at age thirteen, after which he got excused from all such activities by way of notes from his mother.

That was nearly fifty years ago, and the memory of what

physical exercise is, and what it feels like, has all but completely faded from George's memory. He drives everywhere whenever possible, even to the corner shop, always parking as close as he can to his destination. He constantly wrangles on the phone with the Timetabling department over where his classes are to be held – he wants to minimise the distance he has to walk to every class, so he complains every time his classes are put in teaching rooms across the other side of campus. He even complains about how far away the library is from the department, even though it's only a few hundred yards, and he has instigated a move for the University to create a library delivery service for lazy – or, as he puts it, busy – academics. He waited years to bag the office closest to the men's toilets, even though it isn't one of the bigger ones, because that saves him having to walk up and down the corridor all day to empty his bladder.

'Why in God's name would I want to do that?' was what he always says when asked to play tennis, or participate in some other athletic foolishness. He says it in a genuinely puzzled voice. 'I'm essentially a bibliophage,' he allegedly once said to Compton, 'a pure intelligence accidentally shackled to this monstrous world. If I had to be tied to something physical, it should have been a desk, not a human body.' When George says such things the tone is very much tongue-in-cheek, but no-one thinks the content is far from the mark.

Walter swears that he once asked George, years ago, if he wanted to join the Humanities cricket team, and George smiled and said, 'The Germans aren't invading, so there is no need for me to train to go over the top, is there? The bulldozer has been invented, and for the tasks that it's ill-equipped for there's still a plentiful supply of unemployed young men with muscles, so I'll get on with the life of the mind, thanks all the same.'

George has stopped himself from becoming fat by the simple expedient of not eating much. Eating isn't something he is interested in anyway – in fact, he's not much interested in anything outside philosophy, except maybe some history. (It is impossible to imagine him being interested in sex. He does have a wife, but once you've seen her it's even harder to imagine him being interested in sex. In fact, once you've seen her it's impossible to imagine yourself ever having an interest in sex again.) Also, he always said, not eating much prolongs your life, a claim which current research backs up, as George now insists on telling everyone. However, the combination of a long-term lack of both exercise and food has resulted in George's body becoming very weak, and he looks much older than his years. People are loathe to physically touch him for fear that he will crumple. People are loathe to close a door near him for fear that the resulting puff of air will blow him away. Some people are even afraid to raise their voices to him for fear that he'll physically fall apart once the vibrations strike him. His stick-thin limbs would disgrace a bird, and his lack of subcutaneous fat means that his skin looks extra wrinkly, like a three-D scale model of a landscape shaped by ancient water flows. Not even the students call him 'Scrotum', because it's just too obvious, although some students find 'Ballbag' hard to resist, on account of George's last name, which is Bagnall.

'Is there going to be any fallout?' asks Ren.

'Not unless the restaurant complains, which they probably won't. It's not like they never ever have loud drunks in there who get a bit violent.'

'Poor old George. Hope he's all right.'

'He says he's fine. Right as rain apparently. He's coming back in tomorrow.'

'Really? Why doesn't he take a few days off to rest up?'

'He doesn't want people to think he's past it. Besides, rest is a word without application in George's life. There do not exist the necessary divisions between suitable activities for the word to have any meaning.'

'Whereas my life has some very clear divisions, such as between the drunk and sober periods.'

'Quite. Speaking of that, you look distinctly feculent. Did you put a lot away with the Beagle?'

'Quite a lot, yes.'

'I presume he made a pass at you?'

'Why do you presume that? Because of my obvious irresistible sexual magnetism, or because he's known for it? Has he done it to you?'

'No, I'm not young enough for him. He's known for it. And you do have irresistible sexual magnetism, although only to old queens. As soon as you went after him people said don't leave Ren alone with Hedley.'

'Why is Beresford so against him? Does Beresford have a son studying philosophy at his University?'

'No, Beresford is just an embarrassing, belligerent turd-turkey who is constantly spoiling for a fight. About things he knows nothing about. Which is most things, not just philosophy.'

'Yes, but it's perhaps more embarrassing that our department has members who know less philosophy than Beresford does. He knows much more than Verna Leach, for instance. If you had to choose between her or Beresford to teach on any central area of philosophy, you'd pick him.'

'True, but then I'd pick most second-year undergraduates over Verna in that sort of situation.'

'The same applies to Tony fucking Shaver,' said Ren. 'And Adelia. How can we be a credible department with people like that in it?'

'Tony, Adelia, Verna, none of them are even philosophers, really. Adelaide Newman, at least, did some real philosophy at Cambridge, even if she did go off the rails later. But those three, I doubt any of them have ever taken an analytic philosophy module. If they did I expect they got a poor mark. Are you aware yet that Tony's undergraduate degree is in Sociology, not Philosophy?'

'You're fucking kidding me. How is he teaching here? That explains a lot.'

'He did a few subsid Philosophy modules as part of his

Sociology course, I gather, in things like Marxism and Foucault, and got friendly with one of the radical lecturers in the Philosophy department, who encouraged him to do a Philosophy PhD.'

'How was he allowed to do a PhD in Philosophy on the strength of that?'

'It was at the University of Chippenham in the mid-eighties.'

'Say no more.'

'The topic of his PhD was something like "A Foucaldian Analysis of Worker Power Struggles in British Trade Unions 1945-1955".'

'That explains why he's such an expert on metaphysics then. Why is he wasted teaching Marxism, and Philosophy of the Social Sciences? He should be teaching Plato and Aristotle. How did we ever give him a job?'

'Derek's fault, really. Adelaide was on the hiring panel, and she was of course determined to hire whoever was the most sympathetic to feminism, plus she'd previously been at Chippenham so some of her old partners-in-arms tipped her the wink with Tony. Derek was also on the hiring panel as the analytic, but he knew of Tony through left-wing circles, and thought him politically sound, even if he wasn't analytic. The outside person on the panel was a sociologist, who thought Tony was marvellous, so that's why we got him rather than Leighton Hyde.'

'Leighton Hyde applied? As in the rising-star-of-cognitive-science-Leighton-Hyde?'

'Yes, Walter, Martha and George had to fight to even get him on the shortlist. But with that hiring panel he stood no chance.'

'So just when was it that the department took a nosedive? When we hired Tony? Or Adelia? Verna? Or even Derek? Or does it all go back to Adelaide, the first bad apple?'

'In Walter's view it all goes back to Adelaide's appointment. He says she's the original cancer at the heart of the department.'

'Adelaide Newman,' said Ren slowly and dramatically. 'She sits there in the gloom of her mephitic office, a hulking, malevolent spider spinning its web. In the heart of darkness. Like Marlon Brando. Very like Marlon Brando, if you're looking at her.'

'You do put things rather fancifully,' said Compton. 'But I like it.'

'The big bull dyke suzerain of all that has gone wrong.'

'With the department?'

'With philosophy. Maybe with everything. Well, with the department. Let's not overstate her influence.'

'Yes, and she's becoming a forgotten figure in her field, which she doesn't like.'

'The menacing, sussurant voice. The baleful glare. The commanding way she manages to never have a class with more than a dozen students in it, all of them starry-eyed feminists, studying her own classic text, and nothing else. It's amazing how she achieves so much with so little personal charm, and so little effort. She doesn't even try to pretend she likes any of her academic acolytes. It's clear that she resents them for stealing her thunder.'

Adelaide's influential book went by the name of *Irrational Women*. In it she lambasted traditional ideas of rationality, which she said are male-centric, and Western. Women's thinking, with its emphasis on intuition, is different to men's, and superior. Philosophers need to get with the program, and dump, or radically change, their conception of rationality, though the details of how this would proceed were notably absent.

'I've been having the occasional flick through Adelaide's famous book the last few weeks,' said Ren. 'Obviously it's terrible, but what did surprise me was how slight it is. It can't be much more than thirty thousand words. About four papers worth. The way her fans talk about it you'd think it was this mammoth, comprehensive survey of the whole of philosophy. Have you read it?'

'Yes, I thought it would be prudent to when I joined the

department. It's basically a con job. Some tendentious descriptions of a few big ancient philosophers, looking at sections that no-one has taken seriously for hundreds of years, some light analysis of a few more modern feminists, and that's it.'

'So why is it so big amongst the feminists?'

'Seems to me it's because to them she has philosophical credibility. Remember that Adelaide went to Cambridge, and in those days she was an actual, if very ordinary, philosopher. She's read Plato, Aristotle, and the like, and has a poor but passable understanding of them. And same with the big union powerand eighteenth century philosophers. So she can write about them with some apparent credibility. That makes her look distinguished. Here's a real-life analytic philosopher who knows this stuff who's telling us what we want to hear. Verna Leach couldn't do that, she's a former council clerk with a degree from a Poly who wouldn't know her Malenbranche from a tree branch. Nothing she could write on any ancients or moderns would have the same sort of credibility, even amongst her fellow feminists. Whereas Adelaide can talk the right sort of talk. And, as you may or may not know, she wrote a book before that, called *Language and Object*, a fairly normal analytic book based on her D.Phil. It was very poor, nobody thinks it's any good, but it's something else that gives her legitimacy.'

'Let me get this straight. She has credibility with people who despise analytic philosophy and think it's a terrible mistake, because... they think she's good at analytic philosophy?'

'Precisely. Consistency's not their strong point, that's an analytic hangup. Anyway, she provides some analytic gravitas for them to justify their hatred of logic and reason.'

'She did her graduate work at Cambridge as well, didn't she?'

'Yes, she did her D.Phil there, the one that became *Language and Object*. After publishing that she was dreaming that she was going to be a great Professor of Metaphysics.

After all, she's been to Cambridge, she's a female trailblazer, and she's got a book out with Musgrave, in those days one of the leading academic publishers. But the book is not much good, and she doesn't know that she only got the publishing deal because her supervisor convinced a friend who worked at Musgrave that it will strike a blow for female equality. So she never manages to get a permanent post anywhere, which is not surprising, as according to both Walter and George, who knew her from conferences in those days, she came across even then as the angry crusading lesbian always glowering at everyone, and no-one could ever hear what she said because she mutters and grunts.'

'Like she does now.'

'Like she does now. So she moves around doing part-time tutoring at various places for ten years or so, not publishing much, getting more and more disillusioned, and she blames everything on sexism, even though the same places that have rejected her are hiring other women, women who are much better at analytic philosophy than she is.'

'Like Martha?'

'Yes, women like Martha who are good philosophers, who are being hired on the basis of their work, not because they're female. So she's not getting anywhere, and she must know by now that she's not really that good at analytic philosophy. She's no longer a trailblazer and she knows that they are plenty of woman around now who are much better at philosophy than she is, so there's no novelty in her any more. Even the most right-on places, which are increasing in number, who want to hire an analytic woman are going to hire these new women, not her.'

'So obviously she should find something else in life to do. But, knowing her, she's not going to do that. And it's not like she can find a husband with money.'

'Yep. By now, so the story goes, she's angry with analytic philosophy, which has betrayed her, and she's developed a pathological hatred of men, which apparently all started at

Cambridge where she had to deal with the academic men there. I expect there were a lot of smug pricks there, you know how bad some Oxbridge types are now, imagine what they were like back then. She blames men for her dream not coming true, but she has great longanimity, and she will make it happen. She's been getting more and more into feminism which is really starting to take off now, and she realises a pseudo-serious scholarly book giving feminism some academic respectability is just the ticket for her. She dashes it off, and her earlier contact at Musgrave, who's now very high-up and much more Continental than before, laps it up and makes a song-and-dance of it. Bingo! She's suddenly a big name in feminist circles, and she goes straight to a Senior Lectureship at the University of Chippenham, which has turned, as they used to say in those days, very Marxism-lesbian.'

'And eventually we get her.'

'Yeah, Grayvington finally decides to get on the feminist bandwagon and forces the Philosophy department to hire her as a Professor at an inflated salary. Even though by that point she's no longer the flavour of the month. In fact by then she's been left behind by all the new postmodern bullshit, and she looks distinctly old-fashioned in those sort of circles, but of course Grayvington doesn't know this because they're clueless about everything. So she's already become a museum piece, revered, but not a subject for current research, but Grayvington comes to the rescue and gives her a plum job.

'And she takes the place downhill.'

'She does indeed. While she can't quite bring herself to take seriously shit like Lacan and his penis which is equivalent to the square root of minus one, although apparently, his defenders say, it's not the penis he's talking about but the phallus, and the phallus turns out to be whatever it is that the child imagines the father to have that makes the mother desire him rather than the child, and so on, and so on, rubbish piled on top of rubbish...'

'Adelaide?'

'Yes, sorry, back to Adelaide. While she can't quite bring herself to take seriously shit like Lacan, she will hire people who do. Since she was forced in we've had more of the flim-flammers forced upon us, and they're impossible to get rid off. And once they get some numbers they breed, and they take over as much as they can, moving up the food chain. I mean, research is just a joke to them, they have no interest in it except to the extent that it allows them to gain power, so many of the new breed are happy to move into management as soon as they can, although they haven't done quite so well at that at Grayvington as they have places like Chippenham and Uttoxeter. But even the ones who want to stay doing research, and by that I mean research in quote marks, they get onto as many committees as they can, and immediately set about adding and changing rules to make everything as progressive as possible. They're totally ruthless about it, and they are having some success at Grayvington doing that. That's why there's no point trying to compromise with them, or appeal to their better nature. They will steamroller you given half a chance. Your new friends in your TITE class sound like that. Give them a few years and they'll be running the gulags here.'

'Welcome to sunny Solevtsky,' says Ren. 'Don't bother packing a toothbrush.'

2000-01
Semester 1
Week 4
Friday

It's another Friday afternoon, and the Fabulous Lorenzos have again spent most of it uselessly discussing their TITE group project. They've been in a spare teaching room in the Psychology building. Miles had to come outside to meet them all, to show them the way to the room. You can't ask anyone to come into the Psychology building without guidance, because they'll go missing for days, and eventually be found crying and gibbering in a corner somewhere. Student rumour has it that the building itself was deliberately designed as a maze for the purposes of a psychology experiment, though in truth the reason why it's a rabbit warren is that it's been extended so many times, in very haphazard ways. It's been due to be demolished for years now; one day it will be knocked down, but that day keeps getting put off.

Grayvington University started life in 1891 as a few departments in some office space and townhouses in the unpromising suburb of Baron Heights. This location was chosen mainly because it was on the railway line, and there were cheap places for rent, as business was not booming in Baron Heights. Some free land behind these streets was then acquired, which formed the basis for a new campus, which was christened 'Greenwood Glade'. The first stage of the campus building works was completed in 1902, and the new campus was opened, in the absence of the Prime Minister who had to cancel at the last minute, by Larry Lorenzo, a popular local music-hall entertainer.

By 1910, at the heart of the campus there stood (as it still stands today) the magnificent Terminal Building, named in honour of Grayvington's railway heritage, and the fact that the University is a stop on the railway line. The Terminal Building was constructed from sandstone, and was lavishly laid out inside with wide corridors, huge rooms, large windows, quality marble staircases, and superb oak and walnut parquetry floors. Unfortunately the huge expense of creating the Terminal Building meant that little money was left over for the rest of the campus, so the other buildings were hastily thrown together using the cheapest building methods of the time, with little in the way of proper design.

Greenwood Glade wasn't large enough to encompass the inevitable expansion of the University that took place over the next century, so by the 1930's the University was spreading out further into the dismal houses and offices of Baron Heights, as well as constructing ever-taller buildings on Greenwood Glade, whose green grass and trees have gradually disappeared as the concrete has expanded. The original campus was poorly designed, and on top of that further waves of expansion have been arranged in an even more incompetent fashion by highly-paid professionals. The current campus is a dirty, confused, higgledy-piggledy, concreted mess, an architectonic parody of a hungover student's bedroom, with a range of the worst architectural styles from various decades on display. For instance, the soot-blackened Blake Tower, unmistakably a product of sixties campus brutalism, is flanked on one side by a rickety old house from 1920, which still serves as the campus' increasingly outdated health clinic, and on the other by a glass-and-steel inside-out ultra-modern Science Lecture Theatre, which has only been recently completed (and which only came in at three times over budget, which isn't bad by Grayvington standards).

Like most British Universities no provision has been made (or ever will be made) for the fact that it rains a lot in Britain, so students and lecturers are used to arriving in over-crowded lecture rooms with sopping wet umbrellas and raincoats which have nowhere to go. Ventilation is inadequate, so the rooms fog up with all the moisture, and many of the old rooms smell of mould, a smell that no commercial company has ever been able to remove.

In 1982 the University purchased, on the quiet, but to the dismay of those few academics who heard about it, the nasty old Grayvington council offices, located in the suburb of Remington. The council was selling these because it had itself purchased, at great expense, some prime office space in the city centre, in order to move the bulk of the Council's operations closer to the Town Hall. The council had wanted to do this for years, but had never previously been able to find a sucker willing to buy their old offices in Remington, as Remington had become a desolate and difficult-to-access part of the city, due to the way various railway lines, railway bridges, and new roads had intertwined.

It was thought that the University would shift some departments to Remington, but in an unexpected move it decided to transfer most of its administration and bureaucracy there, although the Vice Chancellor retained his enormous and luxurious suite of offices in the Terminal Building. No academic departments made the move, which was a relief to those departments, but there was concern that moving the bureaucracy to its own fiefdom would create a monster. This concern would have been more widespread, but the University's secrecy over the whole matter meant that quite a lot of academics, and almost all the students, were, and still are, unaware of the existence of the Remington campus, which perhaps gives you an idea of the usefulness of those bureaucrats. (HR, of course, is located there.)

Remington is now better known, by those who know of its existence, as 'Canberra'. It is the scene of countless computer system disasters, and the bureaucracy has grown so much that there are now rumours that the University intends to purchase a second admin-only site. Canberra, like its Australian namesake, is not a place that anyone visits willingly, although for a while older townspeople would turn up asking about paying their council tax.

Baron Heights, meanwhile, has become, since the seventies, a place uninhabitable for anyone except undergraduates, drug addicts and petty thieves (the extensions of the last two categories greatly overlap. In fact the extensions of all three categories have been known to overlap). The civilians who previously lived there have been gradually forced out by the endless noisy parties and inconsiderate behaviour of the students. Even the lecturers who owned houses in Baron Heights due to its convenient location have mostly gone, and the grad students long ago learnt to rent elsewhere. Those who have made the mistake of hanging on for too long only stay there now because to sell up and move from Baron Heights would mean taking a considerable financial hit, as property prices there have being stagnating for decades. The only buyers are landlords who specialise in student properties, and the student property market is at the bottom of the heap because most students want cheap share houses which they don't have to look after, so the landlords don't bother looking after them either. And because students are bad at paying rent, there are endless disputes about who is responsible for the rent, which landlords get caught up in, so no landlord with any class or aspiration goes there.

The petty thieves like Baron Heights because students are easy prey, despite the fact that there's usually always someone home watching daytime TV. Students are always leaving their doors unlocked, or even open, they're often drunk or stoned, strangers are in and out of the houses all the time, the students leave valuable stuff just lying around, and they're always losing their stuff anyway. Half the time a student has something stolen from them they don't even realise that it's been stolen until days, or even weeks, later. This situation will only worsen in the years ahead, as more and more students come to Grayvington with desirable and easily lifted tech, such as laptops, smartphones and iPads, although by that time some of the more well-off students will start to bypass Baron Heights and choose to live in high-end purpose-built student apartment blocks in other parts of Grayvington.

'What a waste of an afternoon,' says Ren, as they walk out of the Psych building, with the rain starting to fall. 'There's no point properly researching these topics, Balderstone is just going to fail anything that's done right. One of us is just going to have to hold their nose and write the sort of fustian nonsense that he wants.'

'That sounds like you,' says Miles. 'You know more about this sort of thing than any of us.'

'Alternatively, we just use Burroughs' cut-up technique,' says Ren. 'We write out all the right buzzwords, cut them out, and then randomly draw them from a hat.'

'Sounds good to me,' says Miles. 'An afternoon's work that we can use for years.'

'But is any of us really going to stand up in class and say such words?' says Ren. 'And defend them? I just can't do that.'

'I'll do that if necessary' says Lily.

'Let's just go get a drink,' sighs Ren. 'Shall we go to the staff club, or the student bar?'

'I have to go get a train,' says Lily, putting up her umbrella.

'Going to your love-nest in London, I expect?' says Miles.

'I'm meeting up with Jason, yes,' says Lily.

'A fuck-fest in a love-nest,' says Douglas.

'Douglas!' says Ren.

'Sorry,' says a sheepish Douglas.

'You boffins do come out with the most disgraceful sleaze,' says Ren. 'I shan't be sending any of my illegitimate children to study science. First you have J. B. S. Haldane talking up Stalin, and now we have Oram, his career barely underway, already casting slurs on the reputations of fine young ladies.'

'Actually, we're going to see the ballet,' says Lily.

'Heavens to Betsy,' says Ren. 'Two lesbians. I never would have defended your honour had I known how sordid things had become with the bluestockings.'

'Bye-bye boys. Enjoy your drinks.'

As Lily goes off, Douglas says, 'The student bar? Mind you, I'm not really in the mood any more.'

'Neither am I,' says Ren, trying not to stare too obviously at Lily as she disappears into the distance.

'I've got too much work on to go drinking,' says Miles.

'Well, we're a sorry lot, aren't we?' says Ren. 'Let's just go and work on a Friday night then, and say goodbye to our youth and freedom.'

'I'm not even going to do any work,' says Douglas. 'I'm just going to go to bed early. And I barely had a youth, or freedom.'

The umbrella-less trio separate, and trudge off in the rain (from which there is, of course, no shelter, as this is Britain). The glow that all new lecturers have for the first few months is starting to fade. Ren passes undergraduates, not that much younger than he is, chattering excitedly to each other as they head to the bar, and he realises sadly that already there's a vast gulf between them.

'This old man, he sings. 'He played one...'

2000-01
Semester 1
Week 5
Tuesday

The dawn creeps over the top of the houses on Ren's street like a burglar jumping from roof to roof, looking for a weak spot. Has he left the upstairs bathroom window open as usual? Ren always appreciates being able to see Eos' arrival when he's sober. It partially makes up for having to get up with only four hours sleep under his belt, thanks to a very late night working on tomorrow's lecture.

What's forcing him to get up early is that today is a lucky day. Not for him. For today. The day itself, Monday, is lucky, for it's been granted the immense honour of hosting the second Philosophy Departmental General Meeting of the semester. Tuesday, Wednesday and Thursday are all jealous as can be, although Friday, of course, doesn't give a shit, because it's Friday.

It's because this meeting will take up hours and hours of valuable time that he was forced to work until the wee small hours last night. He would be crankier about this, except that as this is only his second ever departmental meeting it still has some novelty value to him. The novelty of departmental meetings will wear off soon, but for now the prospect of wasting hours of his life listening to a bunch of windbags boring on as though it's the Olympic boredom tryouts doesn't fill him with the gloom it will later on. He remembers sitting in his first departmental meeting earlier on in the semester thinking that he is fortunate to have made it to twenty-eight before he's ever had to do this sort of thing, and thanking Christ he doesn't have a job which requires him to sit in meetings every day. But then he got a

PhD precisely in order to avoid having a job that requires him to sit in meetings every day, so it's himself he has to thank, not Christ.

He also remembers feeling somewhat wistful at the first meeting because he realised that as much as he had tried to avoid it, he's having to grow up. It was hard to deny that when you were sitting around a polished mahogany table in a fancy boardroom discussing, with people with grey hair, matters that would affect other people's lives, overlooked by portraits of what looked like distinguished scholars (although in reality they're probably just former University bureaucrats). His extended childhood is being left behind. Unfortunately. Perhaps there is still time to join a band.

Ren sits down across from George.

'George, why are you here? You have the perfect excuse not to come,'

'I'm fine,' insists George. 'Rumours of my demise are much exaggerated,' he chuckles.

'The rumours may be premature, but they won't be exaggerated if you can't have a rest when you need one.'

'Pshaw. You youngsters go on the sick if someone breathes on you too close.'

'But why come to a departmental meeting when you don't have to? Isn't getting old misery enough?'

'It might be unpleasant, but if you're not at the meeting to vote, you might regret it later. The world is ruled by those who stay awake in committee meetings.'

Ren, like George, stops himself looking at the Continentals after George has made this point. Verna has turned her head their way, and is listening in.

'I take your point. Still, you don't look well.'

'He never looks well,' says Walter.

'You need,' interrupts Verna, 'some natural herbal remedies.'

'Oh God, here we go' says Compton.

'You don't have to stop whatever treatment your doctor is giving you,' begins Verna.

'I'm not having any treatment. There's nothing much wrong with me.'

'Of course there is. You just take the herbal medicine in addition.'

'And dance around the room three times, chanting the magic words,' says Compton.

'Look, herbal medicine is starting to show good results in scientific trials.'

'No, it's not,' says Ren. 'Those results are feeble, and they can never replicate them anyway.'

'I thought science was a grand narrative and a conspiracy?' says Compton. 'Isn't it a bad thing to be showing some results in a scientific context?'

'Science just needs some corrections made.'

Ren decides to change the subject. There's not much point in starting a serious argument just before a meeting is due to start. 'How come we're not in the same room as last time?'

'We only get into one of the boardrooms if we're very lucky,' says Walter. 'The meetings are usually always in here.'

'Here' is one of the drab teaching rooms, with wobbly, veneer-covered chipboard tables.

'Don't expect a good a lunch as last time either,' says Martha.

'The downhill slide continues,' says Ren. 'Last week in my lecture the overhead projector broke.'

'If you think there's a downhill slide happening, wait until you see the agenda,' says Tristram York. Ren takes a look and his heart sinks.

The mood is further soured when the Head of Department – Robot – comes in. Robot is a man who takes departmental business extremely seriously. Plus he has no small talk, unless it involves the latest philosophy clishmaclaver, which he discusses in the most po-faced, ungossipy way possible, thus negating the whole point of it. You have to admire Robot for taking the job as Head of

Department seriously, but everything he is involved in – and that includes just sitting near him – becomes highly unpleasant, simply because of his miserable presence.

The mood becomes even more algific when Adelaide Newman comes in. She grunts at Verna, says nothing to anyone else, and sits as far away as she can, studiously ignoring everyone, even the Continentals, who are all sitting together. Her presence is something of a surprise; she rarely attends departmental meetings. Perhaps Robot had told her to start turning up. Nobody else would have had the balls to do so, but then nobody else wants her to turn up.

The atmosphere improves a bit when Derek Lucas comes in talking and laughing loudly, accompanied by Bill Porterfield. Derek never lets anyone's disapproval, not Robot's nor Adelaide's, dampen his mood and stop him broadcasting his humorous opinions as vehemently as he can, and Ren has to admire him for that.

Derek isn't the easiest person to talk over, but Bill, not the most demonstrative man, found it harder than most. It's difficult to tell whether Bill even likes Derek. Perhaps Bill has been waiting all these years merely for a gap in the conversation so he can tell Derek that he's a cockhead. Watching Bill tramp silently alongside Derek, Ren is reminded of an old hymn:

A mute companion at my side
Paces and plods, the whole day long,
Accepts the measure of my stride,
Yet gives no cheer by word or song.

More close than any doggish friend,
Not ranging far and wide, like him,
He goes where'er my footsteps tend,
Nor shrinks for fear of life or limb.

Bill is someone who appears not to know much about anything in Philosophy except for an obscure seventeenth century contemporary of Locke's called Robert Langston. This is the only topic that Bill ever publishes articles on, and he's been supposedly working on a book about Langston for at least seventy-five years. Not that he publishes many articles on Langston – the non-existence of any modern discussion of Langston's work makes publishing on him difficult, as does the complete modern lack of interest in anything Langston had ever said on any topic at any time. Langston had not been in any way a colleague of Locke's (or any other figure of note from that period), and had not engaged Locke in any verbal or epistolary disputes, preferring to ignore what he thought was an overrated talent, and plow his own peculiar furrow, producing bizarre theories, such as his view that everything was ultimately made of fire. (The argument apparently went something like this: Every physical thing has some amount of heat. Heat is produced by fire. Therefore objects must, in some way, contain fire. But fire would not burn and produce heat if it was confined to the space between the elements. Therefore elements, and thus objects, must themselves be fire, only temporarily transmuted into a different form. Langston also thought that some of these temporary forms, like wood, transmuted back into fire more easily than others, like water, but even water was really made of fire. This argument, Ren thought, while clearly idiotic and a piece of logical Swiss cheese, was no more idiotic than some of the others from that time.)

As a result, all Bill could manage in the way of publishing was to get the occasional article in somewhat inconsequential, historically-based journals, like *17th Century Philosophico-Historical Studies*, and even then only when his friend, Frederick Millard, refereed them. Some had wondered whether Porterfield had invented Langston himself, as no-one had ever heard of him before, but then one day (so Compton says) Millard came to visit the department, and he seemed to know about Langston.

But maybe, Ren thought, he was in on the whole thing.

He could write articles about Langston, and Porterfield would have to referee them, because no-one else could, just as he always gets to referee Bill's articles, and that way they keep getting each other published for years, at least until some grad student decides to look up Langston's work and finds it doesn't exist.

No, of course Langston exists, he decides, there's no great shortage of obscure seventeenth century philosophers one could choose to work on if one wants to be the world expert on somebody that nobody else has any interest in studying.

Last in is Simon Pastygill, a young Senior Lecturer, a publishing success, and a rising analytic star. Or, as Ren thinks of him, a spotty and pale weed with a creepy, lopsided smile, who's had inexplicable publishing success, and who speaks what Compton refers to as 'extreme Welsh'. Pastygill regularly confuses people when he speaks, not because of his accent, but because of his habit of asking sardonic questions in a rhetorical tone of voice which leaves it unclear whether or not he's expecting an answer. For this, and other reasons – in Ren and Compton's case, his constant complaining about the corrosive effects of capitalism – he is generally avoided. Although Pastygill is an atheist, Compton has dubbed him 'creeping Jesus' in honour of the way he will suddenly appear beside you, and the way he makes public pronouncements about the evils that follow from the possession of money. Ren, on the other hand, usually refers to him as 'Pantywaist'.

One of the other reasons Pastygill is avoided is his tendency to turn all conversation around to his passion for church architecture, especially Welsh church architecture. Pastygill travels extensively in Britain and Europe seeking out churches to view, and is always ready to offer his opinion, should it be sought on such a matter, as to why English and Scottish churches, though they have their undoubted merits and are definitely worth visiting, fall short of Welsh churches on three or four points of interest. Pastygill had never been known to offer a view on the merits of Continental churches versus Welsh churches; perhaps he does have an informed opinion on this matter, complete with half an hour's worth of pros and cons, but no-one has ever been foolhardy enough to enquire, or to let the conversation get that far.

According to rumour Pastygill has a list of all known churches in Britain and Europe, and is ticking off the ones he has already visited. The walls of his office are covered with pictures of churches, which at least makes a good impression on the students, although it makes some of them wonder if he's a religious nutter. One of Compton's tutees once asked him this question; allegedly Compton replied with, 'Pretty much, although in his case it's socialism rather than Christianity.'

Robot calls the meeting to order. There is one apology – Panos Costadopolous, known as 'Costa Brava' to his colleagues, a nickname he revels in, although perhaps only because it's better than being called Costa del Sol. Or perhaps it's just because he's shameless – he is known for constantly slipping off to the Continent for a short break when he shouldn't, coming back even more sun-tanned than before. As Robot does not announce what Costa's official reason is for missing the meeting, everyone expects that he's gone off to the Continent again. No-one is quite sure whether to be pissed off with him, or admire him. Although those people who have been lumbered with having to do his marking in the past are definitely in the former category.

'First item on the agenda is a proposal to change the dates that essays have to be handed in for next semester, says Robot. 'You will see from the first appendix at the back of the agenda that we have three deadline schemes on the table. These by no means exhaust the possible schemes, and it may be that during the course of our discussions we come up with some more to consider. You will see a list of pros and cons for each proposal.'

Robot drones on and on. And on and on. And on and on. Then every possible problem with each of the schemes is considered. Will scheme two not give the students enough time between essays? Does scheme three give too much time between essays two and three? Does scheme one require essays to be submitted too early for first years to be able to handle (assuming this scheme will be applied to semester one next year)? Won't scheme two be confusing for the students because one of the deadlines is on a Friday, rather than the usual Thursday? Can it be on a Thursday? No, because of administrative and other reasons that Ren has already forgotten.

Ren expected this fairly simple matter to be over and done with within five minutes, but an hour has gone by, and there's no end in sight. Derek Lucas and Tristram York are the main culprits. Ren can't imagine that either of them really has much interest in this issue, but it seems that each has nothing better to do than wind the other up. Robot is incapable of drawing matters to a close, and insists on considering in detail everything that is said, no matter how trivial, and even if it's said merely in jest (his jest detector, it appears never got switched on like it was supposed to).

After an hour and fifteen minutes has gone by, lunch, coffee and tea is brought in by the catering staff, and left in the corner. By this stage everyone is exhausted, even – perhaps especially – the innocent bystanders.

'Perhaps we'd best take a break at this point, and have some lunch, and come back and consider this further after we've eaten,' says Robot.

Ren looks around, unable to believe what is happening. He is unsure whether it's his place to say anything, but surely something has to be said? He has a lecture to finish writing.

'Excuse me, Grant,' he says, 'but we're an hour and a quarter in, and we're still on agenda item one, out of eighteen items. I don't see how we're going to get through the meeting at this rate. I was told the meeting should take two hours, three at most. I have a lecture to finish writing this afternoon, so I can't sit around all day debating these issues endlessly. Perhaps we should move on and revisit item one at a later stage?'

Robot looks peeved, but finally says, 'All right, Renford. I'm not sure we are going to get any resolution on agenda item one today, so we'll move on with the rest of the agenda after lunch and try to hurry it up.'

As the meeting breaks up for lunch, Derek laughs and says, 'Ren is discovering that everything in academia proceeds at the proverbial pace of a shelled gastropod.' Well, yes, Ren thinks, but in this case it's mainly because of you. Derek clearly isn't in any hurry. No wonder he doesn't publish much. He's renowned for endlessly rewriting his papers, regarding them as never quite good enough to send off, no matter how many years he'd spent polishing them, and no matter how good everyone else thinks they are. Ren doesn't want to be one of those academics who think in decades, but everyone says that's how you end up, no matter how much of a hurry you are to start with.

If I'm still here at Grayvington in ten years, he thinks – hell, if I'm still in academia in ten years – then I'll go down to the science area, take what the students call the 'Elevator to Oblivion', and hurl myself off the top of Bleak Tower. Bleak Tower, real name Blake Tower, is the monstrous, soot-stained, sixties-era concrete high rise in the science area that, as whispered rumour has it, extra-depressed students used to alleviate their suffering. Alleviate with extreme prejudice, that is. 'The Concrete Cure', the student wags call it, nodding towards the Tower as they say it. It's a pity I can't legally hire a hitman to take me out if I'm still in Grayvington in ten years, Ren thinks. That'd get me a move on.

Lunch consists of unpleasant triangular sandwiches. The bread tastes like no bread he's ever eaten before, not even cheap supermarket bread. Some sort of hardened industrial foam, perhaps, that's been sprayed with a reagent earlier today to bring about some temporary softening. The fillings are possibly real food, but it's hard to tell because they have been laid out by one of those TV science teachers who are determined to explain to kids just how much space there is between heavenly objects. There's also a variety of brown objects that vaguely resemble food, and vaguely taste like food, if you're engrossed in conversation and not paying much attention.

Much of the food, or 'food', is vegetarian, and there are 'Vegetarian' labels all over the platters, lest a poor vegetarian accidentally ingest the soul of a chicken, and be forced to undergo The Concrete Cure (there are some crimes that even non-retributivists can't forgive). There are none of the passable chicken sticks he had the previous meeting. Only the bigwigs get to eat average quality food. To get chicken sticks at University you have to be a mediocre academic who has given up on research. Or be a professional – or to be more accurate, useless – bureaucrat who can't get hired in the private sector. Then you get sandwiches made of real bread. Cheap supermarket bread, to be sure, but wheat-based, at least.

After lunch the meeting carries on, somewhat speeded up, and minus agenda item one, and minus Adelaide, who seems to have decided that turning up and sitting in silence for ninety minutes is as much as can reasonably be expected from her. After another hour they have got through seven more items. Derek and Tristram continue to act as though the sole purpose of the meeting is to make sport with one another. This is going to be a long forty years, thinks Ren. Time to check the academic job situation in Hawaii, perhaps.

At the current moment George is explaining why he thinks the Teaching Subcommittee needs to have an extra meeting in March.

'The University's Postgraduate Committee meets on March twenty-three, so if the Teaching Committee can meet a week or two before that they can discuss the issues that always come up in that meeting concerning funding. Last year we failed to...'

George stops talking, looking lost in memory.

'We failed to what, George?' says Robot.

Ren has no idea of what George is about to say, because he has not being paying attention to this agenda item. Or any of them, if truth be told. For the last twenty minutes he has been nodding off every few minutes, and then waking up as soon as he feels his head dropping, and all his attention has been focused on trying to stop himself falling asleep. No matter what he does, though, he can't. He has tried pinching his legs with his fingers as hard as he can, but even that doesn't prevent the constant nodding off. He's tried singing songs in his head. He's tried thinking about Lily naked to arouse himself. He's even tried to scare himself with the idea that Robot will block his probation if he is seen to fall asleep in a staff meeting. None of those tactics have worked. The narcoleptic spells are relentless, and cannot be stopped. His urge to put his head down and sleep is becoming overwhelming.

He isn't someone who normally suffers from narcolepsy. Today is just a combination of lack of sleep and extreme boredom. He wonders whether he should excuse himself, go to the bathroom, and throw cold water over his face.

'George?' says someone else.

'We. Failed. To...' says George, slowly. 'Prepare.'

George's head then does exactly what Ren's head wants to do, which is to crash onto the desk in front of him. It's almost like his and George's head have a psychic link, and the overwhelming desire his head has to collapse has bullied George's head into doing so first.

After a second of frozen horror, George rolls onto the floor, and pandemonium sets in, which is somewhat quelled when Martha Gelber, the building's first aid person, takes charge, and the departmental administrator, Wendaline Clugston, runs off to phone an ambulance. There's no danger of a narcoleptic episode now for Ren. George is unconscious and breathing heavily.

'If this is just an issue with his oesophagus then I'd hate to see something serious happen to him,' says Ren, who thinks no-one can possibly look this bad without something serious having happened to them.

Martha tells the rest of them to leave the room. The meeting is finally over.

'Good old George,' says Compton. 'He took one for the team.'

Later Ren goes to see Compton to find out if he has heard anything more about George's condition. He hasn't.

'I notice,' Ren says, 'that Robot is always talking about doing what's best for the department. With any decision, he always says he's "guided by what is best for the department". Yet every decision he makes seems designed to fuck us up.'

'He is telling the truth in a way. The deviousness comes in with what he means by "the department". He doesn't mean, as most of us imagine, the members of the department. He has no interest in what is best for us lecturers. He means "the department" in a more abstract sense. As a metaphysician you'll understand that the department is not numerically identical to its constituent members. Even if we ignore the students, the buildings, the wider academic and administrative context, and suppose that a department is made up of nothing more than the academics in it, it doesn't follow that the department is the self-same thing as the current members. Because academics can come and go, and the department remains in existence, so they are logically distinct beings.'

'Sure, the department is an entity, of some sort, which is something over and above, or at least, non-identical to, the things that make it up at any one time.'

'Yes. But even that's not what Robot has in mind, because thinking that way still ties the department's existence in some close way to its members. But Robot thinks of the department in an even more abstract fashion. Perhaps he's even a functionalist about it, like Sydney Shoemaker and the mind. The department is a node in a functional system, which takes inputs, such as students, money, admin staff and office space, and produces certain outputs, such as students graduating, good teaching evaluation scores, research papers published, grants won, editorships awarded, keynotes given, etc.

'Or getting in grad students, because they come with money attached.'

'Yes. That's more like what Robot has in mind. So when he says he wants what is best for the department, what he means is, what produces the best outputs relative to the inputs. Which to some degree is a reasonable way to think. To some degree it is the way he should think. But he is misleading us when he creates the impression that he wants what is best for us as a group of co-workers. He has no interest in that at all.'

'He certainly doesn't. It's fair enough for a Head to regard the department's performance as important, sure' says Ren. 'But Robot doesn't take us into account in any way. He doesn't care how a change in admin procedures or teaching will affect our research, even though that's one of the outputs he should be worrying about. We're just getting pushed to do more and more of our work after-hours. That seems to be a long-term trend, but it's not sustainable.'

'It isn't, but he doesn't care about sustainability, except in the bullshit green sense. He doesn't even care about the output metrics, really. All he wants to do is to impress the senior management, so he can get up there himself and double and triple his salary. That's why the long-term sustainability of our workload doesn't worry him. He figures he'll be a Dean or Pro-Vice-Chancellor by the time people start breaking down. He'll be long gone, and in clover.'

'Well, in a way it's good to know that that will never happen. He'll never get that high up. He's just too miserable to be around. Even Senior Management won't be able to stand him. On the other hand, that means we get stuck with him for a long time. It would be good if another place tried to poach him.'

'That would be good as long as he accepts. But he could use an approach from another place as a way to get more money and power from Grayvington.'

'Now you're really depressing me. I'm going home to not drink and get even more depressed.'

2000-01
Semester 1
Week 6
Tuesday

Ren and Miles are having a coffee at the cafeteria when a haughty-looking man with a beaked face, who looks to be in his mid-to-late thirties, sits down next to them.

'Hello Miles,' he says.

'Hello Lucius. Lucius, this is Ren, who is a new lecturer in Philosophy. He's doing the TITE with me.'

'Hello Ren,' says Lucius, without much interest.

'Ren, this is Lucius Birch, a senior lecturer in my department.'

'Pleased to meet you, Dr Birch,' says Ren. 'Miles has been telling me about you. You've been doing very well, I hear.'

'Fighting the good fight. As we all must do,' says Lucius in an abstracted way. 'But don't tell me you're some sort of metaphysician?'

'That's me, I'm afraid. Boring old non-political metaphysics.'

'Such a waste of argumentative talent. Don't you ever want to turn your attention to something that matters? Like the minimum wage?'

'Well,' begins Miles, 'Ren's not...'

Ren kicks Miles under the table.

'Perhaps I should,' says Ren. 'What other pressing topics should be grabbing me?'

'Well, there's the decline of income equality. There's global warming. The much-needed championing of Hugo Chavez and Venezuela. The great Satan. Racism. There's no end to the list, is there?'

'It would seem not.'

'Why don't philosophers lecture on the need for more union power, for example?'

'I'm not sure my Metaphysics students would feel that that was an appropriate topic for a Metaphysics class.'

'You're the lecturer. Persuade them that it is. These are the real cosmic issues.'

'Union power is a cosmic issue?'

'In a manner of speaking, it is. Which one is a universal issue of our time, a matter of extreme gravity, of interest to the entire human race? The decline of union power, or Descartes saying we can't know the external world?'

'That's epistemology. And Descartes thought we could know the external world.'

'You need to shift these perceptions. If you teach the same old stuff you just entrench the existing power structures. How is that freeing students' minds?'

'Thinking about the basic structure of the world seems pretty cosmic to me.'

'Imagine if any aliens came to earth. What would they be interested in? The power structures on our planet, or what Aristotle thought about teeth? There's your cosmic importance right there. And if you really want to stick to metaphysics, why not teach Venezuelan metaphysics?'

'Is there such a thing?'

'How do you know if you haven't looked? Why haven't you looked? Venezuela is flowering under Chavez. I bet you amazing things are being done in their schools of metaphysics. I'm going in a couple of months to the annual Venezuelan Conference of Psychology. It's going to be an eye-opener. A pity Miles couldn't come.'

'Goodness me Miles, you're not really going to miss an opportunity like that, are you?'

'Well, I don't really have the research funds at this stage in my career...'

'Put in an application to the Faculty,' says Lucius. 'See if they'll support you. Which I think they will, if I have a word in the right ear.'

'But I have to be giving a talk at the conference to be eligible for overseas travel funds. And it's way too late for that.'

'I'm sure I can use my influence to get you a speaking slot even at this late stage,' says Lucius.

'Chance of a lifetime, Miles,' says Ren.

'I'm really not sure I have the time,' says Miles. 'There is this TITE course which requires a lot of work. Doesn't it, Ren?

'Oh, yes, I suppose it does. Pity though. You might have even got to shake Chavez's hand.'

'But then I'd never be able to wash it again, would I?'

'Do I sense a little political scepticism, Miles?' says Lucius.

'Ah, well, just a little joke. I do admit to being a bit uninformed about all the latest global political developments.'

'Perhaps you should spend more time talking politics with your friend Ren.'

'I find Ren's political judgements can be, shall we say... off-piste?'

'But it's not about repeating the textbook, is it Miles?' says Lucius. 'As we always say to our students. You have to make up your own mind.'

'You mean, make up your own mind about what type of socialism is best?' says Ren.

'Exactly. Be a free thinker.'

'Within reason,' says Ren.

'Yes, within reason,' smiles Lucius.

'So,' says Ren. 'If you had to choose one, would it be Lenin or Trotsky?'

'Lenin,' says Lucius. 'Trotsky was great, but ultimately it was Lenin who got the job done.'

'Yes,' says Ren. 'Trotsky was ruthless, but Lenin even more so. What about Fidel or Che?'

'Well, that's a hard one. Fidel stayed the course and kept Cuba Communist for a very long time. But then Che was more of an intellectual, like me. So maybe Che.'

'Do you have Che pictures on your door?'

'No, I took them down a few years ago. Didn't want students to get the wrong idea about my research.'

'Very prudent. Ho Chi Minh or Mao?'

'Ho Chi Minh. He really gave it to the Yanks.'

'So you really think academics should be more pro-active in their leftism?'

'Definitely. You don't have to be that open about it if you don't want to. In fact, that might often be the best policy. But we all have a duty to further the struggle, in whatever way we can. Including undermining our enemies, and always making it difficult for them.' Lucius drains the last of his coffee. 'I have to go get ready for a class. Nice meeting you, Ren.'

After Lucius has left, Ren says, 'So, you still think he's totally objective in his research? In his research which coincidentally always comes up supporting progressive conclusions?'

'Uh... that was a bit worrying, I admit. I didn't realise at first that he was quite so political. I have been trying to extricate myself from his circle, but they keep trying to draw me in.'

'Just tell him he's an evil Commie, that should do the trick.'

'You're happy to isolate yourself, and be identified as right-wing. I don't want to be isolated. And I don't want to be called right-wing, because I'm not. Psychology's much more collaborative than Philosophy. If you get frozen out at an early stage then you're finished.'

'Jesus, he's the one who should be isolated. He likes mass-murderers.'

'There are members of my department who are openly members of the Communist Party. And we're not just talking people from an older generation. There are two younger members of the department in it as well. That's the reality of modern academia. You can't be a Nazi, thank God, but you can still openly be a Communist.'

'You certainly can, like those office doors you pass that have pictures of Che, or Lenin, or the hammer-and-sickle, on them. Some mass-murderers are all right, apparently. Anyway, I'd better go. I'll see you this afternoon at TITE.'

'So Jakobsen treats Saussure's dichotomous formulations dialectically, right?' says Balderstone. 'He insists on the close relationship between form and meaning within a state of dynamic synchrony.'

'What are "dichotomous formulations"?' asks Miles. Ren briefly raises his sleepy head from the desk and shakes his head at Miles.

'Langue and parole for instance,' says Balderstone. 'Or, ah...' He looks through his notes. 'Synchrony and diachrony,' he says eventually.

'What are...? Oh never mind,' says Miles.

Ren stirs. 'I'm going to ask the question that everybody's thinking,' he says. 'Dr Balderstone, why are you wearing a dress?'

'I'm glad you asked me that. Very glad. It needs to be discussed.'

'I'm not glad he asked that,' says Lenora. The Panopticons have become noticeably less keen on Balderstone since the Flying Lorenzos started scoring points off him. 'He shouldn't have done so. Being a transvestite is your business. What you wear to class is not a topic for discussion. Ren is trying to subjugate you by placing you in the category of the Other.'

'I'm not a...' begins Balderstone.

'Transvestite?' says Ren to Lenora. 'Isn't that an offensive word by now in your circles? And I didn't say he was a tranny. I'm just curious as to whether he's making an educational point.'

'Well,' says Balderstone.

'If, on the other hand,' says Ren, 'Dr Balderstone's attire is based on his own private aesthetic, sexual, or political preferences, then I'm sure we can all take the opportunity to applaud him, and maybe give him a medal for bravery.'

'The dress is making a point,' says Balderstone.

'You shouldn't call it a dress,' says Millicent. '"Dress" is a gendered term that reinforces stereotypes.'

'What should I call it then?'

'You should have thought of a name.'

'So what do you call it when you wear a dress then?' asks Ren.

'I, er...'

'You call it a dress, don't you? Why must you oppress women?'

'The reason I'm wearing the dress is to make us question our gendered assumptions,' says Balderstone. 'Some men like to wear dresses.'

'Didn't we all know that by the age of fourteen?' says Ren. 'Especially when you lived door to the guy I lived next door too.'

'The point is that men who like to wear dresses shouldn't feel the need to hide their preferences away. Why shouldn't they wear dresses openly?'

'My next door neighbour never hid it away,' said Ren.

'That's enough, Ren.'

'He used to ask my mother for style advice. Of course, this was before I had taken your course, Creighton, so I didn't know that he was being sexist in not asking my father.'

'I'm wearing this dress to show solidarity with men who like to wear dresses, and with anyone who refuses to conform to gender stereotypes.'

'And some people like to dress up as chickens,' says Ren. 'Yet they face prejudice just because they can't lay eggs every day. There is this great ocean of suffering.'

'I'm going to suggest that you think about doing something similar when you lecture,' says Balderstone, carrying on. 'You should think about undermining any negative gender stereotypes the students have.'

'Are you going to wear that dress outside this classroom?' asks Miles. 'Like wear it to the shops?'

'I wasn't planning to, no.'

'But surely the attitudes outside campus are worse than on campus? Isn't there a crying need to educate the general public more than our own already enlightened students?'

'I think it's best to start with our students, and let attitudes filter through to the rest of society.'

'That could be too late,' says Ren. 'A genuinely transgressive hero would be out there in the world wearing his dress, at Tesco, saving real lives. Not here in the comfort zone, preaching to the converted.'

'I don't think the point would be appreciated in Tesco,' says Balderstone. 'The people there would just think I'm an ordinary transvestite.'

'Hang on,' says Ren. 'If they'd think you're just an ordinary transvestite and not pay you any attention, then is there really such a problem to start with?'

'Well, not everyone is prejudiced. But there are prejudiced people out there. Maybe not on one visit to Tesco. Maybe the more marginalised types on the fringes of society.'

'Yes,' says Miles. 'Prison's the place to find them. You need to go give a talk wearing your dress in a prison.'

'I don't need two smart-alecks in my class,' says Balderstone.

'Get out, Miles,' says Ren. 'Come back when you've learned to be more supportive. Like Dr Balderstone's D-cups. They're helping, you're not.'

'He needs three,' says Douglas.

Everyone turns to look at Douglas in puzzlement. 'I mean, if he doesn't need two smart-alecks in his class, then maybe he needs three.'

'Timing,' says Ren. 'As in, work on.'

'You think it's funny,' says Balderstone. 'That's a very juvenile attitude to take. These are the sort of attitudes we need to be eradicating in our students.'

'We also need to be educating the older generation that the word "transvestite" is not acceptable usage,' says Millicent, looking at Balderstone.

'Yeah, it's now "chicks with dicks",' says Ren. 'Kindly refer to yourself as that from now on, Dr Balderstone.'

'There are very troubling attitudes from many of the males in here,' says Lenora.

'"Males" is a gendered term of oppression,' says Ren. 'We prefer to be called Humans Or Possible Humans Most Of Whom But Certainly Not Necessarily All Are In Possession Of Semen Squirting Equipment Which May Not Always Work That Well And Anyway Is An Accidental Rather Than a Defining Feature.'

'Can't you shut him up?' says Millicent to Balderstone.

'A troubling attitude,' says Ren.

'What term do you prefer, Dr Helminth?' asks Balderstone.

'"Cross-dresser" is better, though that also has derogatory connotations.'

'What's derogatory about "transvestite"?' says Douglas.

'If you call Dr Balderstone a transvestite,' says Ren, 'it contains the faint suggestion that he is gaining a perverse sexual satisfaction from wearing his dress. And if he is doing that then it's none of our damn business. Nor should we pass judgement on him if we discovered that he was. It can get awful lonesome in the Staff and Academic Development department. Wearing ladies knickers may no longer do the job.'

'That's enough from you,' says Lenora. 'Really, that's quite enough. I'm putting you under warning.'

'Has Dr Balderstone been sacked from this course? Have you told him yet?'

'It doesn't need to be my class for me to put you under warning.'

'Then I'm putting you under warning too. A get-a-grip warning.'

'I'll not tolerate this sort of bickering in my class,' says

Balderstone. 'I haven't finished discussing my attire yet.'

'I know. You're going to give us another political lecture on the ethnic necklace you're wearing. Am I right, Dr Balderstone?' says Ren.

'I'm glad you're not entirely lacking in astuteness,' says Balderstone. 'This is the symbol of Yamaluta, worn by the Heshka-skian tribe.'

'Everyone knows that,' says Ren. 'It expresses their love of late-era Lyotard and their ineffable sadness over the decline of structural Marxism in northern Germany.'

Malcom Ascaris is roused from his slumbers enough to say, 'Shut the hell up, you mouthy gobshite.'

'As the Yamaluta would say, "Well played, sir",' says Ren.

'Enough,' says Balderstone in a raised voice. 'The Yamaluta is the symbol of...'

'Come and see the violence inherent in the system,' whispers Douglas to Ren.

Balderstone glares at Douglas.

'Timing, dear boy, once again, timing,' whispers Ren theatrically back to Douglas.

'The Yamaluta symbolises the illusory nature of experience. How we should not trust what we see or are told. It enjoins us to look behind the apparent.'

'Good advice,' says Ren. 'I'm glad you wore that, otherwise I might have fallen for what you were telling us. You're wearing your own personal self-underminer.'

'I'm wearing it in solidarity with the Heshka-skian,' says Balderstone. 'Their wisdom, along with many other non-Western traditions, has been marginalised.' Balderstone looks at Ren. 'Especially by analytic philosophers.'

'Guilty as charged,' says Ren. 'There's no arguing with a necklace, is there?'

'Dr Balderstone, you need to get control of this class,' says Lenora, looking at Ren. 'Dr Christopher is constantly making a mockery of it, and you're letting him get away with it. It's impeding our progress.'

'Old-fashioned discipline. Hear hear!' says Ren.

'Dr Helminth, if I may,' says Miles politely, 'both you and Dr Balderstone have been arguing in this class that we need to get away from old-style lectures where it's all about the lecturer telling the students what's what. Let the students speak, you've been saying. It's all about a conversation. Don't silence dissent, and so on. Now you're saying that Ren needs to be silenced, and the great man be allowed to speak unchallenged.'

'I'm not saying he can't be challenged. Just not by...'

'Not by Ren, you mean? Because he doesn't have the right views?'

'That's not what I'm saying. Ren is not entering into the spirit of this class.'

'So he needs to have the right political views to pass the course?' says Lily. 'Is that what it comes down to?'

'I'm not saying that,' says Lenora. 'Anyway, that's not my decision.'

'He does need have to have the right political views,' says Malcom Ascaris, awake again. 'We wouldn't let a Nazi pass the course if he's spouting Nazism. So politics is relevant. Political truth is relevant. If Dr Christopher rejects the political truths that are being revealed in this course then he has failed.'

'Truth?' says Lily. 'You're talking about truth now, when last week you were telling us that truth is a social construct?'

'Political truths are different than the grand narratives that pass for truth in science and economics,' says Malcom.

'So there are truths, but only in politics?' says Douglas.

'The truth can be a matter of social pragmatism. Seen from the viewpoint of absolute historicism.'

'That isn't helping.'

'Put it this way,' says Malcom. 'The social construct that underpins this course demands certain responses.'

'So that social construct can't be challenged?' asks Lily.

'It can be challenged, but only from within its own terms,' says Malcom.

'Isn't that just another way of saying that you have to have the right politics or philosophical beliefs to pass?' says Lily.

'And why can't you challenge this social construct?' says Douglas. 'Isn't challenging social constructs a good thing? I still don't get what a social construct really is.'

'No, you don't,' says Malcom. 'But whatever you think of this social construction, it forms the basis of this course. So you have to operate within its terms to pass.'

'I've got the message Malcom, thanks,' says Ren. 'I have to have the right politics to pass. Thanks for clearing that up.'

'Malcom is not in charge of this course,' says Balderstone, 'and it is not about having the right politics. But it is about having the right spirit of enquiry.'

'The spirit that Derrida possesses, rather than John Searle?'

'I don't know John Searle, but as I have previously said, Derrida's questing intellect would be a good model, yes.'

'Or George Monbiot?'

'I suppose so.'

'All right then. Here's some enquiry in the required spirit. It's not what I think, but it's the sort of thing I'd imagine you lot might. Isn't wearing that native symbol an appropriation of someone else's culture? Like you get some of their supposed wisdom just by the shallow surface action of wearing an item of clothing? Isn't it the same as wearing a Native American headdress and claiming you share the Navaho spirit?'

Balderstone looks unsettled by this, but shakes his head.

'I'm not claiming to possess the wisdom of the Heshka-skian. I'm just drawing attention to their views.'

'It might be said that you're trivialising their views, and bigging yourself up by a pretend solidarity. Isn't that the sort of thing you'd say, Lenora?'

'No,' says Lenora uneasily. 'It seems reasonable to me to draw attention to alternative ways of thinking. It's the sort of thing we should be doing in class.'

'So in your next class you'll wear a gimp suit and a Navaho headdress?'

'You're the ones trivialising things,' says Balderstone. 'You show a continued hostility to alternative ways of thinking.'

'I didn't say anything about those ways of thinking. It's your behaviour I'm challenging. It's glib, and surface, and patronising. And some of your comrades might say that what you're doing is appropriating other cultures. Raping them like any other Western imperialist.'

'A better effort, Dr Christopher, but I don't think that idea is going to fly.'

'On what basis do you decide such things?'

'Well, let's see what people think. Anyone like this idea?'

A couple of hands go up from the Wetlanders, and then go back down.

'So you're running it up the flagpole to see if anyone salutes? Or if the right people salute? How is that a serious basis to decide on things? This is a University course. A course for University lecturers no less. And that's all you have as a basis for deciding on an idea?'

'That's just a straw poll to see if it's worth debating. That's not how we decide.'

'So how do you decide anything? You're not too keen on logic and argument and empirical evidence.'

'Not on your ideas of those things. But I will give you credit for that idea. Although it's rather a weak idea, it is in the right spirit.'

'Give it time. You'll all adopt it eventually. You try on new ideas like hats, discarding the ones that go out of fashion every few years, and you'll grab whatever bad ideas are lying around.'

'Drawing attention and identifying with suppressed cultures is never going to be a bad thing,' says Lenora.

'When you run out of other things to complain about you won't be so fussy. You lot draw on increasingly ridiculous ideas, and in ten years times it's only going to get worse. God knows what you'll all be spouting then.'

Balderstone calls a break. During the break he beckons Ren over.

'Dr Christopher, I do have to object strongly to your continued disrespectful interjections. You're on your way to failing this class, and you know what that means for your position at this University.'

'And I object strongly to what you are teaching. You're supposed to be improving our professional performance, not trying to turn us into postmodernists and political activists. You completely disregard the relevant empirical evidence in this field.'

'I should let you know that I will be making a formal complaint to your department about your behaviour.'

'Complain away. I've already complained about what you are up to.'

'My course has the support of the University.'

'You'd better hope that's really true. But I'll tell you what. Next week I shall come embodying the spirit of your teaching. I hope you'll be pleased.'

After the seminar the Lorenzos decamp to the nearest coffee bar, where they sit next to Douglas' colleague Garrett Slade.

'The University can stuff this fucking titty teaching course into the Vice Chancellor's combined vagina, anus and mouth, wherever he keeps that hidden. In his armpit, probably,' says Ren.

'Back of his head, under his hair. Feeds straight into the brain,' says Miles.

'You said that very quickly,' says Lily.

'You find out strange stuff in my field,' says Miles.

'Always something new to masturbate over, right?' says Ren.

'Children, please,' says Garrett.

'The titty. Jesus,' says Ren. 'It's hard enough being a new

lecturer having to work up all these new lectures from scratch. I'm writing them on the fly, I'm usually up to the early hours, and I'm still finalising them minutes before the lecture. And all you're guided by is your fallible sense of how last week's lecture went. Plus you have all the other rubbish you have to deal with during the week, and students, and of course you somehow have to find time on top of all that to do your research and publish papers to make a contribution to the Department's REF score.'

'It takes so much longer than I thought to write a good lecture,' says Miles.

'Me too,' says Lily.

'It's almost worse if you know the topic really well,' says Ren, 'because then you have so much material that you have to spend so much time hacking it all away. I can't believe how it takes much time it takes to cut away all that excess material, and re-shape what you have. But usually it's worse if you don't know the topic backwards, because then you have to desperately mug up in the week on the topic, and you never really understand it properly in those circumstances.'

'But that's just the job,' says Garrett. 'It's tough in those ways to start with, yes, but it gets tougher in other ways later on too. You have to be able to cope with all that, otherwise you can't be an academic. Academics aren't ordinary people with ordinary jobs.'

'Sure, I'm not really complaining about any of that,' says Ren. 'That's just the job we do, it's a challenge, but an enjoyable one, and if you're up to scratch you cope with it. Late nights aren't a problem for me personally anyway. What I am complaining about is having this stupid titty course thrown on top of everything else. I really needed to spend this afternoon working on my lecture for tomorrow, which is still miles from being coherent. Instead I've had to waste a valuable afternoon in the charming company of Balderdash, which means I won't get much sleep tonight.'

'But isn't it a good idea to have a course on improving

your teaching?' asks Garrett. 'You know how many bad lecturers there are out there. I supported the idea when it was mooted.'

'That's not it,' says Ren, starting to realise that the older academics had been sold a bait-and-switch, and they have no idea of what is going on under the guise of a postgraduate teaching qualification. 'That would be a good idea, and that's what the titty should be about, improving lecturing. But that's not what's happening. In practise it's just a brainwashing exercise where Continentalists force you to mouth their platitudes. So not only do I have valuable time wasted, I have to spend that time being exposed to them trying to indoctrinate me.'

'Continentalists?' asks Garrett.

'Fans of European bullshit artists like Derrida and Foucault. Progressive politics in the form of word salad, all made deliberately unfalsifiable.'

'Oh. That sort of thing. Really?'

Garrett looks at his younger colleague for a response.

'Yes,' nods Douglas, shuddering. 'It's worse than you can imagine.'

'But they're doing other things to improve teaching, though, right? It's not just that sort of thing.'

'The only thing they're doing that seems like it might be any good is some video work. Which is going to be for one afternoon only, later on this term,' says Ren.

'Yes, otherwise it's all this awful "critical reflection",' says Lily.

'Can we make some sort of official complaint, Garrett?' asks Miles. 'I'm going to ask my Head of Department to do so.'

'Me too', says Ren.

'I suppose so', says Garrett. 'But you'd need to get some proper documentation about it. We can't just complain on the basis of cafe hearsay. And I'm not sure what it would achieve. The SADE are likely to just say that this is their domain, and we should butt out, and they don't go around trying to tell us how to run our departments.'

'But we're experts in our field,' says Miles. 'They're not experts in their field. They know nothing about University teaching or education in general.'

'Except that now they've been given those positions,' Ren sighs, 'they are the experts. You'll never get rid of them without a big fight. Those sort of activists never concede ground voluntarily. And if one has to go they make sure the replacement is another one of them.'

'I've got to go,' says Miles. 'I'll see you all on Friday.'

'Friday?'

'For a Lorenzo work session? Remember?'

'I'd forgotten,' says Ren. 'Another afternoon goes missing thanks to TITE. Forget doing your jobs, just make sure you all turn up for the indoctrination sessions. I think I will get Balderstone the L. Ron hat after all.'

2000-01
Semester 1
Week 6
Wednesday

Ren runs into Tristram in the corridor.

'And how are you settling into the job, Ren?' asks Tristram.

'It's rather hectic, but no great complaints so far, other than having to stay up all night writing lectures, and having to do the TITE.'

'Ah yes, I've heard stories about the TITE. Luckily for me I missed out on having to do it. Are you enjoying the company of our delightful departmental Continentalist colleagues?'

'Who could not fail to be charmed by such illustrious company? The things I have learned from my intellectual betters. Language is not real. The signifier is the presence of an absence. Or is it the absence of a presence? There is nothing outside the text. Deconstruction takes place as the experience of the impossible. I have learned the important Lacanian term "extimacy", although I cannot for the life of me recall what it means. I've learned that a couple of vague lines about semiotics can somehow form the basis for a sweeping denunciation of the global capitalist system. Truly an education. Of a sort.'

'And this is the great Ren sarcasm, which is already famous? Or at least much complained about. I've heard that Verna already wants you out.'

'Verna? You mean that angry woman with the spiky hair and the broken tooth? I thought she was some sort of council representative, here to keep an eye on the plumbing. What about the great Adelaide?'

'I don't think she has deigned to notice you yet. That's what she's pretending anyway. She affects not to notice much, which gives her the excuse to genuinely not notice much. But I'm sure she has you filed away under "Minor cockroach" somewhere.'

'Another great Professor who's only interested in you if you have a pair of tits.'

'Have you filled up the shelves in your room yet?' asks Tristram.

'Almost. It's great having so many shelves, I can actually find things now. Hell, it's great having my own office instead of sharing with twenty other postgrads. I can actually get some work done instead of wasting my powers of concentration on trying to filter out other people's stupid conversations. Hello.'

A student has tentatively come up to them.

'Dr York, can I ask you a question about your Philosophy of Mind module?'

'Of course, ask away,' says Tristram.

'I don't really understand what Dennett's view of qualia is. You didn't say much about his view in the last lecture.'

'Dennett doesn't believe qualia exist at all. That's why I'm not going to say much about him.'

'Not at all?'

'Not at all.'

'Well,' Ren says, 'some prefer to say that Dennett's view should be expressed as the view that qualia do exist, but they don't have many of the properties commonly attributed to them.'

'Yes, some say that,' says Tristram, 'but the fact is that Dennett denies them so many properties that in effect they don't exist.'

'What sort of properties?' says the student, as Ren becomes aware of a slinking sort of motion beside him.

'Tristram's rather intolerant today, wouldn't you say?' Simon Pastygill semi-whispers into Ren's ear. 'Then again, he's often very intolerant.'

'Properties like being incorrigible, ineffable, private, and directly accessible,' says Tristram to the student.

'You know you said that quite loudly?' says Ren.

'He thinks the traditional conception of qualia is incoherent,' says Tristram.

'I've heard some complaints about Tristram's interpretation of various philosophers,' whispers Simon, only slightly softer.

'Still quite loud,' says Ren. 'Anyway, that does seem to be what Dennett thinks. Qualia don't exist.'

'I really hate Dennett,' says Tristram. 'He doesn't have any arguments. Just his silly intuition pumps.'

'I don't think he can hear me, do you?' whispers Simon.

'Isn't he trying,' says Ren, 'to give us a plausible, science-like explanation of consciousness? Whether it's plausible is another story, but that sort of thing isn't conducive to the usual deductive argument form.'

'But that means he skates over various problems,' says Tristram. 'What about the sort of objections that Ned Block comes up with? Dennett doesn't argue back, he just handwaves back, and tells another story.'

'Perhaps a bit unfair to say that he doesn't argue back,' says Ren, 'although I agree it's not quite the same sort of rigorous argument that he's been presented with. He's saying that those arguments are beside the point.'

'Which means that he just conveniently ignores the detail,' says Tristram.

'Of course, one can overdo detail,' says Simon, with a pointed look at Tristram.

'Certainly. Some people's papers are just a mass of detail with nothing interesting to say about the bigger picture,' says Tristram, with a pointed look back at Simon.

Simon and Tristram are yet another pair of departmental members who greatly dislike each other. Simon dislikes Tristram because he talks with a plummy voice, has a superior, bemused manner, and because, for all his cleverness, he doesn't publish much (although, unlike

Derek, he does publish sometimes). Tristram dislikes Simon for the same reason as everyone else, because he's a creepy little cocksucker whose mediocre papers get published in volume because the backwater field he did his PhD in has become hot property recently. And each sees the other as getting dues that should be going to them.

'Uh, I have to go to a class now,' lies the student, who's not sure what's going on, but who senses the unease and wants to get away.

'Oh yes, me too,' lies Ren as well.

'And me,' lies Tristram.

'Looks like it's just poor old me without a class to go to,' says Simon. 'What will I do now that the conversation has ended?'

'You could go suck your own cock in your office,' mutters Tristram to Ren as they walk along the corridor.

'We should be encouraging him out of his bad habits,' says Ren. 'Not letting him stay a prisoner of his basest desires.'

2000-01
Semester 1
Week 6
Thursday

Ren drops by Compton's office for a chat.

'I was thinking about our discussion about Robot, and how he misleads us when he says his concern is the department,' Ren says. 'We agree that by "department" he means something abstract. He has no interest in us as fellow workers, even though he creates the impression he does. It makes me think that academia is moving away from the community of scholars conception, where we're like partners in a law firm, towards the supermarket model. Here's your boss, he tells you the jobs that need doing, you do them. Which is fine for a supermarket. I've worked in a supermarket, the boss tells you to stack shelves, you stack shelves, and then you go home at five. Boring, but easy. But that's not what I spent all those years doing a PhD and a postdoc for. One of the attractions of academia was that you'd be an independent scholar, in a like-minded community of fellow scholars, working in partnership, not an office drone being told what to do all the time by someone using your back as a stepladder.'

'Well, that's a nice conception of academia, but the reality is that with any bunch of egos you're often going to get people in there who want power over the others, either for its own sake, or for the glory, or the money, or for ideological reasons, or, most commonly, a combination of all those things.'

'Sure, but that applies double to doctors and lawyers, and they manage to have partnerships.'

'Yes, although you, being young, and junior, wouldn't be

a partner in those places at this point. And those partnerships, especially the law ones, are always having power struggles.'

'Okay, but still, the conception of an academic department I like is where we work as partners. Where we make decisions based on our mutual benefit, within, of course, the constraints of the University system and the commercial need to provide a good product.'

'I'm not saying I disagree,' says Compton. 'I don't disagree. But academia is usually not like that. Twenty to thirty years ago most academic departments in the UK were dominated by one big Professor who decided everything. You wouldn't have liked that, I'm telling you.'

'Probably not. Although at least they were usually the best people in their field, which Robot hardly is.'

'Hmmm. Not sure they always were the best. Departmental politics is not a recent invention. And look at the European University system. Most departments there are controlled by a Big Man. Yet everyone with any familiarity with that system says that the Big Man is usually a Big Phony, a talentless egomaniac who got the position through patronage, and who isn't letting anyone else near the power. At least here you have departmental votes on most matters.'

'Votes?' says Ren. 'The votes almost always go the way Robot wants, because he makes clear the consequences if the vote goes against him. And if the vote does go against him, he and the higher-ups just wear the department down until we finally vote the way we're supposed to.'

'You've noticed that then? Yes, the departments here are a bit like soviets. Soviet were like the Russian local councils that existed under the Communists. In theory they were independent of the ruling Bolshevik high command. In practise, they always voted the way Lenin wanted them to. Eventually, anyway, Because if they didn't, there was trouble. Or take Proletkult.'

'Proletkult? You mean that Bolshevik arts organisation?'

'Yes, it rose up after the October revolution in Russia. It was popular, and gained for itself a measure of independence and power, although it was mostly funded by the Communist state. Eventually it got ideas above its station, and Lenin had never liked its philosophy anyway, so at that point Lenin reined it in, and merged in into Narkompros, the People's Commissariat for Education, effectively dissolving it. That's another threat that hangs over departments. Play ball, or get merged into a bigger entity who don't see things your way.'

'Should we be letting that sort of thing affect us, though?' says Ren. 'You can't be worrying about those sort of possibilities every time you need to make a decision. That just leads to cravenness and timidity. The University isn't that powerful.'

'Those sort of considerations are what a lot of departments have in the back of their mind. You may be right that they overestimate what the University can do to a rogue department, but that's the way they think. And departments do sometimes get shut down. That also stops them getting too rebellious.'

'But it seems to me they're mainly stopped from being too rebellious because the University puts their own man or woman into place as head of Department. It's hard for a department to speak as one against a University proposal when its Head is on the University's side.'

'Yeah, except they can't always appoint a company man, some departments have none. But they'll always avoid appointing a trouble-maker, whether on the left or the right. They prefer a Blairite who's progressive but who isn't allergic to money and business. The main things they want are, don't appoint anyone who might say something non-progressive, and don't appoint anyone who might rediscover their Trotskyite roots and have a sit-in. That's why the likes of Derek Lucas and Tony Shaver will never be made Head, any more than we will.'

'What about Verna? Would the University trust her?'

'I think so. Things are heading her way, so she'll play the game. She's been toning down the Communism recently, and turning up the feminism.'

'In other words, toning down the economic Marxism but turning up the cultural Marxism?'

'Yes. Postmodernists are opportunists, and she wants to get ahead. But I think she's too thick to get anywhere, and she still comes across as too working-class, even though she's tried to smooth herself out. Of course, it doesn't matter if you come across as working-class as long as you have compensating attributes, like intelligence, or good new ideas, or charisma, but she has none of those.'

'But then Adalia has plenty of polish, but I can't see her going anywhere.'

'She doesn't have the desire. She has a nice life, a rich husband, she's prominent in the arts. She isn't as political as Verna. She isn't going to waste her time clawing her way to the top of the University hierarchy.'

'So who's likely to be next Head of Department if we can manage to get rid of Grant?'

'My money's on Simon.'

'Pastygill? You've got to be fucking kidding?'

'It seems ridiculous I know, but he's the only real candidate. Assuming the department doesn't hire another person in who becomes Head, which they may do if Grant were to leave. Walter's too old, he's near retirement, and he did it long ago without much distinction. Same with George. Adelaide won't do it again. Martha would do it, but reluctantly, only if there's no-one else. Panos, well, you can't be Head of Department from the Costa del Sol, can you?'

'And how can you enforce marking standards when you give all your students Firsts?'

'Quite. Bill's a useless old duffer who the University and Robot wants rid off. Tristram gets everyone's back up, and is a gadfly. We're too right-wing. Derek and Tony, as we said, can't be trusted not to be bolshy. Verna, well, not only is she too thick, the analytics wouldn't wear it. Adalia, as before.

That only leaves Simon.'

'I'd struggle to take him seriously as Head.'

'Maybe, but you wouldn't kick up a fuss about it, would you? Not like if they tried to make Verna Head?'

'I suppose not. But Simon isn't polished, is he?'

'He may not be very polished, but he makes up for that with his dullness.'

'But he's no better than the rest of us when it comes to criticizing his colleagues. He cloaks it in this pretend naivety, but we all know when he's having a go at someone.'

'He criticises, yes, but the point is that he's less public about it. He likes to whisper his criticism rather than shout it. The University hardly wants someone who is incapable of criticising their colleagues to be Head. But they want someone discreet. Simon is someone who isn't going to publicly clash with the administration, even when he disagrees with them, which he will at times given his attitude to money. But he'll keep disputes to the back room. That's important. The University doesn't want grandstanders in charge of departments. Also, he's ambitious.'

'Is he? He doesn't seem that way.'

'You're not watching him closely enough. Underneath the surface naivety there's another control freak leftist lurking. No-one takes him seriously now, but watch out for him.'

2000-01
Semester 1
Week 7
Tuesday

'It's like you're asking for trouble,' says Lily.

'Moi?' says Ren. 'I'm such a shy and retiring type. Why are you hanging back?'

'I'll think I'll let you go in first.'

'And you'll come two minutes later and pretend to be taken aback. It's all right. I've always said that you find out who your true friends are when you put on a false beard. False beard, false friend detector.'

As Ren prepares to walk into the class a feeling of apprehension come over him. Has he gone too far? He's wearing a mini-skirt, suspender stockings, boob tube, native American headdress, false ginger beard and a goose necklace. Too late to back out now, though. He's already been seen in the corridor by some of his classmates. He walks in breezily. As he sits down there is laughter, and some angry murmuring. Balderstone is glaring at him.

Miles, who's in on it, grins. Even Adrian Vespula laughs. Douglas is blinking a lot. The other Panopticons look angry.

'I'm just a working girl,' Ren sings softly, in a pretend absent-minded fashion, just loud enough for others to hear.

Lily comes in and tries not to smile. She sits well away from Ren.

Balderstone starts up, reading from his notes.

'Today, er, we're going to talk about the importance of, um, power-sharing within the traditional lecture construct, with reference to Gramsci. We're going talk about...'

He pauses, as though he is wishing that this is not today's topic.

'Talk about tearing down barriers between lecturers and students, and tapping into the store of wisdom that students possess.'

The Lorenzos sense that Balderstone is trying to think of alternate words, but he doesn't have the wit to do anything else than stick to his written script.

'This might be uncomfortable for some of you,' he reads, in a reluctant, mechanical tone, the tone of a man who knows that what he is saying is about to be turned around and fired back at him, 'who have come up through the University system expecting that lecturers talk and students receive.'

'But aren't you going to ask Dr Christopher what he's playing at, dressed like that?' demands Lenora.

'Last week you said we what we wear to class isn't a subject for discussion,' says Ren.

'If it concerns someone's private sexual inclinations. But if you walk in wearing a Hitler T-shirt, that's a different matter.'

'Hitler, Hitler. Where would you lot be without Hitler? Anyway, I'm hardly wearing a Hitler T-shirt. I'm following Dr Balderstone's orders. I'm wearing these clothes not only to draw attention to the right of cross-dressers to wear what they want, wherever they want, but also in honour of those poor unfortunates who walk the streets, forced to make a degrading living from prostitution. Or is it those feisty feminists who empower themselves by choosing prostitution as a positive career choice? I can't remember which week it is. The headdress I wear in solidarity with Native American tribes in honour of their neglected wisdom concerning the health benefits of eating a diet mainly consisting of meat, guts and fat. Did you know that they were really keen on beavers' tails, which were especially fatty? Nutritional acumen that has long been ignored.'

'Do we have to listen to any more of this?' Lenora asks Balderstone.

'What was the good doctor just explaining to you now?

Power-sharing. Tapping into the wisdom of the students. Dr Balderstone isn't going to shout me down. He's not trapped in the twentieth century. You need to listen more closely to his words. The lecturer isn't a martinet any more. And I have taken on board his sage words from last week. The ginger beard I wear to express my sympathy with my burnt sienna brethren, such as Dr Balderstone himself, who suffer silently under the yoke of intolerance. As Creighton has so passionately urged, we should all should be wearing outfits like this to our lectures to raise the consciousness of our students.'

'What's the goose for?' asks Adrian, unable to help himself.

'That is the Sankofa, a Ghanian symbol. It means that mistakes can be rectified, and one should look to the past for solutions. Literally, "return and get it". That's why the goose looks backwards. Jnana that is under-appreciated these days. And I thought a goose looking at its own arse would make a fine symbol for this class.'

'You wouldn't get away with wearing all that to one of my classes,' says Lenora.

'Really? You're really claiming that you can tell students what not to wear after what Dr Balderstone said to you last week? You're sounding a bit like an old-fashioned disciplinarian. Do you set a curfew for them as well?'

'But you're not wearing any of that to make a sincere and valid point, you're wearing it to be a smart-arse.'

'So students aren't allowed to be smart-arses any more? Might hit enrolments. You'd better speak to the Admissions Department.'

'That's enough,' says Balderstone. 'Dr Helminth, I would expect that you do not tell students what they can wear, unless they come in with a Hitler T-shirt?'

'What about a Che T-shirt?' says Miles.

'He wasn't a mass-murderer like Hitler,' says Millicent.

'Oh, but Mr Guevara was indeed a mass-murderer, and an enthusiastic one at that,' says Ren.

'You're a liar,' says Millicent.

'Ask Malcom. I bet he knows,' says Ren. Malcom refuses to look at Ren, and stays shtum.

'Stop it now and listen to me,' yells Balderstone, banging his fist on the table.

'Sounding a bit authoritarian, Creighton,' says Ren. 'Haven't you heard about the new ways? Lecturers aren't the bosses any more.'

'Dr Christopher, you have come to this class wearing an outfit that demonstrates your bad faith.'

'You're quite right. The beard doesn't go with the top, I know. My feminine intuition tried to tell me that when I looked in the mirror, but I wasn't in touch enough with my feminine side to get the message. I appreciate your candour.'

'Shut up. Your sarcastic attitude indicates that you are continuing to refuse to take on-board the lessons of these classes, and that will count against you at the end of the course.'

'Is the goose included in your condemnation? He'll take that hard, sir, he will.'

'Take that ridiculous beard off.'

'I've longed for you to say that. It can't come off quick enough. Begone, Itchy and Scratchy. That's what I call him, by the way.'

2000-01
Semester 1
Week 7
Saturday

The Lorenzos, plus Miles' new girlfriend Tanja, and Jay, a scientist friend of Douglas's from some other science department which Ren didn't quite catch, are at The Head of Steam, a railway-themed pub in the city centre. Railway-themed pubs are quite common in Grayvington, due to Grayvington's important railway heritage, or Important Railway Heritage, to give it its proper name, although as far as Ren can see, the history of rail in Grayvington is no different to a dozen other towns. It just seems to be, he thinks, something for the town and University to latch onto to make themselves seem more important, as there isn't much else to boast about. The University even has a graphic of a steam engine as its logo, despite the fact that the University itself has never had any involvement in railways, either in practise or research, for the whole of its existence, until five years ago when it decided to start pouring money into research on solar-powered railways. The University now has now a Solar Railway Institute, headquartered away from Greenwood Glade and Baron Heights, in one of the old toy factories in Tinfields.

Toymaking is the only other claim to fame that Grayvington has. It started in the 1880s, with Rollinsons, highly successful makers of toy soldiers, doll's houses, rocking horses, jigsaw puzzles, Noah's Arks and sailing boats. Then in the 1920s Gambols was formed by three ex-employees of Rollinson's. They made, inter alia, model railways, toy cars and children's bikes, initially of high quality, and then of diminishing quality, until eventually all the manufacturing was moved to Taiwan in the 1960s, before the firm eventually went bust in the 1970s. Rollinson's itself never survived the loss of three of its best employees, and it was sold off in 1935, and incorporated into a Sheffield toy firm who moved all its employees and useful machines up north.

Grayvington's third great, if great is the word, toy company was Bonkers Toys, established in the late 1940s, makers of all sorts of poor quality novelties, magic sets, X-ray specs, itching powders, as well as their own comic, *Sausage Gravy*. The best that can be said for *Sausage Gravy* is that it has its fans, including Ren.

The town and the University are less keen on proclaiming this other heritage, if heritage is the word, for their own, perhaps because they don't like being called Toytown, the nickname that is sometimes given to the city and the University by their rivals. Tinfields, the fashionable inner-city suburb that contains all the old toy factories and offices, now converted into trendy apartments, offices and restaurants, is better known to the locals as The Toy District, while the large, desirable houses in the posh suburb of Cownmouth, which were built by the toy barons at the height of their profit (and usually just before their downhill slide began), are known as the Toy Mansions.

The Lorenzos are socialising on a Sunday night because Lily was away on Friday and Saturday night in London visiting her boyfriend Jason, the soon-to-be-Professor. Ren reminds himself not to make any, or too many, digs at Jason, as he has been doing in the last few weeks. Sarcastic remarks won't break them up, but they could make it obvious that Ren is carrying a torch for Lily, and he doesn't want to seem sad, or put Lily off him.

He has, of course, looked Jason up on the internet, and while Jason's intellectual performance is credible, at least as credible as a man who writes about phony garbage like the economics of climate change can be, he seems somewhat lacking, if his picture is anything to go by, in the 'Cor blimey' sphere. He can't imagine Lily staring at Jason's tight jeans and feeling a little shaky. He can't imagine Jason roistering 'til the early hours, then carrying Lily off to bed over his shoulder and giving her a good seeing-to. It's easier to imagine Lily carrying him off to bed over her shoulder. And him being unconscious when he's thrown onto the bed. And whimpering when Lily tries to wake him up.

The conversation has turned to the TITE. This is a topic that Tanja does not enjoy, while Jay, Douglas's friend, who has an annoyingly loud voice, relishes the fact that he joined the University the year before TITE was brought in.

'Speaking of TITE,' says Douglas, 'our group project is not getting far. We need to have a proper meet up and do some work on it, and not just go off to the bar instead like we have the last few weeks.'

'Look, about that,' says Ren.

'What?' says Douglas.

'I might as well tell you now. I'm going to pull out of TITE. It's just a bunch of cock. I'm not wasting my time on any more of it.'

'Will they even let you pull out?'

'I don't see how they can stop me. And I've had a closer look at my contract. It doesn't say that I have to complete TITE within the probationary period. It doesn't say I have to pass it. It just says that I have to undertake it. Now, the word "undertake" is a bit vague. If you look at dictionary definitions it's not at all clear that it means the same as "complete". One definite meaning it has is to begin something, as opposed to completing it. So legally I don't think the University can insist that I must complete TITE to get probation, as long as I've started it. Which I have. I'm just going to suspend my enrolment for a while. You should all do the same too. Don't waste any more of your time listening to Balderstone's drivel.'

The other academics look uneasily at one another.

'I don't know if it's wise to piss the University off,' says Jay in a voice that Ren wishes was about a hundred decibels quieter. 'There are other ways they could make trouble for you.'

'I think I'll stay on the course, says Douglas. 'Just want to get it over and done with.'

'Me too,' says Lily.

'Modern academics are such cowards,' says Ren, shaking his head. 'Well, I hope you all enjoy the company of that nice Mr Balderstone for the rest of the academic year, as he puts his cock into your ear every week. And the Panopticon fascists. Not to mention the grisly Wetlands. You'll learn a lot from all of them. Perhaps you should have them all around for tea sometime, and they can tell you off some more, and point out more things wrong with you.'

'But the group project is going so well,' says Miles with a smile.

'Yeah, sorry I won't be able to contribute to that, but in fact you'll be better off without me, as I can't write the sort of shit that's required. I just can't do it.'

'Neither can we,' says Lily.

'Maybe Jay could join you instead.'

'No fucking fear,' says Jay, in a booming voice that echoes across the half-empty pub, which is full of metallic railway paraphernalia, as though he's trying to bring it all to life so it can transport his voice to Scotland in order that the people there can hear him say 'No fucking fear' as well.

'Well,' says Ren, who swears he can hear tiny 'fucking fear' flutter echoes still bouncing around, 'all the Head of Department complaints are due to be made to University management, so maybe the course will be better next year, or the year after.'

'I've got to give it to you, you are a hard-core bastard,' says Miles. 'Leaving the course will go down like a cup of cold sick with Balderstone, especially on top of the complaints you've organised.'

'Hope he doesn't take it out on us,' says Douglas.

'He wouldn't dare now that he's under the microscope,' says Ren. 'He'll be in the doo-doo if he tries that. Kapshar and the other Heads are pissed off with his course, partly for being a load of shite, and partly because it takes so much time away from their new lecturers, without teaching them anything useful. Even your big shithead Sadler is on side.'

'Is this what academic life is really like?' asks Tanja. 'It seems like a war zone. I thought artists were bad.'

'A war?' says Ren. 'By academic standards this is a small skirmish.'

Ren isn't that happy about discussing these matters in front of Tanja, but he can hardly ask her to leave, as this is a social, not a work, get-together. He goes off to the bar and gets a round of drinks for everyone, and comes back with some proper pork scratchings.

'Hey look, they have real scratchings here. Great pub,' he says.

'You and your blinking pork scratchings,' says Miles. 'Is that your main criteria for a pub? Whether it has proper pork scratchings? What about the lack of good ale here?'

'Do I have a beard? I couldn't give a flying Scotsman about ale. I've told you, to me it all tastes like it's been soaking with some old socks for three years in a tub in the basement, and sometimes the landlord pisses in it. You look at some of those landlords of the real ale pubs you go to, and you tell me that they don't look exactly like the sort of person who would do that. Or maybe they bathe in it. Once a year, mind. Most of them look like that's about as often as they wash.'

'I think they toss in all the old cigarette butts every night as well,' says Douglas.

'There you go,' says Ren. 'He's a physicist. He knows all about this science stuff.'

'Just because you drink like a girl,' says Miles, indicating Ren's lager.

'Hey,' says Lily, who is drinking ale.

'All right, you drink like a poof,' says Miles.

'Hey,' says Jay, who is also drinking ale.

'There you go Miles, you're the one drinking like a girl

and a poof. Hoist by your own petard. You'll have clean Jay's steam whistle later on tonight.'

'Hey,' says Tanja, half-heartedly, after a little pause. This sort of banter isn't really her thing, but she feels obliged to join in.

'Don't worry, I'm sure Jay will let you watch,' says Ren.

'Ren,' says Tanja, who clearly wants to change the subject to something more deserving of her attention, 'what do you think of the idea that you can never know yourself?'

Ren sighs. Why did Miles have to bring Tanja along? Is it because he thinks it's nice that Tanja can talk about her pet interest, philosophy, with Ren, even though if Miles paid more attention to their discussions he'd see that what Ren says to Tanja deeply frustrates her?

Miles met Tanja, a serious blonde who is older than him, a couple of weeks ago at a function at The Tantamount, which is the main art gallery in Grayvington, where Tanja works as a curator. She's quite artistic, but not in a good way. Miles is somewhat artistic himself, but he's more of a traditionalist, whereas Tanja is someone who, as befits her job, always has an eye out for the latest trends. Before she arrived Ren was humming the tune to 'Dedicated Follower of Fashion', wondering if Miles would get the dig, but he showed no sign of it.

Ren is not keen on Tanja, partly because she doesn't seem right for Miles, but also because she's another philosopher manque, and Ren has had his fill of them. Whenever he goes to parties, there's always someone there who fancies themselves as a philosopher, and as soon as they hear Ren is a professional one, they spend all night trying to talk to him about it. Which is okay for a while if they're someone charming and clever, who really does know a bit about philosophy, but usually they're a bore who drones on and on with a lot of half-digested Continental crud. Ren finds it difficult to get away from such people. They buttonhole him in an intense fashion, and provide no opportunity for him to exfiltrate. One of their tricks is to say, when his glass is getting empty, 'Let me get some more drinks for us,' to prevent him using the excuse of needing a refill as his chance to get away.

Ren is reluctant to be rude to manques, lest he confirm the Continental view that analytic philosophers are all rude and arrogant. If it's early in the evening he's usually willing to spend some time with them, gently sorting them out (they rarely have any worthwhile ideas of their own), but this is usually a mistake, as it gives the manque the impression that the two of them have an intellectual bond, and the whole evening must be given over to their fascinating conversation, the distorted recount of which the manque will be boring their friends with for years to come. (The friends don't like listening to the manque's views on philosophy, which is why manques are so keen to talk to real philosophers.) The longer it goes on, the harder and harder it becomes to get away without causing offence, as the manque's delusion that they're proving their philosophical worth tonight becomes more entrenched. Sometimes offence is eventually caused when Ren starts to lose patience with his interlocutor's 'arguments' – which usually boil down to one or two dubious claims which the manque is totally convinced of – which are repeated over and over as though Ren just hasn't heard them properly yet.

It's not just the manques who Ren doesn't want to listen to. He's not really that keen on discussing philosophy after work with anyone, even his distinguished colleagues (and when he does feel like it, he'd rather it be with someone good, like Compton). When you spend all day, every working day, doing the same topic, then you want to talk about something else when you go out. Especially seeing as you usually have to do some more philosophy when you get home, before you can go to bed.

It seems to Ren entirely reasonable that one would want to talk about things other than philosophy when you've just spent all day doing it, but as it happens almost every other philosopher is not like this. At the end of the day they can't wait to talk some more about... philosophy. Kripke, Brandom, Unger, van Fraassen, Dummett, Peacocke... they're interesting, but not that interesting. Too many philosophers take all this stuff way too seriously, Ren thinks. It's not mentally healthy to be that way. They probably even dream about it. Most of it's nonsense anyway. Why devote your whole life's mindpower to nonsense? When you look through an old philosophy journal from a hundred years ago to see what the average paper was like back then, it's just embarrassing. The pages of today's philosophy journals are just next century's recycled toilet paper.

But the ones who do philosophy 24/7 are the ones who get ahead in modern academia. The ones who network incessantly, who write articles on the latest hot topics, who go to all the conferences, who live and die by their publication counts, they're the ones who are starting to dominate the profession now. The gentlemen, who had time to think, who had some perspective on life, are dying out. Not that they were that much better, really. They were just bad in a different way to the way the young philosophers are bad. But the young philosophers, his generation, are definitely duller. Their lameness and piousness is just too embarrassing to bear. It's awful being in their presence for more than a few minutes. Ren avoids them socially whenever possible.

But he can see why the supernerds, as he calls them, like talking philosophy all the time. Doing analytic philosophy at the top level is like undergoing a bruising workout at the best mental gymnasium in town. Nothing else comes close, really, at least in the Humanities and Social Sciences. In History, admittedly, you need to understand a lot about how the world works, and human beings, and know an awful lot about shit that's happened. And to do top-level Economics you need to be brainy and knowledgeable, and know maths. So maybe he's over-egging it a little. Still, as someone once said (Will Self?), analytic Philosophy requires an extreme mental dexterity, a God-like power to understand difficult, alien concepts and views, and an ability to hold fiddly, complex, Rube Goldberg arguments in your head, like nothing else does. (Or something along those lines, although it wasn't meant in an entirely complimentary way.)

But it also requires taking seriously, for your whole life, obviously absurd views, like scepticism about induction, or scepticism about the external world, or ludicrous attempts to deal with these 'problems' – philosophy has no end of 'problems' – like direct realism, disjunctivism, and Popper's response to Hume. Someone who spends their whole life on absurdities is, Ren thinks, the modern equivalent of a medieval theologian.

(It's a good thing he didn't say, as you might have expected, 'As those medieval theologians who spent their whole life arguing about how many angels can dance upon the head of a pin', because no-one ever actually debated this. That was a joke. A calumny even. It never happened. In fact, medieval theologians, and medieval thinkers in general, were much more knowledgeable and sophisticated than contemporary society thinks. They didn't believe in a flat Earth, for one thing. That the Earth is round has been known since the Ancient Greeks, and Aristotle, who worked it out himself. The 'Renaissance' that you learnt about at school is, apart from the great painting, mostly an exaggerated cartoon. A lot of what is attributed to the Renaissance actually comes from the medievals. So really, Ren shouldn't have even thought 'the equivalent of a medieval theologian'.)

Anyway, Philosophy may be a first-rate mental gym, but who, except a supernerd, wants to spend their whole life in a gym, especially one that makes you do annoying and silly exercises for forty years to build muscles that are entirely useless, and your only company is other supernerds? At least historians put their brains to use studying real events. But then he could have ended up writing about 'Shipbuilding practises in northeastern Norway, 1485-1510', so perhaps it's for the best that he didn't do History. But he's got to get out of Philosophy. Five years, he tells himself. Five years.

'Ren? Are you listening?' says Tanja.

Oh yes. Tanja's question. Ignoring it hasn't made it go away like he hoped it would.

'Can you ever know yourself?' says Ren to remind himself of the question. 'Do you mean fully? No. Do you mean at all? Yes.'

The blunt answers are an attempt to put Tanja off, although he knows that won't work.

'I mean at all. I mean, how can you know yourself at all?'

'Well, firstly there's introspection, which even if it isn't perfect, does produce some knowledge of yourself, unless you're just going for all out global scepticism, in which case we're hardly going to be restricting our attention to ourselves.'

One of the things to do with philosopher manques who incline towards scepticism is to make them aware of how their type of scepticism won't just be restricted to the sphere they are determined to be sceptical about. Not that they ever really get this, but it can get them off your back with a clean conscience.

'And secondly,' says Ren, 'there's the observation of your own behaviour. If you can know other people, to some degree, by observing their behaviour, then you're no different.'

'But how is that knowing yourself? I mean, truly knowing yourself?' says Tanja.

'What does the word "truly" add here? How is knowing yourself different to knowing yourself truly? Do you mean knowing every aspect of yourself? As I said, you can't know yourself to that extent. You can't know anything to that extent.'

'I mean, knowing what you're really like?'

'Are you assuming that what you're really like is completely different to what you seem to be like? What justifies that assumption? It's possible, but you can't build it into your view that it's probable, seeing as you're so sceptical about having any knowledge of what we're like to start with.'

One of the things that really annoys philosopher manques about Ren, and most other analytic philosophers, is that they don't talk like the manque wants them to talk. This can get the manque off your back after a while, unless the manque is drinking. Which they usually are when such conversations start up.

'But we can't know ourselves. Can we? I mean, how?'

'I just went through that.'

'But our vantage point on ourselves means that we're hidden from ourselves. We are in our own blind spot. There's no mirror we can hold up to see ourselves.'

Ren suspects that Tanja is, as usual, getting this stuff from some art catalogue she's recently been looking at.

'So you say. What reason is there to think this is true?'

'Well...' Tanja is somewhat stumped at this point. Lily gets out her little makeup mirror and starts looking in it, adjusting nothing in particular. Is this sarcasm by deed? Heresy by deed? Even if it isn't, Ren is impressed. But worried. He doesn't need Lily doing clever things that will make him fall for her even more. And right now he has to listen to Tanja for a few more minutes, just for the sake of his friendship with Miles.

'We're always presenting a mask,' Tanja finally says, as though she has dragged something up from memory. 'Aren't we? Even to ourselves.'

'Maybe, depending on how we unpack that claim.'

Ren kicks himself for using 'unpack that claim', a horrible modern cliche.

'But isn't that an issue with our knowledge of everyone else too?' he continues. 'I thought you were saying this was something peculiar to our knowledge of our own self? If this is a bar to knowledge, isn't it a bar to knowledge of every person, not just us? Isn't it in fact worse with other people, because you don't even have access to their conscious thoughts, like you do with your own own?'

'You're not listening to what I'm saying. I'm saying that the reality of who we are is always blocked by, er, by the reality of what goes on. And, er, how we see things, right? And that prevents us seeing clearly, doesn't it? Prevents us seeing at all. In this case. With ourselves. We can't see the back of our heads. So how can we see our minds? Why don't you take that into consideration? You philosophers just can't see the bigger things we can't see because you're always looking at your navels.'

Miles, Douglas and Jay are having their own, much more interesting conversation. Lily, because of her table position, is having a harder time screening out Ren and Tanja's discussion. She yawns. It doesn't look a very real yawn. It's possibly done for Ren's sake.

'Well, I want to get the parameters of what we're discussing settled first,' says Ren. Manques hate this sort of thing. They want instant profundity. 'Is this a problem that only applies to our knowledge of ourself, or does it apply to our knowledge of everyone else too? By the way, I presume we're talking about minds here. Normally philosophers say there's problem with knowledge of other minds, minds other than our own, not that there's some unique difficulty with your own mind. Because if you can know other minds better than your own, then why can't you just use whatever methods you use to achieve that, such as external observation, on yourself?'

When Tanja looks at him blankly, he says, 'Put it this way, such a view would imply that others know your mind better than you do, so why don't you just improve your knowledge of your own mind by asking them about yourself? I presume you don't have anything like this view in mind, though.'

Ren's tactic is to be just harsh enough to force Tanja to leave the conversation voluntarily, and to think twice about engaging him in philosophical conversation again, but not so harsh that she complains to Miles about what a bastard Ren is.

'I don't,' says Tanja uncertainly. 'Why can't you just talk about what I do have in mind?'

Because what you have in mind is brumous pile of shite, thinks Ren, and even my first years would think you are hung up on apparent profundity. They'd also think that you lack the required application to think through anything. Anything, apart from the material on the Michel Mouse Art History degree you did, but that's not setting the bar very high.

'Because I don't know what you have in mind. I'm trying to eliminate some possible views so I can get closer to what you're saying. Is this just general scepticism about knowledge of the mental, which is a scepticism I don't share, or is there some argument here concerning your own mind in particular? If the latter, I'm not getting what the argument is. Talk about not being able to see the back of your own head in the mirror is suggestive, but hardly a fleshed-out argument, or even a fleshed-out description of a problem.'

'Arguments are the problem. There's no argument, just the impossibility of seeing this,' says Tanja.

She's starting to talk loudly because the pub has filled up a little more, and the others are talking loudly, and the pub has a lot of hard surfaces which bounce noise around the room, making intelligible conversation harder.

'You academic philosophers miss everything, you think everything has to be an argument. Or a description,' she says. 'Why must it be a description? Always arguing, never listening.'

Or perhaps she's getting louder because the drink is making her more annoyed with Ren. Or perhaps she's remembering a conversation with some wonderful empathetic visiting artist, and that memory is making her realise more vividly what a blinkered reactionary Ren is. He's such a disappointment. She wants a philosopher friend, but not this sort.

'But I just don't know what it is that you are putting forward,' says Ren.

'I'm explaining it to you now,' she says slowly, in order to be helpful. 'The problem is, you can't see what's in front of your face because of your training, right? You're bigoted, you need to, um, open your mind to alternative points of view. Art would help you, you see, if you stopped using language all the time, it's a barrier to understanding, right? You need to let your visual mind influence your thoughts, and stop being so left-brained.'

Tanja's raised voice has attracted the attention of Lily again, and Miles, who is starting to look uneasily at Tanja. While Tanja is busy berating Ren (who is trying to send a telepathic message to Miles to replace Tanja with a round of drinks), Lily gets Miles' attention, and points to his crotch, and then at Tanja's mouth, to indicate that Miles should stuff his cock into her mouth to shut her up, and, like, why hasn't he being doing more of that so they don't have to hear Tanja bore the hell out of them again?

Tanja doesn't see this, but Ren does, and he immediately breaks the world record for the fastest erection ever attained by a human adult male. It won't go down as the fastest recorded erection, of course, because no such records are kept outside of certain public school circles, but nevertheless, it is the fastest erection ever achieved, which God, if God exists, would be glad to attest to. Well, perhaps not glad, Ren thinks, but he would reveal the truth if asked. (Actually, thinking about it, he wouldn't. He'd clam up. But he'd know, in his heart, what the truth is.)

Tanja breaks off, perhaps unsure of where this shit is going, or perhaps she was subliminally aware of Lily doing something in her peripheral vision.

'You know,' says Ren, getting back into the conversation straight away in the hope that it will make his erection go away before he has an accident in his trousers, 'you'd be better off talking to someone like Tony Shaver about this sort of thing.'

'Who's Tony Shaver?'

'He's Tony Shaver. Or, to give him his full name, Tony Fucking Shaver. A guy in my department. He's much more simpatico with this sort of stuff than I am.'

This is not really true. Although Tony Shaver is a massive bullshit artist, even he would find this sort of talk painful. He's more into sociology of science than hippy-dippy kaleidoscope talk. But Ren would be glad to make Tony suffer. Also, talking about Tony Shaver is proving to be an effective rod size-reducer.

'Miles, have you told Tanja about the QAA?' asks Lily.

Ren, glad of a chance to escape from Tanja's preoccupations, starts banging his forehead against the table. 'The QAA. The QAA. The fucking QAA,' he drones.

Tanja looks annoyed, knowing that the previous conversation is over, and this one is about to take off whatever she does. 'All right then, I'll bite,' she says. 'What's the QAA?'

'You don't want to know,' says Lily. 'Seriously, don't ask.'

Tanja frowns at Lily, because she doesn't want to ask. They're the ones making her.

'Too late,' says Ren.

'The QAA is a review process that the government does every few years,' says Miles, who is not very attentive to his girlfriend's moods, 'supposedly to ensure teaching quality in UK Universities. Sounds all right in theory, right?'

Tanja nods, because she is supposed to.

Ren demurs: 'It doesn't sound all right in theory to me. The government running anything is a bad idea, especially when it's a Labour government. And the more complex the industry, more absurd the whole idea is. Hygiene in restaurants they can just about cope with. Anything else is a disaster. We don't have government inspection of the quality of washing machines, for a good reason.'

'Well, anyway,' says Miles, whatever you think of government inspections in theory, in practise the QAA is a total disaster. Have a guess how many times the QAA people have observed our teaching in Psychology.'

'I've no idea,' says Tanja. 'One hundred?'

'Nope.'

'Two hundred? Fifty? Five hundred? I've really no idea.'

'The answer is... zero.'

'Zero? What? What do you mean?'

'Zero. They don't watch any teaching. There's a fortune spent on QAA, and enormous amounts of time goes into it, but none of it involves watching anyone doing any lectures or any teaching of any sort.'

'What do they... investigate then?'

'It's all just a massive box-ticking exercise,' says Lily. 'Do you do this? Do you do that? All the things they think teaching should involve. But no actual investigation of what the actual teaching is like.

'Not that there's much point them doing that either,' say Ren. 'Why think that two or three people appointed by the government going to listen to the lecturers in a department can give you any sort of definitive verdict? Won't they have their own subjective reactions to a lecturer? And how good are they at teaching themselves?'

'So why is it such a big process if it's just answering some questions on teaching?' asks Tanja.

'That's what government bureaucracy is like,' says Ren. 'You won't believe how enormous it has all got, just, as you say, to ask some questions about teaching. In my department they've had to put a whole room aside just to store all the documents required. And we're spending about eighteen months' worth of manpower on it, worth about sixty thousand pounds. Just for the endless filling in of the endless forms. For a smaller department. Across the University sector, with hundreds of Unis, each with dozens of departments, we're talking an enormous number of millions per round spent on useless form-filling. All that is money that could have been spent on much better things.'

Tanja is looking goggle-eyed at Ren.

'It doesn't even measure anything worthwhile,' says Lily. 'It's not even really claiming to be measuring teaching quality. It's just assessing how well a department measures up to what the department itself claims its teaching goals are. Not that it even does that. Most of the time it has to assume that the department is telling the truth, and it doesn't really have any way of knowing that. So it's not really even measuring how well a department measures up to its own goals. But that is the intention. To assess how well a department measures up to its own teaching goals, rather than measuring how well the department teaches.'

'Yes,' says Jay, 'which also means that if one department makes bolder claims than another department, then the first department could get a lower QAA score than the second even if it's the better teaching department.'

'And what they are measuring changes every time,' says Douglas. 'I discovered that what they're asking us this time is different to what they asked us last time. So the QAA scores, even assuming they really did tell you about the quality of a department's teaching, don't tell you anything about that department's teaching quality over time. Any change in scores is just as likely to reflect a change in the questions asked this time, rather than any change in teaching quality.'

'You know what really pisses me off?' Jay almost shouts. His scientific researches have enabled him to hit the exact frequencies that makes his voice resonate throughout nearby galaxies. 'In most other fields the inspectors, who come from that field, think that they should look after their own field to some extent, so they give all the departments good scores, or pretty good scores, unless you really are a bad teaching department.'

Ren can feel the wooden walls on the other side of the place shaking as Jay speaks. Is he an amateur opera singer? A trained histrion? He looks the part, with his shaggy black hair, and his theatrical moustache, goatee and jowls, which the goatee fails to disguise (the goatee fails to disguise the jowls, that is. The goatee isn't meant to disguise itself, or the moustache).

'But in my field,' Jay continues, 'they take it all really seriously, they're true believers, the stupid bastards, so they give out some undeservedly low scores to show how pure they are. Stupid, stupid, bastards.'

Jay's enunciation, you have to admit, is excellent, but it's not really a conversation that Ren wants advertised to everyone else in the place. Some of the other patrons are throwing annoyed looks their way, but as is the way with loudies, Jay is oblivious to this.

'So,' Jay goes on, 'one good department in one field might get a much lower score than a poor department in another field. It's so unscientific that all just becomes a worthless exercise.'

Ren shrugs. 'You lefties only have yourself to blame,' he says in a low voice, in the hope that this will make Jay speak more quietly. 'You always think the government can fix things, but usually it makes things worse. No situation is so bad that the government can't make it a disaster.'

'But has it improved teaching?' asks Tanja.

At that the academics all burst out laughing. Jay laughs like he's in a theatrical version of a spoof of a Hammer Horror film. In fact he looks like he's currently performing five nights a week in a theatrical version of a spoof of a Hammer Horror film.

'Christ no,' says Miles, wiping his eyes. 'It hasn't made teaching any better at all.'

'All it's done is removed all the old internal incentives we had as academics to teach well, and replaced them with external incentives,' says Lily the economist. 'External incentives don't work as well as internal ones.'

'Especially when the monitoring systems for those external incentives are so poor,' says Ren.

'So is this like the RAE that Miles was telling me about the other day?' asks Tanja, who is fascinated now, despite herself.

'Sort of,' says Miles. 'The RAE is another government inspection, but it concerns research rather than teaching. It's called the Research Assessment Exercise. It's bad, but it's not in the same league of badness as the QAA. Every seven years a department has to submit up to four papers, that is, articles, or books, from each academic.'

'Who assesses the work?' asks Tanja.

'A couple of people from that discipline will read all the stuff every department in that discipline submits, and then they give each piece of work a score,' says Ren.

'How can so few people make such big decisions like that? Is that your objection?' asks Tanja.

'That's one of the objections,' says Ren. 'There's no way that a few people can accurately assess the quality of so much work published in so many sub-areas. That's just a joke. Nobody really thinks they can. So really, in practise, the assessors base their scores on where the books and articles are published. Better publisher, better score. Better journal, better score. They pretend they don't do that, because officially they don't, officially they definitely don't, but everybody knows they do.'

'Not that that's a bad thing, it's better than trying to do it themselves,' says Douglas. 'But it's not like you can really say that because Paper A is in a supposedly better journal, it's better than Paper B.'

'Yeah, take *World Science*,' shouts Jay, as though he wants the editorial board of *World Science* to hear his pointed comments all the way from Grayvington. 'It's one of the biggest journals in the science world, but it has areas it likes to publish, and areas it doesn't like to publish. And lots of stuff they publish isn't that good, but it's trendy.'

'And *World Science* has cliques that run things, and they get each other into print,' says Lily in a quiet voice, like she'd also prefer Jay to keep it down. 'Buggins' turn. Like a lot of journals. Each revolves around its own clique, and the interests of its usual referees, which are often drawn from that clique.'

Tanja is looking disillusioned, but she also looks like she's appreciating having the scales fall away from her eyes. Universities are fucked-up places just like everywhere else. (At least, they are when the government gets involved, although that is not a thought that occurs to her. The thought, the mistaken thought, that occurs to her at this moment is that it's no wonder that academic philosophers like Ren are so small-minded, having to deal with all this bureaucracy.)

'And who's to say what's a better journal anyway?' says Ren.

'Yes,' says Lily. 'Determining that is very difficult if there's no agreement, which there usually isn't.'

'There is this move in some fields, especially in the sciences, to try to make journal rankings more objective,' says Miles. 'One way they're trying is by citation count. The journals that get the most citations, that is, mentions in articles and books, are the best. But that's like trying to say that the best music is the stuff at the top of the pop charts.'

'Also, a lot of material gets a lot of mentions only because it's being held up as an example of what is wrong,' says Lily.

'Yeah,' says Ren, 'in fact the Arts and Humanities Citation Index did a study of the years, seventy-six to eighty-three, I think it was, and found that the most cited twentieth century author in the major humanities journals, by a long way, was Lenin. Also in the top ten were such idiots as Heidegger, Sartre, Derrida and Foucault. And most of the others weren't much better, Barthes, Levi-Strauss, etc.

'*Das Kapital* is always in the top ten or twenty of those lists of the most cited works every year,' says Miles.

'What's bad about that?' says Jay.

'You're fucking joking, right?' says Ren. 'Marx at number twelve, Robert Conquest at, who knows where? Seven thousand? And usually at or near the top is Kuhn's *Structure of Scientific Revolutions*, which is still trendy despite Kuhn's obvious inability to distinguish between the logic of science and the history of science.'

'In science the citation counts aren't much better,' says Jay. 'It's rewarding those who make the most noise, not those who do the best science.'

'At least the RAE is attempting, however imperfectly, to directly measure what it's supposed to measure,' says Ren. 'Research quality, that is. Unlike the QAA, which uses highly indirect measures of teaching quality.'

'In my view there's only one good thing about the RAE, and that is that it hasn't been overcomplicated like the QAA,' says Lily. 'It's straightforward. Here's some work, let's see how good it is. Even though they're mistaken in thinking that they can so easily assess that work, at least that's all there is.'

'For now,' says Ren. 'But that won't last. It's government. And there are vested interests. Government doesn't like things being simple. It thrives on things being unwieldy and over-complicated, all of which enables it to expand. If you think it's going to stay simple you're fooling yourself.'

'I agree,' says Jay. 'Because the RAE is causing all sorts of problems for Oxford and Cambridge. They don't do as well in the RAE as they expected they would, because they're full of old grandees who don't publish so much these days. So they're pressuring the RAE to change the criteria, to include things like "marks of esteem", like getting keynotes.'

'What are keynotes?' says Tanja.

'Getting a keynote means being invited to present a keynote lecture at a conference, that is, one of the prestigious longer speeches that everyone is expected to turn up to. Oxbridge wants this to count in the RAE. They have so much clout that I expect it'll be included in future RAEs. Which will defeat the point of the RAE, which is that it's not supposed to be about reputation, but about the actual research that is done in that RAE period, not basking in the glory of research done in earlier periods.'

'You just wait, eventually they'll start including things like being an editor of a journal, and all sorts of other shit,' says Miles.

'But does any of this really matter?' asks Tanja.

'Yes,' says Miles, 'because how much research money the government gives your department depends on your RAE score. And departments with a lower RAE score sometimes get given the axe.'

'The other problem with the RAE,' says Lily, 'is that it encourages publishing for the sake of the RAE. It's not like there's any shortage of academic papers in the world. People are publishing material that no-one is going to read, or needs to read, just because the RAE says they have too.

'Gore Vidal once said that the world doesn't need any more novelists,' says Ren. 'What it needs is more readers. That applies to the academic world in spades. Tens of thousands of papers coming out, that no-one, except the author and a referee or two, ever reads. Journals are overwhelmed. Referees are overwhelmed. Refereeing is getting worse, academics hand over their referring duties to their grad students because they don't have time to do it. Because of the demand to publish, more and more journals will start up, and put out more and more papers that no-one will read. We have an epidemic of over-publishing, which is made worse by the government.'

'Why do you all put up with it?' says Tanja.

'Good question. We shouldn't,' says Ren. 'But, like I said earlier, academics are cowards. They're all wedded to their salaries and their pensions. They've assumed they have a job for a life and as a result they've got themselves nice houses with big mortgages. Funny how the middle-class left always ends up in the nice positions. So most academics would be in financial trouble if they lost their jobs, so they don't take any risks.'

'But why do the Universities themselves let the government push them around?' asks Tanja.

'The Universities sold their soul to the government,' says Ren. 'In return for letting government have some power over them, the government guarantees their existence, and their funding. It's not like the Universities couldn't operate as private industries, they could, but then you'd have all the uncertainties you get with running a private business. There'd be no guarantee that you'd have the student numbers you needed next year. Perhaps they'd all migrate to some new place. And there'd be no guarantee that the students you do get can afford to pay you what you needed. But under the current arrangement those risks are greatly reduced. The government pays the student fees. Competition is reduced because the government controls the market, and the quotas, so the status quo changes only very slowly, if at all. Grayvington, for example, knows that, unless it's incredibly stupid with its money, it will still be in business in thirty, forty, fifty years time, at the very least, and probably a lot longer, because it has the government behind it.'

'Okay, I can see the attraction of that.'

'It's a good deal for them, especially for the Vice-Chancellors, who get paid huge money by academic standards to operate as bosses in a sheltered market. But the problem is that the government wants more control in return for the money and the guarantees it's giving. It's gradually been taking away power from the Universities, and that's going to ramp up over the next few decades. This is not something that gets commented on much, because most academics are left-wing, so government control over industry seems so natural to them that they barely notice that it's an issue. Of course, they'll complain about what *sort* of control the government should have, but they don't really see the fact of government control as an issue.'

'But you can't just let industries do what they want, can you?' says Tanja.

'Let's not have that discussion now,' says Ren.

'Well, okay. But if, like, you academics don't like what the government is doing why don't you just all stand up against them? Right? Protest. Why don't you just not cooperate with the QAE and RAA?'

'QAA and RAE. Like I said, academics are cowards, and

no-one wants to be the first one to stand up and be shot down..'

'Then why doesn't the Union do anything?'

'The Union complains a bit, but the Union is useless. It has no credibility. It's run by hard leftists who are mainly interested in boycotting Israel. Last week it put out another report on why Israel is the most evil country in the world. The only practical thing it's capable of doing is making placards saying "Evil Tory scum".'

Tanja looks dubious, but Miles defends Ren. 'That's true, unfortunately. Look, I don't agree with a lot of what Ren says, but the Union isn't very effective, and the academics who oppose the RAE and the QAA don't want to rock the boat.'

'Sounds like you mostly agree with me then,' says Ren.

'Well, I would disagree somewhat on the matter of how academics view the RAE and QAA,' says Miles. 'While some academics hate them, some think they're good things.'

'That's true, some academics do think that,' says Ren. 'So we are in agreement.'

'The real problem is the Vice-Chancellors and the managers,' says Jay, like it's his turn for a rant. 'If the Union was in charge then things would be better. Although I don't suppose you agree with that,' he says, shooting a sardonic glance at Ren.

'The Union, no, but the academics yes,' says Ren. 'I think we'd be better off with the academics back in charge. They might be a bit incompetent sometimes at running things, but the move to professional management has been a disaster for Universities. Would you, as an economist, agree with that, Lily?'

'Definitely,' says Lily. 'So many people said that academics can't run things, you need professionals, or academics you turn into professionals with high salaries to match, but they've made just as many, if not more, bad financial decisions, and other bad sorts of decisions, as the old academics did. The old academics were much more careful with money. Look how many Universities have currently got themselves into serious debt now that they've been taken over by supposedly proper professionals, who don't know very much except how to spend money.'

'And even worse than that, the modern managers are slowly squeezing the life out of the sector,' says Ren.

'Are you sure you're not left-wing?' says Jay. 'I heartily endorse those sentiments.'

'Well, I'm sure we can find much to fight about later, but let's celebrate our current agreement.'

Ren and Jay clink glasses.

'I'm sure we can. They say you're a mouthy gobshite,' says Jay, with an extra-loud emphasis to make sure that Ren's parents hear this opinion of their son, 'and they're not wrong, but you're not all bad.'

'Anyone's gob need filling with some more shite?' asks Lily.

'Are you buying a round, or offering some speciality services?' asks Jay.

'I'm offering to buy you some of the landlord's speciality services from the tank in the basement that according to Ren he brews the ale in,' says Lily.

'Where he also keeps an assortment of gimps, and monkeys that have escaped from the Psychology labs,' adds Ren.

'So that's where all our monkeys have got to,' says Miles.

'Then a pint of the landlord's finest, with extra shiza,' says Jay.

'Liquid pork scratchings for you, Ren?'

'Liquid pork scratchings? Be still my beating heart,' says Ren, 'the woman plays you for a fool. If there really was such a thing then I'd already be a limp-limbed shell of a man lying on dirty sheets in a filthy scratching den, barely responding to the overtures of those of my timid friends who dare not indulge themselves, lest they be lost and be never able to eat a square meal again.'

'That's not that different from your current life, you

know,' says Miles. 'Replace the scratching juice with alcohol and that's pretty much you to a tee.'

'Except that you're lying in the even filthier bed next to me. With even gaunter features.'

'I never said I was timid.'

Lily finally gets an order out of everyone, and acquesting she goes.

'So given your analysis, Ren,' says Miles, 'why don't you be the one to put your head above the parapet? Are you a coward too?'

'I'm too junior for it to have any effect,' says Ren. 'I'm only a few months into the job. And I'm still on probation. It has to be people who are more senior.'

'Or maybe you're just a coward?' says Douglas.

'Maybe I am,' says Ren. 'All talk and no action. Thinking of the pension again. At twenty-eight.'

'Well, at least you're walking the walk on the TITE,' says Miles. 'Gotta salute you for that.'

'Yes, best of luck with your new career in the service sector,' says Douglas.

Miles starts to add something to that, but Ren interrupts him. 'No, don't say it,' he says.

'Don't say what?' says Miles.

'I know what you're going to say. That I have to start practising saying "Do you want fries with that?". Say something more original.'

'That's a bit hard, because garages don't have petrol pump attendants any more,' says Miles. 'There's always clerking in an insurance office. Or is that all computerised these days?'

'The young man carbuncular arrives, a small house agent's clerk, with one bold stare,' says Douglas.

'I'm not pimply,' says Ren.

'One of the low on whom assurance sits, as a silk hat on a Bradford millionaire.'

'Bradford? Are you slagging your own off now, northern chemist?' says Ren.

'Not my words. One of your philosophers, wasn't he?'

'That's it, I shall take up as a poet. Specifically, dirty limericks. Here's one of mine that I've always been quite fond of:

There once was a man with a whim
To make use of his counterfeit limb
He procured a girl
Turned her round with a twirl
And stuck it right up her big...'

Ren coughs instead of finishing. Lily has come back with the drinks.

'Not like you to go shy, Ren,' says Miles, his eyebrows raised.

'Don't be coy on my behalf,' says Lily. 'I'm pretty good with limericks myself. Here's one of mine I made up last year. How does it go again? Der-der-der, yes, that's it.

Said a hugey who called himself Bryce
Self-fellatio would be very nice
With his penis in place
In the hole in his face
Hit the back of his throat in a trice.'

The table is in uproar at this, laughing, gasping, spilling drinks, coughing. Ren is doing all of them, and in addition his old fellow has undergone another rapid phase transition. It's so stiff and tall it could act as the structural support for a skyscraper. Pour some concrete on it and you've got an instant addition to the New York City skyline. Even Gay Jay will have a boner over that. And Tanja has even cracked a smile.

2000-01
Semester 1
Week 8
Monday

'Come in,' says Ren.

A sullen-looking student with curly black hair and a black hoodie shuffles into the room, and sits in front of Ren's desk.

'What can I do for you... Sebastian, isn't it?'

'Seb. I wanda ask about been allowed to miss fis week's Metaphysics lecture and seminar on Fursday. I fort I should ask because you marked that guy absent who'd been on a ski trip last week, even though he'd told you where he'd been.'

'I see. And where are you off to?'

'I'm going to a protest camp?'

'Protest camp?'

'Yeah. We're going to learn more effective ways of protesting.'

'How much are they charging for this?'

'Six hundred and fifty quid'

'That's a lot of money.'

'Well, we get to network wivv ovva activists as well.'

'I hope you're not spending too much of your grant on this. You've got to eat.'

'Here's the fing. I got the money off my Dad. He works in the city. I told him it's for a ski trip wivv some of my mates from school. Vere's supposed to be firteen of us going.'

'I remember now. You went to Crace School, didn't you?'

'It's pronounced "cray". The "c" is silent.'

'How could I forget the pronunciation of dear old Crace School?'

'It's not a dear old school, I fink it's a lot of fascist fugs.'

'Really? But isn't your headmaster well-known for his radical views?'

'Yeah, he's good. And most of the masters too. But it's a fascist structure.'

'Well, perhaps this is not the time to pursue the matter of the structure of Crace School. Do I take it that you want me not to register you as absent for this week?'

'Fat's right.'

'I can't do that. You can only be excused for your absence if it's like a medical issue, or a death in the family, that sort of thing.'

'But my friend Jonty Forpe represented the University in the UK University Hockey Championships, and he got let off attending classes for vat week.

'Yes. There is that. The University feels that it has to allow students to miss classes if they are representing the University in sports events. It's not a decision that goes down well with all academics, but as the student is, in a way, officially representing the University then it's hard to see how the University could mark that student as absent without authorisation for doing so. Attending a protest camp doesn't really come under the same category.'

'Fat doesn't seem fair to me. Fis is part of my political education.'

Seb's pronunciation is winding Ren up something chronic, but as bold and reckless as Ren generally is, he isn't bold or reckless enough to pass comment on the pronunciation of his students. Not even a little bit of advice to Seb along the lines that while Seb is never going to set the world of intellect alight, his deliberate refusal to pronounce the digraph 'th' properly makes him look even more fick than he really is. (Or lazy – it's just so much work, man, to, like, be movin' ma tongue all the time.)

'I wouldn't worry about being marked absent. You don't have to come to all your classes. Officially, you're supposed to come to eighty per cent, not counting classes missed for legitimate reasons, which allows you some leeway for improving your extra-curricular skills. And you can usually get away with missing a lot more than that, although officially I'm not supposed to say that. So if you decide not to come to class, then you'll be marked absent, but you may feel that it's worth missing this week's classes for that. That's your decision, though.'

'But I've missed some classes already fis semester.'

'How many, exactly?'

'Er, quida few. Fere was a protest march in London I had to go to.'

'Had to?'

'Yeah, it was about Israel, I fort fat as a University student I had a responsibility to go. Fat's the fick and fin of it. And fen there was the trip to Amsterdam with the RTS.'

'RTS?'

'The Radical Finkers Society.'

'I understand. Too much serious protesting makes Jack a dull boy.'

Seb looks at him suspiciously, not sure if Dr Christopher is making fun of him or not.

'It had been arranged ages ago, so I had to go frew wiv it. But I told Derek – Dr Lucas – about fat and he marked fat one down as an auforised absence.'

'Did he now? Look, I suggest that you do go to some of your outside activities, but you need to keep the number of them in perspective, and bear in mind that your grades might be affected. I won't pretend that I didn't do lots of extra-curricular activities and cut a lot of classes, but I then had to take the hit of my grades being affected. So will you.'

Even as these words are coming out of his mouth Ren is wondering whether it's wise to be telling students even this sanitised version of his undergraduate career. Seb brightens.

'So I can frow a lot of classes and still get a good degree?'

'I didn't say that exactly. What marks are you getting at the moment?'

'Mid 2:2. Well, lower-mid 2:2.'

'So to get a 2:1 you're going to have to improve significantly, and start getting marks in the mid-to-high 2:1 range at least. Do you think that's a possibility?'

'It's possible.'

'Is it at all likely, though?'

'Let me fink it frew.' Seb stays silent for a few moments. 'To be honest, I fink it's not going to happen, whevver or not I try. I won't have any trouble keeping up a 2:2, fo. So why should I try any harder fan I am? My degree's basically already determined.'

'If you think like that you might end up with a third.'

'Probably won't vo, will I? So fat's not a fret hanging over me. It's hard to do 2:1 level work. At least for me it is. But you have to have brain damage to get a fird here. Even when I write a load of rubbish at the last minute on a feory I know nuffing about I still scrape a 2:2. So fanks for the advice, but why I should I bovver trying harder? I'll just coast frew the year, do what I want, and get my 2:2.'

Ren thinks about various noble speeches he could make to try to convince the young man in front of him, but then decides that with this guy it's a waste of time. Which is a bit worrying. He's supposed to get this cynical ten years into the job. Not in his first semester. But he'll save his his noble speeches for someone who's worth it. Maybe one will come along eventually.

2000-01
Semester 2

2000-01
Semester 2
Week 3
Tuesday

Ren knocks on Compton's door.

'Compton, what's all this cuggermugger I hear about Verna winning a grant?'

'It's true.'

'But how?'

'The postmodern sisterhood. They look after their own.'

'But even by their standards she's dumb. Wouldn't they give it to someone a little brighter?'

'You overestimate the intelligence of the ranks. There's not much there. And it's partly about loyalty, and politics. Verna might have fencepost levels of intelligence, but she can be trusted to write what she's supposed to, and remain an acolyte, without straying off the reservation, as they say.'

'So what's it about?'

'You haven't seen? I've got the description bookmarked. Here, let me print it out for you. You'd better sit down while I do this, it's going to be a bit of a shock.'

After the printing has finished Compton passes Ren a piece of paper for perusal.

Hector Drummond

'Recon(cept)ualizing the Vacuum Cleaner:
God, Slave, Function, Liberation'

Verna Leach

*Vacuum. Cleaner. Clean. Vacuum. The diffraction of the void.
The nothingness of space at the heart of the assemblage. A womb?
To give: birth: to: [multiple possibilities]. A parallax view of a
revolutionary machine with an atomic energy-driven core.
Liberator, or captor? Is it our tool, or we it's?*

In the political ecology of things the humble/mighty
vacuum cleaner has been ignored, but nothing played a
bigger part in womens' lives in the twentieth century. This
project explores the metaphysicks, the politicks, the
in(tra)fusion of this mash-chine from a postmodernist
perspective, sucking in Foucault, Irigaray, Derrida,
Baudrillard, Kristeva and Lyotard. A multiple-
meaning/multiple-conclusion approach has been derived
from the recent breakthroughs of Hoskaveda, allowing the
fullest/weakest focus/pan on the Booth/Kenney invention,
which created a Russian revolution/holocaust in the
suburbs of the privileged/enslaved. Calibrations are reset,
and a machine is created anew, only this time in the form of
word's and idea's, which create their own powerful force
and irresistible attraction.

'This is utter bilge. How much money was she awarded
for this?'
'One hundred and fifty thousand pounds.'
'One hundred and fifty thousand pounds? This cannot be
real.'
'It's real.'

152

'How is she going to spend that much money on this baloney? The result will be a few papers that you could write up in the pub one afternoon once you've knocked a few back.'

'Three years of teaching and admin buyout for her.'

'Three years? THREE FUCKING YEARS? No way is this real. This is a prank. You're shitting me, aren't you?'

'Plus she gets a PhD student funded to do this with her.'

'A PhD? On some fake bullshit on vacuum cleaners?'

'Could have been worse. She could easily have got two or three PhD students out of it.'

'This doesn't even read like something Verna could have written. It may be idiotic, but it shows a bit more invention than she's capable of.'

'Well spotted. The word is that Adalia helped her write it. Reads much more like something Adalia would write, rather than Verna the Learner.'

'So is Adalia on the grant as well?'

'No, she was just lending a hand, as a favour. So she is of course mightily pissed off that Verna has landed such a big grant with it. Big by Philosophy standards, anyway. They're not speaking. Not that Verna will care.'

Ren screws the piece of paper up and throws it at the wall. 'The whole grant system has gone insane.'

'Conquest's third law of politics,' says Compton. 'The simplest way to explain the behaviour of any bureaucratic organisation is to assume that it is controlled by a cabal of its enemies. Or parasites, I would add. In this case that is, to some extent, literally true. The Continentalists, for instance, who are both enemies of scholarship, and parasites, have infiltrated the system. It's Kimball's "long march through the institutions" in action. Once they get in to the system, they're very difficult to get out, and they work hard at getting more of each other in. In a way, that's also what the Robotikin has done. Got himself into the system, so he and the people like him can give each other grants. Did you know about his grant from a few years ago?'

'I knew he had one, but I don't know the details.'

'Philosophy of architecture. Not as loopy as Verna's of course, but still total dejecture. A complete waste of taxpayer's money. I can't even tell you what it's about because I can't remember, it's like trying to grab hold of fog. Something about structural integrity, I think.

'Isn't philosophy of architecture a bit like philosophy of sport? A kind of artificial field invented, or expanded, by people desperate for a field that isn't too hard to make a name in for yourself?'

'You might say that. I couldn't possibly comment. Robot has this little group of philosophy of architecture people who all refer to each other's work, and referee it. Outside of that group there isn't a person on Earth who would have the slightest interest in anything that lot say. No other philosophers care. No architects care. It's of no relevance to anyone handing out money for architecture projects, public or private. Even the members of the group wouldn't be interested if they weren't making a career out of it. Yet Warhol was awarded two-hundred and twenty-five thousand pounds for it, all paid for by Uncle Sucker.'

Ren just sits and shakes his head, completely donnered.

'Didn't you know?' says Compton.

'I didn't know he got that much money.'

'That's why he has so many PhD students. Most of them are funded through his grants.'

'Is that why his students are all so dull? Because they have to work on his boring ideas?'

'I expect that's the reason.'

'I don't even really get how you can work on someone else's ideas as a grad student in Philosophy,' says Ren. 'In science, sure. You run some experiments as directed by the PI. But how do you write on a philosophical topic as directed by the PI? It's got to be your own work or it's not a PhD, so the PI can't just tell you what to write. But your ideas are unlikely to be that close to the PIs. What if you end up thinking up ideas that are very different?'

'In theory you go with your own ideas if they end up differing from the PI,' says Compton. 'But often in practise the PI will guide you closely. Especially if it's someone like Robot. It's not really your PhD. You take his skeleton, and add a bit of flesh to it. With writing joint papers it's even more fraught. If you want to appear on a joint paper you'd better be mighty fictile and agree with the PI. And the PI will expect you to subordinate your views to his or hers. You're right that this sort of funded collaboration doesn't really work in Philosophy. Two or three philosophers who find that they have similar ideas on something can collaborate, but hiring in collaborators? Do you hire the best candidates, or the ones who agree with you? It's just more examples of philosophers pretending to be scientists.'

'And Verna is pretending to be God knows what.'

'Pretending to be an intellectual, I think.'

2000-01
Semester 2
Week 4
Wednesday

Ren's in his office recovering after giving a lecture, which had gone well enough but will require some extra explaining next week, on top of the extra explaining he was already going to have to do because of the previous week's lecture which he didn't have time to cover today. But he can't get on with writing down everything he needs to write down while it's still fresh in his mind, because now he has to go to meet this week's visiting speaker, and then host the weekly departmental seminar.

Being in charge of the seminars was one of the admin jobs he was given when he arrived at Grayvington. New, young members of the department are often given this role. One reason for this is that it's a job that doesn't require much knowledge of University procedures and rules, or much familiarity with University politics. But it's also felt that it's a way that newbies can get to meet more senior members of the profession, and that will help them make a name for themselves – networking is as vital in the Philosophy profession as it is everywhere else – and that in turn helps improve the department's name. It also means that the visiting speakers get to interact with some new blood, who genuinely want to listen to what the speaker has to say, and who genuinely want to go out to a restaurant with them afterwards, rather than the speaker having to deal with the same tired old farts who are bored of departmental seminars and who just want to go home as soon as the talk is finished.

But there are some downsides to giving the job to a

newbie. Some of the more distinguished and older guest speakers, especially overseas ones, aren't so keen on having to spend time with wet-behind-the-ears kids fresh out of their doctorate, and expect to be entertained by the more eminent and interesting members of the department. Thus it was understood that if a really big name came to speak then someone more senior would be given the job of looking after them. However, this policy hasn't been a great success in the past, as there is, unfortunately, no-one in the department who is both eminent and interesting. (This is perhaps why none of senior members of the department are taking the job of hosting a very big name in the field, Tyson Kipnis, who is coming to give a talk in a few weeks. Or perhaps it's because Tyson has a rep for being difficult.)

Another problem is that the seminar organiser has to book the speakers for the next academic year, and newbies don't have the contacts or the knowledge to do a good job of that, so whoever has the job depends greatly on the rest of the department recommending people they know who might be interested, and who will give a decent talk. This is something the other departmental members can't always be bothered to do. (It's not their job this year, okay?) If prompted enough they might recommend an old friend, who will usually turn out to have nothing much to say, or someone whose written work they have admired, who as often as not will turn out to be a terrible speaker and gruesome company.

Ren has already been surprised at how dull salaried philosophers can be. At conferences, as a grad student, you can get a mistaken impression of them, because there are always a few who are fun, who stay up drinking and talking shit with the grad students, and letting their hair down. It's easy to think that lots of other philosophers are like that. (Maybe a lot were, back in 1972.) But eventually Ren will come to realise that such philosophers are few in number. At those conferences he and the other grad students never noticed that they weren't socialising with the one-hundred and fifty other philosophers who have gone to bed early, or who are having torpid conversations with each other over dinner somewhere in a stuffy restaurant far away from the conference bar and the postgrads and the minor members of the profession. In the whole country there are really only three philosophers with permanent positions who are any fun, and even they are gradually becoming jaded as various responsibilities, both academic and familial, are piled upon their shoulders.

So most of the philosophers Ren has to wine and dine are not scintillating company. (Thankfully he doesn't have to do much entertaining of any of the snake-oil merchants that the Continentalists have got in to do talks, because Verna, not trusting Ren to keep things civil, usually looks after them.) Often only a few other colleagues come to the dinner afterwards. Sometimes no-one else comes if the speaker is really dull, or unknown, or it's essay-marking time. In that situation it can be hard work to keep the guest entertained. Most of them expect you to do the work of entertaining them. That's partly because they're often people who are socially awkward to start with, but it's also because they feel that they've done the work of giving your department their talk, so now it's your job to entertain them, on behalf of your department, and be interested in them. But that's not easy when you've nothing much in common, and they're less interesting than the curtains, and they have no knowledge of any topic that would engage what Ren likes to call a 'spirited person'.

Usually what a speaker wants to do most of all after their talk is to discuss the material they have just presented. This is fair enough, as one of the points of going to another department to present your work is to get some feedback on your views (as well as getting the chance to promulgate them). So you really want some discussion of the ideas you've just spent the last few months working on, however critical. Usually there's a few people around who are happy to talk to the speaker about their views, or attack them. But if no-one else is at dinner other than the speaker and the organiser, then that duty falls to the organiser. If the topic is something that you, the organiser, is interested in, then all might be well. But if it's been some boring old tosh that you paid no attention to, or you just had more important things to think about, like the next Test match, or people you might be able to have sex with, or writing down good band names on your piece of paper so the speaker thinks you're taking notes, then you're in a jam. (It's generally a good idea to pay some attention to the speaker's talk when you're the organiser.)

The only way out is to pretend to have some idea of what the speaker had said, but ask him or her to explain things all over again just to be absolutely sure you've understood it properly, and then act like everything they say is most fascinating. The speaker may well realise that you hadn't listened the first time, but even so, they'll still run through it all again, because (a) they want to talk about it, and also because (b) they know, just as you do, that this will fill in the time until they go to their hotel, or the train station. (But not their car; no-one in British philosophy ever drives to give a talk, except Ren and his departmental colleague Compton Hart, so it is invariably the train station that speakers who aren't staying overnight will go to.)

2000-01
Semester 2
Week 5
Thursday

'Take them all over,' says Derek.

'All of them?' says Simon.

'The state?' says Bob. 'Yes.'

'All the public schools?' says Simon.

'No more private schools,' says Derek.

Ren, who has just finished talking to a student nearby, has overheard the conversation, and joins the trio.

'Are you saying that the state should commandeer private schools?'

'Of course,' says Derek. 'Don't tell me you're so right-wing that you're holding a torch for the bloody public schools?'

'Right-wing? Jesus, you lot are so out of touch with ordinary opinion that you think sending your kid to a private school must be criminalised. No wonder civilians think academics are political cranks.'

'Didn't you get sexually abused at yours?' says Derek.

'Unlike you I went to state school.'

'If a state education is good enough for most people, why isn't it good enough for everyone?'

'Yeah, why should a few people get a superior education?' says Bob.

Derek gives Bob a look.

'Well put, Bob,' says Ren.

'They don't get a superior education.' says Derek. 'They get an unbalanced education.'

'At my state school I just got a mediocre education, with leftist indoctrination,' says Ren. 'I had to educate myself to learn anything.'

'You don't have to just take them over in one go. Another method is to just gradually bring them under your control by way of increasing regulation,' says Simon, who usually speaks slowly and with bizarre emphases on certain words. 'And the teachers they'll have to choose from in the future will mostly be left-wing, because that's the way University graduates are heading, so they'll be taken over by stealth.'

'Don't frighten the horses, that's always your way, isn't it, Simon?' says Derek.

'Unless your aim is to actually frighten the horses, then yes, that's my way,' says Simon, in his quiet but slightly hammy way. 'Choose the effective path, rather than the melodramatic one.'

'I think you'll find that Derek's aim mainly is to frighten the horses,' says Ren. 'He doesn't want to make an omelette without breaking some eggs. That's half the fun of it.'

'It's just that you have to establish early on who's boss,' says Derek. 'Otherwise the old bosses will have too many opportunities to stymie you.'

'So we all agree that the state should completely take over the Universities as well?' says Ren.

'What? No,' says Derek.

'Of course not,' says Simon. 'That would be awful.'

'A disaster,' says Bob. 'The state couldn't possibly run the Universities. Imagine having a government bureaucrat in charge of Grayvington.'

'So it's imperative that the state does not run even a single University,' says Ren, 'because the state is full of idiots who don't know what they're doing, but they must nevertheless be put in charge of all schools?'

'It take specialist skills to run academia,' says Derek. 'Only academics are in a position to know how to do it properly. Not the government, they'd make a complete mess of it.'

'Conquest's first law of politics: everyone's a conservative about what he knows best. In our field, it's best to let Universities manage themselves, and the government know-nothings should butt out. But in that pretty similar field over there, which I don't know so well, I reckon the government know-nothings should run everything.'

'Oh come on, it's not the same thing at all,' blusters Bob.

'You mean the school's are even harder to get right?' says Ren. 'You may be right there.'

'We're the experts on Locke,' says Simon. 'We're the experts on Joyce. We're the experts on physics. We're the people who know the students best. We're the ones who should make the decisions.'

'Sure, but schools can say the same thing. They know their students the best, they know the parents, they're the ones in the best position to make the decisions for their students.'

'You can hire a lot of educational experts who make better decisions than teachers,' says Simon, 'and that's what the state's done.'

'You can say the same of lecturers. The state could easily hire a panel of top philosophers who tell us what to teach. But would that be a good idea? Do you want a panel setting your curriculum for you? And the idea that the state does a good job of hiring educational experts is horse feathers. The whole field is full of poor quality, unempirical, politicised dross, and the government education department that sets the national curriculum is full of third-raters, despite the fact that that department takes a significant proportion of the whole education budget. Thank God there are still some schools that can provide some variety in what is taught.'

'Why should richer students get a better education?' says Bob.

'I thought the argument was that the state is better at education? Or is it that you want to cut down private schools because they're better than state schools?'

'What it is, is that public schools suck up too many good students,' says Derek, 'leaving those at state schools at a disadvantage.' He is about to elaborate further on this when

Verna comes up looking angrily at Ren. Ren assumes she has come to join the battle against him, but it turns out it's something else.

'Ren,' she says. 'I have a bone to pick with you.'

'What?'

'That graduate seminar you came to yesterday. Your behaviour wasn't acceptable, and you need to be told.'

'Huh?' Ren racks his brain. He didn't misbehave at that graduate seminar yesterday. What on Earth is this misbegotten hag going on about? 'What are you talking about, Verna?'

'You asked Lauren a question.'

'Yes. And...?'

'You asked her a question after her talk. That's not acceptable.'

'I don't understand. I asked her a question in question time. When the floor had been thrown open to questions.'

'Yes, but you shouldn't have asked her a question.'

'I shouldn't have asked her a question... in question time?'

'It was threatening.'

'I'm not following you. It was a normal question, in fact a fairly softball question, asked in a normal tone of voice. How was it threatening?'

'It was threatening because you are a staff member asking a graduate student a question.'

Derek and Bob make their excuses and slip away.

'Still not following you. Isn't the point of these graduate seminars to give grad students the chance to experience a philosophy talk? Where people ask them questions? Isn't that what we all want when we give a talk? To discuss our ideas with other philosophers?'

'It's intimidating for a graduate student to have to answer a question from a staff member. Especially an analytic staff member.'

'I asked her an easy question, and she answered it without any trouble. Did she say she was intimidated?'

'No, but it's the principle that matters. Graduate students can find it a hostile experience to be asked about their work by staff members.'

Simon decided that he is better off elsewhere too, and he glides away silently.

'This is stupid. The grad students beg us to come to their seminars. They're desperate for us to pay them attention, and ask them about their research. And they want the experience of facing questions before they have to do it for real, in front of a real audience, who might ask them much more hostile questions. That's why I went. You sent out an e-mail practically ordering us to come to this week's.'

Verna seems to be unmoved by what Ren has said. 'I didn't say you could come and ask questions.'

'You just want us to come and sit there and listen? Like it's a lecture, not a seminar.'

'That's right. Unless you're someone sympathetic to their viewpoint, you should just listen. In respectful silence. Not harass them.'

'But you asked a question.'

'I'm not a hostile questioner.'

'Neither am I. I asked a straightforward question. Practically a practise question for her. It was hardly Bertie Russell or Freddie Ayer getting vicious and trying to knock someone down and destroy them. And why do you count as non-hostile?'

'I'm female. I'm not analytic. And I'm her supervisor.'

'Then you're the last person who should be asking questions in a seminar. You've had many opportunities to talk to her about her research. The point of the seminar is to open it up to others. To let her get used to taking questions from people who might not agree with her. Or people who haven't understood things, and need more explanation. This is a University. These are graduate students, for Christ's sake. It's not a sheltered workshop.'

'That is offensive talk.'

Ren thinks better of letting her know what real offensive

talk looks like.

'Really, you just don't want the wrong people asking awkward questions,' he says, in a slightly harder voice. 'Or even non-awkward questions. I don't think she had any issues with answering questions. It did her good. You're doing her no good trying to hide her. She's not a shrinking violet first-year grad student. She's a third-year, and can cope.'

'You're being aggressive. This is what we don't want students being exposed to.'

'You're the one being aggressive. You came over to me to berate me over nothing.'

'You're still being aggressive. This is the sort of behaviour that needs to be stamped out.'

'Is your hypocrisy deliberate? Or do you genuinely believe that I'm being the aggressor when I'm just defending myself against your aggression?'

'I need to speak to the Head of Department about your unacceptable violent male attitude.'

Ren shakes his head. 'I seem to remember you saying the same sort of thing about him last semester, so I'm not sure how well that's going to work. Adelaide's not Head any more, remember.'

'Then I'll take it higher up. The Dean is not so keen on your sort of bully-boy tactics.'

'Can't have people asking questions at a University after all, can we?' says a fed-up Ren as he walks away.

2000-01
Semester 2
Week 7
Wednesday

Ren shoots Compton a look to say sorry, I owe you one. Compton looks back, amused. He seems to be saying, don't worry, this is worth it for the story. They're at the Terminal Building cafeteria entertaining Tyson Kipnis, who is giving the departmental seminar this afternoon. Ren has roped in Compton to help him cope with Tyson, who seems to be, as his reputation has it, a tinge on the eccentric side, to put it mildly. Tyson has been travelling with his wife, who is reputed to look after him almost all of the time, but on this occasion she has had to leave him in the care of Ren, because she has an urgent errand to undertake. Ren overheard her asking Wendaline Clugston (the department's administrator) where the nearest pharmacy is, and Ren worries that maybe some of the medicine that keeps Tyson marginally sane has been lost.

Tyson is a seventy-year-old American with a straggly beard, paranoid eyes, yellow British teeth, a strong New York accent, and a unique combover. He has a small amount of thinning hair left, and he's let this grow long at both the front and left side of his head. The combover is created from both of these rugs, but even with both there is still nowhere near enough hair to cover the large area of bald scalp. So what Tyson has done instead of a standard combover is to create what Ren can only call 'the graph paper look'. Thin strands from the front of his head are drawn back across the bald patch, like lines of longitude on a globe. These are interweaved with thin strands of hair from the side of his head, which intersect the other strands at ninety degrees, like lines of latitude, so he looks like he has a net on his head. The whole lot is presumably kept in place by some sort of hair product, and judging by the greasy looks the strands have, this product is something old-fashioned, although perhaps that's just what his hair is naturally like.

Ren cannot think why Tyson bothers with this hair arrangement that is, even by combover standards, ineffectual in the extreme, until the logic of it suddenly strikes him. Oranges. Oranges! That must be it. Oranges are usually sold in netted bags made of thin orange-coloured twine. The deep orange colour of the twine fools our perceptual system into thinking that the oranges inside the netting are a darker shade of orange – and thus are riper and juicier – than they really are. You notice this when you open the netting and you're disappointed that the oranges are somehow lighter-coloured than they appeared when they were in the netting. That must be the sort of effect that Tyson, in his mad way, is going for. He knows full well that he cannot hide his lack of hair with what he has left, but he believes he can fool our perceptual systems into thinking that he has more hair than he really does by creating the hair equivalent of an orange bag.

This is, after all, the man who created his own fiendishly complicated system of seven-dimensional parietal logic, which no-one can properly understand. This is the man, after all, who recently declared that his seven-dimensional parietal logic was, all along, really a seventeen-dimensional logic. Even his supporters have professed themselves unable to understand what the fuck he's talking about now. His fame in twentieth-century philosophy is assured, so no-one knows why he feels compelled, at his age, with his problems, to constantly tour the Philosophy departments of the western world giving talks, especially seeing as he was, until five years ago, famed for his reclusiveness. He doesn't get paid anything for the talks other than expenses. Is it some sort of therapy? Or making up for lost time? But he gives no indication that he enjoys travelling around giving talks. If anything, he seems to dislike it – it's a difficult business at his age, and he's socially very awkward. And mostly he stays in budget hotels (except for the big conferences, when he gets put up somewhere better).

Ren and Compton are asking him questions, but not getting much sense out of him. He keeps asking Ren to go up to the counter and buy him a cupcake. So far he has six of them, which he has lined up on the table. He isn't eating them, he's arranging them and talking to them like they're toy soldiers.

'So, Tyson,' says Compton, 'de Rossi and Parfitt say that your M4 entailment is only valid if you assume the structural equivalence of P2 and S7. What do you say to that?' says Compton.

'Those two, what do they know?' Back to the cupcakes. Mumble, mumble, mumble. Rearrange the cupcakes. Laugh. Mumble. Ren and Compton raise their eyebrows at each other. There's been a lot of that today.

'And, er...' tries Ren, 'Oswold Osbourne and Anthony Iommi say that it all leads to the negation of the double Blackmore rule.'

Eventually Tyson looks up from the cupcakes.

'What do they know about the double Blackmore rule? I've been teaching that since before they were born. I first taught that so long ago that I don't even remember it any more.'

He fixes them with a cracked stare, keeping his eyes up long enough for them both to see how bloodshot and mad they look. His eyes look older than the stars, old enough for so much to have gone wrong with them and the brain tissue they're connected to that there's nothing fixable left.

'Remarkable,' says Compton. 'Not many people know about the double Blackmore rule outside of Aston.' But Tyson is oblivious to their probing. He's too busy mumbling and playing with the cupcakes. Ren tries to see if he can decipher what Tyson is saying, but he can't. He wonders whether what Tyson is mumbling is just gibberish.

'So I take it you're not bothered by, er... Stavely Makepeace's psychological criticisms then?' says Ren.

Compton mouths 'Who?' at Ren.

Tyson fixes Ren with a baleful glare, the veins in his bloodshot eyes seeming to pulsate under the fluorescent lights. 'I don't know half these modern pygmies you're referring to,' says Tyson. 'Nor do I want to. Go and get me four more cakes.'

'Four? You want four more?'

Another glare. 'Perhaps you're right. Going to need six, aren't I?'

When Ren comes back with six more cakes Tyson has cheered up a bit, in so far as he is cackling more often as he plays with the cakes. Compton seems to have decided that there is no more need for psychiatric evaluation, and is no longer studying Tyson intently.

'I said eight more,' says Tyson.

'Um, actually, you said six.'

'Are you deaf? Eight.'

Ren looks over at Compton, who grins and says, 'He definitely said eight.'

Tyson doesn't appreciate Compton's intervention. 'What are you grinning at, jackass?' he says to him. 'Go and get me another eight. You shouldn't be letting your friend pay for everything anyway.'

Compton obediently trudges off.

'Ha, ha, these will do nicely,' says Tyson, taking the six cupcakes. He's a whirl of activity now, talking in what sounds more like the clown language Grammelot than English. Ren doesn't dare interrupt.

Compton comes back. 'Sorry, they only had seven left,' he says.

'Seven?' shouts Tyson. 'Seven? Why would you think an odd number is of any use to me? Are you trying to jinx me?'

He takes one of the cupcakes Compton has placed on the table and puts it on the floor near his foot.

'Bam!' he yells, as he violently squashes the cake with his

shoe.

'You see what I can do?' he says to them. 'That could have been a whole world, and I've just crushed it.'

'All those cream miners, squashed flat,' says Ren.

'I don't think the Galactic Cleaning Company will be too pleased with the mess,' says Compton.

'Shut up, shut up, shut up.' Tyson turns his attention back to the cakes. The whole table is covered with them, and Ren and Compton have had to move away from the table to give Tyson room for his manoeuvres. They chit-chat quietly to themselves, keeping their worried eyes on their prestigious guest, who is getting more and more animated. Ren wonders whether they should get him out of this public area, but he doesn't really want him in his office. God knows what he might do in there, and he'd probably want to take the cakes with him.

'Uh huh hah,' says Tyson loudly in a triumphant, bird-like voice, as he completes another cake rearrangement. He giggles in a high-pitched voice. They look blankly at him. 'It's all coming into place now,' he beams.

'Great, Tyson, great,' says Ren, who is about to finally suggest they make a move, when Tyson raises his fist and violently flattens a cake.

'BAM!' he shouts as he does it. Cake shoots everywhere. People look over at them, but it has all happened so fast that no-one else in the place knows what has transpired.

'You see?' Tyson whispers excitedly. 'Do you get it now? All my work, you and I and he and Monkman and all the fritters thought it was about logic, but no, no, no no. Ha. Of course not. Code. Instructions. In code. Flat stuff, and all. You know code? You won't know this code. Telling me what to do, how, when, what, why, up, down, when, why, repeating myself, over and over, when, how, why. It's after the Universe shifts. Folding the wheel again. Have to know it, otherwise you get caught in the shift. Torn apart. Unless you're a super strong. Know how to roll with it.'

'The soup?' says Compton. 'Yes, I think you do get a roll

with it.'

Ren kicks him under the table.

'Souperman, souperman, souperman, shut up, shut up, shut up. A message from the future. Or another Universe. Maybe from the future me. I'm all there, I'm everywhere. Even in the soup. Think I didn't get the reference? Pots and pans all spick and span. The shift, encoded the answers into the formulae. They're all here now.' He points to his head. 'In here. The clarity is so intense now, it hurts. Jesus, it's burning my mind. BAM!'

He has squashed another unfortunate cupcake with his fist. People look over again, puzzled now. Tyson starts laughing hysterically, grabbing bits of squashed cake and putting them all over his face and hair. Ren and Compton try to get him to leave.

'Can't you see? Can't you? It's all around, the evidence, you dummies, put this stuff in your eyes, it shows you the truth,' he says, offering them some squashed cake. People are looking over at them uneasily.

'We'd really better be going, your talk starts soon,' says Ren.

'BAM! BAM! BAM!' shouts Tyson, expertly squashing three more cakes.

'You'd better stop that now,' says Ren ineffectually.

'These machines kill fascists,' shouts Tyson, holding up his fists.

'Hadn't we better tell everyone the news about what you've found?' says Compton. 'At the talk? You can tell everyone! Let's go.'

'Yes! Tell them! Tell them all. Spread the news to the elect, and infiltrate the electrical circuits. The chosen will understand the code. The fritters will be finished with. Binoculars! BAM! BAM!'

Two more cakes bite the dust before they manage to get him away from the table and out the exit. Ren avoids looking at the cafe staff on the way out.

'The ones who don't get the code will be rearranged, of

course,' says Tyson as they're going up the stairs.

'Well, that's nice to hear,' says Ren.

They get to Ren's office. He's not sure what to do. Despite what they told Tyson, the start time of the talk isn't for another thirty minutes. Tyson isn't currently in any shape to do it, even though he has calmed down considerably, and is smiling beatifically. Where is his frickin' wife? Should they get him to a doctor?

'What strange garb you wear,' says Tyson. 'Are you fifth century?'

'No, I'm, ah, just ran out of normal clothes to wear today,' says Ren. 'So I just grabbed these.'

'You don't fool me. But I'll take your little secret to the grave. Anyway, I'm just going to take a little trip to another world for some more revelations,' says Tyson. 'Back soon.'

He lies down on the floor on his stomach and goes immediately to sleep.

'What do we do?' says Ren.

'He needs a doctor,' says Compton. 'But the NHS...'

'Yeah, we don't want to spend all night in A&E to get two aspirin.'

'What we need is his wife to come back. She'll know what's up with him. And she should have his medicine. And we shouldn't wake him now.'

'I have no intention of waking him now,' says Ren. 'Let him sleep.'

Twenty minutes later Tyson, face down on the floor, starts singing. 'Hello carpet my old friend,' he croons to tune of *The Sound of Silence*. He looks up. 'You two still here? You're keen.'

'How are you feeling, Tyson?' asks Ren.

'Fine, a little subdued now, but okay. I'm sorry if I got carried away earlier, I get a little excited sometimes. Ideas take hold of me. The power of ideas. Still strong in me after all these years. Some better than others.'

'Do you want to go back to your hotel and rest now?'

'Whaddya talking about? We gotta talk to do.' He looks

at his watch. 'Oh, good timing. Starting soon. Let's go.'

'Are you sure that's wise?' says Compton. 'You seem...'

'What? I was a bit overwrought, that's all. I'm fine now. Back to the sober logic. I came all this way, not going to back out now, not with all those fans waiting for me.'

'Well, okay,' says Ren, 'but let's cut the talk short if you start to feel... unwell again.'

'For a young fellow you worry an awful lot. You're like my brother, he was always worrying. Then he got killed in Korea. Worrying won't stop a bullet that's coming to blow half your brain away, will it? Come on.'

Ren gives Tyson his overhead slides, which Tyson had left in Ren's office earlier, and they take the pile of photocopied handouts. As they walk to the seminar room Ren starts to think that maybe going ahead with the talk is a bad idea, but trying to stop Tyson from giving his talk could be even worse. And if the talk doesn't go ahead then Ren would have to sit with Tyson waiting for his wife to turn up. Might as well let him talk in that case. And having others around might be a good idea – if he has another turn they can help.

The seminar room is packed, and uncharacteristically noisy. The audience consists of most of the Philosophy staff, apart from Grant, but including the Continentals, apart from Adelaide. Also in attendance are some people he doesn't recognise who are probably from other departments, plus Alan Pettigrew, quite a few grad students, and even some undergraduates. The physicists are not here – Beresford has thankfully stopped coming since Hedley's talk. Many of the audience have been lured not just by Tyson's intellectual reputation, but by the rumours of his eccentricity. In addition to the well-known rumours, there are also whispered ones, privy only to a few, that hint at more unsavoury behaviour.

When he sees the size of the audience Ren's heart starts to sink a little. He was hoping for a smallish crowd of only those with a serious interest in higher-order logic. He's not happy having undergraduates present in case Tyson goes off the deep end again, but there's nothing he can do about it now.

Ren doesn't do the big buildup. It doesn't seem wise. Instead he just says, 'I'm sure Tyson Kipnis doesn't need any introduction, so here he is.'

Tyson starts to address the audience. Ren thinks he looks deranged, and he fears the worst, but to his surprise everything is all right. That isn't to say that Tyson makes much sense. He rambles, gets confused, and appears to have no clue what his talk is even about, and the audience is shocked, but really, that all comes as a gigantic relief to Ren, who knows it could have been much, much worse.

Tyson finishes early, after about forty minutes. Then it's question time. This could be tricky. Derek Lucas's hand is up first, as it always is. Ren usually mixes up the order of questions so Derek doesn't always get to go first, on principle, and also because Derek, although he usually asks good questions, does tend to go on and on. But no-one else is offering to ask a question, so Derek it is.

Derek's question is, as usual, very long-winded, but it does contain some serious challenges to Tyson's position. Or rather, to what is generally taken to be Tyson's position, going by his earlier, saner work. (There's no telling from today's talk what his position is, or even what subject he was lecturing on.) Tyson appears to pay no attention to Derek as Derek rambles on, enjoying the sound of his own voice. Tyson looks out the window as though what's outside is very boring, but not as boring as Derek.

'Phah,' says Tyson when Derek has finally finished. 'Really? No. Just no,' he says, flicking his fingers in contempt at Derek. 'Not worth wasting my time answering that. Next.'

Derek sits there open-mouthed. He cannot believe what he has just seen and heard. No-one can, except Ren and Compton. Even Derek himself wouldn't ever respond to a question like that. The Continentals look outraged, but despite their pursed lips Ren can see that their eyes are shining in triumph. The big analytic star showing his true analytic colours. Arrogant and dismissive, like all of them. This will feed their gossip for years. Hell, it will feed their gossip for the rest of their careers. (None of them noticed that Tyson's talk made no sense. All talk of logic seems like gibberish to them.)

'What?' says Derek. 'You can't say that. You've got to do better than that. This is not a Continental seminar.'

Ugly murmurs break out from the Continental section of the audience at this.

'Just joking, of course,' says Derek, smiling sweetly at them, while his face makes it clear that he thinks they should shut up because the action today doesn't concern them. 'Excusez-moi.'

Tyson is looking at his fingernails, unperturbed.

'I think,' Ren says, in his capacity as host, giving Derek a meaningful look that he knows everyone else except Tyson will see, 'that if Professor Kipnis isn't feeling up to answering some questions today, then it might be best if we don't press him too hard on those ones, so that he has the energy to concentrate on questions he feels he can tackle today.'

Derek grumbles, but accedes. The Continentals continue to mutter.

'Right, anyone else?' asks Ren. 'Tristram, thank you, the floor is yours.'

Tristram puts on his usual bemused smile and adopts the self-deprecating tone he sometimes resorts to. 'Well, I expect my question won't fare any better than Derek's, but I was wondering about the issue of how your stack operators are going to remain consistent if you're assuming a polyordinal lattice. I mean, obviously, assuming we're talking about a Polokowski logical space.'

Tyson sighs. 'I explained all that years ago in my book *The Logic of Parietal Geometry.*'

175

'Actually,' says Tristram, 'It was called *The Geometry of Parietal Logic.*'

'That must have been what the British version was called. The answer's all in there. Any more up-to-date questions?'

'Well,' says Tristram, 'it was your views expressed in that book that I wanted to talk about.'

'You,' says Tyson, pointing at an undergraduate. 'You got a question for me?'

The frightened student thinks for a moment, and, feeling forced to answer, says in a halting, primary-school voice, 'Did you study logic as an undergraduate?'

'Study it? When I was an undergraduate I was teaching it. I've been studying logic since I was five years of age, kid. Maybe earlier. You know I went to Randolph at age sixteen? By eighteen I was in charge of the advanced grad student logic classes.'

Ren asks for some more questions. Not surprisingly, no-one is very keen to ask one. The only person putting his hand up is Alan Pettigrew.

Alan is a former civil servant, now retired. He turns up most weeks with a couple of plastic shopping bags full of newspapers. No-one knows why he has the bags. There is a spectrum between eccentric and mad, and in Alan's case there is a lot of week-to-week movement of the swingometer that points to his position on this spectrum. There is usually a short discussion each week in the staff club as to what position Alan was on that day. A few months ago he was definitely on the milder end, talking lucidly, asking some reasonable questions, making some half-decent witticisms. Recently, though, he's been starting to show signs of becoming unglued again. And when he goes downhill his jokes go from being lame to indecipherable, and he chuckles at them more. So Ren isn't that keen on calling on Alan. But Tyson takes matters into his own hands.

'Question,' he says, pointing at Alan.

'My question is this,' says Alan in his mumbling, breathless monotone, which is worse than usual today. You can also tell it's a bad day because he's fiddling with the newspapers in one of his plastic bags, which he has on his lap. 'When I used to work in the civil service we had a work rota where we'd all fill in the shifts we wanted to do, or had to do, and as you can imagine, it got very complicated, didn't it, and we came up with numerous systems, and no-one could decide which was the best system, so we tried to devise a method that could determine which was the best system, but we came up with two of those, so how could we decide which was the best one of those, so we spent a few months trying to come up with a system that could tell us that, but that was beyond the range of our abilities, and how did we know that there'd only be one of those systems? So Jock Landers, who was a bit of an expert on logic, got talking to this Oxford chappie who was a whizz at logic, and he used to work on radar in the war, and he said that with radar systems you've got a similar problem, because of the calibration needed, although Ted Sanders reckoned it wasn't similar at all with radar, and he said the problem that Jock was on about was due to an issue with the electronics, but then that leaves us in what is a similar situation, isn't it, because how do we decide between Jock and Ted? Mmm? So my feeling is that perhaps we can't, or for all intents and purposes we can't, so we're left with relativism, aren't we, and if it isn't relativism of facts, it's relativism of knowledge, because even if there are facts we can't get at 'em, can we? I used to talk about this with the old Professor who was here years ago, McConogill, and he wasn't very keen on this talk, but then I'd say to him, how do I know you're right? And he'd say, Well Alan, he'd say, think about it like this.'

Alan rambles on in this vein for ages. It's material the philosophers have heard before quite a number of times. It doesn't form anything remotely like a suitable question for Tyson's seminar – in fact it doesn't even form into a question at all – but it's filling in the gaps for now, while Ren points at people and silently asks them whether they want to ask a question. No-one gives a firm commitment to ask one. While

Ren is doing this Tyson silently rises from his seat and goes over to Alan, who looks up at him, but doesn't stop talking.

'Don't mind me', says Tyson, who takes one of Alan's newspapers out of a bag. He takes it back to his seat, sits down, and starts reading it. Alan is looking most flustered, but keeps talking, like his language centres are on autopilot. He looks like he wants to get his newspaper back and tell Tyson off, but here he is finally being given the chance to talk and talk in front of a large captive audience, he can't let that chance go, he has to ignore Tyson, as hard as it is when one of his newspapers has been taken without permission, and just let the words flow for as long as he can.

'And what if it all comes around in a circle? What if one of the systems you've now reached turns out to be the same as one of the systems you started with? That puts you in an impossible situation, doesn't it? I mean that could happen, it may not be very likely, but it's logically possible, as you fellows say, and that means you're trapped in a loop and you can never get out, and do we not know, I mean we can't, can we, we might be in a loop like that now, we don't know we are, but we don't know we aren't, you might as well toss a coin, mightn't you, all these things you think you know, but really we don't know anything.'

'Oooh, nasty bus crash,' says Tyson, turning a page. 'Twenty-four killed. Tragedy.'

'Is it all an illusion, and does it all goes back to Plato and the cave?' says Alan, getting really rattled now, and making less sense than ever. 'It always does, but Plato thinks there's truth, but is there? How do we know they're even in a cave? Maybe it's the bottom of a well. Maybe it isn't either, it's both, no, not both, but not either either, but it could be both, but not really because maybe there's no truth.'

Alan is starting to mumble now, and his words are gradually getting harder and harder to make out.

'So maybe they're not even there, and the flames can be described as flames or as turnips, who's to say that's wrong if we call them turnips? Well, not turnips perhaps, that's not a good example, but something that's like a flame but isn't a flame, but isn't a turnip either, but isn't that far removed from a turnip, I mean, who decides? Is it a flame? Is it a turnip? Does a flame or a turnip look upon the situation and decide which it is? Do we know who or what is deciding? How do we do that?'

'I get it,' says Tyson.

'You do?' says Alan. 'What?'

'I get what the newspapers in the plastic bags are for.'

Alan says nothing. Tyson lies on the floor, and starts placing sheets of newspaper on top of him.

'Please don't do that,' says Alan.

'It's a tramp kit, isn't it?'

'What?'

'It's a tramp kit. You carry the bags around and whenever you need to sleep you just take out the papers, and hey presto, instant bed?'

Alan looks flustered and angry. His lip starts quivering, and he looks like he's ready to attack Tyson. Ren thinks he'd better step in now. Secretly he's enjoying this bit of drama, which is a welcome relief from the usual seminar tedium, and he suspects that most of the audience is secretly enjoying it too, even if they're affecting to be appalled, but he'd rather not have another physical fight on his hand as seminar organiser.

'Right,' he says, 'we're going to wind things up early today, I think. Tyson, please give Alan back his newspapers. Thank you for coming everyone, and can we have a big hand for Tyson Kipnis.'

(Later on Ren is praised for his decisiveness here. He wasn't decisive, of course. He should have stepped in earlier. He only seemed decisive by philosopher standards. Most other philosophers would have still been umming and aahing long after Alan and Tyson had finished punching each other.)

There is some desultory applause, but mostly there's silence. Then everyone pours out of the room, clearly because they want to start gossiping about what they've seen as soon as possible. Tyson just lies there under the sheets of newspaper. Alan goes and snatches them back, helped by Ren. He stuffs them back into his plastic bag, but they don't fit now because he hasn't folded them up properly. He stalks off out of the room, furious.

Ren's not sure what to say. Eventually he says, 'Come on Tyson, let's go.' Tyson gradually rises to his feet without a word.

Ren corrals a group who are still gossiping in the corridor. 'Can you lot take Tyson to the staff club? I'm going to put a note on the door of the Philosophy office in case Tyson's wife comes back there and finds it all shut up for the day.'

When Ren arrives at the staff club he is appalled to see that Tyson is drinking a glass of wine, and has a wine bottle in front of him. Who the fuck bought him that?

'Tyson? Are you allowed to drink on your medication?'

'What medication?' says Tyson. 'I'm not on any meds.'

'I heard your wife mentioning earlier that she was going to the pharmacy, so I just assumed...'

'She's the one on meds.'

'Any idea where she is? She's been gone a long time.'

'She's probably gone crazy by now,' says Tyson, knocking back his wine and pouring himself another, as though, with his wife gone, this is the last ever chance he'll have in life to get loaded. 'She gets like that if she doesn't have her meds.'

Am I really supposed to babysit this mad fucker, wonders Ren. And his possibly, or possibly not, mad wife, if she ever turns up again? Can I, a junior squirt, tell a venerable and distinguished professor that he's not allowed to drink? Ren notices that the Continentals have come to the staff club and are keeping their beady eyes on Tyson, just waiting for him to create some more juicy gossip.

'Perhaps you should go easy on that,' tries Ren. 'It's been

a long day.'

'Listen sonny, I've run departments, chaired prestigious committees, edited the best journals in the world, testified to the White House, advised three US Presidents, and won the Dalkeith medal for outstanding intellectual achievement. You're not going to tell me that I can't have a goddam drink after giving a talk. How many Dalkeiths have you won?'

'None, but how many times have you had to be committed?' is what Ren is tempted to say, but he just goes off to get a beer instead. When he comes back he is unsure of which conversation to join – the after-seminar party is a big one tonight, with plenty of people from outside the department in attendance.

'Did you hear Tiddles is off to East Anglia?'

'Poor chap. Is he taking something for it?'

'Tyson, you can't surely be serious about dropping the law of lesser consequences?'

'No law is safe from me. I'm a law unto myself.'

'If the Dean's wife won't put up with him anymore I don't see why we should either.'

'I heard she clocked him one. Giving you any ideas?'

'Well, if I hit him in the same spot there'll be no evidence.'

'I swear it was the same food they serve the students. Pigswill's too good a word for it.'

'Did you see the Continentals taking notes at the talk?'

'Notes? I bet they had a secret camera recording the whole thing.'

'No-one told me Frank was going to give a talk to the grad students. How do they feel about it?'

'Not happy, because now they'll have to waste time reading his stupid book in advance to have a clue what he's on about.'

'Would you say Tyson is more mad or less mad than last time you saw him give a talk?'

'I would say the talk was slightly less mad, but the eyes look slightly more mad.'

'He did rather put Alan's nose out of joint, so he's done one thing right.'

'If we've got rid of Alan on top on of getting rid of Sadler then that's a result.'

'Never heard of him, but I hear there's a famous guy in Chemistry who's just as mad as this guy. Wasn't your supervisor a bit loopy too?'

'Only on Monday mornings and Friday afternoons.'

'Have you heard Raven's lunatic plans about taking over a Scottish University and connecting them up with a solar-powered rail link?'

'The guy's insane. If I had a wife that looks like his I'd be spending all my time in bed instead of dreaming up megalomaniac ideas.'

Ren sits down, uneasily, on the edge of the group. He can see at a glance that Derek is in a malevolent mood after his treatment by Tyson, and that George is shitting himself over what Tyson might do when provoked by Derek.

'What was that fat guy on about, huh?' Tyson is saying. 'Calling me a degenerate medievalist. I'd like to get medieval on his fat ass.'

'What fat guy would that be?' asks George.

'The fat guy who was fat. And a guy,' says Tyson.

'I don't remember a fat guy, Tyson,' says George. 'And no-one called you a degenerate medievalist. Or a degenerate modern. Or a degenerate anything.'

'The hell. The fat guy at the back with the dirty T-shirt. Where's the organiser?'

Tyson looks around and finally spots Ren. 'You. You must have seen him. The fat guy at the back. Greasy hair. Nasal German voice.'

'Right', says Ren. 'Fat guy. Don't remember him.'

'Course you do.'

'Perhaps his comments were so worthless that my memory of him was immediately erased by my brain,' Ren says in a lame attempt to lighten the mood.

'Fuckin smartass. You can remember. You're just being a

prick.'

'Maybe, ah, maybe you're remembering another talk you did recently?'

At this Tyson looks furiously at Ren, but says nothing. He pours himself another drink, and takes a big swig. After a few moment's uncomfortable silence, Derek, in full-on mischief-making mode, says, 'I'm surprised you're not still at Randolph University, Tyson. That's where you made your name. I thought they loved you?'

'Fuckin Randolph,' says Tyson. 'I'd like to take the dirty slug-sucking cockroaches and strangle them with a horse's cock.'

Talking of horses' cocks is clearly thirsty work because Tyson pours himself another glass from someone else's bottle (his is now empty). George kicks Derek under the table, but to no avail.

'Didn't they offer you enough money, Tyson, is that why you left?' Derek says, before getting up to go to the bar, well away from any fallout that might occur now.

'Keyholes,' says Tyson enigmatically. 'That's what it all came down to. Keyholes. I'll say no more. You get a good perspective on things by looking through keyholes. They're like looking into other Universes. Philosophical kaleidoscopes. Most of my best work has been powered by the keyhole. Meditative. Enlightening. I want to go back there to keyhole space.'

While Tyson is expounding on the metaphysical poetry of keyholes, behind him Derek is miming the actions of someone who has crouched down to peer through a keyhole, while simulating, in exaggerated fashion, the having of a furious wank. Suppressed titters can be heard, which confuses Tyson.

'Coburn and those other cunts couldn't understand it,' he says, by way of explanation. 'A fucking chemist in charge of the place. Saw everything in the basest way.'

'Well, that was predictable,' whispers Ren to Compton, as Niall Raven, the Vice Chancellor comes into the room.

'You never see him when you need him...'

'What do you mean? He's never needed,' whispers Compton.

An angry, bespectacled forty-something man in an immaculate suit walks over to Derek, who is still bent over and carrying out his impression of Tyson, with his back to the VC. The sight of the VC's determined strides causes the mood in the group to abruptly change, which confuses Tyson even further.

Raven puts his hand firmly on Derek's shoulder.

'I'm not sure that's setting the best example to any guests who may be in the club tonight, Dr Lucas,' says Niall, in a severe tone of voice, a tone which Fourier analysis would reveal to contain the coded message 'You're getting sacked in the morning, wanker'.

'Argh,' shouts Derek, who in his shock falls from his crouched position onto the floor.

Tyson turns around to see what was happened, and sees Niall standing over Derek.

'What have you done to him, you greasy goose fucker?' he shouts.

'It's all right, Tyson,' says a panicked George. 'He's the Vice Chancellor.'

Tyson grabs George by the shirt and shakes him. 'They're all the fucking same, these chemists,' he shouts. 'Don't you see? Give them a bit of power and they start fucking us over.'

'Really, it's all right,' whimpers George, who is getting more crumpled by the second.

Tyson lets go of George, who sags and shrivels, and turns to Raven. 'Leave him alone, you maggotty slimeballing shitscreen.'

'I don't know who you are,' says Raven, 'but that language is not acceptable. You'll have to leave.'

'Not this time, chemistry man,' Tyson shouts. Then he screams, 'It's payback time.' He picks up his empty wine bottle and hurls it at Raven. It misses him, but hits the wall behind, making a tremendous smash, and glass splinters everywhere.

Then Tyson tips his table over, taking George with it, and screams, 'Open the cages! Free the animals! Everyone out! RUN!'

Tyson runs at Niall, and mimes throwing a punch at him. Niall cringes and shields himself from the blow that doesn't come, which gives Tyson the opportunity to kick Niall's legs out from under him.

'No more bars,' shouts Tyson. 'Ever.' He runs to the door. 'I'm never coming back to your little world. Free yourselves or die like gooses.'

Niall, Derek and George are all lying on the floor amongst the debris. George is clutching his chest. Before anyone can say anything, Tyson puts his head back through the door.

'Sorry, geese,' he says.

With a heavy heart Ren decides that as seminar organiser, and as the youngest and fittest departmental member, he'd better be the one to chase after Tyson. Someone else will have to look after George.

It's dark outside the staff club, and there's no sign of any bearded old philosophers running around going berserk. Ren takes a guess at which way Tyson went, and runs. Ten minutes later, after he's covered a lot of territory but seen no sign of the crazy old bastard, he hears some screams and commotion coming from the direction of the student bar. He hesitates. This won't be good. Maybe he should just leave Tyson to his fate. He's probably already been trussed up by security. Except that the Uni bar doesn't have security guards, and the general campus security is good for nothing but discovering broken-into buildings six hours after they've been broken into. In the end, it's curiosity more than anything else that drives him to investigate. What kind of story to tell will it be if just ends in 'And then I went home to watch TV'?

Outside the bar he finds outraged students milling about. He can see some guys scouting around the area, searching.

'What's going on?' he asks a random group of students. There's something in the corner of his visual field that is disturbing him, but he doesn't want to look just now.

'A flasher,' says one of the students. 'That's what we heard.'

'An old flasher with a stiffy,' says another. 'Must be a Professor.'

'I didn't know Professors of that age could get stiffies,' says a third student.

'Jase told me he heard the guy had no trousers on,' says the first student, over the others.

Ren knows what the thing in the corner of his eye is without having to look at it now, but he briefly glances anyway. A pair of trousers lie discarded near a bush. Did Tyson take them off there, or did someone, discovering them somewhere else, drop them there?

The students are bursting to fill him in further.

'He was wanking while watching those ladies there, and they saw him, and then he ran away.' The student points. Ren groans inwardly. The two women are Millicent Bartonella and Lenora Helminth, who are directing the search parties, looking grimly satisfied.

Everyone is too excited and flustered and giddy to look properly, so they don't see what Ren now sees, which is Tyson sneaking back behind a nearby bush. The dark night means that visibility is poor, but Ren definitely gets a brief glimpse of nothing but white flesh and black hair below Tyson's belt line as he moves into position.

Ren is now faced with a moral dilemma as daunting as anything to be found in a moral philosophy class. Forget abstract intellectual exercises where you are forced to choose between diverting a runaway trolley to kill one person rather than the five it's heading for. Forget the issue of whether you should dynamite the pregnant woman. This is an urgent, real-life moral dilemma, with real consequences.

Should he shout, 'There he is, burn the witch,' and watch as the pack goes for Tyson? Or should he shut up, and let Tyson enjoy his few last moments of freedom twanging the wire before he's locked up for good? And maybe slink off home? Or go inside the bar for a quick beer while the crowd at the bar has thinned, as most of the customers have come outside for a look?

It's not really much of an ethical dilemma, though. Clearly Tyson needs to be apprehended for his own, and everybody else's, sake. Ren sidles away from the students and walks causally over to Tyson's bush, trying not to draw too much attention to himself. As he gets closer he can see Tyson's face peeking through the bush, looking at the students. Some slight rustling at groin level gives him an idea of what Tyson is up to, which puts him off going any closer.

'Tyson,' he says quietly.

Tyson either doesn't hear him, or ignores him.

'Professor Kipnis,' he says, a little more loudly. Tyson still doesn't respond to him.

'Is that the Dalkeith medallist Professor Tyson Kipnis, who has run departments, chaired prestigious committees, edited the best journals in the world, testified to the White House, and advised three US Presidents?'

Ren thought that was sure to work, but Tyson's gaze remains fixed on the females present, a group that includes Millicent and Lenora, which you'd think would give anyone an instant soft-on, but then Tyson has gone doolally.

'Is that the Randolph keyhole wanker?' Ren says a little bit louder still.

That gets Tyson's attention. And everybody else's – they all swivel around to look around at Ren. Lenora, faster than the rest at seeing what is going on, strides towards the bush. But quick as a flash, Tyson has grabbed something off the ground. A pre-prepared weapon. He comes around the side of the bush to screams and gasps from the crowd, not only because he is naked and erect below the waist, which isn't a good look for a man his age, and not only because his face is twisted grotesquely, but because he is waving something white around his head. As something brown flies out of it Ren realises that the white thing is Tyson's underpants.

Only his years of playing cricket save Ren – he instinctively sways his head backwards as the loose packet of sludge hurtles towards him like a thunderbolt from a vastly earlier, and more primal, cricketing era. He gets his face underneath the trajectory of the semi-solid tracer bullet just in time, courtesy of all the years he has spent evading bouncers in the nets. His cricket career never went anywhere, but he is now immensely grateful for those wasted hours spent after school when he and his friends would bounce balls of string-covered cork at each others' heads at tremendous pace.

Like any good batsmen Ren keeps his eye on the ball, or streak, as it passes by a centimetre or two above his nose, which enables him to get a good, if upside-down, view of it hitting Lenora smack in the chest as she rushes towards Tyson. He also notices some other small smidgeons of poo spraying around the area at the same time, some perhaps coming off the main body in flight, some perhaps coming from the generous smear on the underpants, but none of them hit him. He will later swear that he saw a small fleck hit Lenora on the cheek microseconds before the main motherload struck her. The central poo, as is all too evident, was not the firmest stool, which has made the resulting splat on Lenora's white blouse – and neck – all the more ruinous.

As a hit on an immediate enemy, from Tyson's point of view, it's an effective blow. The hunting party's leader has been stopped in her tracks, and is standing there, huge breaths gasping in and out, her arms pulled up away from her body, wrestler-style, far away from the damage, her day of fighting over and done with. And the others are too stunned to move.

In terms of Tyson's wider strategy, though, it wasn't perhaps the wisest move. But Tyson is now in a primeval mood, wanking, shitting, mis-perceiving, over-reacting, running and fighting like a gorilla... would never dream of doing. He looks more like an escapee from the opening scenes of 2001, and his scraggly beard hits just the right note.

Ren decides that his swaying back motion can be continued for another fraction of a second, just enough to cause him to topple over onto the ground on his back. That allows others to rush past him to do the dirty work – possibly very dirty work – of tackling Tyson. He sees Tyson's hairy white bum disappear into the distance as he runs off at a surprising pace, a once-canny fox gone senile, pursued by a baying crowd of drunken student hounds, hungry for his blood.

'Tally ho,' murmurs Ren. Tyson is going to be ripped to shreds.

He sees Millicent and a couple of other students pull out their mobile phones. 'Don't call the cops,' he shouts as he picks himself off the ground. 'Call an ambulance. He's mentally ill, because he's lost his meds.'

'He's a male patriarchal rapist,' says Millicent sternly. 'He physically assaulted Lenora in the most degrading way, just because she's a woman.'

Lenora is standing in the same position, still gasping, arms still held away from her body, apparently unable to move.

'He needs to be locked up,' says Millicent.

'He needs medical help, not a jail cell.'

'Why is it not a surprise that you're okay with sexual assault?'

'What? I'm not saying what he did was all right, it wasn't, I'm just saying that he's gone insane.'

'But if he's insane then we need the police to help catch him. Who knows what he might do?'

'Okay, but those guys who are after him should be able to get him. If they can't then we'll have to call the police. But first we need to call an ambulance.'

'But what's the point of calling an ambulance if we can't

catch him?' asks a student.

Although Tyson does need to go to hospital rather than jail, the main reason Ren doesn't want to call the cops is because he doesn't want this making the newspapers. But he doesn't want to say that in front of students. Millicent lifts up her phone again. Ren hears shouting.

'Wait,' says Ren. 'They've got him.'

'Have they?' asks Millicent.

'Well, it sounds like it. Listen.'

As well as shouting, a high-pitched wail can also be heard. Which everyone knows has to be the mad Professor. Ren is about to run off in the direction of the noise when the wail stops, and the hubbub dies down. He stays to keep an eye on Millicent and her phone. They all stand still, listening. A little later the mob arrives back. Tyson is walking placidly along with them.

'How did you get him to calm down?' asks Ren.

The guys in the mob look sheepish. Finally one says, 'Let's just say he had a little accident.'

After taking a moment to digest this news, Ren realises this is the moment to say something.

'In view of that development,' he tells the members of the mob, 'it might be prudent on your behalf not to run off to tell the newspapers about this. Not unless you want to forever be known, everywhere you go, as the guy who was ejaculated on by a mad old half-naked visiting Professor in a bar fight. That would stay on the internet until the end of time. Best to have this as a story you can tell at the pub, or at dinner-parties. It's up to you, though. You can choose public shame, and never having a girlfriend again, or you can choose to have an amazing drinking story to impress people with.'

Ren scans their faces. They look like solid engineers, or at least science students. No shifty-looking sociologist types, who might run to the papers. But then you wouldn't expect a sociologist to try to physically tackle Tyson in the first place. Although they might as part of a mob. Leftists like marching in the middle of mobs. But he can tell from their faces that none of them will be talking to *The Guardian*, or *The Daily Gravy* (the local rag), or even the student newspaper, *The Digger* (referred to by some students as 'The Hairtrigger').

Millicent comes over. 'I'm going to call the emergency services,' she says. 'I'm going to tell them exactly what's happened. If they decide to send police around as well then that's their decision.'

'You can do that Millicent, if you want. You can either do that and then have an interesting conversation with the VC tomorrow when he finds out what you've done, or you can let me handle it.'

Millicent fumes for a few seconds. 'All right, you sort out the mess for now. But I'll be talking to the VC tomorrow about the possibility of pressing charges against this vile quasi-rapist.'

'Okay, good idea Milly,' says Ren, who knows that Raven, despite his progressive credentials, is never going to let this story get out, or let the Uni be seen to be persecuting someone who is mentally ill. He also knows that Millicent hates being called Milly. 'Why don't you go and help Lenora get cleaned up.'

Millicent helps, from a safe distance, Lenora go into the bar to use the toilets. Lenora, still in shock, is walking at about half a mile an hour, like she's been bombed, and is covered in blood and human gore. The crowd outside the bar is big by this time; it magically parts to let Lenora through, like she's Jesus the Pooh.

By the time the ambulance arrives, Tyson, who has his trousers back on thanks to Ren – putting Tyson's trousers back on isn't a memory Ren is going to cherish – has been happily chatting to a bunch of students about logic. They are hanging on his every word. Not that any of them are much interested in logic, and none of them understand it, they're just enjoying being part of the general weirdness of the night. This story is going to get around campus, but generally students can be trusted to follow the old adage of what happens on campus, stays on campus. (Parents especially must be kept in the dark).

2000-01
Semester 2
Week 8
Wednesday

Ren, Compton and Walter are at the cafeteria.

'No, I've heard nothing more about Tyson other than that he was quickly transferred to a private hospital in London,' says Walter.

'Thank God for that,' says Ren. 'If he'd stayed at the local hospital then the story might have leaked out.'

'But I have heard that your TITE colleagues, Tilly...'

'Milly. Millicent.'

'Millicent. And the other one, who took the full force of the depth charge...'

'Lenora. Or as I now call her, Jesus the Pooh.'

'They've been demanding that action be taken against him, preferably criminal charges. But, of course, as Tyson was on the psych ward the University couldn't do that.'

'Not after all the high-profile campaigning the University's been doing on understanding mental health,' says Compton. 'Getting in actors like Roger Horse to lecture us about how awful our attitudes to screwed-up people are. Even evil political fixers are forgiven as long as they say they get depressed sometimes.'

'As long as they're on the left, of course,' says Ren.

'So putting Tyson in jail would be viewed as a return to Bedlam,' says Compton. 'Not going to fit with the latest narrative.'

'Sometimes the left hand doesn't know what the extreme-left hand is doing,' says Ren. 'How's George doing?

'Says he's fine,' says Walter.

'That's what he said last time,' says Ren.

George's collapse was supposedly about his oesophagus again, not his heart, but no-one except himself thinks he's in good shape.

'Don't tell me he's taking his classes this week?'

'The show must go on, he says.'

'George Bagnall as Freddie Mercury in his last days. Not a comparison I ever thought I'd make.'

'Well, he does have the body for it,' says Compton, to puzzled looks. 'As in thin and gaunt.'

'Has Robot had a go at you for not looking after Tyson properly?' asks Walter.

'He has,' says Ren, 'but I said that if it was so well-known that Tyson was mad then why was he invited to give us a talk? And why didn't Robot turn up himself to help keep an eye on him? I'll be very glad when this term is over. Just a bit over a week to go and then I'll have completed my teaching for this academic year. I'm only hanging on for Friday night next week.'

'Congratulations, by the way, on getting your paper into the *British Journal of Metaphysics*,' says Compton.

'Thanks,' says Ren. 'Just a minor piece, really, And I've a long way to go before I catch up to Robot. I was counting his list the other day. He has seventy-five publications, and probably some more that have been accepted recently.'

'If you do philosophy properly you're unlikely to ever catch up to Robot,' says Compton. 'He just writes the same papers over and over again, and still gets them published. He really only has five papers, yet somehow he has stretched that out to seventy-five publications.

'It's five good journals, ten okay ones, fifteen mediocre ones, twenty bad ones, and the rest are book chapters,' says Walter.

'Because so many of his papers are in his obscure area that no-one cares about, no-one's really sure how bad the journals they've never heard of actually are,' says Compton.

'And all the referees in that area are friends with each other,' says Walter. 'They all accept each other's work.'

'That's one way you can get ahead with publishing,' says Compton. 'Robot's the master at that. Find a niche area, make friends with everyone in it, then you all have to referee each other's papers because no-one else can, and you each give a yes to the other's work.'

'Even if you know it's the same rehashed paper your mate writes every time,' says Walter.

'The Continentalists, of course, are the real masters at this,' says Compton.'

'And Grant's book chapters are just commissions from his network, they're not even really refereed,' says Walter.

'One thing that keeps it in check is if those people fall out,' says Compton. 'Which, being academics, they often do. Then they end up as bitter rivals, desperately trying to keep the others' work from being published.'

'Don't editors have tactics to get around the mutual back-scratching?' asks Ren.

'Well, sometimes they get referees from outside the area, but then those referees will often make bad decisions because they don't know what they're doing,' says Compton.

'Some editors will just make executive decisions not to publish a piece that the referee has said yes to, either because they've looked at it themselves, or they'll come up with some other reason,' says Walter. 'But editors having that sort of discretion is being clamped down on, because it's thought to be too subjective. So some editors are now just declaring, not very loudly, that they aren't publishing in certain areas.'

'Not that they say it like that,' says Compton. 'If pressed, they'll say they're preferring pieces in their central areas. But that's not going down too well either. But they can do it because of the huge number of articles that get submitted to them, that gives them scope to reject articles that even two referees have said yes to.'

'One other thing journals do is they don't use a referee for a piece if that referee is from the author's own department or University,' says Walter. 'Even if the paper is submitted to the referee without a name or department, the referee might still know it's by their colleague. It makes sense to not let that happen, but that does nothing to stop the alliances that exist outside departments, which are usually even stronger than any departmental alliance. Members of the same department are just as likely to dislike each other than like each other.'

'But that has to be done,' says Ren, 'because with the RAE it's to a department's advantage, both financially and otherwise, to have the members getting work published, especially in better journals.'

'It does have to be done, yes' says Compton, 'but the non-departmental alliances have no such block. Not that you really can block them. We want academics to network and get to know other academics from outside their own departments. You can hardly demand that referees not know anyone.'

'It wouldn't be hard to recognise Tyson's submissions these days, would it?' says Ren. 'They're the ones written in pooh mixed with semen.'

'He'd be better off submitting those to the sort of journals that Verna and Adalia get published in,' says Compton.

'They'd be accepted there straight away,' says Ren, 'on the basis that the author is making a strong political statement with their materials, and because the content is incomprehensible gibberish.'

'And also he's a full-blown member of the latest celebrated minority,' says Compton, 'people with mental health issues.'

'You mean nuts?' says Ren.

'You can't say that any more,' says Walter.

'It's short for Noncomformists Under Tremendous Stress.'

2000-01
Semester 2
Week 9
Friday

A feeling of abandon begins, and spreads. Since morning began the celebratory sap has been climbing, and now it's the afternoon the amrita is starting to bubble up into the brains of the students, making them giddy with anticipation. It's one of the University's primal days: the last Friday of the last semester, and a sunny one at that. Lectures are finishing, the Easter hols are nigh, the academics' halos are slipping, and celebrations are in order. Of the chug-a-lug variety.

Quite a lot of students decamped days ago, but there are still more than enough to fill up the student bar and spill out onto the grass area in front of it. The air outside the bar is more alive than it ever has been, as the students drink and talk with more life, animation and passion than most of them do for ninety-nine per cent of their days. Why don't we behave like this every day, they're all thinking. This is the way we will live every moment from now on, they think, and continue thinking, until they wake up the next morning with a faceful of carpet and the feeling that they have been speared right through the head with a javelin that has sunk into the floor below them, pinning them there until the agony dissolves their mind into a puddle of stale, tepid beer.

Ren, Miles, Lily and Douglas are walking to the student bar. The latter three have just had their last TITE class of the year, so they're feeling like they're justified in behaving like students on this glorious last day of term.

'No more of Balderstone the bastard until October,' says Douglas.

'No more having to see Lenora, Malcom and Millicent

until October,' says Lily.

'Hang on,' says Ren. 'I thought I told you all not to carry on with TITE next year. You won't need to for probation purposes.'

'Well, we'll see,' says Lily. 'That hasn't been decided by the powers-that-be yet. And if we've done a year we might as well do the second year and get the professional qualification.'

'The TITE's about as professional as my arse,' says Ren.

'Isn't that an unfortunate comparison?' says Miles. 'Seeing as your arse has often worked in a professional capacity?'

'I've told you before, I never got paid for all that.'

They can hear the merry chatter of the students before they can see the bar.

'I can taste the first ale already,' says Miles.

'You mean you can smell it,' says Ren. 'Particularly nasty batch they have in at the moment, Badger's Backside I think it is.'

'Cougar's Cloaca is the latest one,' says Lily.

'Dingo's Dong, it's an Australian one,' says Douglas.

'Miles?' says Ren after a pause.

'Do I have to?'

'Nobody's forcing you.'

'It has to start with E,' says Lily. Because Lily has said this Miles is not going to back out. 'Elephant's Egress?' he says.

The only thing missing is the clinking of glasses, because today the bar is using disposable plastic cups.

'Drinking lager in plastic cups is just about bearable,' says Miles. 'But ale? Just not right. Ale drinkers, being more responsible generally, should be allowed glasses. They're called lager louts for a reason.'

'I agree Miles, but propose that said ale drinker must also be chaetiferous, which rules you out.'

'Chaewhaterous?'

'Bristly. Bearded.'

'You and your prejudice against beards.'

'On the contrary, I'm saying the bearded ale-drinkers are the more responsible members of the cervisial community, so I'm complimenting them by comparing them favourably against clean-shaven ruffians like you.'

'But beardies who drink lager are more likely to be violent,' says Lily.

'See? She's the prejudiced one.'

When the quartet walk back out of the bar with their drinks they spot some of Miles' psychologist colleagues sitting on the grass, including Lucius Birch, so they join them. The introductions are made. Ren notes that these psychologists aren't the nice ones that Miles has previously introduced him to; they seem to be Lucius's people. Ren suspects he's not going to warm to them. There are also some sociologists in the group who he recognises, including Harry Smales, a scowling, grey-haired man of about fifty who, despite the sun, wears a thick grey scarf wrapped around his neck. Lucius and Harry and some of the others have an aura of ageing, disaffected public schoolboys, still nursing their grudges.

'Are there more of you turning up?' Lucius says.

'No, why?' says Miles.

'I notice you and your philosopher friend have two pints each.'

'There's a large crowd at the bar, and not enough staff,' says Miles. 'So getting two pints now made sense, saves going back so often.'

'So that explains why you had vodka put into the beer as well?' says Lily.

'Today is not the day to drink catlap,' says Ren. 'Go hard or go home.'

Fifty minutes later and most people have been going hard. Only a couple have gone home. There have been two additions, one – Compton – very welcome, and one – Malcom Ascaris from Politics and TITE – very unwelcome. Then someone else turns up. Obviously Lucius's girlfriend, because she kisses him. She turns her face and... the warmth of the day is chilled a bit. The sun goes behind a metaphorical cloud. The birds stop twittering. It's Lenora Helminth. Somehow, this isn't a surprise. Next round then.

Twenty minutes later, in all the milling about, Ren finds, to his displeasure, that he and Compton are now sitting next to Lucius, Lenora, and Harry Smales. Ren notices that in Lucius's presence Lenora looks happy, or, at least, she looks like human sacrifice is preying less on her mind than usual. Harry, however, is clearly not a happy man.

'Labour should grab the initiative while it's shitting on the Conservatives,' Harry is saying.

'Yes,' says Lucius, 'raise taxes, and re-nationalise all those industries that the evil witch set free. Who's going to object to that, outside of a few capitalists?'

'I'm going to object to that,' says Ren.

'Er... is there a joke attached to this?' says Lucius.

'No joke,' says Ren. 'Unless you're wanting to destroy the country for a joke.'

'Oh dear. We have a Tory on our hands. Who brought him?' says Harry.

'Hang on,' says Lucius. 'You told me you were socialist.'

'I said no such thing, you just assumed. I simply asked you some questions to see what your views were. Only a fucking idiot would be a socialist after the century we've just had. And you don't even stop there, you're an actual Communist. You take Lenin and Trotsky to be great visionaries and leaders.'

'There's nothing wrong with Communism,' says one of the grad students, a lad whose face looks like he's tried so hard to clean it that it's been turned red by all the rubbing. 'It just hasn't been tried properly yet. Every time it's been implemented it's been taken over by tyrants and ruined. We haven't had real Communism yet.'

'Oh Jesus, that old one,' says Compton. 'How old are you?'

'It's true. Lenin and Trotsky were building a better

world, and then Stalin and the US wrecked it.'

'And black is white,' says Ren.

'Lenin and Trotsky were evil bastards,' says Compton. 'Some of the worst people who ever lived. Hitler, Stalin, Mao, and Pol Pot may have been worse, but Lenin was still a mass-murdering scumbag. As was little Leo.'

'Lenin basically invented modern totalitarianism,' says Ren.

'I think you'll find that was Stalin,' says the boy with the red-scrubbed face, who Ren decides to call Sunburn. 'Read a history book.'

At this point Lucius and Harry are looking a little embarrassed by their young comrade.

'These are the historical facts,' says Compton. 'I'll take you over to the library myself and introduce you to the Russian history section if you don't believe me. Mass murder and terror were part of the package right from the start. They were totally integral to it. Lenin knew that there wasn't a hope in hell of the Bolsheviks staying in power unless they ruthlessly suppressed all their enemies. He even deliberately started a huge civil war because he thought it was the only chance he had of succeeding. He murdered and terrorised enormous numbers of people. Aided by Trotsky, Kamenev, Zinoviev, all of them. It didn't go bad because it drifted from its course. It was bad right from the start. It's bad in its essence. The badness is built-in, at the core. As it has to be. The only way you can maintain a one-party state where everyone's private property and rights are taken away is by murdering anyone who dissents, or putting them into a Siberian gulag, and ruthlessly maintaining a rule of terror. And that's what Lenin did.'

'Lenin didn't kill anywhere near as many people as Stalin,' says Sunburn.

'That's like saying you're not that bad a serial killer because you didn't kill as many people as John Wayne Gacy. Stalin just applied the same techniques that Lenin had, only on an even larger scale.

'And also against his fellow Communists,' says Ren. 'Lenin needed them on-side, so he didn't murder any Party members. And he considered them his people. But by the time Stalin had an iron grip that no longer applied, so he tortured and slaughtered Party members as well. In their thousands.'

'Anyone see that new series on TV last night?' says Miles desperately. 'What's it called... the one with the guy from that other show from last month...?'

'You can bad-mouth Stalin, that's fair enough,' says Harry, ignoring Miles. Ren estimates that Harry was about the same age as Malcom McDowell's character in *If...* when it came out. Harry probably still has the poster up in his room. 'He went a bit too far. But Lenin had to do what he did. If he didn't, the monarchists would have restored Nicholas as Tsar, and things would have been back to the bad old days.'

'The Tsar wasn't ever coming back,' says Compton. 'The February revolution was leading towards democracy, before Lenin launched his coup d'etat in October.'

'And even if the Tsar had come back,' says Ren, 'which he wasn't, but even if he had, it would have been better than having the Bolsheviks in charge. The Tsar's regime was mild compared to Lenin's. And he would have had had so much less power if he'd come back.'

'Those were different times,' says Lucius, with a face like thunder. 'The Imperial War was happening, killing millions, and destroying Russia. There were a lot of hard-line rebel groups of different political stripes all jostling for power. If a new government didn't assert its authority then the result would have been anarchy. And Russia's always been a violent country. Strongman tactics were the norm. If Lenin hadn't been tough then the Whites would have come back and killed all of the Reds. A few hundred thousand dead in a civil war was a good result compared to how things could have gone.'

'Okay, take the way the Bolsheviks treated the Church,'

says Compton, oblivious to, or maybe just ignoring, the fury that Lucius and Harry are directing at him. 'The Orthodox Church wasn't presenting much in the way of opposition to the Bolsheviks. But they might do. And the Bolsheviks wanted to destroy religion anyway. So they smashed the Church. The Orthodox Church. And the Catholics. And the Jews. Put thousands of bishops and priests and nuns on trial on trumped-up charges, and then had them tortured and killed, on Lenin's orders. They were the original show trials. Stalin just copied Lenin later on when he had his own show trials.'

'The Church burned heretics,' says Lenora. 'So it placed itself into the middle of the struggle for freedom. It should have been helping the Bolsheviks, not opposing them.'

'Yes, the Church was reaping what it sowed,' says Harry, who is giving Compton the death stare. 'Look at how many people it's tortured and killed. Lenin may have been rough, but the Church had to be taken down when the chance presented itself.'

'Glad you're not denying it,' says Compton, looking pointedly at Sunburn, who has decided to keep quiet for now. 'It had been hundreds of years since the Russian Orthodox Church had burned any heretics. And the Church was offering little resistance to the Bolsheviks. What Lenin really couldn't stand was the idea that there might be an area of mental life that he didn't control. Something you modern Leninists also hate. As Ren said, Lenin really set the template for modern totalitarianism. Hitler, Mussolini, Mao, Pol Pot, Ho Chi Minh, Tito, Hoxha, Ceausescu, they were all just copying his methods. As you lot would, given half the chance.'

'Fuck you, you Tory cunt,' says Harry.

'Not exactly a denial,' says Ren.

'You wouldn't be an academic if I was in charge. You'd be clerking in the shittiest office in the land.'

'That's your euphemism for you'd have me killed, I presume. You just don't want to say it in front of the ladies.'

Mind you, thinks Ren, the way some of the females, like Lenora, are glaring at Compton he's not sure they aren't thinking the same thing. He wonders what Lenora would be saying if she was recklessly drunk like the others.

Suddenly all the psychologists and sociologists, except for Miles, stand up, as though a signal has been pre-arranged. Then they stalk off to another part of the grassed area.

'Brave Sir Robin ran away, he ran away,' sings Ren at them as they leave. Then he turns to shouting at them in a Russian accent. 'Comrades, never forget role of false consciousness in counter-hegemony. Way to crush bourgeoisie is grind between millstones of taxation and inflation.'

'We're enemies of the people now,' says Compton.

'Enemies of the proletariat,' says Ren. 'Didn't you see the calluses on their hands? Sons of the toil, that lot.'

'Whenever they were talking I got shivers up my spine,' says Lily. 'Not good shivers. The sort of shivers I expect you get when you hear a knocking on the door at 4am.'

'4am? Won't that be Jason?' says Ren.

'At 4am Jason's knocking on my door,' says Miles. 'I have to triple-lock my place to keep him out.'

'Is it wise to be making enemies with people in other Humanities departments?' asks Douglas.

'Don't care,' says Ren. 'I'll be gone from academia within a few years.'

'Doing what, exactly?' says Douglas.

'Don't know exactly, but something more exciting than teaching nominalism to uninterested kids destined to work in call centres, and having Communists as colleagues. Besides, Sociology and Psychology aren't in Humanities at this University.'

'Miles,' says Compton. 'I can't say I'm too impressed with what I've seen so far of your department.'

'Well, says Miles, 'some of them are grad students, not lecturers. Plus half of them were from Sociology, not

Psychology. But look, my department's not all like that. Those are just the extreme lefties.'

'Meaning the rest are just your standard lefties?'

'Hmm, well, there are other extreme lefties, I admit, and the rest are standard lefties, yes. Although we do have one guy who is more of a centrist.'

'Who's that?' says Ren.

'Ray Hawser.'

'Isn't he about to retire?'

'Well, yes. But mostly the rest of our department are concerned with psychology, not politics.'

'But when I last saw your not-so-political colleagues they were all raving on about arresting George Bush,' says Ren.

'But you have to admit they talk a lot of psychology.'

'Yes, they do, I suppose that's true. They talk shop an awful lot. Or at least they talk about each other, and people in their field. But the other half the time it's politics. Psychology and left-wing politics, that's all you get from most of them.'

'Your department's not much better, though, is it?' says Miles. 'Whenever I've been around them they're talking shop, all the time, interspersed with left-wing politics.'

'The sad fact is,' says Compton, 'that while most academics might be intelligent and knowledgeable about their own fields, although even that's not a given, they have very crude and simplistic political beliefs. They generally know little about politics. Or economics. Subtleties and complexities elude them in these fields. But they assume that because they're intellectuals their half-baked, fresher-level opinions about politics must be insightful and sagacious, when in reality your average car mechanic has much more realistic and sophisticated views.'

'I think part of the problem is that they hardly ever get exposed to different opinions,' says Ren. 'Look at the way Lucius's lot ran away when tackled.'

'You were pretty fucking aggressive towards them,' says Miles.

'Just giving back what they like to give out,' says Compton. 'They can dish it out, but they can't take it.'

'They don't like it up 'em,' says Ren in his best Dad's Army voice.

'They're not used to being disagreed with in such a forthright manner,' says Lily. 'Academics, at least the ones outside Economics, do live in a political bubble.'

'That's only going to get worse,' says Compton. 'The few conservative or non-left-wing academics there used to be are all retiring or already gone.'

Ren stand up and shouts at Lucius's mob in a Russian accent again: 'Comrades, need remind you that base and superstructure in dialectical relationship, da?'

'I don't think they can hear you, Comrade Ren,' says Douglas.

'I'll shout louder then,' says Ren, 'while you go and get your round. Get me another lager with vodka in it.'

'That's two drinks, Ruskie. I'll get you a lager.'

Ren turns and shouts: 'Objective reason for revolution lies in development and intensification of conflict between productive forces and relations of production.'

Ren continues to shout Communist slogans at Lucius's lot as they keep drinking.

'I'm not sure they can hear me,' he says.

'I think they can,' says Lily.

'Here Miles, hold my drink,' Ren says.

He walks over to them. 'Comrades,' he shouts, 'objective conditions for socialism on campus have been met by exploitation of oppressed Sociology scarf-wearers. This is tangible source of oppression. Surplus value has been extracted from scarf to greatest possible extent. Nyet?'

He turns to walk back. He hears a shout of 'Harry', and seconds later it feels like a lion has jumped on his back. Or maybe a sloth. Someone is grabbing him around the neck, and is trying to wrestle him to the ground.

'Look at the violence inherit in the system,' Ren shouts. He can't see who it is, but he can see that Harry is missing from Lucius's group, so it must be him. Harry is stronger than Ren thought he would be, perhaps because he is filled with righteous rage at the heretic, but Harry has spent his last few decades sitting down and talking about Communism and socialism while drinking. The only exercise he has got in years is standing on picket lines, and selling the *Socialist Worker*. Ren, on the other hand, is a sporty type, and as a graduate student he took advantage of the flexible hours and his free college gym to regularly work out, so he's currently strong, much stronger than Harry. (He is very drunk, but so is Harry, so they both cancel out on that score.)

'Little cunthead,' whispers Harry viciously in his ear.

'Bourgeoisie incites workers of one nation against another in endeavour to keep them disunited,' Ren says loudly in his Russian accent, making sure his audience can hear him. Harry's has been trying to get his arm around Ren's neck to strangle him, but Ren is using his chin to prevent that, so he's still able to talk.

'Stop it Harry, you silly cunt,' he hears Miles saying. But nobody moves to do anything. He can see Lucius sitting watching with academic interest, stroking his chin, as though he's at the cinema watching two dinosaurs wrestling on the screen and thinking of how he can draw out some psychological or sociological significance for a journal article. If it was two students wrestling then the other students would have broken them up by now, but perhaps because it's two lecturers none of the students dare come near them. Or perhaps they just want to see what happens. Ren can hear excited chatter from the students.

'You're fucked, Thatcher boy. We're going to fucking screw you over right and proper,' says Harry, a bit too loudly for his own good. But Ren can hear the worry develop in Harry's voice as Ren starts to overpower him.

'In social order dominated by capitalist production even non-capitalist producer is gripped by capitalist conceptions,' Ren intones. This seems to go down well with the audience, some of whom are chuckling.

Ren has managed to get a hold of Harry's arms, and has forced him to the ground. He sits on top of Harry, holding his arms down with his hands, and feels the intensity of the fight in Harry sag.

'Revolutionary dictatorship of proletariat lies between capitalism and communism. More proletariat presses bourgeoisie, more furiously bourgeoisie will resist.'

Ren pins Harry's arms to the ground with his knees in order to free up his own arms. Then he starts doing 'the typewriter' with his fingers on Harry's chest. This is an old schoolboy trick where you stab both your fingers into the other person's chest in imitation of a typewriter. If you can do it hard enough it's a bit painful, ticklish, and very annoying.

'Technical apparatus of production and distribution,' says Ren as he types, as though he is typing out a book, 'functions as system which determines product of apparatus as well as operations of servicing and extending it.' Students are laughing at this, so he keeps going.

'Get the fuck off me,' snarls Harry, who wriggles, but all the fight has gone out of him.

'Communism is Soviet government plus electrification of whole country, based on static electricity derived from wearing scarf in summer.'

Lily comes and bends over them. 'It might be a good idea,' she whispers to them, 'for you both to stop, and for the sake of appearances to get up, shake hands, and pretend if was all in good fun.'

'Who says Lenin have gulags? Lenin open doors of all corrective labour camps!' Ren shouts, as he gets off Harry, who sulkily gets to his feet.

'You're a dead man,' Harry whispers. Ren grabs Harry's arm and lifts it up in triumph.

'Freedom to scarf wearers, who power Russia to start international revolution!'

Some in the crowd cheer. Harry shakes his arm free and

stalks off back to his group, but is bewildered to find that Lucius and Lenora have disappeared. But some of the sociology grad students clap him on the back.

Ren is surrounded by students who shake his hand. He tries, not very successfully, to do a Cossack dance. A student buys him a triple vodka. He looks around for Lily, but she's gone.

2000-01
Semester 2
Week 9
Saturday

An uneasy feeling gradually comes over Ren as manic dreams flit through his head. He feels like he is unable to lie down. Try as he might, he cannot make his body stretch out. He realises that he is running, or jogging, in a stooped-over fashion, and has been for hours. He can't stop. He can't stop because he can't unbend his body at the thorax and make himself stop. He is permanently stooped from being bent over while running. He'd give anything to be able to straighten out properly. Or even bend all the way so he falls over, but he can't bend any further either. He tries to will himself to fall to the ground, but it just makes the stoop more rigid. He's going to be stooped for years, as a result. Perhaps even forever. He starts to cry at the thought of this. It's so awful. His body has been disfigured, just when he's in his prime.

Hours later, he wakes. There's something not right with the way he's lying down. Maybe he really can't bend any more. Maybe he has got a permanent stoop. His legs feel wrong, like they've changed weight. They hurt too. Everything hurts, especially his head. Something very heavy must have fallen onto his head, and crushed the back of it.

He opens his eyes. A blazing light torments them, but he can just make out a word: 'Options'. Indeed. What are his options? He can stay still and remain in pain. He can try to move, and risk disaster. He can try to die now, to escape this personal torture camp, but in the absence of anything like a cyanide tooth that's a tall order. 'Options': it's not much of a message.

Then he makes out some more words: 'Robert Sheckley'. Oh. It's a book spine. He opens his eyes more fully. He's looking at the bottom shelf of the bookcase on the landing halfway up his stairs, before the stairs turn right. He's lying on the stairs, his upper body on the mid-stairs landing, his lower body on the steps below. It's morning. He's been asleep halfway up the stairs all night. How did he even get home? Gradually he drags himself up the rest of the stairs, trying to ignore the throbbing in his head, and the cold stiffness in his body – he suspects he hasn't moved a muscle all night – and into bed.

Then he wakes again, to find the future is upon him. Three hours later in the future, to be precise (or as precise as we need to be.) He feels terrible, but at least he's no longer in mind-rending agony. Eventually he drags himself downstairs and takes some codeine and paracetamol tablets. It's such a shit, he thinks, how great days, days that are so great that you celebrate them, end up being followed by the worst days of your life. Like the day he finished his final undergraduate exams. The day after that was so bad that he would have gladly thrown himself into a pit of spikes just to end his suffering. He would have gladly bashed his own brains in with a hammer had there been one lying nearby. Except that he wasn't capable of moving at all that day until 6pm, even to get up find some painkillers. In what way does the Universe deem that a suitable reward for someone who worked so hard to do his exams? Not that he actually did much work himself. But even if he had, the result would have been the same: a blinding, killer headache. A scant reward for effort.

He thinks of those poor bastards who get vomiting hangovers, something he never does. Why should a student who's been studying hard all year and going easy on the booze until after exams be rewarded by the Gods with a morning bed covered in foul-smelling brash? And then have to run to the toilet all day for technicolour yawns, which makes their headaches even worse? If the Gods do exist, they must be those Greek buggers.

If he could only catch that bastard who's always fucking him over. Ren the Celebrator, he's the bastard. Boozy Ren the Celebrator, always celebrating something or other with alcohol. Oh, I got another paper accepted, let's go to the bar and get hammered. Oh, I just bumped into an old friend, we must celebrate with firewater. Oh, it's Friday, such an unusual occurrence cannot be allowed to pass without an alcohol-based celebration. Give the guy an inch and next thing you know he's destroying my head and liver. If I could only catch him... but I can't. He's never there to be caught. I'm never around when he acts up. I leave messages telling him not to, but he ignores them. It's like trying to see the back of your head in the mirror, as Tanja would say. It can be done, but only with an elaborate system. And Ren the Celebrator is good at evading systems. Especially when he's with that other bastard, Miles the Other Fucking Celebrator. My friend Miles the Done-In also hates Ren the Celebrator and Miles the Other Fucking Celebrator, but he's also powerless against them. Ebriection is the last thing on their minds when they start knocking them back. (Well, in a way it is on their minds when they shout, 'Let's get fucked up.' But it's Miles the Done-In and I who get fucked up, not them.)

Then he thinks about what happened last night, and the PPP descends upon him. The dreaded PPP, scourge of the over-imbiber. The PPP is the 'post-piss paranoia', a term from his undergraduate days. He buries his face in his hands. God, the embarrassment. Is he going to be sacked? Raked over the coals?

It's that asshole Ren the Celebrator again, fucking him up in public.

No. Stop it. He can't go that way, evading responsibility for his own actions, even his own drunk actions, like a leftist who says, 'Social forces made me do it.' Or a drug addict who says, 'I found myself taking drugs again. They were too strong for me to resist.' Or one of Theodore Dalrymple's shifty criminal patients: 'I watched as the knife went in.' It was him, all along, all him. He's Ren the Celebrator. A stronger dose of paranoia sweeps like a wave over him. He can't show his face in public ever again. He can't even show his face in his own kitchen. He goes back to bed and hides under the sheets.

After another nap another future arrives and he feels a bit better again. The codeine has now kicked in. He feels a bit happier when he reflects on the details of what happened last night. He did little wrong. Harry jumped on him. Attacked him. That's assault. Not that has any interest in prosecuting Harry for a bit of argy-bargy. As for himself, all he did was engage in mild self-defence, while trying to make light of it all. Yes, he did sort of provoke Harry, but a bit of light-hearted parody doesn't excuse being jumped on and strangled. He's in the clear, surely? Anyway, is there likely to be any complaint made? He isn't making one. Harry won't be making one. None of the academics there will be either. The students are unlikely to, it was good entertainment for them. Rumours will spread, sure, but even if he gets hauled in he has witnesses to say he was jumped, and he did nothing wrong. So he's in the clear, right?

But then what happened later on in the evening? He remembers more frenzied drinking in the bar for a while, as people bought him vodka, but at that point the grainy Super 8 runs out. He's tried to tell Ren the Celebrator before not to get plastered in the student bar, where students can see him, to move on somewhere else, but Ren the Celebrator doesn't always listen. Or maybe they did move on somewhere else. He just can't remember. He tries to clear his mind and relax, to let his memory improve its retrieval tasks, but there's an irreparable fault with the access to his later memories. Or perhaps the relevant memory slots got wiped overnight. Or perhaps they were never laid down in the first place.

He calls Miles to get his view on the public perception of the wrestle with Harry, and to see if he remembers the later events. And to see if he knows how Ren got home. But there's no answer. He thinks about calling Lily, but remembers that she's seeing Jason today. And she disappeared anyway. Depression and paranoia sweep down on him again like an unwanted afternoon shower when you're out walking on the dales. He's acted like a buffoon in front of Lily. Even if she and Jason ever split up, which seems a remote prospect, he's surely put himself out of contention with his tomfoolery. Ren the Celebrator strikes again. Bastard.

2001-02
Semester 1

2001-02
Semester 1
Week 5
Thursday

'Come in,' says Ren.

A young woman enters. Ren recognises her as the student from his Metaphysics class he calls El Whino. She's the one with the twisted face who always looks moody, and who's always asking petulant questions in a querulous tone of voice. The one who's angry that she can't understand what's going on. He feels an ancient weariness in his bones, like he's walked a thousand miles, a thousand years, on a quest only to realise that he's going in the wrong direction. The wrong fucking direction all along. His feet have been worn to the bone, he has canulus dipthermia – 'slowrot' – throughout his body, the forces of darkness are going to win, and his life, which started off so promisingly, is being exposed as a cruel joke. Just take the damn magic ring-amulet-stone-necklace-KISS badge and get it over with. Shove it up my arse and zap me to death with it.

'Angela isn't it?'

'Yes.'

'What's your last name?'

'De'ath.

'And your middle name?'

'Ophelia. Ofy for short'

'So you're Angela Ofy De'ath?' The Angel of Death. Of course. She's come to deliver her judgement on me. She can't understand mereological essentialism, so I must die. Except that he only imagined the second part of that conversation.

'What's your last name?' he asks for real.

217

'Saunders,' she says.

'So what can I do for you this morning, Angela?' says Ren half-heartedly, even though he knows that she's come to complain. Most probably about the mark for her Metaphysics essay which she will have recently got back.

'I wanted to talk to you about my Metaphysics essay,' she says in a voice that sounds like it's supposed to be laden with menace. One of Lord Nasty's crew, I am. His right-hand man. Right-hand woman. Right-hand something.

'Sure, let's have a look at it,' says Ren. He's determined not to say anything about her mark. 'Any particular section you wanted to discuss?'

'It was the mark it got that I really wanted to discuss,' she says, like she's running the University herself, and is going through the proper procedures before she can give Ren his marching papers.

'Oh, let's have a look then. Fifty-eight. Well, that's not too bad. Almost a 2:1.'

'Except that I usually get 2:1s in my other essays. So why am I not getting a 2:1 in your class?'

'How often do you get a 2:1 in your other essays?'

'Pretty often.'

'That's not very precise. What percentage is 2:1s and what percentage is 2:2s?'

'Well,' she says, fuming at this line of questioning, 'it's about sixty per cent 2:1s.'

If we adjust for her exaggerating, he thinks, that will be more like forty to fifty per cent 2:1s. Maybe even thirty per cent.

'And when you get a 2:1, what sort of mark is it? Are we talking sixties and sixty-twos, or sixty-eights?'

After a few seconds, she replies, 'Sixties and sixty-twos.'

'So a fifty-eight is in your general mark area. Hardly unusual then.'

'But this is as good as any of those essays. So why didn't it get a sixty or a sixty-two?'

'Well, let's have a look through it.'

Ren takes her through the essay section-by-section, explaining why she didn't quite get over the 2:1 line, which is sixty. Normally when he goes through an essay with a student (either one who is complaining about their mark, or with a student who just wants to know how to do a better job next time), the student quickly starts to appreciate that it's not up to scratch. Often Ren doesn't even need to comment much to achieve this realisation. He just reads out the sentences the student have written, and the student will visibly cringe at how poor they are. But Angela doesn't react like that. She talks as though she's done an excellent job.

'But that's an accurate description of endurantism,' she says at one point.

'It's one short sentence. And all you've done is say that on endurantism, objects endure through time. That's not going to help anyone who doesn't know what endure means here.'

'But you know what it means.'

'Of course I do, I'm the lecturer. But with that excuse no-one would have to explain anything in detail, they could just fill their essays with the names of theories and say that the lecturer knows what these mean. But you have to show that you know what they mean. You have to explain in some more detail what a view involves, so that you convince the reader, the marker, that you understand it. You should imagine that you're writing for someone who knows some basic philosophy, like a fellow Philosophy student, but who doesn't know this area. You need an explanation of a theory that will enable them to get a grasp of it.'

'You're saying I can't explain anything? That's just insulting me. You're supposed to be helping me, not insulting me.'

'I'm not saying anything so general. I'm just talking about a few specific examples which are a bit below what they could be, given your talent.'

A bit of flattery might help, he thinks. At least it will help him to suppress the suicidal urge to tell her to get the fuck out of his office and quit wasting his time with her thicky thickness. Unfortunately, as a modern lecturer, rather than a pre-eighties lecturer, he has to stroke this neurotic student's ego, rather than let her digest, by herself, the news that her essay marks bring her, which is that's she's an average student. Or perhaps below average. Her marks might be nothing to be proud of, but they're nothing to be that ashamed of either.

The British degree system, with its crude classification of degrees into 1st, 2:1, 2:2 and 3rd, is supposedly liked by employers because it's straight-forward and easy to understand, but it means that the students who are near a borderline freak out about finishing on the right side of that border. A 2:1 in their mind means an easy life of cushy, well-paid jobs, while a 2:2 means they'll be assigned to the ship's hold, to shovel coal into roaring hot furnaces until they die a horrible early death. Hence, the tiny difference between getting a fifty-eight and a sixty is to them the difference between being asked to come in and put their feet up on the desk, old boy, and would you like a brandy and a cigar, compared to having hot needles plunged into their eyes while their intestines are ripped out via their bowels by wolverines with specially sharpened teeth.

'Look at this description of perdurantism, for instance. "Perdurantism is the notion that objects aren't all there, when they exist, they have parts but these parts are time not space parts." That's a bit jumbled, and the marker can't tell from it how well you really understand perdurantism.' (Looking back at the essay Ren considers that a fifty-eight is pretty generous, really, for this tripe.)

'If I don't understand it properly that's your fault. You didn't explain it properly.'

'Well, I spent quite a lot of time explaining this, as clearly as I could. Most of the other students didn't have any trouble with it.'

'So it's just me, is it? You're saying I'm dumb, and everyone else in the class isn't? My friend Julie found this bit hard too.'

'I'm not even saying that you don't understand it. I think perhaps you do, but you needed to spend some more time working on this section to make your understanding clearer to the reader.'

'You need to go slower in class. You cover things too quickly.'

'When I do that too many students complain that it's too slow, and too easy. I need to pitch it at a suitable level for University students.'

'So you're saying I'm not University level!'

'No, you're doing fine, just a bit more work and you'll be doing really well.'

'I put so much work into these essays already.'

'Really?'

That slipped out. Mistake. Ren thought she couldn't look any more offended, but he was wrong. 'You're insulting me again,' she says, sounding like she's about to cry. 'I come here for help and you just insult me. Now you're saying my essays look like they've had no work put into them.'

'No, no, I wasn't saying that,' says Ren, although that's exactly what they read like.

Ren doesn't mind spending time with students who are struggling if they're genuinely interested in learning. Or even if they just want to get a better mark, and are prepared to listen. But someone who just wants to blame their lecturer for everything, and is pretending their own inadequacies don't exist, doesn't belong at University. She'll be one of those students who thought she had to go to University because that's what everyone does now, or that's what her parents told her to do, and she's chosen Philosophy because there's little else she can do. She should, of course, have chosen Sociology, where her lack of intellectual ability and her feelings of inadequacy and rage at everything around her would fit in nicely. But Philosophy is stuck with her now.

After another five minutes of hurt feelings being piled on

top of outraged feelings, Ren tries to placate her once again, and once again he makes everything worse.

'Look,' he says, 'Philosophy isn't for everyone. In fact most people don't have the ability to look at things in the way required in Philosophy.'

'Now you're saying I'm no good at Philosophy?' she says with a rising note of hysteria in her voice, which is now quite loud. 'You're supposed to teach me how to do Philosophy, and all you do is tell me that I'm rubbish at it?'

Ren realises that he has two options at this point. He can continue on with this, as she deliberately winds herself up at everything he says, which will culminate in her running out of his office and straight to Robot's office while screaming about Ren, or he can strangle her here and now, and throw her body out the window. That will cause him trouble, sure, but both options will cause him trouble. The question is, which will cause the least trouble? What he really needs is a fake fire alarm button under his desk. He can secretly press it, and everyone has to run outside, and then he's rid of her, for the time being at least.

A knocking is heard at the door. Saved! He's saved! A mercy mission has arrived. It's Adalia Greenflower. Normally he'd do everything but bar the door to keep her out of his office, but today the welcome mat is out for her. On some strange literary-metaphysical level of Platonic reality he has opened a secret cupboard and got out a red carpet, which he unrolls for her.

'Adalia, come in,' he says with genuine sincerity.

'Oh,' she says. 'You have a student. I can come back later.'

'No, no, we're just finishing up, come in.'

'It's not important. Just some admin.'

'If it's admin we need to sort it. And I have some urgent admin I need to talk to you about. Okay Angela, I'm sure your next essay will go even better now that we've had a look through this one.'

'But I want you to re-mark my essay. I'm not happy with

the mark. I demand it be re-marked. By someone else if you don't change the mark.'

'I'm afraid we don't do that, as Adalia here can confirm.'

'Er, yes, that's right,' says Adalia, looking about her as though she's weighing up making a sudden run for it.

'Essays are not re-marked on request, otherwise we'd never get anything else done, and it wouldn't be fair to the students who don't ge re-marked. We only revisit marks if there's been some procedural irregularity, which isn't the case here.'

'Well, I'm still going to go to Professor Kapchar to complain about this.'

'You can try, but he'll tell you the same thing. It's general University policy. Just because you want a higher mark is not a reason for us to give you one. You need to learn from this one and just get that little bit extra next time.'

Angela storms off in a huff, worse than the one she came in on. Ren figures he has about twenty minutes before he's sacked, and he's not keen on spending that twenty minutes with Adalia, so he gets rid of her after ten minutes. An hour later and he's stopped worrying. These days there's no end of screwed-up, flaky students who have no real interest in their chosen field of study complaining about their marks. Robot should give her short shrift.

On the other hand, Robot has no backbone, except when kicking down, and he'd love the chance to get Ren in the shit. So maybe he should worry. And maybe he should worry about where this supposed dream life as an academic is heading. Is this going to be the rest of his life? To be kicked around every term by students and his Head of Department? He can see that power is already draining away from ordinary academics towards – or back towards – the Heads and the Deans and the Pro Vice-Chancellors, and towards the bureaucrats, who are being hired in ever greater numbers. And towards the students. Not so much to the good students. Mostly to the bad ones.

And the admin jobs are going to get even worse in the

coming years. Being in charge of the weekly departmental seminars is a stroll in the park on a sunny day compared to being in charge of assessment, or admissions, or any of the other admin jobs. (The only other easy admin job is being library rep, but it's looking like no-one is going to be allowed to do just that in future.)

He knows the job is still better than most jobs. But it's not the dream job that grad students convince themselves it's going to be as they slave away at their doctorates. We all fooled ourselves. And if he keeps slaving away at his papers and gets ahead then his reward will be a little bit more money. Or none at all – if you get promoted from Senior Lecturer to Reader, which requires a great deal of successful research to have been carried out, then your salary increase is exactly zero pounds and zero pence per year. The job title itself is reward enough, apparently. Although they won't even let you put a sign saying 'Reader' on your door here. Only Professors are allowed a sign with their rank displayed on their door. And you don't even get your alloted place in the hierarchy on the departmental web pages any more – they've recently been made politically correct, so that the names now appear in alphabetical order, rather than being grouped into 'Professors,' 'Readers', 'Senior Lecturers', and so on, as they used to be.

But promotion will mean that he'll be lumbered with more of the responsibility for the running of the department, and he'll have to make more of the decisions that will make people hate him. The more he advances the more hours he will have to waste sitting on mind-crushing Faculty and University-level committees, and people say that there are more and more pointless committees being created every year. And all the while he'll get one – or even zero, or at best, two – papers on unfeasibly obscure topics published every year, which only three people will ever read.

Even within the department no-one reads anyone else's papers. Everyone gives everyone else their draft papers, because that's what people in proper Philosophy departments do. In those departments they all read each others' papers and then write helpful, insightful, even brilliant, comments for the author. But in this department everyone has a huge pile of papers from everyone else, which they never read past the first couple of pages. Especially if it's a paper from Pastygill. Or, obviously, Bill, because he just writes bilge about Robert Langston. Or Panos, because his stuff reads even worse than he speaks. Or if it's... Ren realises he could on for a while here.

Occasionally people ask each other, 'Oh, have you read my such-and-such paper yet? Because I was going to send it off to *American Philosophical Letters* soon, and wondered if you had any thoughts on it?' And the other person will say, 'Oh, I've been meaning to read that, but I haven't had time to get around to it, got such a big to-read pile, and with all the essay marking and whatnot...'

There's only one thing to do. He gets in his car, drives to KFC and buys a big bucket of chicken, and then goes to work at home where he can have the Test match he recorded on his VCR last night playing in the background. The only way he can get any work done is to do it at home. He may have his own office at work, but it has a door, and on that door people – students, admin staff, other lecturers – knock all day. Here he can concentrate on Philosophy, interrupted only by the occasional wicket.

2001-02
Semester 1
Week 5
Sunday

It's Sunday evening, halfway through the first semester of Ren's second year at Grayvington, and Ren has asked Miles to join him at the pub.

'Where's Lucy?' Miles asks when he arrives.

'We broke up this afternoon,' says Ren.

'That's too bad. She was nice. Can I fuck her now?'

'No.'

'You forbid it. I understand.'

'No, she just wouldn't have you, that's all. I've spoiled her for other men.'

'Meaning you've somehow rendered her unattractive to other men, or that other men cannot satisfy her after you?'

'The latter.'

'Strange. Most girls don't like halfwits who wear ladies' panties.'

'You don't need to tell me. Being honest on lonely hearts ads isn't a good idea.'

'So you broke up with her, then?'

'No, she broke up with me.'

'Has she spoiled you for other librarians now?'

'No, I'm always up for a spot of rumpy behind the stacks with a pair of glasses. But librarians are sensitive creatures. Too sensitive for brutes like me.'

'Was it your politics? Your refusal to be left-wing in front her friends?'

'Actually she didn't mind that. What she couldn't take in the end was my endless questioning of everything she said.'

'I could see that would be a problem with you.'

'That's what philosophers do, though.

'They're annoying arseholes?'

'It's what academics in general do, so don't think you're exempt. But yes, particularly philosophers. Always questioning everything.'

'But there are times and places for that. Perhaps not on a romantic date. Perhaps not in the bedroom.'

'I'm not like that in the bedroom. It's the day to day stuff she doesn't like. She doesn't understand that for a philosopher, analysing, questioning, even attacking what has been said, is normal. It doesn't mean you have a low opinion of what was said. In a way it's a sign of respect that you engage with the person and what they're claiming. That's what we teach first-years right from the start. If a philosophy lecturer, or a fellow philosophy student, critically analyses what you've said, that isn't an insult.'

'Or it isn't necessarily an insult.'

'Okay, yes. It takes students a while to cope with it, but they do, and they're better off for it. You need to be able to cope with criticism in life. You'll get worse thrown at you in real life. It's good to be able to have the resources to deal with that, and hold your own, without breaking down in a pile of tears because someone criticised what you said. Of course the progressives will eventually kill it, but for now it's a good thing for students to be exposed to criticism.'

'Yeah, especially seeing as students are supposed to be the best and brightest. You're hardly the best and the brightest if you can't cope with a bit of criticism.'

'Not sure "the best and the brightest" really describes our students,' says Ren.

'True, but still, there's not much point doing an Arts degree if you can't handle a disagreement.'

'Definitely.'

'So Lucy has disappointed you. Mind you, she wasn't a student herself, so you didn't have that mandate for critical analysis of her conversation.'

'I wasn't trying to teach her. I was just being myself.

People always say you should be yourself.'

'Oh, that doesn't apply in your case. You should never be yourself.'

'I've had this feeling that I'd forgotten something. Maybe that was it.'

'You're also a total pedant. That's something that philosophers have that most other academics don't. You're all pedants. Especially you. Doesn't go down too well with the ladies. Critical analysis is one thing. Endless pedantry is another.'

'Even my humorous pedantry?'

'Especially your humorous pedantry. A pedant who's an earnest bore she could probably take. But the endless hilarious pedantry at her expense she couldn't, I expect.'

'It was only occasional. And mostly not at her expense.'

'Still. She was a sensitive thing, as you say. Was she good in bed?

'Heavens to Betsy, Miles, a gentlemen does not kiss and tell. Shame on you for asking, you cad.'

'Sorry. So are you cut up about it?'

'A bit, yeah, but it wasn't like it was ever going to be a long-term relationship. But I'm down enough to want to drink tonight.'

'As opposed to when you're happy so you want a drink to celebrate? Ren the Celebrator is in the house. Well, at least you won't have to put up with any more pictures of pussies.'

'You're referring, I hope, to the cute cat pictures she liked to stick onto everything?'

'Despite what you think, I am a gentlemen, and that is what I was referring to. I will not pry into any snap-snap grin-grin Polaroid-type activities, or ask for a look.'

Ren gets some drinks in.

'So how's it going with Andrea?' Ren asks. Andrea works for the Council.

'Ahhh... I was hoping you weren't going to ask me that.'

'Problemo?'

'Sort of. Let's see. As you self-identify as a gentleman, despite much evidence to the contrary, I shall but faintly allude to the fact that she's good in bed.'

'That's not faintly alluding to it, that's baldly stating it.'

'Whatever. She's a firecracker in the sack. Insane. But she has all these animal rights posters all over her flat.'

'As in appeals to save cute fluffy animals? Or militant "Kill all the animal-testers" posters?'

'You might say they're from the more radical end of the spectrum.'

'You sure can pick 'em. Does she go on about it a lot?'

'Surprisingly no. She hardly mentions it.'

'But it's going to be a problem, isn't it, seeing as you work in a department that contains numerous monkey-torturers?'

'Could be.'

'Has she asked about that?'

'In passing. I've played it down. Important research and all that. Which it is.'

'Right. Well, I don't like to interfere...'

'You think I should dump her?'

'That's your business. But there are numerous cliches appropriate for such situations. Don't let the little head, book and covers, and all that. I know she's good-looking, but...'

'She does seem very keen on me.'

'Lots of girls are keen on you, pretty-boy.'

'She even likes to come in and see me at work.'

'Well, it is a fascinating building. All those endless, flouro-lit, dirty corridors in a horrible sixties building. What more could a girl want?'

'She really comes in because she likes to...'

'What?'

'Well...'

'You mean in your office? What have I told you about being a gentleman? No kissy telly. You're not *Cosmopolitan* magazine. And remind me never to sit on a chair in your office again.'

'By the way, speaking of girlfriends, I have some news about Tanja.'

'She's moved to London?'

'No. She's found a new boyfriend.'

'Whoopie-do. Oh. Is it someone we know then?'

'Tony Shaver.'

'His full name is Tony Fucking Shaver. Oh God. Tony Fucking Shaver. Shite. I thought I'd never have to see her again. Jesus, it's my fault, I told her that Tony Fucking Shaver was someone more sympathetic to what she was talking about. She's probably gone and sought him out. Should have kept my fucking trap shut. Flub-a-dub. So anyway, where's Andrea tonight?'

'She's, er... she's away.'

'You're hiding something. Where is she?'

'Just a thing she's got on.'

'Right. Let me guess. An animal-rights convention? A Socialist Workers Party meeting?'

'Just some sort of animal-rights meetup. Nothing big.'

'What is to become of you? Why can't you find a semi-normal woman and not an escapee from your labs? You want a relationship, not a test subject to write a thesis on.'

'Like you could have resisted what she was doing to me at that party.'

'Have your drunken shag, sure, but you don't have to keep going out with a woman just because she took you into the broom closet at a party and used the vacuum cleaner as a sex aid, or whatever she did.'

'This is still just a shag. Only a somewhat extended one. Also, she has plenty of coke.'

'Isn't she just a bag of fun? Is that why your eyes are bloodshot?'

'Are they?'

'You look like you have conjunctivitis.'

'That's my story.'

'So. All it is, you're saying, is a shag, and you just haven't quite got around to telling her the shag is finished?'

'I will tell her. When she gets back.'

'Unless she comes back with some more coke?'

'It will die soon enough. It's purely physical. These things burn out.'

'So do your nostrils.'

'If finding a semi-normal woman is so easy, where are yours?'

'You had to bring that up. I don't charm them out of the trees to the extent you do.'

'I'm just going to suck the marrow out of life for a bit longer, that's all.'

'Just as long as the police don't have to break in to find her and her mates on the floor sucking the marrow out of your bones.'

'Oh pish posh, stop being such an old woman. She's a healthy young woman who likes to fuck, as is right and proper, and I am obliging her.'

'Or, she's a right lunatic who's up to no good who likes to fuck.'

'The common denominator is the important bit.'

'Okay. It's your dick.'

'It goes wherever I go, so that's a safe assumption.'

'I'm sure it will look nice on her mantelpiece.'

'Mantelpiece, what a good idea. We haven't done it there yet.'

'What do your monkey torturers do to their monkeys? Do you think she'll try to recreate that with you once she's got you tied up?'

'I've told her I love animals.'

'She's vegan, right?'

'Yes.'

'Do you have meat in your fridge when she comes around?'

'Yes.'

'It was nice knowing you, Miles. Get us a round in before she ransacks your bank account.'

When the evening has wound up Ren gets on his bicycle, which he came on because he doesn't want a conviction for drink-driving, and because he doesn't want to spend money on a taxi. He has started off at the bottom of the salary scale, which means he gets less money than most of the junior admin staff. That pissed him off, but he was even more pissed off when he found out that Miles and Douglas were both starting off making ten grand a year more than him. Not because they had negotiated anything, or because they were personally in demand, or because their fields were suffering shortages. In Miles' case it was because he had worked for six months after his PhD for a scientific publishing company for a proper salary, and the University for some reason decided this meant he must be put at the top of junior lecturer scale, even though that job was just was just a temporary job while he looked for academic vacancies. In Douglas's case he had simply spent a few months in a temporary job for a scientific firm in Cambridge. When Grayvington asked him to put down his annual salary he just estimated what the annual equivalent would be given what he'd been paid for two months work, and lo and behold he had also been started off at the top of the junior lecturer scale. The geniuses at HR at work – from what he can gather they're all being paid at least twice as much as him.

He takes off rather unsteadily, hiccaburping as he gets going, while forgetting to turn his bike light on. Riding a bike on urban roads when drunk is never much fun, but there's not much traffic late on Sunday night. He is coming down a hill towards his house, going pretty fast and feeling good now that he's nearly home, when suddenly he feels simultaneous sharp – in fact tremendous – pains in his left leg and arm, and he is catapulted across the road. At first he has no idea what has happened, as the lights around him wooze and sway as if now giddily free of his restrictive gaze. Then he feels himself being pulled up by urgent hands, and back across the road to the footpath.

'...really sorry, I'm really sorry,' someone is saying. The first thought that comes to him as his mind recalibrates, and reality is reconstructed, is that he hadn't had his light on, so this man can't be really blamed for opening his car door and knocking him off his bike. (That he had been poleaxed by a car door opening was not a thought that consciously presented itself to his mind, it was, rather, an automatic, non-conscious induction that had been made by his brain and placed in his current operative assumption bank.)

'...but you didn't have your light on, so I didn't see you were coming.'

Ren is somewhat annoyed at this, not annoyed at the content of the claim, which he agrees with, but with the fact that he hasn't got in first with it, and so he can't be quite as heroically Ace Rimmerish as he had intended a second earlier.

'Not your fault, mate,' he says. 'Like you say, I didn't have my light on.' He limps towards his bike and picks it up. His leg and arm are hurting badly, in a sort of numb way.

'I can take you to hospital in my car.'

'Hospital? I don't need to go to hospital. It's not that bad.'

'Are you sure? Looked pretty nasty.'

'I'm fine. No point going to hospital for some bruises.'

'Let me drive you home then.'

'That's very kind, but I only live a few hundred yards away. Nothing to worry about, I'm a big strong boy, I'll just go home and have a soak in the tub.'

'Well, if you're sure.'

Eventually the man, who Ren can't quite see due to him seeming kind of blurry, accepts that Ren is in no need of his assistance, and he drives off. Ren tries to get on his bike to ride it home, but it had become bent somewhere, and won't go properly. He can't quite make out what the problem is, due to his eyesight still being a bit disorganised, so he drags it and himself home.

The closer he gets to his flat the more his leg and arm hurt, although his vision is now back to normal. He gets inside, and takes off his clothes in order to have a look at the damage while he runs a bath. Blimey. Both limbs have huge, angry-looking raised areas, like burial mounds. The skin is not broken anywhere, but the damage underneath looks considerable, and the hillocks are a nasty mottled red colour. Ren starts to think that maybe he'd been too hasty in not accepting a lift to the hospital, it looks like he's suffered some muscle damage. He's getting stiffer by the minute. He lets the bath run for a while before deciding that he does need to go the hospital. He unplugs the bath and calls for a taxi. He knows what A&E departments are like, so he grabs a novel to take with him.

The taxi drops him off outside A&E at Grayvington General Hospital. He hobbles to the reception desk, where he is greeted by a long queue, despite it being a Sunday night. Good thing he'd brought the novel. Maybe he should have brought two.

After an age spent staring at the other sad cases in the place and thinking up fanciful diagnoses for what ails them, he gets to the counter. 'I think I have muscle damage', he says. Don't want to oversell it, but don't want to undersell it either, he thinks, in case I become an eternal low-priority patient, destined to never get seen because there's always someone in more urgent need than me. They don't feed you in A&E, so eventually you'd just waste away to the point where they did have to see you, and then they'd tell you the cure is to go home and eat, because they don't feed you in A&E.

As expected, he isn't one of the urgent cases who is straight away transferred to waiting for hours in his own curtained booth. Rather, he's transferred to sitting on a chair in a communal waiting area, where he will wait for hours to be transferred to his own curtained booth, where he will wait for further hours on his own for a nurse to see him and make an initial, inexpert diagnosis, whereupon he will wait for more hours for a harassed-looking quacksalver to appear and say, 'Nothing we can do, go home and rest'.

That, at least, is the worst-case scenario, he thinks. More likely is that I'll be out of here in half an hour. He starts to get less confident of that prediction when he sees a shocked-looking man with deep cuts all over the top left corner of his face being directed to a booth, and being left alone to wait with just a bloody towel. Has he been glassed? Whatever the cause, he's clearly very drunk, despite his best efforts to appear sober.

That was a thought. They could probably smell the alcohol on his own breath, and tell that he's drunk. Would that result in him getting shunted down the priority list? And are most of available doctors working in the children's A&E section, which is separate to this one, where deserving and adorable mites with fevers and kidney conditions and asthma are lovingly looked after by kind and considerate doctors and nurses, who all get a well-deserved glow from treating innocent children with halos? If he were a doctor or nurse on emergency duty he knew he'd rather be treating cute kids with real medical conditions than a load of horrible drunken thugs who had smashed each others' faces in, or randy middle-aged men on drugs with multiple gerbils stuck inside their bottoms, or short-sighted DIYers with nails through their hands.

He takes another look at the people around him. While there are a few with visible injuries or conditions, with a lot of them you can't tell what the problem is from a glance, which meant that it's possible that that man sitting uncomfortably over there does have a dildo lost somewhere in his rectal region, patiently waiting in the dark heart to eventually hear Dr Stanley say, 'Dr Dildo, I presume'. The woman he's sitting next to looks fine, but it isn't the done thing to ask her what her problem is, in case she says, 'My arse and my vagina have somehow swapped functions,' or 'My nipples leak petrol,' or 'Mind your own fucking business.'

But you know what, Ren thinks, I'm happy. The reason I'm happy is because I have bought a book to read. Nobody else has had the foresight to do that. Admittedly it's quite hard to bring a book with you to hospital when you've been walking along the footpath and some loose masonry has fallen on your head, but Ren thought that even if he had driven a nailgun through his arm he would still find the time to pick up a paperback before he left. Nothing too heavy, obviously. You're not going to be feeling like reading Kant in hospital, sure, but someone a bit breezier, like Hume or Stove, would be fine. Or some science fiction to take your mind out of its depressing surroundings. Everyone else is looking around morosely, as the microseconds are strung out, or else they're trying in vain to be interested in reading a car magazine from 1996.

But as the night wears on he realises he isn't happy any more, because what he hasn't had the foresight to bring with him are painkillers, and he is starting to get a headache from the booze wearing off, and his wounds are throbbing very painfully now. And before long he isn't up to reading any more. The clock ticks over to 4am. He just sits there on the chair, in a sort of half-doze, thinking about Lucy, and then Lily, and then Lucy, and then Lily, and so on. There is no point complaining because the place still has quite a lot of other people waiting, but eventually he does enquire, very politely, but is told officiously to go and wait some more. He asks if they can give him any painkillers, but they said they can't unless the doctor prescribes some for him. Could the doctor prescribe some for him? Not without seeing him, no. He'll have to wait some more.

At 7am he is woken up from his stupor. He realises he's been sitting there with his eyes open watching the waiting-room scene while superimposing various bizarre dream-like activities over it. The Goth across from him with the filed-down incisors hadn't really gone over to the water cooler tank and bitten into it, creating a leak which has gone everywhere, and the water was really acid, and everyone had to stand on their chairs, and then the legs on the chairs were gradually eaten away by the acid. Though the twat really does have filed-down teeth.

The number of patients has gone down a lot. The stream of new arrivals greatly slowed after 3am, and the nurses are finally moving him into a booth. Tail-end of the night now, he reasons, so it shouldn't be long before he is seen. But before too long he can see, through the gap in his curtains, a whole new stream of people who have started coming in. Bloody hell. Now it's morning accident crowd. Is he going to get shunted down the priority list again? It's like TITE all over again, an unproductive waste of time, and he's tempted to get up and walk out, to cut his losses and get some sleep instead, after taking some much-needed painkillers. But having made it to the booth, which feels like a victory, he is reluctant to give up such hard-fought ground.

But it looks like he has been shunted down the priority list again, because time ticks on as he sits all alone in his booth, convinced he's been forgotten about because he's out of sight.

Finally, at 10am, he's seen by a doctor. He's in a bad way, feeling sick and cold, with a headache, and his damaged limbs are feeling painful and numb at the same time. To his disgust, after all that waiting, the doctor spends three minutes with him, says there's nothing we can do, possibly minor muscle damage with swelling which will go down eventually, go home and get some rest. I've been more damaged by the wait than by the car, Ren thinks angrily. Should have just had the bath. Fucking useless NHS.

'Can you at least get me some painkillers?' he asks.

'I'd have to prescribe them,' says the doc, 'and that would mean a few more hours of you waiting around for the on-site pharmacy to send them through. Possibly four or five hours, in my experience. You're better off just going home and taking some there. What's your job?'

'I test out defibrillating paddles. I'd like to do a spot

check of these ones here, with the help of your administrators, so if you could please send them in one by one,' is what Ren feels like saying. Instead he says, 'I work at the Uni. And I have to teach in a few hours' time, so I'd better go.'

'Can't you take a day off?'

Ren gives him a look. 'We don't do that,' he says, like he's in the Marines.

Ren expects the doctor to clap him on the back and say, 'We have the same attitude here, no golf afternoons for us,' but he just looks concerned and says, 'Are you sure you're up to teaching today? You don't look well.'

'It's just some first-year classes. I'm not going to infect anyone with anything. And I'm tired, but it's not like I'm going to collapse while doing open-heart surgery with a scalpel in my hand.'

2001-02
Semester 1
Week 6
Monday

Later he realises that he should have taken a sick day and stayed at home. Doing those classes felt like he was doing open-heart surgery and he was about to collapse at any moment with a scalpel in his hand. Seminars can be hard enough even when you're fit and well, mentally sharp, and know the material well, and none of that applied to him today. The classes are on Ethics, a first-year lecture course that Bill Porterfield has been forced to do.

Forced, because Bill Porterfield is no great expert on Ethics. In fact, no-one was quite sure what field Bill Porterfield is an expert on, outside of his interest in Robert Langston. So Bill doesn't want to do Ethics, and the department doesn't really want him doing it either, but nobody else in the department has any expertise in Ethics, or any interest in teaching it, other than Verna Leach, but she can't be trusted with it. So it's Bill who has ended up with it this year.

The reason why no-one in the department specialises in Ethics is that whenever a new Lectureship comes up, either the analytics get to choose, or the Continentalists do. The Continentalists always choose someone on the basis of how Continental they are, so none of them are ever suitable material to take a fairly analytic course like Ethics – the analytics certainly don't want to let a Continentalist or a postmodernist run a course like Ethics, because it would immediately be turned into Applied Political Protesting With Incoherent Ranting Analysis.

The analytics, on the other hand, although they know,

every time, that they should hire a lecturer who can fill in some of the teaching gaps in the department, always end up going for whoever they think is the best researcher, who'll publish the best papers, improve the department's research standing, and provide good conversation about the sort of philosophical topics the analytics are interested in. (Luckily for Bill Porterfield he's been in the department for decades, and has never been subject to these criteria.) This means that no ethicists ever get hired, because people who do Ethics are usually considered a bit second-rate and woolly. Of course there are some very good ethicists around, but they're all at better places. Grayvington never gets any good ethicists applying, and anyway, most of the analytics want other metaphysicians to talk to, not ethicists. So they never hire any. Thus Introduction to Ethics is always badly taught. It's been passed around from one person to another, and often they try to foist it upon a new lecturer, as long he or she is an analytic philosopher.

As the newest analytic lecturer Ren had been tapped up for it himself, but although he had suggested at his interview that Ethics was an Area of Competence for him, after he had been given the job he made it clear that he barely knows any Ethics. There's meta-ethics and normative ethics, isn't there, and, er, that's about as much as I know. Moral statements are just boo or hisses, I sort of know that one too. Of course I could mug up on it, but seeing as you want me to teach other courses, plus there's the TITE I have to do, it doesn't really seem feasible that I should do that one as well, I'd have to spend the whole term in the library, bang goes all the papers I'm trying to finish up and get out to journals, if Bill did it last year then I'm sure he could do it again, such an experienced member of staff, he must know it well by now. How many times has he taught it previously? At least six times over the years? Well, there you go then, be a shame to take it off him, should be a doddle for him. Glad that was so easily sorted out.

But he hasn't got out of having to take seminars for it,

and that's what he has to do today.

Having taught a lot of seminars as a grad student, and having talked a lot about seminar teaching with other seminar leaders, he is aware that there are three types of seminar groups: the Rollers, the Fords, and the Funerals. The Roller groups are those where there's a sufficient proportion of students who are keen, smart, interested in the topic, have done their preparation, and most important of all are happy to talk, and debate, and listen to each other, and who don't need much prompting or correcting, and can handle being disagreed with. Even two such students can make a seminar group a good one, a seminar that purrs along like a Rolls-Royce, never breaking down. A Roller seminar is a pleasure to teach, which you come out of feeling refreshed, or at least not too different to how you felt when you went in.

The Funerals, the seminars everyone dreads, including the students, are the ones where the students won't talk. Sometimes it's because they haven't prepared, haven't done the readings, or haven't even been to the lecture. Some students are just shy. Some students are very unsure about their philosophical skills and knowledge and are too scared to speak up. Some students are very unsure of themselves in general. Some are a bit dim, at least by University standards. Some are intimidated by the seminar leader. Some are hungover. Some just dislike the philosophy staff, and consider talking to them uncool. Some are enrolled in other departments, and are taking just the one 'subsidiary' Philosophy module because their department forces them to take some courses from other departments, and they have no clue what's going on; they just want to say nothing and scrape a pass.

Sometimes the outside students in a first-year class are East Asian students from the Commerce Department, or the Physics department. The problem with these Asians is that they're not used to having to give their own opinion – they want to be told what to think. This is, everyone says, a result of the deference that youngsters are expected to show to their wise elders in East Asian culture. Ren thinks that any such Asian subsidiary student should be made to sign a disclaimer before doing any Philosophy module that says, 'I acknowledge that the Grayvington Philosophy department contains no wise elders, and the opinions of any elderly (or non-elderly) members of the department are worthless.'

The other problem with East Asian subsid students from faculties such as Economics and Chemistry is that even if any of them are bright (which they are often are) and also willing to contribute in class (which is much less common), they usually have poor English, which means that any discussion you do manage to have with them doesn't go very well. Poor English may not be such a barrier in a mathematical subject such as Physics, but, with the partial exception of Formal Logic, it's a great handicap in most Philosophy modules, which are very language-based, and involve making fine and subtle distinctions.

Then there are those students, like El Whino, who do Philosophy because they don't know what else to do. Students who want to go to Uni but who don't know what subject to do usually do either Philosophy or Sociology (or English, or Theology, although not that many Unis offer Theology). The better ones do Philosophy, the thicker ones Sociology. The ones in the middle often do English, but outside considerations can sway them towards Philosophy or Sociology – the more progressive ones do Sociology, for the obvious reason, whereas those who vaguely (but unrealistically) aspire to getting a well-paid job in London, but who don't want to limit themselves to working for *The Guardian* or *The Indy* – not that they'd ever really manage to land a job there even if they did do English – do Philosophy.

Most of the haven't-a-clue-what-to-do students who choose Philosophy discover, sooner or later, that they have neither interest in, nor aptitude for, the subject, and they soon come to realise that the bright kids who do enjoy it are on another planet to them. At this point they switch off, and sourly resolve to keep receiving their grant for the rest of their degree, and collect a 2:2, or at worst a 3rd. Instead of pointlessly studying their texts any further most of them take up more 'extra-curricular activities' instead. Some spend their time partying, some throw themselves into a sport or a University society, some seek out more romantic and/or sexual liaisons, or a future husband or wife. Some do things that look good on their CV to make up for their 2:2 or 3rd.

Unfortunately some of these students while away the best years of their young adulthood watching daytime TV, day after day. These are the ones making the biggest mistake of all. In Ren's view, spending your University days watching daytime TV is a mistake on a cosmic scale, regardless of whether you do it ironically, or whether it's because you're constantly stoned. If you're going to cruise your degree at least have the decency to get some stories out of it. Even if your story is, 'I was in the Tennis Club and I used to steal from the bar', that's better than 'I used to watch Countdown every day, and every time I would jerk off over Carol Vorderman, and I felt so sad doing it that I'd just come all over the sofa and not even clean up afterwards, so the sofa ended up this crusty, smelly mess and I had to throw it out, but the rubbishmen wouldn't take it.'

And then there are the saddest cases of all, the students who just lie on their bed all day looking at the ceiling, feeling depressed, and having anxiety attacks. There never used to be that many of these types, but since the progressives took over the school system, and parenting, and everything, and since dual-parent working became the norm, the number of these poor fuckers is increasing every year. This type of depressive manages to do nothing at all except regularly put in their requests for essay and exam extensions – most of them manage to summon up the energy to do this on time. Even the ones who don't get their extension requests in on time are always retrospectively granted them later on, on the grounds that a depressive can't be expected to get their request for an extension in by the extension request deadline. (Retrospective extension requests are always granted because depressive and anxious students are untouchable, and cannot ever be failed or kicked off the course.)

So they are a varied group, the students who are doing a Philosophy degree because they couldn't think of anything else to do. But they do all have one thing in common. Whether they are jolly or sad, they all skip seminars as much as they can, and when they do come they are usually determined to say nothing, and to let others do the talking. So a seminar that has a preponderance of these sorts of students in it will be a Funeral, unless, as everyone hopes, there are a few bright and keen students who can do the talking required.

A room full of students who won't talk is the academic equivalent of getting very constipated and consequently having to try desperately hard to force some pooh out. The atmosphere is rather strained, like everyone's girlfriend or boyfriend has left them for their best friend, but we're not mentioning it. In his early days, when he was a less experienced seminar leader, Ren would end up losing his nerve when faced with a Funeral and just start giving a virtual lecture instead. That was easier to do with his own lecture courses, where he could talk intelligently for hours about the topic and at least give the students some useful information, even if they're failing to develop their own speaking, arguing and critical skills. But that wasn't so easy to do with a course that he didn't know that much about, like Ethics. Although he exaggerated his lack of knowledge of Ethics in order to avoid having to lecture in it, he is pretty hazy on the details, and he isn't about to do any more mugging up on it than he should have to for a first-year seminar.

He wouldn't have been able to cope with a Funeral today at all, except that there is a reading for this week, which he already knew, and which everyone was supposed to have read. Which, of course, most of them, in all three of today's classes, haven't, because it has never happened in any Philosophy seminar at Grayvington ever in the modern era that more than three students have attempted to read the set reading, and usually they've only got through a couple of pages. After the third page the reading could consist of nothing but entries from the telephone directory, and nobody would say anything about it.

'I've sort of skimmed it, didn't have time to read it properly' was what students usually said. In this situation one thing you can do is to go through the reading, slowly, with the students, section by section. This isn't just a time-filling tactic, it's a good way for the students to learn. He remembers one of his old undergrad lecturers who used to take the students line by line through Aristotle. You need good students for that level of analysis, though. No point trying that with Sarah from the University Ski and Champagne Society.

(Also, if you, as a seminar leader, go into class with a reading you don't know that well, then reading it slowly allows you to get a grasp of what it's about as you go, and you can pretend you know it. But it's a bad idea to try to wing it with a reading you don't know at all, and any seminar reader fool enough to do it once never does it again.)

Ren hasn't re-read this week's reading recently, but it's a piece he knows fairly well from his teaching experiences as a grad student. It's a paper by Judith Thomson arguing in favour of abortion. Suppose somehow a violinist gets attached to your body, and uses your body for sustenance. To remove the violinist would kill him. Don't you still have the right to remove him from your body? The argument has a lot of stages, so Ren can take the students through it slowly if he needed to.

He didn't need to with the first group, which is always a Roller class. There were at least five good students who joined in with the discussion. Normally Ren tries to bring out the non-talkers as well, but today he didn't have the energy, it was a struggle enough just to stay awake, and he let those five get on with it.

That went well, but by the end of the class he is feeling terrible, exhausted, with a parched mouth, and his injured leg and arm ache. He has to change rooms for the next seminar, so he goes off limping, hoping no-one will notice, to the next room he has to teach in, which thankfully isn't far away. He sits down and rubs his leg under the table. The ache is making it hard to concentrate, and the hangover isn't helping much either, and he is virtually asleep on his feet. He doesn't know how he is going to get through the next two classes if they aren't good groups. Especially the last one. Groups that meet later in the day are always the worst, and so far in the course that group been keen to play up to the stereotype.

The second class is less good than the first. It's a Ford. A Ford Focus, at his estimate. Not a Mondeo. In fact, a somewhat older Focus, really, with squeaky brakes. It could have been a brand new Mondeo, or even a slightly used Roller, except that it is spoiled by a student who doesn't understand things properly, isn't keen to let anyone else speak, and gets on everyone's tits. Normally this would annoy Ren, and he would make a concerted effort to quieten this student down and bring others in, but today he doesn't mind so much because at least someone else is doing the talking. Talk away, arsehole, he thinks. Tick tock. Tick tock. Occasionally he says, 'Let someone else speak for a change, Phil,' but inside he's raising a Lucozade toast to Phil.

He lets them go five minutes early, pretending that's a favour to them, and sits there wondering whether he has enough time to rush to the cafeteria to get a Lucozade. God, how he wants a Lucozade. The cravings an alcoholic feels for another drink are but nothing compared to his craving for a Lucozade. He could taste that sweet amber liquid now, pouring down his throat, with its molten bubbles, soothing all his fears, enveloping him in a warm glucose glow. He wishes he could ask one of the students to get him one. He'd gladly pay twenty quid if someone offered him one right now. Or even the worst machine coffee ever made. He should have bought a Lucozade before the classes. There is no way he can make it to the cafe in time now. If it was yesterday, there'd be just enough time, but today his left leg and arm – especially his leg – are are so painful and stiff that it would take him half an hour.

The glorious thing about a Lucozade, he thinks, is that you can just have it there, in public, in class, and drink it right in front of everyone without them batting an eyelid, without them knowing that it's reviving you from the dead (for a while, at least) like a magic elixir, charging up your brain like a vodka. You couldn't do that with a beer. Or a vodka.

As he waits in the empty room, he wonders whether he could risk taking a peek at his bruises and mounds. When he last had a chance to, in his office, they'd become spectacularly horrible. Better not, though. Don't want a student to walk in while I'm peering intently down my trousers with a look of horrified astonishment on my face.

The third class trickles in. There are only seven there. This gives him an excuse to start five minutes late, as they wait for more to come. No-one does. Sometimes a smaller class can be a good thing, it makes it feel more intimate, and usually it's the sulkiest, energy-sucking students who haven't turned up, which improves the atmosphere, and the good students enjoy the increase in the average IQ of the room.

But sometimes, usually with a Funeral class, a lack of numbers is a bad thing. The students who have turned up are not much better than those who haven't turned up, and they start to panic. You can see it in their faces. I should have gone home, their faces say to each other. Sometimes they say it out loud. 'I should have gone home too,' they'll say, in a semi-whisper, perhaps hoping the seminar leader will say, 'You can go home if you want, today's class is sort of optional.' They're worried because they don't know the reading, they don't know the lecture material, they think they're no good at Philosophy, and they don't like talking in public, and now it's going to be much harder to hide.

Then, at seven minutes past the hour, after they have finally started, another student comes in. Ren is glad, because it sort of justifies his decision to wait five minutes before starting, even though late students shouldn't really be waited for. He can see the look on this student's face as she walks through the door. Where is everyone? Oh shit. Is it too late to sneak off? No, he's seen me. Damn it, I should have gone to the bar, now I'll have to say something and I haven't a clue. That'll teach me for being conscientious. In future stay in the bar. Ren agrees with her. In future, stay in the bar.

The class is ghastly. These are the worst, or at least the most clammed-up, students. Ren probes away at them for a while, hoping to bring some of them out, but has no joy. So he begins his analysis. He works methodically through the text, section-by-section. Explain a little. Ask some questions. Explain a little more, ask some more questions. But nobody is biting. The atmosphere is frosty. The students' horror that the smallness of this class will force them to say something has frozen them all up, and they all know what each other is thinking, and that's reinforcing their fears, like a feedback terror loop.

No-one wants to be the one who has to talk. Everyone is making a bigger effort than everyone else to say nothing. Gone are any attempts at looking intelligent but shy, to convince the seminar leader, with a look, that while they aren't worth asking any questions of today, they're really a very good student who is listening hard, and who will hand in an insightful essay that will more than make up for their reticence in class. The students today are prepared to look as thick and uninterested as possible, as long as it puts Ren off asking them questions. One is looking out the window the whole time. Another is looking at her phone. She looks like she's about to start typing a text message on it, should Ren dare to ask her something.

Ren wants this to end even more than the students do. He could say he doesn't feel well, which is definitely true, and leave the room, but he isn't going to do that, for the same reason that he turned up today. You don't duck out of your classes. Before they're assigned you can try to get a lighter load, that's acceptable, although too much trying will get you a bad name. But once you have your teaching assignments, you do the job.

Of course, taking your seminars is less important than taking your lectures. While it is important that students turn up to most of their seminars, because that enables them to develop various skills, no individual seminar is important in the way that an individual lecture is. So in theory, an academic cutting a seminar was less of a big deal than cutting a lecture. But still, you just don't do it. You have to turn up, and do a good job. Similarly, you don't walk out of a seminar halfway through, unless you're about to vomit blood all over the carpet. And it's better if you do vomit blood all over the carpet, because then the students will think it reasonable for you to cancel the rest of the class, whereas if you just walk out they'll be suspicious. (And they have cheap, dirty carpets in the teaching rooms at Grayvington. After a couple of days the stain would barely be noticeable.)

So, as ill as he felt, Ren isn't going to cut the seminar short. In theory he could have showed them his Technicolour bruises – they would have earned him a hall pass. But that would mean stories about him spreading all over the campus, getting more lurid by the minute.

So for all these reasons he keeps going, although it's mostly because he's stubborn and not wimping out is a matter of pride for him. Also, he'd been bladdered last night, so it's really his fault. He'd feel guilty about blowing off classes because of that. It's never a good idea to drink too much the night before you have classes, and he had ignored that. But if you are going to burn the candle at both ends, then do it. Don't burn the candle at one end, and then say you're too bushed to attend to the other end, sorry, got to have a lie down now. Work hard and play hard, that's his motto, not play hard and then go to bed with a cold compress when the shovels and pickaxes are handed out, saying you're feeling a bit peaky.

All these thoughts briefly flit through Ren's mind as he starts to flag. He tries to buck himself up for the final stretch. What he really needs is a Christian. Could any of these unlikely types be a Christian? It seems doubtful. Most students go along with Thomson's argument, but sometimes a Christian will, quite reasonably, take issue with the idea that the situation with the attached violinist is analogous to that of a pregnant woman. He can't ask outright whether anyone is a Christian, but he tries to tease it out of them. Even the most reluctant Christian could afford him another ten-fifteen minutes of worthy debate, and then he could finish early.

But the shutters have really come down now. Even the two students he'd managed to get grunts out of have shut up shop for the day. Twenty five minutes left, their expressions seem to be saying. I can stone-face it out for the last half of the class. Next week I just won't come.

It's ridiculous, Ren thinks. We all just want to go home. But we can't say it. Whatever he says in this seminar isn't going to make any difference to these students, even if, as seems unlikely, some of them are better than they seem. You can't presume that just because a student is quiet that they're less bright than the talkers. Not at all. Often the talkers are dimmer than the others. Often the brightest students are shy. He wasn't a big talker as a first-year, realising that he knew little, so he has sympathy for the ones who are quiet but who look intelligent, and who are clearly listening hard. But he has a good look at each student in turn as he talks, and his hopes are dashed. As he drones on, boring them and himself senseless, he thinks longingly of his bed.

And then, a miracle. One of them has started speaking. It sounds like... can it be true? Yes! He's talking like he's a Christian. God has sent his cavalry after all. Not the student Ren would have picked. An olive-looking guy with a baseball cap, and chains, and sports jacket. Probably Greek, and brought up in a religious household. Not what you would call articulate. Halting and confused. But he's speaking. Ren feels like Oliver Sacks at Beth Abrahams, as the first encephalitic patient on the ward responds to L-DOPA. He tries to prevent a big Robin Williams-style grin from spreading across his face. Play it cool, he thinks, don't scare him off. Act as though a student like you talking in a seminar is the most natural thing in the world, and no big deal.

Ren doesn't know whether this guy really is much of a Christian, or whether he's just worked out that he can play this role as a way to pass time. Or to look like he's contributing more than the Sleeping Beauties in the rest of the class. Perhaps he's willing to assume any role in order to rise above being cast as just another cadaver.

It isn't a great conversation, it's stilted, and full of misunderstandings, and it takes great effort from Ren to keep it going, but keep it going he does. It sounds like the guy is parroting things his parents have said, but in this situation it doesn't matter what you bring to the party, as long as it's alcoholic. Fifteen minutes to go. Then the girl next to him starts chipping in a bit as well. Ten minutes to go. Ren has to do some talking. Then a late burst from the Grecian. Not bad. With three minutes left on the clock, Ren calls a halt.

Some of the others, the ones who don't run off scowling as quick as they can, look at the Greek guy appreciatively, with admiration, and maybe a bit of jealousy thrown in. He looks happy, and even a bit smug, as though he has had the balls to go up and chat to Miss Universe at a party. For a brief few minutes Ren even starts to feel good about seminar teaching. Normally after taking a Funeral you feel like what a godawful waste of your young adult life and your glorious talent this job is, but now it's like he'd just presided over a Roller.

Ren sits and waits while everybody else leaves before he risks moving. His leg is like a dead thing. Perhaps it is dead. It did look that way on the damaged part of his thigh. Maybe he should go see his GP for a second opinion – that A&E doctor didn't really give it a proper examination. He stands up, with real difficulty. He remembers long, all day-hikes he did in the Scouts. What a piece of piss they seem now, compared to the struggle he's going to have to get back to his office.

After he is sure everyone is gone from the corridor outside he drags his leg out of the room with him, like he's suffering from alien leg syndrome. *A cold dead thing, like nothing on Earth.* His happy glow dissipates, and the usual feeling you get after taking a Funeral class returns with a vengeance. The thought of doing this sort of thing for another forty years is almost too much to bear.

2001-02
Semester 1
Week 6
Friday

'Come in,' says Robot.

'You asked to see me?' says Ren.

'Yes, come in Renford. Take a seat.'

Ren walks over to the chair, disguising the limp in his bruised and battered leg as best he can. The leg is painful, and he still feels pretty bad. He hasn't managed to catch up on any sleep yet, so he's in a very cranky mood. This better not be about that fucking Angela Saunders sad-sack.

'What is it?' he says.

'A student has written a letter of complaint about you,' says Robot, holding up a hand-written letter.

'Was it Angela Saunders?'

'I can't say who it is.'

'Can I read it?'

'No.'

'Well, in that case I'm not going to stay,' says Ren, getting up. 'I don't listen to anonymous complaints, especially when I'm not allowed to see the details.'

'Sit down,' says Robot. 'Student complaints are serious matters.'

'They are? Because my tutees are always complaining about your teaching. Perhaps someone needs to have a talk to you.'

'This student writes that she's not happy with your teaching.' Ren can see that underneath his worried persona Robot is rather pleased with this development.

'She? So it is Angela Saunders then.'

'I didn't say that.'

'What's the actual complaint? Because lots of students complain about teaching. Is this just a generic complaint, or is there a specific charge?'

'Well, she says that you, er, you haven't...' Robot takes a look at the letter. 'You haven't explained things well.'

'That's not a very specific complaint. And the other students aren't saying that.'

'She also says that you haven't given her sufficient attention when she's come to see you.'

'I can hardly answer that if you won't tell me who it is. I don't like this trial by anonymous complaint. If it is Angela Saunders then I have given her time. The same is true if it's anybody else. I spend too much time, too much of my supposed research time, talking to students, giving them individual attention, holding their hand, giving them a slow-motion replay of the lecture that others don't have the benefit of. It's rarely the good, or the diligent, students who come to see their tutors. It's mostly the not-so-good students who are neurotic about getting their 2:1. The ones who need someone else to wipe their bum for them.'

'That answer doesn't give me much confidence that you have an appropriate attitude towards the students. Remember that you are still on probation. There is no guarantee that you will get your permanent position, and these are relevant issues in deciding that matter.'

'I can assure you that no students are getting the brush-off, and I give all who come sufficient time and energy. In fact, I put a lot more time and energy into those students than many of the other lecturers, from what I've heard. Including you. I've had students complaining that you are impossible to get hold of. And Adelaide, unless you're one of the sisterhood's proteges. Is this something we should discuss? Panos is always on the Continent. Derek just ignores the students, unless they're attractive young ladies.

'I'll have to ask you not to fling around irrelevant accusations in this formal context.'

'Formal context?'

'A written complaint has been made against you. While this is not an inquiry, I am asking in my official capacity as Head for your view of the matter.'

'As I have already said, if I am not given the name of this student, or the details of the accusation, then it's hard for me to answer, but I assure you again that I have performed my duties correctly and diligently. I'm not joking about the students complaining about other lecturers, including you. If student complaints are to be taken seriously, why aren't they being taken seriously?'

'All complaints are taken seriously, but written complaints are considered more serious. You have received a written complaint. Anyone else who receives a written complaint is treated in the same way.'

'But you won't let me see the letter, and you've failed to give me anything concrete, so I don't see what more I can do other than give you my word that I'm doing a good job. Does the student have a history of making complaints?'

'I can't reveal that, and it's not germane to to the matter at hand.'

'It may be very germane if she does this a lot. I'm being accused of something vague, by an unknown person, who may or may not be a nuisance complainer with personal issues. What more do you want me to say other than the assurances I've given you?'

Robot looks at his watch. He appears to have lost patience.

'Thank you for those assurances, Dr Christopher. That will be all. For now.'

2001-02
Semester 1
Week 7
Thursday

'Let's sit over there in the far corner away from the students,' says Miles as he and Ren get their coffees.

Ren limps after Miles. The side of his left leg has been turning spectacular colours, but it's feeling a lot better than it was last week.

'Are you trying to make me walk so I have to suffer?'

'No, just don't want any students listening in.'

'Miles, they've already heard plenty of shameful stories about you.'

'How have they heard?'

'There's a team of your female admirers who stalk you.'

'Really?'

'No. Or maybe yes. How would I know? Aren't you supposed be the departmental object of desire? With all those females students – what is it, eighty-five per cent female in Psych?'

They sit down at a table away from the students.

'Well, I did get a few saucy comments on some of my teaching evaluation forms last year,' Miles says.

'Lucky old you.'

'"Dr Honeywell can pour honey over me any time he damn well likes", that sort of thing.'

'Is it your pig pheromones? All I get is "Too fast" or "Too slow"?'

'Are these bedroom or lecture comments?'

'They could be comments on my driving, so far as I can tell. So, have you broken up with Animalia?'

'Who?'

'The one who has an abattoir spot reserved for you. Andrea the Animal. You were going to break up with her when she got home from her animal rights meeting last weekend.'

'Ah, yeah, that's what I wanted to tell you about. I haven't managed to do that yet.'

'Her she rigged your balls up with remote-controlled explosives?'

'She certainly did something explosive to my balls the other day.'

'Oh God. Here we go. Little Miles, along with his two ovoid mates, is running the show again.'

'Well, I did tell her I wanted to break up.'

'And little Miles fought back valiantly, with her assistance.'

'I suppose that is what happened. But it wasn't just her assistance. You see, when I phoned Andrea and told her, she came over and brought a friend with her. I was a bit surprised, and then she and her friend took their clothes off, and started doing rude things to each other in front of me.'

'I see.'

'Do you think you could have resisted that?'

'No, I don't suppose I could have. Although it would have depended on how mad the friend looked.'

'She didn't look mad. At least I don't think she did. Hard to tell at the time, I wasn't really paying attention. So I'm not really that bothered any more about breaking up with her.'

'Fair enough. Enjoy it while the last grains of sand trickle away. At least you won't have to worry about getting them pregnant.'

'Why not?'

'Too many humans already, you see. They won't be getting up the duff. Not unless you can convince them you're half pig. Which may not be that hard. But why am I giving relationship advice to you? You're supposed to be the psychologist who understands how the mind works.'

'But we don't. That's why we psychologists do

psychology. Psychologists don't understand people, or their behaviour, or themselves, so we study psychology to try to get a clue as to what's going on. We're all mentally or emotionally deficient in some way, and we got interested in psychology as a way of trying to work out what's gone wrong with us.'

'I thought it was psychiatrists who were all supposed to be certifiable?'

'They're like us on steroids. But you philosophers are supposed to be the wise ones, so you should have some good advice. Not that I'm asking for it.'

'Wise? Does anyone in my department seem wise to you? Do any of them have much of a grip on the world?'

'Now you mention it...'

'I do have one bit of wisdom for you. A truth revealed through countless deaths. Never trust a loony leftie.'

'All right Eisenhower. I'll bear it in mind. By the way, I wanted to ask you. How do you keep that annoying eccentric who turns up to your departmental seminars from coming to the staff club after the talk? We're having a similar problem.'

'Alan Pettigrew his name is. There's no mystery, we just told him members of the general public aren't allowed in the staff club, it's staff and students and visiting academics only. No-one's mentioned that anyone can come in as long as a member signs them in.'

'But don't you sometimes take other members of the general public who turn up for talks to the staff club with you? Hasn't he noticed that?'

'Sometimes we do, but I don't know if he's noticed. Maybe he has, and he just accepts it. You should come to our next talk. It's Rialto Magnussen talking about rat consciousness, you'll probably be interested. He cuts bits out of rat brains to see what happens to their behaviour afterwards.'

'Well, I have a bit of a problem with your seminars.'

'Too specialised? Assume too much background in

philosophy? Too much logic notation?'

'No, no, nothing like that. The problem I have with your seminars is to do with the wine and cheese after the talk.'

'But we don't have any wine and cheese after the talk.'

'Yes, that's the problem. Why don't you?'

'I don't know. We just don't.'

'We do. We have plenty of wine. Decent stuff too. Cheese also pretty good, not that I'm bothered about that. I can usually get through at least a bottle's worth, sometimes more, before we go to the staff club. And sometimes I grab a bottle when we head off.'

'You think Philosophy should do that?'

'You'd get more people coming.'

'We don't want people who come just for free wine.'

'They won't just come for the free wine. That may be what tips the balance into whether they come or not, but they will listen to the talks. No-one wants free wine that much.'

'Graduate students do.'

'Yes, but I'm talking about academics with a salary. Academics don't want to waste their time listening to a talk they're not interested in just for some wine. If they come, they'll be interested in both. And it looks better if you get more people turning up. Makes your department look like the centre of something. So why don't you lot start having wine and cheese afterwards?'

'I don't think I have the power to make that happen.'

'Most departments do it. Economics does it. Physics does it. Sociology and Politics do it. They all do. So why can't Philosophy?'

'We don't have as much money as other departments. But anyway, why should the taxpayer pay for academics, who already get a decent salary, to quaff wine? That's just depeculation.'

'It's not defuckulation. It isn't about the taxpayer paying you to drink. Departments already have their budgets. So the amount the taxpayer has stumped up is already fixed.

Your job, as a drinker, is to transfer the loose money that isn't already committed to the important things to the wine budget. So that instead of that loose money being spent on things that benefit non-drinkers, it's spent on things drinkers like, like wine and cheese. And preferably more wine and less cheese.'

'Sounds rather like sophistry. If Parliament decided that fifty per cent of the money that goes to running Parliament each year is to be spent on wine for the MPs, it would seem pretty obvious that taxpayers are being stung by boozy MPs. You couldn't say, well, the Parliamentary budget is already fixed, and this is just how MPs are internally arranging the spending of that money.'

'But we're not talking anything like fifty per cent of the budget. We're talking a very small proportion that would otherwise get frittered away on some pet scheme of the Head, or taken back by the central admin. Fifty per cent on booze is not a proportionate amount, but less than half of one per cent is. Wine is essential to help the after-talk go well. Think of how much important work gets done after the talk, over a few drinks.'

'You're going to end up one of those Vice Chancellors who gets the University to pay for an amazing wine cellar which only you are allowed to ransack,' says Ren.

'Like our own dear VC, you mean?'

'Raven? Has he done that?'

'Yes. Well, from what I hear it wasn't him, it's a tradition that was established at the founding of the place. But he's taking full advantage,' says Miles. 'There's a huge cellar under the Terminal Building with like a million pounds worth of good wine down there, or maybe more. He, and only he, can bring up whatever he likes to entertain guests at Carthradean Hall.'

'Carthradean Hall? What's Raven got to do with Carthradean Hall?'

'Don't you know? That's where he gets to live, because he's the VC.'

'What? I thought he lives in town.'

'He has house in town as well, but his main residence is Cathradean Hall.'

'The VC really gets to live in Carthradean Hall?'

'Yes.'

'Is this a copy? Or a place with an ironic name?'

'No, the real Cathradean Hall, as in gigantic, ornate, amazing historic mansion in the country. Not the whole thing, of course, but he gets to live rent-free in a luxury apartment within it, away from the tourists,' says Miles.

'Oh Jesus, Mary and Joseph. This is on top of his salary being one of the highest in the country?'.

'Yes, not to mention he gets a free chauffeur to drive him to the Hall and back every day. Not bad for a mediocre political scientist. You sure you don't want to be left-wing? Then you could join the Union and protest.'

'The University system is hardly the free market, is it?' says Ren. 'Who gets to decide his salary? His mates on the University Board, that's who.'

'Yeah, it's disgraceful. You know he got a raise last year that was worth more than our entire year's salary?'

'What does he even do?'

'He runs around chairing pointless meetings, and coming up with pointless initiatives to waste more of the University's money.'

'You sure you still want to be left-wing? What about your Union mates? What are they doing about executive pay? Nothing at all, other than the occasional bit of ineffective whinging to *The Guardian*?'

'Yeah, the Union is a waste of space,' admits Miles.

'About as much use as an armless man at a wankathon. Why is the Union always going on about Israel? It's always fucking Israel, every second time you hear the Union raise an issue it's bloody Israel. It's the only democracy in the Middle East, the only one that isn't run by murderous loonies, and anyway, what the cunting fuck has Israel got to do with academia in the UK? Why don't they try to do something about the issues they're supposed to be concerned with? Why don't they realise that the reason there is so little enthusiasm for the Union is because it's always acting like a branch of the International Socialists?'

'That's because it's run by the same people who ran the International Socialists Society when they were students.'

'Well, yes. That's why I'm not going to bother to renew my membership next year. It's a waste of money. And where does all the money go? Many thousands of academics at this place putting in well over one hundred quid a year each, much more for senior people, that's hundreds of thousands of pounds the local Union branch gets every year, and what do we get in return? Very little. Except a few cheap small black and white flyers about Israel. Where does the money go? Is it all sent to London to be donated to the Labour Party? I'm not letting them raid my bank account every year just to help re-elect Tony Blair.'

'If you want the Union improved then you could always get involved yourself instead of just complaining.'

Ren shakes his head in disbelief. 'You think the Union would let a libertarian like me get anywhere near them?'

'A what? A libertine?'

'Libertarian.'

'Well, whatever you're calling yourself, I don't suppose they would let you get involved.'

'Look, I gotta go. But do me a favour, mate.'

'What?'

'Check under your car for bombs every time before you turn the ignition on. But otherwise give my best to Animalia.'

'I will.'

'On second thoughts, don't. Don't ever mention my name in her presence. Certainly do not ever mention my address.'

'You know, the thought of death at her hands just makes the double pussy and arse seem all the sweeter,' says Miles in a mock tone, which unfortunately for him sounds much the same as his normal tone to someone who doesn't know him well. The reason this is unfortunate is because a group of female students has just come to sit near them, a local geographical fact Miles has failed to register until Ren draws his attention to it with a raise of his eyebrows. The girls are looking open-mouthed at him.

'Gotta go too,' says Miles hastily. 'Class. Let's run.'

2001-02
Semester 1
Week 8
Wednesday

For some reason Ren can't get onto campus in his car today. There are witches' hats blocking off all the entrances. He finally finds a parking spot off-campus and walks from there to the University. It's not what he wants to do as his leg, although much better, still hurts if he walks too much.

When he arrives he sees that there are police cars on the campus. He hobbles towards where the commotion seems to be. It's the Psychology Building, which has been taped off by the police. He asks some students if they know what has happened.

'The rumour is that it was animal rights activists who broke in, in the early hours. They've trashed the place, smashed up all the computers, and let all the experimental animals out.'

'I heard they liberated, as in kidnapped, the animals,' says another student.

'I hope they took the animals with them rather than just letting them loose,' says a third student. 'You wouldn't want chimpanzees running around the grounds here. That won't end well.'

Ren can't get in to the Psychology building, so he goes to his office and rings Miles' office, and then Miles' home. Miles isn't answering, but that isn't a surprise, he's probably got his hand full at the moment. He can't raise him on his mobile either, so he sends him a text and an e-mail. He wonders whether he should inform the police about Andrea, but decides that Miles will be telling them about her, and he has a busy day with a lot of teaching on which he needs to get on with.

When Ren gets back to his office in the late afternoon he sees on the internet a report saying that five people have been arrested in connection with the attack. Miles still hasn't been in touch, but there's no mention of any harm done to any psychologists, so he's presumably okay. Perhaps he's at the police station telling them all he knows about Andrea. Or is he lying low at home, pretending Andrea is nothing to do with him, and not answering the phone?

By evening time Miles still hasn't got back to him, so Ren drives around to his place. Miles lives in the suburb of Campdown, in a semi-detached house. His car is outside, so Ren knocks on the door. There's no answer. He walks around to the back of the house, and tries the back door. It's unlocked, so he goes inside.

'Miles,' he yells. He hears a rattling sound from upstairs. Like metal being shaken. He runs upstairs and opens the door where the sound is coming from. Inside there's a metal dog cage on the floor of a bedroom. Miles is inside the cage, naked, and trussed up and gagged with gaffa tape.

'Goodness me, a prize turkey all ready for Christmas dinner. What a treat. Listen carefully, Miles. This is very important.'

Miles stays still, his frightened eyes wide open, looking at Ren.

'Have you got any cranberry sauce in your fridge?'

Miles eyes crinkle in anger, and he shakes the cage as best he can while making what noises he can with his mouth.

'All right, all right, let's get you out. Are you unharmed?'
Miles nods.

'Good. I should be able to force the door. It's got a padlock on it, but the metal around it should be breakable.'

While Ren attempts to force the door open, he sings to himself. 'I was right, I was right, I was right.'

There are two places where a padlock could be fitted on this cage, on the upper and lower parts of the door. Only one padlock has been fitted, to the upper part. Ren can't get this section to break, but he can force open the lower part of the door enough for Miles to squeeze through. Ren unwinds the gaffa tape from around Miles' head.

'Andrea!' Miles gasps.

'No!' says Ren. 'I never would have guessed if you hadn't told me. In fact, I refuse to believe it. You're maligning the poor girl. Someone in an Andrea mask, perhaps, but never Andrea herself.'

'Shut up, you fucking cunthead. Has she done something else?'

'Only killed most of your department, sparing only you and Lucius.'

'Bullshit. If she'd spared Lucius you wouldn't be so happy. What did she really do?'

'Trashed your department, apparently. Destroyed lots of computers, and kidnapped the test animals. Stay put, I'll get a knife from the kitchen to cut your ropes.'

When Ren finally comes back, Miles says, 'Why did you take so long?'

'I was looking for your camera. Where do you keep it?'

'Somewhere you'll never find it. Just cut the ropes. I feel ghastly.'

Ren has also brought a towel, which he throws over Miles' mid-section. While he is carefully cutting through Miles' bonds he says, 'So, sex game gone wrong? Or gone right?'

'Last thing I remember is being in bed last evening with Andrea and her friend Coyote.'

'Coyote? You went to bed with a woman called Coyote?'

'She's quite sexy, if a little unhygienic. I remember getting sleepy and then waking up in the daytime in here.'

'Drugged? Good to see a traditional black art coming back into fashion. They're not all bad then. Or perhaps you were just drunk? Keep your hands still while I finish this last bit.'

'Did you say they've destroyed our computers? Is that

for real?'

'That's what I've heard. I don't know any details except campus rumour and what's been on the news. Five people have been arrested. There were police all over campus today. The security department, it seems, didn't notice a thing.'

'They wouldn't. They might do a walk once a night around the campus, but that's it. This has been a previous concern for our department with its animals. In fact, that's why all the real test subjects are located off-campus, at a private and secure location. Even I don't know where it is. The decoy animals we have in the department are not used for much, and we don't stick probes in their brains.'

Miles' hand are now free.

'Right, now for your feet. Then we'd better call the police.'

'What? No fucking way are we calling the police.'

'Not calling the police? But you're involved. You were kidnapped. Sort of. If I hadn't have come around you might have died.'

'I don't care, we are under no circumstances calling the police. I am not going to be known for the rest of my life as the guy who got tied up in a dog cage by animal rights activists.'

'Is this because you don't want to be seen as a victim?'

'I don't mind being a victim. But I'm not going to be a comedy victim. If they had sliced open my belly, or tortured me, then I wouldn't mind being a victim. It would enhance my status, I'd be a brave survivor. I could show people my scars. If you'd have left it a week before you came around and I'd almost died from a lack of water, that would have been all right too. But, fucking hell, you come around the same day, that makes it all a joke.'

'I'm very sorry I was so thoughtful and rescued you promptly.'

'It wasn't that prompt. But thanks, though, I do appreciate it. But I just can't be forever known as "dog cage man". Not without any real suffering involved.'

'Well, it does smell like you've pissed yourself.'

'Couldn't help it. It's the pooh I've been fighting to keep in. But that's not enough suffering. The brave dog cage man who spent a week in the cage, great. But the dog cage man who spent half a day, and pissed himself, that will raise nothing but laughs. So no police.'

'You want Andrea and Coyote to be free to do this, and maybe worse, to someone else?'

'They'll be free to do it anyway. They're only going to get a slap on the wrist either way, aren't they?'

'Thanks to you progressives having taken over the punishment system, that's true. Yesterday you might have denied that. Funny how being personally involved can make you see past the propaganda.'

The ropes around Miles' feet are now cut. He gingerly gets to his feet, and hobbles off to the toilet. When he comes back, he's still hobbling.

'You might need to go to the hospital,' says Ren. 'Being tied up all day might have damaged you.'

'No, no and no,' says Miles.

'You know you're going to get investigated by the police, being Andrea's boyfriend?'

'I was never her boyfriend. Just someone who shagged her a few times.'

'Won't people in your department say that they saw her with you?'

'I don't know. I never introduced her to anyone. We will have passed a few people in corridors occasionally, but that's it. You're the only University person who met her who knew who she was. Even if the police want to talk to me, I'm not telling them about what happened here.'

'Are there security cameras in your building?'

'No.'

'Won't they find your fingerprints at her place?'

'Why would they dust for fingerprints at her place? No crime took place there.'

'A criminal conspiracy might have.'

'I doubt they'll dust for prints at her place. Her lot don't meet there, and the police will know who the other members of her organisation are. And even if they did dust, my fingerprints won't be on file. This stays here. You keep your mouth shut forever more. Even after I die. You take this to your grave, otherwise the grave is where you'll find yourself.'

'I'm beginning to regret involving myself in your sordid penile affairs.'

'You can spend the rest of your life laughing to yourself about how you were right if you want, as long as you keep your mouth shut.'

'Can I one day write a disguised novel about what happened?'

'Definitely not. Look, one day we can look back on this and laugh...'

'I'm laughing now. But if I was you, I'd want revenge.'

'I do want revenge, but it's out of the question. I just hope she gets some jail time.'

'You keeping quiet about this means she's less likely to get jail time.'

'The pub!' cries Miles. 'Let's go to the pub to celebrate my freedom! I'm paying.'

'That was seamless,' says Ren. 'You sure you're up to the pub?'

'What I'm not capable of doing is not going to the pub right now.'

'We could just stay and drink here.'

'After so long in that cage I need to see people.'

'It was only half a day, you said. You spend longer in your office without seeing anyone some days.'

'It was more like a day, really.'

'Half of which you were unconscious for. But I get it. You want to be in public so I don't go on about calling the police. Very well. Clean yourself up while I go downstairs and drink your best whisky.'

2001-02
Semester 2

2001-02
Semester 2
Week 3
Monday

Ren has brought a coffee from the cafeteria and is looking for a place to sit when he sees Miles at a table, so he goes over and plonks himself down next to him. Just as his posterior hits the plastic he realises that Lucius Birch, who is a Professor these days, is also sitting at the table. It's an unpleasant surprise, but perhaps also the opportunity he's been waiting for.

Lucius, as haughty as ever, doesn't look too pleased with Ren's appearance.

'Well, well, well, it's Miles' right-wing philosopher friend,' says Lucius icily. 'Eaten any babies today?'

'Babies plural? I can't get through more than half a baby a day. Have you ever tried eating one? More meat there than you'd think.'

'Do you eat their bones too? Or grind them for bread?'

'Lucius,' says Miles.

'Just a joke,' says Lucius. 'I am jesting with the young philoquester.'

'It's all right, Miles,' says Ren, 'Professor Birch sees right through to my black heart, so let us not muzzle the great Leninist truth-teller.'

'You don't have a black heart. Just an absence of a heart,' says Lucius.

'My, he's feisty today, Miles. Are you not feeding him?'

'Feeding? All of us psychologists are living on nothing but coffee at the moment,' says Miles, trying to change the subject.

'Then you should come over to my office and try some

babies. Had a shipment come in from South America this morning. I can't stand by and see you starving creative types living in poverty.'

Ren puts a bit of an emphasis on the word 'creative', while looking pointedly at Lucius as he says the word. Lucius's face gets a strange, perhaps slightly disconcerted, look on it in response. Interesting, Ren thinks. Time to probe a little further.

'So what study can we expect next, Professor Birch, that will put us fascists in our place? Will you be showing that small business owners demonstrate a greater propensity to torture seabirds? That Labour voters' hearts are two sizes bigger than those of Conservative voters? That even psychopaths are better at distinguishing babies from old sacks of rubbish than Conservative MPs are?'

Lucius doesn't ride to the bait. Instead he says, meekly, 'Oh, ah, nothing we want to talk about now.' Then, in a more friendly tone, he says, 'So, er, how's it going over in the Terminal Building? Are those renovation works finished?'

'Yes, all finished.'

'They must like you Humanities people, seeing as they're making a very nice building even nicer.'

'Either that, or the administration is getting it ready for when they completely take the building over.'

'You think they'll do that?'

'I'm certain they'll do that within ten years. It'll be said that we need a dedicated space designed with Humanities' needs in mind, which means they'll build us an uncomfortable and cheap modern building with small rooms, while they commandeer more of the Terminal building. But tell me Lucius, what did your last study show again? The one you got in *World Science*? Didn't you claim to show that foreigners were rated as having a stronger accent after people had been given *Mein Kampf* to read?'

'I don't really have... well, it was after they'd been reading *The Daily Mail*.'

'Lovely bit of research. I've actually been having a read through it. It would be interesting to see the raw data. Can I come over sometime and have a look at it?'

'I, er, well, no, I can't. I don't make raw data available. Look, I need to go, got some work to do.'

'Well, I'm sure Miles is looking forward to helping you out with the organisation of your next study. Getting a cognitive man on board might give you some ideas.'

'Oh, there's no need for Miles to get involved. Anyway, nice to see you both. Bye.'

'Well Miles, what do you make of that?'

'See, he's not so bad really, he warmed to you eventually.'

'Yes, he noticeably warmed to me, didn't he? Right after I started talking about his research in a less-than-reverential tone. Funny that. Almost like he didn't want to talk details with me.'

'He didn't have time for an argument, I expect.'

'Tell me, Miles, have you ever seen any of the raw data from any of Lucius's studies? For example, the sheets filled out by his test subjects?'

'No. Why should I have seen that?'

'And who is it exactly who runs his studies?'

'He does. And sometimes some grad students, I think.'

'Have you ever seen him or them running these studies?'

'No, but I wouldn't normally expect to. Don't tell me you're doubting Lucius's studies just because their results don't fit in with your politics?'

'Why don't you take a close look at some of them? For example, he had one in *Scientific Dispatches* a couple of years ago where he says that participants in a study who were exposed to pictures of the American flag gave responses to the questions that indicated they were more receptive to violent attitudes than the group who were exposed to the Swedish flag. Do you really trust him to be objective with that? Take a really close look at his results with that one. A lot of it is just too good to be true. The effects are too large to be believable, in my view.'

'But maybe that's because you're expecting there to be no such results. They're only surprising to you.'

'Well, the results are also not as messy as you'd expect. All very neat and clean. Not much in the way of outliers. That's very unusual. Also very typical of faked or doctored results.'

'Jesus, that's a strong claim.'

'I'm not making any claim. I don't know. It just seems to me that his results are so unusual that they meet the criteria for further investigation. Can you take a look for me and see what you think? You're the psychologist, and you're good at stats, you'll have a better sense of what is too-good-to-be-true than me. And maybe have a sniff around his grad students, see what their involvement has been.'

'You have to be joking. I'm not going around asking questions like that. That could be the end of my career.'

'I don't mean direct questions. Just try to indirectly tease out what they've been doing. Does he get them to do any of the studies, or does he run them all? Ask them, for example, what the setup was with that accent study? Were they studying videos? Which videos? Where did he get the test subjects from? You can plausibly ask those questions just out of general curiosity, and because it may help you with your research. The first thing is to find out whether the studies even took place. And if they did take place, who did them, and where's the raw data?'

'I'll have a look at some of his published papers. That's all I can promise at the moment.' Miles looks around and lowers his voice. 'I can't imagine Lucius is a faker, if only because it would be so reckless and stupid. He'd have to know he'd get caught eventually.'

'Seems to me there's not much chance of any faker getting caught if everyone in Psychology has your attitude. Which I expect they do.' Ren gets up to leave. 'Read his papers.'

2001-02
Semester 2
Week 6
Wednesday

'I'm just anxious all the time,' says the student, a stick-thin, unattractive girl whose name is Violet Wells. She's wringing her hands together as she speaks. Getting her just to come in to see Ren, her tutor this year, has been an achievement. 'That's why I haven't handed any essays in or sat any exams this year.'

Violet is looking at the floor. Ren can barely hear her speak.

'Well, as you have a doctor's note for your anxiety, confirming that you have... anxiety... you've been given extensions for all the essays and exams you've missed this year. Even though you didn't hand in any of your extenuating circumstances forms in by their deadlines, which is two weeks after the essay or exam deadline. Normally that means you get zero for that piece of work, but the department has decided that the fact that you failed to hand in your extenuating circumstances requests on time should be overlooked. You have, in effect, extenuating circumstances for your extenuating circumstances form failures.'

'I'm too stressed to deal with forms,' says Violet.

'Well, the department has ruled that you can do your essays and exams over summer. But seeing as the prospect of you doing all of them this summer is somewhat unrealistic, it might be better if you just repeat second year. Given you have medical note I expect the department would allow you to do that.'

'Again?'

'Again?'

'Can I repeat it again?'

'What do you mean, again?'

'I'm already repeating second year.'

'Oh. I see.'

'So would they let me try second year a third time?'

'Uh, I don't know about a third time. The EC committee will have to decide.'

Ren doesn't think it's right that she should be allowed to continue in her degree after so many chances. But there's nothing he can do to stop it. A diagnosis of anxiety and/or depression, which is easy to get, is like a magic spell in a video game, it enables you to keep on going no matter how many times you get killed. It used to be that a University degree indicated a certain level of robustness and reliability on the part of the holder, virtues that employers want. Whatever you thought of the degree in question, at least the possessor of it had demonstrated that they could regularly submit their essays or projects, and regularly turn up for exams and tests. And degree-bearers will have had to regularly attend lectures (they could only get away with not doing that if they were very, very bright). Nowadays, however, there is no guarantee that someone with a degree has those sorts of qualities. There are graduates coming out who have never submitted a single essay in on time, and have had to re-sit most of their exams, and their potential employers are none the wiser.

Some of these students have never even managed to submit their extenuating circumstances forms in on time. But if the department fails such a student then the student magically comes to life and finds the energy to complain. (The temporary discovery of the student's energy seems to be closely connected with the threat of them losing their grant.) The student is then, invariably, re-instated by the University, as Grayvington is the sort of place which goes out of its way to avoid trouble from students or parents who might sue them. Grayvington was sued a couple of years ago by a student who said she was too depressed to do anything other than lie on her bed all day, but who somehow found the motivation to put together a court case. The University quickly caved on that one. (The University might have won in court, but it was too scared of any possible bad publicity to let it get that far.)

'What happened last year then?'

'The anxiety. I just couldn't face coming to classes. I was in a really bad way last year.'

'Did this condition also affect you in first year?'

'Yes, it took me three years to get through first-year.'

'Three years?' Christ Al-bloody-mighty.

'Yes, I was allowed to try again twice.'

'How many classes did you go to in first year?'

'Uh, I didn't go to classes because of my condition.'

'Not in any of those three years?'

'No.'

'How did you pass then?'

'I just got through anyway, without going to classes. Managed to get myself to read some of the literature a few days before the exams.'

Ren can believe this. It's very difficult to be good at Philosophy if you don't go to class, but anyone with half a brain can get through to second year without even going to class. There isn't even a requirement that you pass everything, as long as you don't fail too many modules, and your marks aren't too terrible.

'But to get through I had to do some resit exams over the summer of my third year. I found doing that very stressful. It wiped me out for last year.'

'So if you took three years just to do first-year, how are you still getting a grant?'

'My grant has finished. My Dad is paying for me now.'

'That's going to be expensive for him.'

'Not for my Dad. He works in the City.'

'He's a good Dad to you, then?'

'Not really. I never saw much of him growing up.'

'Your parents were divorced?'

'No, he was just busy. Like my Mum. She had a high-powered job too, so I never saw her much either.'

Ren doesn't want to know this sort of thing, but Violet gives the impression she wants to tell him. He can feel the neediness in her infecting the room. Another modern kid screwed up by absent parents. She's been turned into a very unlikeable young woman by her parents' behaviour, and that's created a further reason for them to stay away from her as she's grown older.

But while he's somewhat sympathetic to her, the fact is that she just shouldn't be at University. A University is a place for intelligent, capable people to study, and do essays and exams. It isn't a place for sad sacks to do nothing but lie on their bed looking at the ceiling all day. University resources should not be used on them year after year. Taxpayers shouldn't be paying for students who won't be students.

It's clearly not good for most of them either. It makes their condition worse, increasing their stress and anxiety the longer things go on. Their failure to do any work leads them to be more depressed, which makes them even more incapable of doing work, which in turn makes them more depressed again, and so on. But the fact that most of these students are roused to action whenever their income is imperilled indicates that they'd be in a better state out in the world of work, where they aren't allowed to get away with doing nothing for such long periods.

'It might actually be best if you suspend your studies for a year or two. Get away from Uni and get yourself into better mental shape. Then come back when you're up to studying.'

Violet starts to panic, and starts hyperventilating loudly. 'Heee haah, heee haah, heee haah,' she goes. Ren doesn't think it's real hyperventilating, but she's clearly distressed.

'What? What's the matter?'

Finally Violet calms down. It turns out that the issue is

suspending.

'I don't see why you're so against suspending,' says Ren. 'The evidence we have before us tells us that it's very unlikely that you will fare any better next year. It would be better for you to get away from Uni for a while, and come back only when you're better.'

'But...'

'But what?'

There is silence for while. Then, finally: 'My Dad won't give me any money if I'm not studying. He wants me to get a degree, but once I have my degree he says I'm on my own.'

Now it's Ren's turn to stay silent. Often with these students money is an important underlying issue, and it seems Violet is no different. As much as she hates being a student, she hates the idea of having to go out into the workforce, or the dole office, even more. She may be lying on her bed all day looking at the ceiling feeling miserable (or she may be having a good time every day; Ren has no way of knowing) but at least she's doing it with a guaranteed income for the year, with no requirement for her to do anything at all. Not even to submit extenuating circumstances forms. Ren's sympathy for her starts to recede a little.

In a way, the condition of these students is caused by the government, or the parents, handing out money and thus creating an incentive for some people to do things they really aren't suited to, and are better off not doing. It's the law of unintended consequences, thinks Ren. Just as the single mothers' benefit results in a lot of women who don't really want babies, and who have no interest in looking after a child properly, having babies for the sake of the money, student grants create an incentive for people who aren't suited to University to go, and to stay there even though it's not working. In the same way, the unemployment benefit creates an incentive for people to be unemployed. If you pay people not to work, it's no surprise that some people will take you up on your offer.

'But it's just going to happen again next year, isn't it?' says Ren. 'Is that what you want?'

'Yes.'

'But why?'

'I won't have to worry about money. I won't have to worry about getting a job. And I'll feel worthless if I don't eventually get a degree some day.'

'Statistically speaking, virtually everyone in the whole history of the human race has not had a degree. It hasn't bothered most of them. Why should it bother you so much?'

'I don't feel like I'm worth anything. A degree will show me that I'm worth something.'

'What does it show you're worth?'

'It shows that I'm capable of doing University-level study.'

'But in five years that's exactly what you've failed to do.'

Mistake. In his growing impatience Ren has said something he shouldn't have. Violet bursts into tears. It takes half an hour to get her to calm down and get her out of his office. That's the other problem with these sort of students – they take up so much time. At least three-quarters of the time the staff spend on students is spent on the 'ECs', that is, the students with endless extenuating circumstances submissions. When a good student comes in to see Ren, they discuss the study topics, the student throws a few ideas around, Ren critiques them, there's a bit of back and forth analysis, and then the student departs in a normal and timely fashion to make some changes to their essay. When an average student comes in the same happens, except they might do a bit of moaning about various other things as well. But generally they also have things to do, and they don't hang around for too long. But the ECs... They're always coming in, in a panic, in crisis-mode, in tears, in a rage, and it takes a long time to get things sorted. At least, you think things are sorted. But two days later they'll be back again for a repeat performance.

Extreme cases like Violet who never come in might seem easier, but then you have to spend time chasing them up, trying to work out what's going on with them, and corresponding with various people in the Byzantine University bureaucracy about them, with definitive decisions about their status always postponed. Ren thought he was going to spend his working hours doing Philosophy, but it turns out that's a hobby for after work. His working hours are spent in a creche for middle-class flakes, holding their hand and saying 'There, there.'

It's worse if you're a young, sympathetic lecturer still on probation who is anxious to make a good impression on your department, because then the flakes gravitate towards you. Ren doesn't come across as very sympathetic so he is spared the worst, but Miles, Lily and Douglas are finding that their niceness (or apparent niceness in Miles' case) means that there is an endless stream of panicky students at their door. Older, grumpier lecturers with established positions (especially Robot and Adelaide) get far few knocks on the door from the frangibles.

2001-02
Semester 2
Week 7
Thursday

I should have taken my car, Ren thinks. I took the train because I wanted to work on a paper on the way to the conference. Which didn't happen, because even though he was in the specially designated 'quiet carriage', there were still people loudly talking to each other, and shouting into mobile phones. There was, of course, no-one policing the quiet carriage, and even if he'd complained to the ticket inspector when he made one of his pass-throughs the likelihood was that the inspector would do nothing, or nothing more than say 'Quiet please', and Ren would have achieved nothing other than earning the enmity of the creeps making all the noise. Now he's in the quiet carriage on the way back home from the conference, and the situation is much the same.

Sitting a noisy quiet carriage is so much worse than sitting in a noisy normal carriage, Ren thinks, because when you're in a noisy normal carriage, although the noise might be annoying, you don't feel that those making it are doing anything wrong, other than being impolite. But when you're in a noisy quiet carriage, where there are people sitting next to 'This is a quiet carriage' signs and making a lot of noise despite that, you start having thoughts about boxing ears and flattening a few noses. 'Makes my blood boil,' he mouths to himself in a Cockney taxi-driving voice.

He's been in this situation before. Asking the miscreants if they could please be quiet as this is a quiet carriage, no matter how politely you ask, only gets them angry. He's been threatened before for this by a group of shell-suit-wearing chavs, straight out of central casting. (Central casting is pretty busy in Britain these days.) He reckoned at the time that he could have taken them all on, the sallow one, the weaselly one, the fat one, the even fatter shouty woman with dreadlocks, but he knew that CCTV footage of him brawling with trevs on a train would not be good for his career. So he has to sit there silently fuming. Quiet carriages may work in some of the more genteel parts of the country, assuming they are any of those places left. But in most of the the country they only make things worse.

And now they're all stuck in the sidings and the freight yards. He'd been counting down the minutes until he could get away from these braying donkeys who broadcast every intricate detail of their trivial daily business, when the train started to get slower and slower as it came in towards the station. And now they've been trapped together for forty minutes, looking at the graffiti. And still the phone calls go on. One woman seems to have called every single person she knows to inform them that she is stuck just outside Grayvington Station. Unless she's on her way to a big birthday party that all her friends have organised for her, Ren's not sure why all of them need to know this. (And if they're all going to the party, one phone call should suffice.) Ren has brought along *Material Beings* by van Inwagen, which was intended to be light reading that he doesn't have to take too seriously, but he should have brought a novel, or some history, because he can't concentrate well enough with all this noise to get anywhere with it.

He has a look through his briefcase for something else he can read that will require less concentration. He's brought along a few philosophy papers from his 'forever pile' – that is, a pile of reading to do that's gotten so big it can never be gotten through in one human lifetime – but he's not in the mood for any of them. He's also brought along some old copies of *Sausage Gravy* which he found in the library, but if he's reading those then it will be even harder to get the noisy people to take him seriously. He decides it's time to look at some of Lucius Birch's social psych papers that he also brought, as he's been meaning to read them as part of his investigation into Lucius's work. He picks one out called 'Dirt and Discrimination: Some Unconscious Biases That Drive Behaviour', co-written with Tobias Woolley from Lilydale University. Ren remembers this paper being reported on in the national and international media at the time. He starts to read it, and is amused at the coincidence – the research takes place in the Grayvington Railway Station, the very station that his train is currently starting to inch towards.

In the article Lucius describes how he set up some experiments at the station. In the first stage of the experiments the station was put into a deliberately messy state: the floors were made dirty, litter was dumped around the place, and the windows had dirt smeared on them. Some of the signs were temporarily replaced with copies that had been broken. In the second stage the same experiments were carried out after the station had been put back to normal.

The studies involved volunteer participants being given a short murder mystery story to read. They were then asked to say who they think committed the murder. More people picked out the black character as the murderer when the station was dirty than when it was clean. The participants were then asked to rate the trustworthiness of various strangers in photos. When the station was unclean the perceived trustworthiness of all the black people in the photos went down compared to when the station was clean, and vice versa for the white people in the photos. This applied to almost every participant in the study, even the black people.

Lucius claimed that this study shows that in virtually every mind black people are unconsciously associated with dirt, crime and slovenliness, and thus that we are all unconsciously racist. This applies even to people who aren't consciously racist. It even applies to black people themselves. The study also supposedly shows that when there is disorder we 'fall back on' stereotypes.

The article is noticeably thin. Not only is it short, it doesn't have much argument backing up these claims, or much on the logic that supposedly links the claims. But, Ren concedes, that's what non-philosophy papers are usually like. Under-argued. And poorly argued.

The response rate of the participants who were asked at the station to take part is eighty-five per cent, which seems abnormally high to Ren. You'd think it would be more like fifteen per cent. Would most train passengers getting off a train, most with places to get to, really agree to take part in a somewhat lengthy and involved study? He knows that thirty-five to forty per cent is considered a good response rate for a standard survey, so eighty-five per cent in this case seems very high. Still, he's not a field psychologist, so maybe it's not so unusual. In any case it's no basis for thinking that Lucius has fiddled his data.

He also notices that there is a lot of simplistic talk of 'stereotyping', as though stereotyping is a one-dimensional, monolithic trait that can be dialled up or down as a whole. As though anyone who starts thinking that all capitalists are rapacious money-gougers will automatically start thinking of all musicians as drug-taking weirdos. There may be someone who thinks both these things, but there's no guarantee that just because one stereotype gets cranked up, all the others follow. And different people will have different stereotypes in their head. (And how does a stereotype differ from a well-established generalisation anyway?) It's very poor that a publication with *World Science's* stellar reputation should have let Lucius get away with such cartoonish material. But then Ren's science friends have been telling him for a while now that *World Science* is going downhill.

But none of this proves anything. Ren looks at the graphs, and looks at what data there is, but it's pretty sparse. There's not much there to be going on with. Maybe an experienced statistician could still find something dubious in there, but there's nothing for him to work with.

There's also no information at all about how these experiments were carried out, and no acknowledgement of those who helped run them. That's not entirely surprising, because science journals as prestigious as *World Science* want to fit lots of articles into every issue, so they want their articles to be free of all excess, unnecessary material, so it's hard to get that sort of thing in even if you want to. But it means that he doesn't even know whether Lucius's collaborator Tobias helped out with running the studies, or did them all, or whether he just did some analysis.

He can't just ask the guy, because that might set alarm bells ringing prematurely. Is this other guy in on the fiddling, assuming there was fiddling? You might assume so, but then it would suit Lucius to find someone naive who has a spotless reputation to publish with, because that would help to deflect any suspicion. All Lucius would have to do is to say that he'll run the study, and the other guy just has to help with the analysis. So the collaborator might have no clue as to what's really going on – he's a collaborator, but not in the French sense. Lucius need only nudge a few figures in the right direction, and then he can send them off to his patsy.

Ren can't wait to get back to his office so he can get on the internet to look Tobias Woolley up. If only his attempt at creating a mobile internet connection had worked – he'd tried to create this by getting a laptop and jury-rigging a connection to his mobile phone, but the connection was too slow to even download his e-mail, let alone browse the internet. Browsing on the train is going to have to wait a few years.

Ten minutes later the train has finally arrived at the platform. As he's walking through the gates he gets an idea – he could talk to the staff at the station about Lucius's study, and pretend he's going to do something similar. Then he can ask them about how Lucius did his study, and who was involved. He could say he's doing 'experimental philosophy', something there's been talk of recently.

He talks to one of the security guards, who takes him to the general manager's office. After a ten-minute wait she shows him in.

'Thanks for seeing me,' he says. 'I'm a lecturer at the University, and I was wondering whether the station would be interested in hosting another psychology-style experiment.'

The manager looks puzzled. 'What do you mean, another experiment?'

'The station hosted a psychology experiment done two to three years ago by Doctor, now Professor, Lucius Birch. He asked questions of volunteer subjects when the station was dirty, and then when it was clean.'

'Dirty?'

'The place was made dirty for some questions, then it was cleaned up for later questions.'

'Nothing like that has ever taken place here.'

'Perhaps you weren't here at this point.'

'I've been in charge for five years. You say this happened two to three years ago?'

'Well, perhaps you were away at the time.'

'Nothing like that would happen without me knowing about it. Is that the article? Let me see it.'

She has a scan through the paper that Ren passes her. 'No way did this happen here. Has he changed the name of the station for some reason?'

'No.'

'Well, I don't know what this about, but this just didn't happen.'

'Perhaps the studies happened more than five years ago, and Lucius sat on the data for a while before publishing it.'

'No. If that had ever happened I would have heard about it.'

'You're definite about this.'

'Absolutely definite. I don't know what this guy is playing at, but this does not describe anything that took place at Grayvington Train Station.'

'Right.'

'Shouldn't there be a date in there saying when the studies took place?'

'There aren't any dates listed.'

'Really? This is supposed to be science, and there's no date? Does it at least say the year?'

'No, that's not listed.'

'Science must have changed since I was a girl. Then it was all about precision, and listing relevant factors. I liked all that. That's why I'm good at running a train station. Dates and times are important here.'

'Okay, well, what I should do then is go and see Lucius and ask him what's going on.'

'I think you should.'

'I'm sorry to have wasted your time.'

'Is this a psychology experiment you're doing on me now?'

'No, it isn't.'

'But you'd have to say that, wouldn't you, if you were. How do I know you're telling the truth?'

'We're not allowed to do things like that. There are ethics forms to fill in. Funding depends on it.' According to Miles, anyway. 'Any experiments that involve deception have to involve telling the subjects at the end of the experiment what has happened, and what was being tested.'

'But what if this isn't the end of the experiment?'

'It is.'

'You just said it wasn't an experiment. Now you're saying it is.'

'No, I mean, if it was an experiment, this would be the end, where we part ways. I wouldn't be allowed to pull the wool over your eyes at this point if it was an experiment.'

'That's if you're telling the truth.'

'You can go on the internet and look up psychology ethics. A department that did anything like that would be in big trouble and would risk getting its funding pulled.'

'But what if all those webpages have been planted... It's all right, I'm just yanking your chain. You go and have a word to your Professor, and ask him what's he's playing at. Perhaps he's doing an experiment on you.'

'Perhaps he's doing an experiment on a lot of people. Anyway, thanks for your time.'

'No problemo.'

On the bus home Ren digests what has just happened. He suspected that Lucius had been fiddling his data, but he never dreamed that he'd be so shameless as to just make whole studies up. But that looks like what he's done. Is there an alternative, innocent explanation? He can't assume at this point that there isn't. Maybe a study was done, and the general manager somehow didn't know about it. He can't challenge Lucius at this stage. He's an arrogant man, hungry for power and advancement. (Miles reckons he's now angling for a Professorship at Oxford or Cambridge, or London.) If Ren asks him about the study he'll try to brazen it out, and he may succeed. And then he'll start covering his other tracks too. More evidence is needed before he goes blundering in making serious allegations.

Then something else strikes him, something that has been niggling at his unconscious but which he's now in a position to see more clearly. A lot of Lucius's papers involved studies that were done at Lancedown University, the place that Lucius was at before he came to Grayvington, even though at the time of these papers Lucius had been at Grayvington for a few years. So Lucius was going back to his old place to carry out his studies. That isn't suspicious in itself, he's presumably got good contacts there, and they're presumably happy to have him come back to do some work, as it reflects well on them. But no-one from Lancedown University is listed on the papers as a co-author. He gets some papers out again to check. Yes, no-one from Lancedown is listed on any of the papers Lucius has where the studies were done at Lancedown University. That's very strange. Some are by Lucius only, some by Lucius and Tobias, and one is by

Lucius and someone else. But why would Lancedown let him come and use their facilities if none of their people were involved? Experimental facilities are usually in demand. Even empty rooms are in demand. Maybe he just hired the rooms out, for himself only. But none of the experiments described require anything much in the way of specialised facilities. He could easily have done them at Grayvington.

It's hardly a smoking gun, and there are possible explanations. Maybe he has family in Lancedown, and he spends time there, and that makes it convenient to carry out some studies at the University. Maybe these results are all from very old studies he did at Lancedown before he moved, and he didn't have time to analyse the data before he moved to Grayvington. There's no dates on any of these papers listing when the studies were carried out – well done the station manager for bringing that point up. But for all he knows that's standard practise in Psychology, although it's pretty piss poor if it is.

Still, this aspect of Lucius's work has increased Ren's suspicions. If Lucius is faking studies then it's very convenient for him that these 'studies' take place away from Grayvington, where no-one from Grayvington can notice that they never happened.

2001-02
Semester 2
Week 8
Monday

Miles has e-mailed Ren to come to a non-descript, out-of-the way pub on a Monday night. Ren assumes this is to do with Lucius – he told Miles on Friday his discoveries about Lucius.

When Ren gets there he finds Miles with two younger guys. Miles introduces them as Ken and Halberd. They're social psychology postgraduates. They're not Lucius's students but they've been working with him on the analysis of some of his studies.

After getting drinks in, they all sit down to talk.

'So,' says Ren. 'Is this about...?'

'It's about Lucius, yes,' says Miles. 'I've told these two what you've discovered. Or possibly discovered, we don't want to jump to conclusions just yet. But Ken and Halberd have been suspicious of Lucius for a while, as I discovered a couple of weeks ago, when we were having a drunken conversation in the pub about fraud in psychology. They've been analysing his work, and they think there are very suspicious things in Lucius's data.'

'Like data that's too good to be true?' says Ren.

'Yes,' says Ken. 'Sometimes, anyway. In the earlier work it looked more credible. Then it started to look more perfect as it went on. But recently it's got more credible again. This suggests, assuming he's massaging or even inventing his data, that he was careful early on to make the data look realistic, then he got blase about it for a while, and then he started being careful again, after realising that he was being too risky.'

'Something else we've discovered is the Cronbach Alpha scores on some of his studies are very low,' says Halberd.

'What's that?'

'It's a measure of the internal consistency, or reliability, of the responses made. Like if a respondent says on one question that they're an atheist, then they shouldn't say on another question that they believe in God. If the internal consistency is low then that's a problem. It means you may have participants who are just answering anything to the questions, and don't care, in which case you can't take the answers as confirming anything.'

'But it seems very unlikely that Lucius would get so many participants who are just answering the questions randomly,' says Ken.

'Low Cronbach Alpha scores can also be caused by questionnaires that have been poorly designed,' says Halberd.

'Lucius's questionnaire's, however, aren't poorly designed,' says Ken.

'So let me guess,' says Ren. 'Another thing that can explain low Cronbach Alpha scores is that the analyst has changed some responses without checking how this affects the overall consistency of that participant's answers.'

'Exactly,' says Ken.

'Hmm, not good for Lucius,' says Ren. 'Did Miles tell you that I noticed that a lot of Lucius's studies were done at Lancedown University, years after he left it, yet no-one from Lancedown was listed as a co-author?'

'He told us, yeah,' says Ken. 'We hadn't noticed that, but you're right, it's suspicious. Not in itself, perhaps, but along with everything else it's adding up to... well, I hesitate to use too strong a word here. Let's just see how we go with some more analysis. There's various other weird things to do with his work which we're taking a closer look at, and we've been setting up some replications of his studies, which we were hoping to do over summer.'

'He heard that they want to replicate his studies,' says

Miles, 'and he tried to discourage them. And now he's subtly trying to sideline them from his analysis team.'

'So what has he been giving you to analyse?' asks Ren. 'Do you ever see, like, responses written in different handwriting? Videos of people giving answers? Anything like that?'

'No, it's always just computer files of results.'

'Do you know anyone who has ever worked on one of his studies, and actually seen it happen?'

'No. These are further reasons why we were suspicious.'

'He loves the limelight, does Lucius,' says Miles. 'He isn't going to go down without a fight, and he'll try to take you all down with him. You guys sure you're prepared to face that?'

'I am a little scared,' says Halberd.

'I'm not,' says Ren. 'Bring it on, data-fucker.'

'I'm worried too,' says Ken. 'Perhaps we should have stayed out of it. But once we joined his analysis team, we had no choice. Imagine if he got exposed as a fraud later on, and it was known that we were on his team. How would that look?'

'So what about this Tobias Woolley guy?' says Ren. 'Do you think he's in on it?'

'We're not sure, but we suspect not,' says Halberd. 'If Lucius is faking everything then Tobias won't be involved in any studies, because there are no studies. And if Lucius just sends him data he's going to assume that it's kosher.'

'Tobias is very political, in a very admirable way, in my view' says Ken, 'but he's a bit gullible, I'd say, having met him at a conference once. Like, you could tell him anything, as he'd believe it, as long as it fits in with his politics.'

'Or maybe he suspects that Lucius is making it all up,' says Ren, 'but he's keeping quiet because the conclusions are politically agreeable to him.'

'Well, who knows?' says Ken. 'This is all speculation. All we can do is dig deeper.'

'It's depressing,' says Halberd. 'I never knew academia

could be so corrupt and political.'

'Oh, I knew that,' says Ren. 'What I never realised was that it could be so much fun.'

2001-02
Semester 2
Week 9
Wednesday

'Well, they've got a lot to protest about,' says Ren to George.

Ren and George are attending a reception being thrown by the University for the visiting Murnesian Head of State. They nervously scan the crowd protesting the visit. There's no sign of the usual protesters like Derek Lucas, Tony Shaver, Verna Leach, Harry Smales or Lucius Birch – they prefer to protest against democracies. The protesters are mostly Murnesian students and migrants who've experienced the semi-Communist one-party Murnesian state for themselves. There are far more protesters than Ren expected – they must have come from all over the UK for this opportunity to protest against the Murnesian government in a free country.

Ren is not happy about being part of the official reception for Ding Pingajing, the current Great Dignitary of the Worker's Paradise of Murnesia. Ding is generally regarded as the Murnesian Head of State, although some Murnesian commentators claim that the real power lies with Fan Jimjam, General Secretary and Inquisitor of the National Peoples' Consultative Committee of the Murnesian Communist Procuratorate. Tonight's reception has been brought forward from Friday, which most people have assumed is an attempt to thwart the protesters, but it's really because Ding needs to get back to Murnesia pronto to see off any attempt by Fan to officially replace him. (The University did consider banning all protest against the Murnesians, but eventually decided that this would look a bit too...

Murnesian.)

Ren is part of the reception because Robot has leant on him to go. Robot has been dropping heavy hints about probation; he's unhappy with Ren for various reasons, such as the TITE situation. Although Robot agrees with Ren that TITE is unfit for duty and needs to be reformed, he doesn't like the way Ren caused so much trouble over it last year, nor does he like the fact that Ren is still refusing to go back on the course (Ren's grounds are that Balderstone is still running it, and nothing much has changed). Ren needs Robot to support him getting through probation – without that support he'll lose his job. Although it would be a very unusual step for a Head not to support a lecturer in such a situation, especially one who is doing well with his publishing, Ren can't be sure that Robot isn't going to fuck him over while he has the chance. Hence, Ren is representing the department at the Murnesian State visit, which no-one else in the department wanted to do.

George has been roped in as well because he also wants to throw Robot a bone – he's refusing to retire on health grounds, even though he's officially sixty-three and near retirement anyway (and departmental gossip has his real age at more like seventy-three). Since his collapse at Tyson Kipnis's talk he's been fine, and carrying on as normal, but Robot, who wants to get rid of him so he can hire in someone more current, who'll apply for grants, keeps telling him he should retire before he dies giving a lecture. George says that he's going to go somehow, so why should it matter if it's in the middle of a lecture? Robot says that staying on in the job will make it more likely that he dies, but George says it's the other way around. Ren thinks with the way George is puffing and wheezing tonight with the effort of walking that he's going to die soon either way. But who knows? Maybe he'll outlive them all with his long-life dieting.

Philosophy is expected by the VC to have a presence at the reception because the Murnesian government has asked the University to set up a campus in Rankpo, one of its industrial cities. The idea behind the campus is that an exact copy of either Oxford or Cambridge will be built. ('Oxford or Cambridge' meaning, of course, the University colleges and buildings – the Blackbird Leys estate is unlikely to be included.) The choice of Oxford or Cambridge has yet to be decided; possibly a combination of the two will be the final result.

Both Oxford and Cambridge have rejected the offer to be involved out of hand, and both have threatened legal action should any of their buildings be copied. But the Murnesian government insists that there are no legal impediments to copying buildings in Murnesia, and has been courting various other UK Universities who might be interested in running the resulting University. Grayvington University is now in pole position to be in charge of 'Oxbridge University at Rankpo', which will earn it a massive fee, enough to outweigh, at least in Raven's mind, any resulting fallout with Oxford and Cambridge. (Raven's thinking seems to be that, as the University's relations with both Oxford and Cambridge are very low to start with, those relations can't get much worse. Also, he considers Oxford and Cambridge to be elitist institutions who need taking down a peg – although he's happy to talk in elitist terms about Grayvington when it suits him.)

As Philosophy has the reputation (whether truly or not) as being of central importance at Oxbridge, the VC has stressed to the Philosophy Department that it is important that Philosophy is represented at the reception. Robot was initially a bit reluctant, as he wasn't sure whether that would go down well in the wider philosophical community, but colleagues from other Universities assured him that no-one would care. It's not like Grayvington philosophers are going to shake hands with George Bush or Ariel Sharon. (Robot, being a kiss-up/kick-down type, would have acquiesced regardless.) So Ren and George got the squeeze to represent the department, along with Robot. The media hasn't been very interested in the Murnesian visit, to Raven's disappointment – he regards this collaboration as an event of historical, world-shattering importance – so there isn't going to be much in the way of publicity, whether positive or negative, anyway. Ren has only seen one camera crew here, and he recognises the woman speaking to camera – it's just a local news show.

The two philosophers walk past the protesters, who are behind barriers. Ren thinks of giving them a thumbs-up sign, but he decides it's best to do nothing. There's no knowing how they would react to that – they're really, really furious, shouting and screaming at everyone involved in the event. The air they're expelling at furious pace from their lungs threatens to knock George over; Ren holds onto his arm to steady him.

'I'm all right,' says George. 'My friends and I used to play cricket on the roads in the suburbs of London during World War II after they'd been bombed. I'm not going to get frightened by an unruly crowd.'

Hmm, thinks Ren, if you really were playing cricket in the war then you're probably older than sixty-three. But he keeps quiet. He's angry that he's been forced to do this event honouring real-life tyrants. He's angry with himself for agreeing to do it. The Murnesian state may not be as bad these days as in the time of the mass-murdering leader Kum Kwat, but it's still a place of terrible abuses (and there still exist forced labour camps), not to mention the fact that Pingajing is a veteran murderer from Kwat's time (as is his rival Jimjam). He wonders whether he can walk in and then sneak out without Robot realising, before he remembers that he and George are supposed to be sitting on the front row. Still, it's a good experience to see all this in action, even if he'd prefer to be with the protesters.

There are private security guards in front of the barriers, although not as many as there should be, given just how many angry protesters there are. The Murnesians are surrounded by their own security people, and Ren can see one of the Murnesian agents filming the crowd, which worries him. Will the video will be used later for identifying dissidents? There are also some white guys in suits he suspects are British security agents. They wear their suits far too well to be suited-up academics.

They go into the Terminal Building and head for Bear Hall, the largest and grandest hall on campus, used only for the finest occasions (and certainly not for student graduations). It had seemed unlikely to Ren that he and George really would be on the front row, but when they get into Bear Hall they see that the seating has been laid out in a semi-circular, concave, arrangement, so there's quite a few seats on the front row. And there they are – two seats with their names on them on the left end of the front row. Grant, meanwhile, has the honour of being seated on the dais along with the Murnesian and Grayvington bigwigs. George collapses into his chair like he's just completed a marathon, puffing heavily and looking a little green.

Bear Hall was originally designed in a mock-Renaissance style, with vaulted arches, but before completion a new architect took over, and the University administration of the day decided that a medieval theme would be more suitable, so some hasty changes were made to create an impression of the middle ages, and the hall was re-christened with its current name. One wall, the one furthest away from Ren and George, is full of stained-glass windows, whose mix of themes infuriates the University historians, but which do look very impressive to the less tutored eye.

Ren notices George's dandruff. It's all over his shoulders. It's so bad Ren can even see it on George's hair. Some of the flakes are rather large. And then he notices that everyone else has large flakes of dandruff all over them. He looks up at the ceiling. It's not dandruff. It's bits of the ceiling falling down.

The ceiling, as the University well knows, is in bad shape. That's one of the reasons why the hall isn't used very much. A full, noisy, humid house will occasionally cause bits of the ceiling to fall off, although it's never been this bad. It looks like the audience at a dandruff convention eagerly awaiting the announcement of a new miracle cure. The University keeps putting off the repair of the ceiling because the whole ceiling needs to be done with just the right sort of repair methods, and the ceiling can't be repaired without re-doing a lot of the Hall, and all of that is going to be expensive (although not as expensive, some people have noted, as a lot of the other things that Raven likes to spend the University's money on). But after today, Raven has been assuring people, the University will easily be able to afford to get the ceiling fixed.

After the audience has settled Raven calls for quiet. This allows everyone to get a good listen to the crowd baying outside. The Murnesians and their security guards look uneasy. Do these complacent Westerners really know how to handle an angry mob? Even Raven looks a little worried as he nervously adjusts his glasses. Ren, on the other hand, is content to stare at a blonde who is seated up on the dais near Raven. This must be Raven's wife. He's never seen Raven's wife before, but it's got to be her. Even the salacious gossip doesn't do her justice. She's stunning, and her languid movements leave Ren mesmerised. How on earth did Raven snag her?

Raven clears his throat.

'I'm proud to welcome to our University one of the world's great leaders, Ding Pingajing,' says Raven.

Pingajing stands up to receive the lukewarm applause of the crowd. He bows.

'Murnesia, as we all know,' continues Raven, 'is one of the world's most ancient countries, a country full of wisdom that goes back millenia, and a wisdom that continues to be displayed every day in the modern age. We still have much to learn from this wonderful, vibrant land, which sets us examples in so many ways.'

George lets out an awful groan. It sounds to Ren like he is trying to suppress a groan of pain, but it sounds to the audience like he's trying to suppress a groan of anger. There's muttering in the crowd. Ren can see Robot making neck-cutting motions to George with his hand. He notices that the Murnesian guards have also seen Robot do this. They're looking at Robot and George suspiciously. What does a neck-cutting motion indicate in Murnesia? Ren smiles at the agents to try to reassure them, but this seems to make them even more suspicious.

Raven pauses. His thunder is in danger of being stolen. He puffs himself up, puts on his most important look, and takes a deep breath: 'This is a historic day. It is perhaps the most historic day in history. It is the day when East and West finally come together in peace and harmony, through the means of a healing bridge built by scholarship. I am proud to announce that Grayvington University will build and manage the historic Oxbridge University in Rankpo.'

Raven pauses. The audience has gone deathly quiet, which provides a dramatic backdrop to the sounds of the crowd outside, who seem to have gotten louder, and – as far as one can tell from the inside – even angrier. The Murnesian guards look to have become even more jittery than before. Raven's wife, Dymphia, however, has closed her eyes and is rolling her head around as though she's in internal ecstasy, and Ren can't take his eyes off her.

Raven makes a little movement with his hands, and a few people cotton on that this is supposed to be the moment for rapturous applause. The clapping takes a while to get started, and as a result never really reaches the thunderous level Raven anticipated. The Murnesians look angry, like they've been disrespected. Ren has a look behind him to see what the faces on the audience look like. While he does this, and while the clapping is dying out, George gets to his feet unsteadily, with one clawed hand out in front of him, and staggers over towards the Murnesians on the dais. He lets out an angry shout, which probably sounds to the Murnesians as though he is remembering the relatives and friends who were murdered by the Kum Kwat regime, taken from their beds at 4am into the labour camps, never to be seen again. The Murnesian security guards draw their guns. Even the British agents put their hand into their jackets.

'George, no,' shouts Ren, who has turned back around to see what is happening. 'Stay away from there.'

Then George, with a face that looks like he knows that death is near, emits an agonised wail, while his shaking index finger seems to be pointing at Ding. As he howls, Ren shouts out that he's having a heart attack, but George's wailing drowns out his exact words. George reaches into the inside of his jacket to hold his heart. Or his oesophagus, whichever it is. Ren gets up to run to him, but it's too late. Milliseconds after George's hand goes into his jacket pocket three bullets are fired at him, and he's killed instantly.

The hall erupts like Ginnungagap has arrived. Guards fire bullets into the ceiling, but this just shoots out some of the lights and causes large sections of the fragile ceiling to fall onto the crowd, sending up clouds of plaster dust, reducing visibility, making things even worse. The screaming and shouting crowd frantically tries to run through the dust for the exit, but this results in half of them ending up on the floor, or getting knocked over into the chairs. More plaster falls, and more dust is thrown up. Some people are completely caked in white plaster. Those who do make it to the exit find that their way is blocked by the security guards from outside, most of whom have run into the building and to the hall to see what has happened.

The recent 9/11 terrorist attacks have made people jumpy, so it's no surprise that serious panic sets in when the sounds of crashing glass are heard in the room. The stained-glass windows on the side of the hall are being smashed through, and protesters wearing heavy gloves and batons start climbing in over the broken glass. Ren tries to get to George's body, but he can't see much through the haze of dust and the frightened crowds, and then he is knocked to the floor by the swirl, and is forced to crawl around just to avoid being trampled to death.

The Murnesian guards, sensing that they've killed an innocent man, and aware that they really don't want any more deaths on British soil, are reluctant to fire directly at the invading protesters, and they don't want to fire at the ceiling again, so they aim their guns off to the side, and shoot again to bring order. This does nothing but create even more terror in the audience, especially as some of the bullets have ended up going through the top parts of the stained-glass windows, resulting in glass falling onto the crowd from on high. The protesters and the guards start swinging clubs at each other. Ren can hear a mix of dull thuds, and the sound of bones cracking. He's going to get caught up in the middle of this. The hired security guards from outside can't get in, as they're caught between the audience trying to get out of the hall, and other protesters who are trying to get in.

Ren heads towards the side of the stage. He knows there's a door there at the back behind a curtain, which leads to a toilet and a small, hidden-away office. Even if the door is locked he can at least hide behind the curtain so he doesn't get caught up in the fighting.

He goes past the curtain and tries the door. It opens. The office behind it, next to the toilet, belongs to Foz McKendry, Research Fellow in History, who Ren knows through the occasional game in the University's social cricket league. (The story about Foz's crooked nose is that it was caused by a solution to a research problem coming to him just as he was facing up to a vicious bouncer, causing him to lose interest in the ball, until the point at which the ball managed to wrest his attention back again by hitting his nose and breaking it.) Ren sometimes comes to visit Foz, which is why he knows of this office's existence. Hardly anyone else does, not least because the door to Foz's office looks like the door to a broom closet. The door doesn't even go all the way to the floor. Foz thinks the room was most likely a storage room before the critical shortage of office space on campus meant that it got converted into an office. It's not an office that anyone else would willingly have, but Foz was desperate to have his own space, however small, rather than be in a noisy postgrad shared office.

Ren automatically tries the handle to Foz's office, even though there's no way he could be in. Surprisingly, it opens. Even more surprisingly, Foz is in his office.

'Hallo Ren,' says Foz. 'I'm surprised to see you here when there's some big event going on in the hall at the moment. In fact I was tempted to take a peek at what's happening because it's so noisy out there, but I thought I'd better not, as I don't think I'm supposed to be here this evening. Besides, I do have this paper I really want to finish tonight.'

'Can I come in?' says Ren. 'Bit of a disturbance going on. Political protests.'

As he says this a Murnesian politician and security guard appear in the small corridor as well.

'We need come in too,' says the politician, having a look inside the room. 'If that preases.'

'Why yes, you can all come in,' says Foz, 'but it'll be a bit of a squeeze. It's not the biggest room.' They go into office, which contains a small desk and chair, an armchair, Foz's cricket bag, and not much else.

'Where window?' says the guard.

'No window in here, it's completely internal,' says Foz. 'I know what you're thinking – I should complain, right? But for a Research Fellow on a two-year contract, this is as good as it gets.'

'What this?' says the guard, indicating a large vent in the top of the wall.

'Just a vent,' says Foz.

The guard goes over to it and rips the vent grille off the wall. Then he tries to get into the vent.

'You're not going to fit through there,' says Foz. 'I know what you're thinking. What does a historian know about spatial dimensions? But it's your shoulders. Anyone can see they're too broad.'

Foz, it appears, is right. The guard gets his body halfway into the vent, and then gets stuck. They can hear his muffled shouting. Ren and Foz try to pull him out, without success.

'Ignore him,' says the politician. 'I need to hide. Quick. Where can I hide?'

Foz indicates the room. 'Nowhere to hide in here, as you can plainly see.'

They can still hear shouting coming from the hall.

'Very important that I hide. Think crick. There always place to hide. In 1940s I once hid inside dead donkey for three hours. Save my rife. Think.'

'If you're the hide and seek expert, then you think,' says Foz, who feels his generosity has been taken for granted. 'I suggest you try the toilet next door.'

'The coffin!' says Ren. 'You can hide in Foz's coffin.'

'His coffin? Prease exprain.'

'The cricket bag. We call them coffins because they're long. Let's take the gear out.'

There's not much gear in the bag, just a bat, pads, gloves and a box (a box is a protector for the gentleman's area).

'It too small,' says the politician.

'Squeeze up. Pretend you're inside the dead donkey again,' says Ren. 'Time to save your life again.'

The politician steps into the bag, and bends down. Ren grabs him and pushes him all the way down, and then does the bag up around him. It's a tight fit, but he gets it closed.

Ren and Foz sit down, Ren on the armchair. The trapped guard shouts out for help again.

'I suppose we should try again with this guy,' says Foz.

'In a minute, says Ren, brushing the plaster dust from his hair. 'Did no-one come to your office to tell you that you couldn't come in this evening?'

'No,' says Foz. 'I did hear that something was going on a while ago, but I thought I'd just keep quiet until it was over. Got to get this paper finished, like I said, and I don't have good internet at home. What's the event?'

'It's the Murnesian state visit. Don't you pay attention?'

'Got more important things to think about. But I thought that guy in the bag looks familiar. He looks like Ding Pingajing.'

'I thought he looked familiar too,' says Ren. 'Don't think it's Ding though.'

They hear shouts from outside in the corridor. Ren grabs a book from the desk and starts reading it.

'During the Protestant reformation,' he says, 'a lot of Benedictine monasteries were closed. In your opinion, Dr McKendry, was this because the monastic vow was seen as...'

The door is wrenched open, and some masked protesters clothed in black rush in. They're momentarily taken aback by the scene in the office, but they quickly grab the security guard and yank him out of the vent. They take a look at his face. Deciding that he isn't one of their targets, they give him a half-hearted punch in the face, and turn to go.

Ren is tempted to draw their attention to the bag. The protesters don't seem to be murderous. If that really is Ding in there, perhaps he deserves a beating. But that would achieve nothing, except to make himself a personal enemy of Ding. The protesters rush out again.

'Are you going to be playing in the Humanities versus Sciences match this Sunday?' says Foz.

'I wasn't planning to,' says Ren. 'But maybe I'll get along. We'll see.'

'I hear Sciences are going to have their new fast bowler from Biology playing this time. He's marvellous to watch. Not so much fun playing against him. Really gets the ball to zip about.'

'What was his name again? Gribben? Cribbens? Gibbon? Gibson?'

'Can't remember. He's played for Oxford against some county sides. Too good for our league, really.'

The security guard gives them a disbelieving look, and sneaks outside for a peek. Three minutes of cricket and history conversation later, he comes back.

'All crear,' he says, unzipping the bag. The delitescent Murnesian removes himself from the holdall. He seems a little ginger, and rubs his bones, but says, 'That was a piece of the pie compared to hiding in dead donkey. Bring back many memories of dark times.' He turns to Ren and Foz. 'You show sang-froide under pressure.'

'Yes, time is ticking away,' says Foz, getting the wrong end of the stick, 'but I think there's still enough time left tonight to do a decent job.'

'He means sang-froid in the face of the riot,' says Ren.

'Oh, that,' says Foz.

'Cruel as crucumber,' says the bagman, who is looking at Ren, and ignoring Foz. 'What your name?' he says.

'My name is Dr Ren Christopher.'

'Thank you Dr Christopher,' says the Murnesian, who bows. 'You save my rife.'

'Nothing to it,' says Ren. 'Anyway, I don't think the protesters were out to kill anyone.'

'Don't be deceived, they deadly dark enemies of humanity who kill mirrions if they have chance. That why we have to riquidate them. Orr of them. We must not ruse.'

'It's so wonderful to hear of your cultural activities, which provide a fresh perspective on our squabbles here in England,' says Ren.

'Ret's go,' says the guard, pulling his fellow Murnesian out the door.

'Do you think I'll be able to stay here for the rest of the evening?' says Foz. 'I really do want to get this paper finished tonight.'

'I don't think that's going to be possible. You'd better save your work, grab your books, and get out of here before the police shut it down for days.'

Now that the danger has passed, thoughts of George's fate bubble to the surface.

'They killed George.'

'Who? You mean old George Bagnall? Who killed him?'

'The security guards. He was having a heart attack, and

they thought he was going to assassinate Ding. So they shot him.

'Oh my. That's what those bangs were. I thought they were fireworks.'

'It happened right in front of my eyes. I think I'm in some sort of a state of shock. Delayed shock. I don't feel right. My body feels all weird. My head's starting to feel weird too.'

'Did anyone else get killed?'

'Don't know. Anyway, get out quick.'

Ren turns to leave.

'What are you going to do?' says Foz.

'I'm going to see if I can find out what's happened to George.'

'Sure. Quite right. Well, hopefully see you on Sunday,' says Foz. 'And if you do come, don't forget your gloves this time.'

'Foz, in order for you to be there on Sunday you'll need to leave this office soon, okay?'

'Sure,' says Foz reluctantly, looking at his screen in a worried way. If he can just finish this section...

2001-02
Summer break

2001-02
Summer break
Early June
Thursday

Compton knocks on Ren's door.

'Er... you might want to go to the office right now.'

'What is it?' says Ren.

'A little present from Murnesia.'

'What?'

'It's best if you take a look yourself.'

Ren hurries along to the departmental office. The whole disaster of the Murnesian state visit is something he'd gladly never think of again, but of course everyone he meets wants to talk about it. It certainly created some media interest in the Murnesian visit, to put it mildly, although obviously not in the way Raven was hoping for. Ren avoids talking about it, mostly because of George's death.

Thankfully no-one else but George was killed that evening, but thirty-seven people were injured, three seriously, including the Professor of Chemical Engineering who has just come out of his coma. Twelve Murnesian politicians and delegates were injured by being clubbed by protesters, two ending up with broken skulls, and most with broken bones somewhere about their person. The protesters who attacked them didn't fare much better.

George's funeral had been spoiled somewhat by the unnecessary presence of the Murnesian ambassador and his wife, and a gaggle of Murnesian security service agents. It was hard to properly say goodbye to George when agents from the same security services who had killed him were sitting nearby, even if the security services had some claim to say that they couldn't really be blamed for opening fire on him. The autopsy report said that it looked like he'd had a massive heart attack just before he was shot – although it was hard to be sure due to the damage done by two bullets which had entered his heart – so he may have died anyway. It turned out that George was really seventy-one, so at least there was the small satisfaction that he had lived a longer life than had initially been supposed.

As they walk along the corridor, Compton says, 'I think it's a small token of appreciation from Ding.'

Gossip has it that Raven is nearly spastic with rage at Philosophy for ruining his 'most important event in human history.' The whole 'Oxbridge in Rankpo' project has been postponed indefinitely following the bad publicity, which Raven regards as a financial disaster, especially now that Bear Hall will have to be completely rebuilt, although many others in the University think the University has avoided a financial disaster, as the latest rumour is that there was never going to be any money up front, and the University was expected to stump up a lot of the cost of building the campus itself. 'Raven's vanity project, it might have bankrupted us,' is the gist of the latest gossip doing the rounds.

Raven, however, is unable to take revenge on Philosophy, due to one of Philosophy's distinguished Professors having been shot dead by the Murnesians, and because Ding is so grateful to Ren. The man in the cricket coffin who looked like Ding, and who Ren saved from a beating, or worse, was not Ding, but Ding's beloved older brother, and political adviser, Dong. Ding and Dong have been inseparable from childhood, and it was Dong who drew Ding into the imaginary delights of the coming Communist utopia in the 1950s. So while an unbalanced Raven fantasises about doing grievous harm to the Philosophy Department, he is currently impotent.

Although Ding is grateful to Ren, Ren's actions during the riot have not been made public. He has been asked by the Murnesians to say nothing, and although he doesn't like the Murnesians, he has no desire to announce to the world that he saved a veteran Communist killer. Foz doesn't want to say anything either, although Foz is not in the Murnesians' good books because he told Dong to go and hide in the toilet. Raven and Robot are the only other people who know what Ren did, plus Compton, who Ren has told under a condition of complete secrecy.

Ren goes into the office.

'Oh,' is all he can say. 'I wasn't expecting that.'

In the office are two life-size white marble statues, one of George, and one of him.

The former statue sees George dressed in a toga, with a youthful, powerhouse body and rippling muscles, posing mightily, with a book held out well in front of him. His face, however, is the face of old George, with his wrinkles, squint, and glasses, so an unkind person may be tempted to speculate that he is holding the book that far away so that he can focus on the words. However, a closer examination of Marble George's eyeline reveals that at the moment that has been immortalised in stone he is looking not at the book but into the far distance, as though he is searching for a glimpse of an ancient, transcendent truth not easily discernible by lesser mortals.

The general effect is of a Disney version of Hercules that's had George's face superimposed. And George's face looks very much like it does on the photo of him that is still up on the departmental website, so there's no prizes for guessing where the sculptor got their inspiration from.

The statue of Ren has him playing cricket, batting, with pads and gloves on. He's in mid-stroke, playing a straight drive, with the bat near his feet. It doesn't look quite right, at least not to a cricketer, because his head is too straight. It isn't leaning over to his right-hand side like it should be with that sort of shot. His face also looks very much like his photo on the departmental website. It's not a bad photo, that one, thinks Ren, and his face in marble doesn't look too bad at all.

'Which one's you, Ren?' laughs the departmental administrator, Wendaline Clugston.

The statues stand atop their own bases. Ren's just has his name on it, whereas George's has his name, and the dates 1938 – 2002, on it. 1938 is the birthdate for George that appears on several old internet sites, but as has been recently revealed, George was really born in 1931.

'Why do you get a statue?' says Wendaline. 'You weren't shot.'

'I was sitting next to George,' says Ren.

'Why doesn't Grant get one? He was there too.'

'A statue of Grant would be otiose, seeing as he already exists in statue form,' says Compton.

'Do you think they expect us to put these in the courtyard?' says Wendaline.

'The dates on George's statue would indicate that,' says Compton. 'I don't know about Ren's. As a junior member of staff, and one who is very much alive, with, one would hope, his best achievements still to come in the decades ahead, I think that putting this in the courtyard would not be appropriate, whatever the intentions of the Murnesians. Ren did, after all, escape entirely unscathed.'

'Totally agree, Compton,' says Ren. 'I think I'll take it home.'

'You'd have to ask Grant about that,' says Wendoline.

'Was it addressed to me, or the department?'

'Let me look at the wrapping.'

Wendoline sifts through the masses of wrapping and finds that the statue of Ren came addressed to Ren.

'It's mine, then. Anyway, I can assure you that Grant will have no interest in claiming for the department a bad statue of me playing cricket. I doubt he's even going to want that one of George. It can't go up in the courtyard, surely? It'll only make people laugh. Hardly fitting for George.'

'How are you going to get yours home?' says Wendoline.

'I'm going to take it right now,' says Ren. Before anyone sees it, he thinks. 'I'll go get my car and park it out the back in the loading bay.'

'It won't fit in your car,' says Compton.

'I'll tie it to the roof.'

'What with?'

'String.'

'String?'

'String. From the stationery cupboard. Can you get a couple of balls, and some scissors, while I get my car?'

When Ren comes back he has brought with him a blanket from his car.

'Let's put this over it to protect it' he says, although really he just wants to hide it from view.

He and Compton carry the statue to the lift.

'Have you seen the latest stories from Murnesia?' says Compton while they're in the lift, which is, thankfully, unoccupied by anyone else other than Compton, Ren, and Marble Ren. 'That Ding is set to be toppled by Fan, because of the shame Ding brought upon Murnesia due to George getting shot?'

'Yes, I saw that. I don't suppose George ever thought that he'd be responsible for the downfall of an Asian dictator. Even if he is getting replaced by a near-identical Asian dictator. Do you think this is real marble?'

'No idea.'

They carry Marble Ren, or Pseudo-Marble Ren, over to Ren's car.

'I'm not sure this is a good idea,' says Compton. 'That heavy base unbalances it. It may even snap off if the statue is held horizontally without any support for the base. Why don't you wait, and get someone with an estate car or van to help you take it later?' says Compton.

'No way. I want this thing out of here immediately, before anyone else sees it.'

Ren puts the blanket on top of the car, to prevent scratches, and they place the statue on top of that. Ren folds the blanket over the rest of the statue, and then winds the car windows down.

'We just wrap the string over the statue, and then through the windows, over and over,' says Ren. 'We need to do it enough times so that the bands of string are thick, otherwise it won't be strong enough.'

'It's going to need to be tight,' says Compton. 'Any looseness could be fatal. You're trying to hide this thing, but if it goes through someone's windscreen and kills them you'll be international news.'

They start tying it, but then Compton looks at his watch.

'Shit, I have to go, got a class to teach. Sorry. You can wait for me if you like.'

'I can do it myself. You go.'

Ren uses up all of the two balls of string tying up the statue, getting it as tight as he can, but he can't do it as tight as he could if he had someone helping him.

Then he drives off, very carefully. All is well until he gets about halfway home, when he can feel the the statue starting to slip around a bit. He pulls over, cuts the knots with the scissors which he's brought with him, and re-does the string. Then he drives the rest of the way home very slowly. He gently pulls up on the apron at the front of his house.

He gets out and looks at the statue on the car, satisfied with himself. A bit of string and bit of improvisation is all you need to handle most things, he thinks. He cuts the string, and pulls the statue into his arms. As soon as he lifts it away from the car, however, he feels the heavy base threaten to get away from him. This is a lot harder with just one person to lift than with two. He can't get control of the base, and the smooth stone slips through his arms. The base hits the concrete hard, and the lower half the the statue disintegrates into rubble.

The Indian man who works in the corner shop across the road runs over to help.

'Oh dear,' he says. 'You should have asked for some help. That is the end of that. Was it expensive?'

'Nothing to worry about,' says Ren breezily. 'Just a joke statue made up by some art students. I'll just keep the top half. Be easier to get in the house now.'

The shopkeeper goes back to his shop, and Ren takes the upper half into the house. It takes him a while to clean up the rubble, and then he notices that despite the blanket, the roof of his car has some nasty scratches on it. It's not easy being a hero of the Murnesian revolution, he thinks. But things could be worse – most heroes of the glorious Murnesian socialist revolution ended up with a bullet in the back of their head. So he goes inside for a sit-down and a coffee and a counting of his blessings.

2001-02
Summer break
Late June
Friday

Derek watches as the last group of undergraduates, including Wren English, leaves the party. Then he yells across the room, 'Fugg you, Compdon, you fugging liggspiddle.' He staggers towards Compton while holding his wine bottle. 'You're a fugging fashist. You should be drummed out of the depardmend for your disguzting views.'

'I think you've had too much to drink, Derek,' says Compton, who is fairly sober, as he intends to drive home. He realises before everyone else that this is not a joke, and Derek is deadly serious.

It's the afternoon of the official departmental end-of-the-academic-year party. The students got their results a few days ago, and the graduating third-years have been invited to mingle and drink with the staff and postgrads in one of the larger departmental teaching rooms, with free wine and cheese laid on by the department. About fifteen to twenty bright and naive students usually turn up for this, happy students who have done well or better than they expected to. Occasionally a disgruntled one comes along who glares at the lecturers they imagine are responsible for them not getting the degree class they thought was their due. But generally it's a festive occasion, with innocent, optimistic students dreaming their dreams of a glorious future, and feeling a little misty-eyed about the department.

One especially wide-eyed type is the eumorphous Wren English, who got a First, and who has been in several of Ren's classes in the last two years. She's been talking to him this afternoon, and if Ren isn't mistaken, is aggressively thrusting her breasts towards him as if to say, 'You're allowed to play with these now.' Thankfully her classmates have just dragged her away to go somewhere else, because Ren is getting very tempted to take her up on the offer.

There is more wine than anyone can drink today, but Derek is trying his best. So is Ren. And so are some of the postgrads. Grant and Adelaide, of course, are not here. Neither is Simon or Adalia, and Panos left absolutely yonks ago for the Spanish beaches, neglecting all his moderating duties, which someone else has had to do. Derek, for once, didn't skip out on his marking, so perhaps he is feeling unusually morally virtuous at this moment. Or maybe he is pissed-off because he has had to do some drudge work.

The Continentals look delighted to see Derek lay into one of his fellow analytics for his political failings, but none of them join in. Derek can cop the fallout himself.

'You're a cund. A right-wing baztard,' yells Derek, his ocular matrices of bloodshot veins blazing like two fiery mazes in Hell, impossible labyrinths which the occupants will never escape from. 'We never should've hired you.' Can you have two impossible labyrinths in Hell, Ren wonders. Maybe one's a reflection of the other? 'Shid knows what politics you're filling your studenz heads wid.'

'I don't proselytise to the students about politics. Neither should you,' says Compton.

'You fugger. You Thatcher-loving fugger,' says Derek, staggering and swaying and starting to foam slightly at the mouth. 'You fug Pinochet up the arz at weegends. Workhouses and chimney-sweeps, that's what you want, isn't it? Goozestebbing, lev, right, lev, right, oh fug, my helmed's come off, well, we'll just have to shoot you for thad, won't we? Oh yes, if you can'd keeb your helmed on then you'll have to be shot like a dog.'

Derek is getting closer to Compton, and he starts stabbing his finger at him.

'That's whad it's all aboud, you Nazi gunner man wid a

gun and big knife to shood people who don'd do whod you dell 'em. Cracken skulls with your gun cos you'd run oud of bulleds and pizzing on the dead bodies and biding fingas off to get at the rings onna the fingers.'

Derek takes a big swig from his bottle, three, four, five glugs.

'You're the disgrace, Derek,' says Compton, who is for once not amused. 'You're the one acting like a fascist. It's never far from the surface with you left-wing authoritarians.'

'Don'd you fugging talka me like that, you'll be oudda here, sag you tomorrow.'

Walter comes over to Derek.

'Derek, that's quite enough. Let's break it up now.'

'Nah, got to tell the right-wing cund some more home truths. We don't wand him here. Drive out the Thadcherites.'

Walter tries to take Derek's arm. Derek breaks free, and raises his arms (and the bottle) in the air, and shouts wildly. 'Oooooh, ooooh, I'm the great Comdon and I say lefties are bad. I'm a bad man becoz Combdon says so. I only freed the slabes and gave all the workers enough money to lib on, but Combdon comes in and says we're liars.'

Tony and Verna decide that that's enough, and they help Walter to remove Derek from the room.

'Ged him out now,' says Derek as he's taken outside. 'If no-one else'll do it I'll throw him oud myself with my frigging pinkie.'

'There you go,' says Compton, 'the left in action.'

'He's just drunk,' says Bill Porterfield.

'He's not just drunk. That was political intimidation, a game the left plays all too well. Why is he allowed to get away with it?'

'Will he get away with it?' asks Ren.

'Of course he will. What's going to happen? Nothing. Even if he's talked to, he'll just say, oh, I was drunk, just made a few personal comments about someone I don't get on with personally. And that will be that. Not even a slap on the wrist.'

'Academics are only human,' says Bill. 'People fall out, get drunk, say a few unwise things.'

'But this isn't a personal matter. This isn't just Derek and I not getting on. This is straightforward political thuggery.'

It's obvious that what Compton is saying is not going down well with some of the postgraduates, particularly a group of three left-wing postgrads, Huey, Dewey and Louie, as Ren calls them (more specifically, Huey Long, John Dewey, and Louis Althusser), who look up to Derek. (Not that Derek is willing to be a supervisor to any of them. Derek doesn't have postgrads because they're too much work.)

It's also not going down well with Zack Paddlemore, a graduate student from America, who Ren has labelled 'Zack of Crap'. (Ren managed to convince people that he'd heard this from someone else. Now everyone calls Zack this, including Zack sometimes.)

Zack is a type who's hard to avoid in a British Humanities department. He's the very fat, loudmouthed, goateed, left-wing American who has come to Europe to escape the oppression of conservative America, and he will loudly tell everyone, at all times, of how awful and right-wing America is, and how you shouldn't confuse him with George Bush, no sir-ree, he's no fascist, and he loves Europe and its progressive culture and its cobblestones, in fact its culture full-stop, because America has no culture other than McDonalds. This sort of walking modern Humanities infestiche always sounds for all the world like he's never lived in the U.S. and has got all his ideas about his own home country from one of those British TV documentaries where an arch-wit goes to America to make fun of enormous donut-eaters who think the best reading material is the *TV Guide*.

Zack desperately wants to hang out with Huey, Dewey and Louie, but his correct politics don't make up for the fact that he's an embarrassment, and they do not want to be lumbered with a girl-repellent. For all his love of all things British and European, Zack has no clue about what passes as cool in Britain or Europe. Or, for that matter, the US.

'Derek's just passionate about politics,' says Zack, in his always full-bore voice. 'I wish people in the States were that committed.'

Huey, Dewey and Louie don't say anything, but Zack is too thick to know when his opinion is not wanted, not even by the leftists.

'I remember when one of our Professors...'

'Blythe, it's probably best to let it drop,' says Walter, who has come back, letting Tony and Verna look after Derek.

'I'm going home,' says an angry Compton.

'Blythe?' says Zack.

'Fucking left-wingers poison everything,' Compton can be heard saying as he leaves.

'Why's he calling me Blythe again?' mutters Zack, flustered and confused, to no-one in particular.

Walter always calls Zack 'Blythe' because there used to be an exactly similar pinguedinous American postgrad in the department before Zack arrived called Blythe Tubshaw, and Walter's ageing memory centres cannot permanently register the change in personnel due to the qualitative identity between the two goateed, maladroit anti-American Americans.

'He thinks you're the ghost of his dead son,' whispers a bum-fuzzled Ren, who's thinks he's being hilarious, to Zack. 'His son Blythe drank rat poison one night by mistake which Walter left out in a Lucozade bottle, and ever since then he's haunted Walter's office. Although only when Walter is trying to sort out admissions.'

'I don't understand what this is,' says Zack.

'You see, Blythe doesn't want any new young people in Walter's life, probably because he thinks he should be the one young person in Walter's life. Although possibly it's because he wants to save them from drinking more of

Walter's rat poison.'

'What is this?' Zack shouts. 'Are you trying to be funny?'

'You want funny?' says Ren, giggling. 'This is funny.' He goes to the corner of the room and gets his satchel, and starts to rifle through it. 'Where is it?' he mutters theatrically.

'What are you looking for?' shouts Zack eventually.

'Your last annual PhD progress report,' says Ren.

'You bastard,' says Zack in a strangled voice. Possibly he's trying to do an English accent. 'You think that's funny? This is funny.' Zack sticks two fingers up at Ren, in his best English finger accent, and storms off.

'For fuck's sake, I'm just joking, Zack,' Ren yells after Zack, but Zack is off.

'Shit,' says Ren. 'I'm too drunk to even gently tease a postgrad.'

'It wasn't exactly gentle teasing,' says Aaron Bach, another postgraduate. Aaron is a Christian hippy who wears clothes made out of burlap bags to indicate his humbleness.

'I know, that's what I'm saying,' says Ren. 'It was a failed attempt at gentle teasing. Failed by reason of drunkenness. A common enough reason for failed degrees, failed marriages, failed attempts at intercourse, and failed attempts at teasing.'

'It doesn't help that Walter still calls him "Blythe"' says a postgrad called Camilla Fortescue.

'Yeah,' says Ren, opening another bottle, 'and now Walter's nowhere to be seen, so we'll forget to tell Walter not to call Zack "Blythe" until the next time he calls Zack "Blythe"'.

'It's not clear that Zack isn't just Blythe with a new haircut,' says Rowan Loder, another spiritually-minded hippy postgraduate. Unlike Aaron, though, Rowan is not a Christian, and unlike Aaron he is not above cracking a few jokes at the expense of his fellow postgrads.

'Derek really went off on one today, didn't he?' says Bartek Sokolsky a Polish postgraduate, after noticing that Huey, Dewey and Louis are not listening in, and Bill

Porterfield has gone. Bartek recapitulates his native country's history by changing his political opinions wildly from day to day. Yesterday he was a Communist, but a few days before that he had been a Randian. 'What brought that on?'

'Leftists like public intimidation,' says Ren. 'Helps with the social ostracism. You'll have to learn that if you want to be a Communist.'

'I'm not a Communist any more' says Bartek. 'Now I'm a syndicalist.'

'Economic syndicalism, or anarcho-syndicalism?' says Ren. 'Presumably not national syndicalism?'

'What's the difference?' says Bartek.

'I could tell you,' says Ren, 'but then I'd have to kill myself. Anyway, what's made Derek extra pissed-off with Compton is that Compton made it clear to the department and to Derek that he would not be rescuing them from Derek skipping out on his exam marking again. Compton's really the only one who can mark Derek's exams these days, so if Compton won't do it, then Derek can't sneak off to Paris and leave Compton to save the ship from sinking, as he has done for the last two years in a row.'

'Lecturers are allowed to just not do their exam marking?' says Bartek. 'Really?'

'No, they're definitely not allowed to do that. But somehow Derek has done it regularly, and has gotten away with it. This year it was made clear to him by Grant, who has just about had enough of him, that this was not on, and that he would face disciplinary action if he did it again. So Derek is in a bad mood.'

The postgrads are marvelling at this gossip. Ren belatedly realises that he is being unwise in drunkenly sharing so much departmental dirt with the postgrads in so public a way. He looks at his watch.

'I'd better go,' he says. He doesn't say where he's going. It's only to the student bar to meet Miles, but he doesn't want any of the department's postgrads tagging along when he's this drunk. Miles, at least, doesn't mind him being a drunken fuckwit, as long as he's amusing.

Ren takes the unfinished bottle of wine with him, swigging it as he goes. He's walking past the University's statue of Engels when a figure gets up from behind it. 'Hey Ren,' it says.

Ren is bewildered when the figure turns out to be Derek.

'Derek?' he says, like he's just discovered a long-lost schoolfriend living as a tramp.

'Can I have a drinky-poo?' says Derek.

Ren nods and passes him the bottle.

'I kind of expected you to be...'

'Whad?' says Derek.

'Well, unconscious, mainly,' says Ren. Or locked up, he thinks. 'What are you doing here?'

'Just going home, thaz all. Taking a while though. Can't remember the besd route to take.'

'Where do you live again?'

'Lidden.'

'Where's that?'

'No, lizzen. Lizzen me.'

'What?'

'Compden's an absolude fugger. Absolude hunerd cent fugger. So fashisd thad he'd have us all gilled.'

'Oh come on Derek, that's absurd.'

'No, he is, really. He's a Dory gunt through and through. You're all right dough, Ren,' Derek says, slapping Ren on the back. 'I lige you. You sdill have promise. Bud you've godda ged away from Comden. Heze ebil.'

Ren tries to take the bottle back from Derek.

'Why are you taging my boddle?'

'Just wanted a drink, Derek. Is that all right?'

'Courze id's all ride,' says Derek. 'Ged id in you, boy.'

Ren takes a drink.

'Nod doo much though,' says Derek, taking it back. 'You're a good guy, Ren. We all lige you. But why do you lige that creep?'

'He's not a creep. He's a good guy who just has very different political opinions than you.'

'He can't be a good guy when he says whad he says. Deregulation. Freedom. More flexibilzity for employers. Bollogs. All code words for screwing the worgers.'

'You seem to agree with him when it comes to some of the more modern and progressive aspects of the left, though. Feminism. Racism. Queer Studies. Postmodernism. That sort of thing.'

'Gorze. All just bullshid broughd in to drain more power to da lefd. Don't agree with it, but idza good polidigal tagtig. Bud id undermines druth and science and jusdice, so izza bad idea long-derm.'

'Look, I gotta go.'

'No, Ren, I haben't finished. We godda thingk of a way to screw that bastard over.'

'Fucking hell, Derek, you're the one sounding like a fascist.'

'Gotta fight fire wid fire. Destroy him before he destroys us.'

'Go home and get some sleep Derek. You're raving.'

Ren makes to take the bottle back from Derek.

'Ged your own fugging boddle,' yells Derek. He stumbles away with it. 'Ged fugging Comden to get you a fugging boddle if you think he's so bruddy great.'

Derek goes off singing a song about the struggle carrying on. Possibly it's *The Internationale*, but Ren's interest in Communism hasn't yet extended to much of a knowledge of its musical works.

When Ren gets to the bar he finds that Miles is pretty drunk too, Miles having been to the Psychology department's equivalent end-of-academic-year wine-and-cheese party.

Ren tells Miles about Derek's behaviour. Miles hasn't got anything equivalent to amuse Ren with.

'You know,' says Ren, 'I think there's another reason again why Derek hates Compton.'

'What?'

'Derek is jealous of Compton because Compton is now the one who's young, relatively speaking, and good-looking and charming, which Derek still wishes he was.'

'Wouldn't that apply to virtually three-quarters of the faculty as against the remaining quarter?'

'No, because most academics are not, and never have been, charismatic and good-looking.'

'Present company excepted, of course,' says Miles.

'That is not for us to judge,' says Ren. 'Whatever the mirror tells you. But I hadn't finished. It's also because Compton is now the rebel. He's the one now rebelling against the majority opinion, not Derek. Sure Derek is harder left than most academics, but I don't think he feels that his opinions mark him out anymore.'

'So he's no longer the sexy dissident?'

'That's it. As David Stove said, the cruelest fate which can overtake enfant-terribles is to awake and find that their avowed opinions have swept the suburbs. Even railing against the higher-ups doesn't mark him out any more because everyone does that now, including Compton. The only way that was left for Derek to rebel was to behave badly and do things like not mark his essays or his exams, but that just made him seem like a selfish prick. And now he can't even do that any more.

'So he got what he wanted, everyone is now left-wing, and...'

'And it's killing him.'

2001-02
Summer break
Late June
Saturday

Ren's brain no longer fits in his skull. It must be monstrously swollen – he can feel it bursting against the side of his skull. If the skull doesn't break soon and release the pressure he's going to die from the pain and the nausea. If he was capable of movement he'd dash his head against the wall to try to break his skull to let his brain expand. Even if that doesn't work at least it might knock him unconscious, and give him a few more hours respite.

There is no longer vision. Or sound. Or touch. Non-existence is now upon them, obliterating them from history. They no longer exist, not even in a possible world. They are no longer even logically possible. Even the rules of logic have been altered by this blinding pain. Everything has been changed by it. No, nothing has been changed, because those old things never really existed. They're not real, and never were. Only this pain is real. The pain is all there is. Either it exists, or there is nothingness. Ren wants there to be nothingness. No pain, no Ren, just nothing. Everything must go.

But he knows the pain is winning. He isn't strong enough to defeat it. He wishes it would just kill him. But it's too clever for that. It's just stopping short of killing him, to prolong the agony for as long as possible. I give up, Ren says to it. I'll admit to whatever you want if you just stop. I'll sign the confession papers sight unseen, Mr Yezhov. I'll never touch the demon juice again if you'll just quit it. I'll never drink again anyway. Why do I put this poison in such toxic amounts into my body? What sort of lunatic would do such a harmful thing to themselves in the supposed name of pleasure? Perhaps if I can just cut this part of my brain out things will be all right, like Rialto Magnussen does to rats. No doubt I won't be quite the same afterwards – I should have gone to Rialto's talk to see what it does to the rats – but at the moment that's a price I'm willing to pay.

Ren goes on thinking like this for a while, when the realisation starts to dawn that he's not in his own bedroom. He doesn't dare open his eyes yet, but he can tell by the way the bed feels, the smell, even the acoustic ambience, that this is someone else's place. Whose? He doesn't remember much from the time he bought a second round of triple vodkas for himself and Miles. There's a hazy memory of some tequilas after that, and that's about it. He's broken his own rule of not getting hammered in the student bar, although at this time of year it doesn't really matter because the only students who were around were the graduating third-years who are leaving. But who on Earth would go to bed with someone as drunk as he must have been? Someone equally drunk? Or someone who really, really fancied him?

He hears the door open. 'Ren?' says a female voice. It jolts him, because he thinks he recognises it, and because it's like soothing honey being poured over his injured brain. It's definitely the voice of Wren English. He's gone to bed with the delectable Wren English and he can't remember? She comes over to the bed, and strokes his head. That hurts, but he doesn't want her to stop. 'I've brought you a coffee and some painkillers in case you need them.'

Ren can't talk yet, but he wants to see her, and he wants those tablets, so he rouses himself to roll over and open his eyes. She's dressed in respectable clothes, and looks gorgeous, if a little crumpled. He takes the tablets and gets a bit of coffee down him.

'You may not remember me saying this now, but my parents will be here soon. We agreed it would not be the best idea for them to find me in bed with one of my lecturers.'

'Srakofta. Bznejus,' says Ren. He's not even sure what these words were supposed to come out as. But he is trying to indicate his agreement. He tries again. 'Howzoon?' It comes out croaky, but audible as English.

'Could be ten minutes. Could be half an hour.'

'Szofajedon,' he says. He tries very, very hard to move. Very slowly his body responds. In three minutes time he has managed to sit up on the bed.

Wren watches him with amused delight. 'Poor baby,' she says, stroking his back. 'I knew I should have dragged you off before you drank all that whisky. Still, didn't do you any harm, did it?' she says suggestively.

It least it sounded like I was up to it, Ren thinks. The funny thing is that even though he feels as bad as any man ever has done outside the battlefield or the torture chamber, he still wants to ask Wren if he can have a quick look at her naked body. What's stopping him is not the impending arrival of her parents, but the fact that he doesn't want her to twig that he can't remember a thing about last night.

In two more minutes he is getting his clothes on. Having lewd thoughts about Wren has woken him up some more, and given him enough adrenaline, or some sort of chemical rush, to enable him to temporarily ignore the pain in his head. Before he can get his pants on he has grown a massive hangover erection, and an intense desire for Wren that seems to be transmitting directly into the pleasure centres of her brain.

'Oh God,' says Wren. 'We have to meet up after my parents go later today. Okay?'

Ren can only nod dumbly as Wren starts to manipulate him. 'Better get dressed. Got to stop this now,' she says, without stopping. Then she takes a deep breath, shudders, and stops. Ren tries to get his trousers on. Just as his brain feels like it wants to burst out of his skull, so to does his schlong feel like it wants to burst out of whatever is stopping it getting bigger and bigger forever.

'Is that going to fit in?' she says.

'I'll just focus on my headache. That should put a stop to things,' says Ren as he completes his penile deorsumversion with difficulty.

She pushes him out the door with a kiss. Once the door closes he straight away feels worse. His desire collapses, and so does his body. His headache comes back with a vengeance, and an unseen person throws a sleep blanket over him. He's not even sure he's going to make it out onto the street. There are stairs to be navigated. He goes down two flights, and the bottom is still not in sight. How big is this apartment block? He can't walk another step at the moment, so he lies down on the floor to have a quick rest.

The next thing he knows is he's being poked. He can feel someone jabbing a finger into his shoulder. Or maybe it's a stick. Perhaps they're keeping their distance from him.

'Are you all right?' he hears a woman say in a fairly posh, middle-aged voice.

'Fuggoff,' Ren says, not really conscious. 'Hangover. Godda sleep.'

'I told you it would be a drunk,' says the male equivalent of the earlier voice. 'Thank God Wren is leaving this awful place.'

Ren rolls over onto his side, away from the direction of the voices, so that his face is against the wall and hidden from view. A little later he hears more voices.

'There he is,' says the woman's voice. 'Disgraceful. Drunks lying on the floor. How I wish you had gone to Durham like I said you should.'

'There were a lot of end-of-degree parties last night,' he hears Wren saying. 'Some of the inexperienced students overdid it. But it's not that bad here.'

'He looks a little old to be a student,' says the male voice.

'A postgrad, I expect,' says Wren. Thankfully her voice is getting fainter. 'Some of them live on nothing but wine and cheese, which has certain effects.'

A little later he dreams of hearing Zack Paddlemore talking.

'Now that you've finished your degree,' Zack is saying, 'you'll have more time to come around and see me in my flat.'

'I don't know about that, Zack,' says a female voice. 'I'm going to be pretty busy this summer.'

'What have you got on?' says Zack, his voice getting mysteriously louder.

'Well...'

It dawns on Ren that this Zack is real, and he's coming up the stairs towards him. He rolls closer to the wall and hides his face and head as best he can, hoping Zack won't recognise him, or his clothes.

'I've got a Tai Chi class I do, and... Oh.'

'Someone's had too much to drink last night,' says Zack. He sounds like he's glad that someone is making him look good. That doesn't happen too often.

'Should we check if he's okay?'

'If you want him to vomit all over you, yes,' says Zack.

The voices fade and then disappear. Later on Zack comes back and rolls him over, saying, 'You want to see something funny, come and see Ren in disgrace.' Zack picks him up and drags him up the stairs to his flat. He can feel his head hitting each step. This has got to be a dream. But he can feel his head being bumped for real. Or is he imagining that? He tries very hard to put his a hand up to his head to check, but Zack is dragging him too fast for him to move his hand there. He knows Zack is going to dismember him if he gets him into his flat.

But will Zack ever get there? The apartment block is too high. Every moment another inch is added to the distance that needs to be traversed. Ren digs down into the moments, dividing them further and further, and more and more inches get added. Soon there will be too many inches for Zack to complete in his lifetime.

Then he and Zack are lost, swimming around in the infinitesimal moments. There are more and more of them being created all the time as the existing ones divide. Getting out will be impossible. He tries to cling on to a moment, but it splits on him, dividing into two smaller moments. He makes a grab for one of them, but that splits too, and again, and again. It's like trying to climb up a mountain of cornflakes. They are lost in a sea of infinity. They are so lost that all talk of being lost becomes almost meaningless. He is being reduced to a point. A point with no point.

He has no idea how much later it is when Wren shakes him awake.

'Ren, wake up,' she says. 'I can't believe you've been sleeping on the stairs the whole time.'

'Well,' says Ren, looking around for any sign of Zack, and taking a second to regain his composure, 'I couldn't remember which flat you lived in. And I don't know your phone number. So I thought it best to just wait for you here.'

Wren gives him an indulgent smile. Ren gets up pronto, pretending that he's in better shape than he really is. He realises that he'd better be in good shape, because Wren, no Daphnean maid she, is desquamating as they walking along the corridor, first her shirt buttons, and then, before she puts the key in the lock, unclasping her bra in the middle to expose her euphoric globes. Ren's conscious mind is saying that he should be in hospital, not having relations, but his disco stick, it appears, has other ideas. 'You just lie back and rest, rummy' it says, 'and let me do the work'.

Later on they're having some food. Ren is fantasising about having a long-term relationship with Wren. He can see them buying a house together, having beautiful kids, and growing old together. Maybe one day he'd even tell her parents that it had been him on the stairs all those years ago. Maybe they'd have already worked that out for themselves. But he's knows it's not going to happen. For one thing, their names are heterographs. She thinks that's cute and says she knew it meant that she eventually had to go to bed with him, but how could he go through life with a wife who has the same name as him, verbally speaking? Wouldn't the marriage be destined to end up like Evelyn and Evelyn Waugh? He can't go through life with everyone calling them He-Ren and She-Wren. Also, she's going to live in Manchester in nine weeks, when she starts a job. Manchester is a difficult place to get to from Grayvington, and vice versa.

Another thing is that, while he may be prone to highly immature behaviour for a man of his age, he doesn't want to hang around with people in their early twenties, which all her friends will be. And because she's still so young she might be a very different person in a year or two. She probably will be after living in Manchester for a few years. She may even mature quickly, and soon find him too immature for her.

'I presume the Philosophy department didn't offer too many opportunities for sexual fantasy amongst the young ladies,' says Ren. 'I mean, Grant Kapshar, Walter Clutterbuck, Bill Porterfield...'

'You've left out the younger ones,' says Wren, smiling. 'But yes, you're right. There was nothing like Miles in Psychology with his hundreds of fans wetting the seats in excitement like at a Beatles concert. Simon Pastygill is weedy. Tristram York only appeals to frigid intellectuals girls, and they aren't too many of them at Grayvington.'

'Plenty of frigid intellectual women in the faculty.'

'I'm talking about students, silly.'

'Students, right. Well, there aren't many intellectuals full-stop amongst the students.'

'Then there's Panos, he is good-looking but he thinks he's a pinup. He's too old to be wearing tank-tops to class. The left-wing girls like Tony Shaver, though.'

'But not Derek Lucas, I hope.'

'Not generally. But I suspect there are a few who do. It's the big, bold personality, and he does have a sort of old-fashioned revolutionary chic charisma about him. But you haven't asked about yourself.'

'Modesty forbids. Also, the answer either way is going to

be unsettling.'

'You have a few. It's not just me. But you are a bit of a smart-aleck. You try to hide it in class, but everyone can tell it's there. Some girls don't like that. They find it threatening.'

'But you don't mind?'

'A man without cheek is not a man at all, in my view.'

'This man is going to get between your cheeks. Right now.'

Eventually they decide that what they will do is stay together for nine weeks and have the dirtiest sex possible for every available minute of that time. Ren was supposed to have finished a book chapter by then, but he figures he'll have at least forty more years to write book chapters, whereas he'll only have about five, possibly ten, more years to do this sort of thing, because after that he won't be attractive to lascivious members of the young nubilia any more. For now he'd rather be between the cheeks than between the covers.

2001-02
Summer break
Early July
Friday

Ren doesn't come in to work until Friday afternoon. He goes to the departmental office to check his mail. The statue of George is still there, under a layer of clothes.

'I thought George was going to be moved somewhere else now?' he says to the departmental administrator, Wendoline.

Marble George has been living in the departmental office ever since it was delivered last year, and is currently used as a coat, scarf and hat stand.

'We can't get rid of it,' Wendoline says. 'Nobody wants to take it. Why don't you have it in your office?'

'Might freak the students out,' mumbles Ren, hurrying off to his office. He's not been in his office for long in when Compton knocks on his door.

'Where have you been?'

'Just taking a bit of a holiday after the end of term.'

'A holiday? What about that book chapter you have to write?'

'Oh, I have plenty of time left to finish that.'

'Last week you were saying you didn't know where you'd find the time to do it, seeing as you had to start from scratch.'

'If I can't do it, I can't do it.'

'Well, you'd better tell Orson now if you're not going to do it, not in two months' time. You don't want to get a reputation for cunctativeness, do you?'

'Er, I guess not. I'll let him know early next week what my decision is.'

'Last week you were desperate to do it. Now you seem very relaxed.'

'And you seem very wound up.'

'You haven't been here. Have you been checking your e-mail?'

'No. My dial-up's not working at home. That's why I've come in, to check my e-mail.'

'My hard disk has been wiped.'

'What? What happened? Has it failed?'

'No. Not failed. Deliberately wiped.'

'Jesus. Who by?'

'That's what we don't know. Possibly Derek, or Huey, Dewey and Louis, but we don't know'

'Did it happen after the party then?'

'Well, I came in on Monday to find that there was nothing left on the hard drive.'

'Shit. Have you got backups?'

'I do, I regularly back everything up onto Zip disks and CDs, so I've only lost a week's work. But Jesus, somebody wiped my drive.'

'Was it definitely wiped deliberately, and not just a drive failure?'

'Yes, IT have checked it and they say it was given an extra thorough wipe. There's nothing recoverable there at all.'

'I can't believe that anyone would stoop to this. So is there any evidence pointing to who did it?'

'No. Just the weak circumstantial evidence that Derek was drunk and angry with me on Friday night. Also, Derek has a key to the main office, where he can get the spare key to my room. On the other hand, Derek is known to be no good with computers. This was someone who knew what they were doing. That points to Tom, who is very good with computers.'

'You mean Dewey?'

'Don't know, the tall one with the glasses. But he has on his side the fact that he doesn't have a key to the main office, so he couldn't have got the key to my room. On the other hand, there have always been rumours that spare main office keys are floating around, so he may in actuality have one.'

'So what's happening? Is there going to be an investigation?'

'Robot has questioned them all. They all deny it. End of investigation.'

'No chance of the police being called in, I take it? Dusting for fingerprints?'

'No chance. Even if we called them they wouldn't come, not for this.'

'What about Derek's outburst on Friday? Has that come up?'

'Grant has given him a bit of a telling off. I mean, Grant doesn't like Derek, and he doesn't at all approve of him shouting at his fellow departmental members, but that's all he can muster. He knows that he doesn't have the power to do anything stronger when all that happened on the surface is a drunken argument, so he's not going to try. As I predicted, he's treating it like a personal disagreement in our private lives, rather than political intimidation. He doesn't approve of my politics any more than Derek does.'

'Has Derek said anything to you?'

'He made a breezy non-apology to me in front of a lot of other people on Tuesday, when he came in because Grant wanted to speak to him. Then he disappeared. He's said nothing to me privately. Other than that appearance, no-one's seen him here all week, not that that's unusual at this time of year. He's probably gone off to Paris again. He said the hard drive had nothing to do with him. Huey, Dewey and Louis are all lying low too. They deny it, too. I feel like Derek is trying to drive me out.'

'Don't you want to go anyway?'

'I do, I'd love to get out of this swamp and go somewhere more fully analytic, and better, but I'm not going to be driven out by Derek. And I'm not sure I'd ever be appointed anywhere else now that it's known that I'm a conservative.'

'Don't let him get to you. He doesn't have that much influence these days. He's burned his bridges with almost everyone.'

'I'm not just talking about Derek. It's the left in general. There's a long-term witch-hunt steadily building up. It's going to gradually ramp up now that all the old Conservative academics are retiring, and being replaced by leftists.'

'I know, but that's no reason to give up now. And you'll outlast Derek.'

'Hope so. Anyway, it's back to the hard disk restoration project for now. See you later.'

2001-02
Summer break
Late July
Thursday

By the end of July, Ren and Wren have become coosters: worn-out libertines. So they take a few days break from their debauches to give their livers and their sore edea a rest. Wren with a W goes to visit some friends. Ren without a W goes to see Ken and Halberd in Ken's flat to discuss progress on the Lucius project.

Ken with a K, and Halberd without a K, have been getting on with attempting to replicate some of Lucius's work. Lucius thinks they've given up on doing that – he thinks they've gone back to doing their own studies – so he's paying them no attention. He's no longer using them to do analysis on his data.

Ken tells Ren what he has learned at a recent conference.

'I was talking to this psychologist who's now in clinical who told me that he left social psychology because the whole field is bullshit. When he was a graduate student he was trying to replicate all these studies that had impressive results, and he never could, no matter how careful he was. So he writes to all the people who did these experiments, asking for more details of what they did, and they all sent back detailed information. Very detailed. In most cases the experiment only works in certain conditions.'

'By "works", you mean getting the desired sexy, political result?' says Ren.

'Yeah,' says Ken. 'So there were instructions like, don't do this test on a computer, it only works if the participants are using paper and a pencil. Or it doesn't work if they use a pencil, it has to be a pen. Or the participants have to be given something else to do after reading the materials, for precisely two and a half minutes. If you make it any more than that, or any less, then you don't get the result you want. And if you more or less people than some specific number in the group then it doesn't work either. And there was... I'm trying to think of another one he mentioned...'

'Didn't you say there was something to do with the words used?' says Halberd.

'Oh yeah,' says Ken. 'On one experiment he was told that he had to use certain exact words when talking to the subjects. If you used other synonyms, even really close ones, then it didn't happen.'

'My favourite was the clothes,' says Halberd. 'On one experiment concerning behaviour in contexts where you are reflecting on your eventual death you only got the result you wanted if the experimenters wore black clothes and had a gloomy manner.'

'Jesus, those sort of factors should discredit any experiment,' says Ren. 'Don't the researchers understand that?'

'Well, this guy did,' said Ken, 'that's why he changed fields. But I don't know if other researchers do.'

'They don't know much about science then,' says Ren. 'Or else they're deliberately ignoring these issues because it that allows them to publish their propaganda in good journals and make a name for themselves.'

'That's a harsh interpretation,' says Ken.

'Is it any worse than the alternative?' says Ren. 'That these supposed top scientists don't understand the basics of confirmation? Either way things are bad. Frankly, it's just dishonest to claim that such-and-such is the case, when in fact that such-and-such only happens in certain carefully-contrived circumstances, which the experimenters have searched hard to find. "People are more X in an Y environment, but only if the environment is Y in the precise ways A, B, C, D and E. And it's 3:37 on a Tuesday afternoon and it's exactly twenty-seven degrees. At the very least you should make all this clear in your paper.'

'But the journals don't want that much detail,' says Halberd. 'And they don't want such qualified conclusions. They want strong conclusions that are supposed to hold up generally. So if you put all that in your paper then it will probably get rejected. And then your career suffers.'

'That's basically an admission that for the sake of your career advancement you're willing to publish highly misleading research. That doesn't constitute any sort of defence.'

'We know,' says Ken. 'You don't have to tell us that it's dishonest. We're putting our careers on the line for the sake of honesty.'

'I have to admire you guys for that,' says Ren. 'It's very admirable. That sort of bravery isn't very common in academia. Look at how Miles has dropped out of sight. He's worried that he'll get caught up in the blast. Or the fallout.'

'If it all goes well then he'll say he was part of it all along, won't he?' says Ken.

'Yes. Mind you, he was part of it all along, to some extent. But it's you guys doing most of the work.'

'Thanks.'

'Might be too late for your field's credibility, though. I mean, if Professor Plum thinks it's okay to publish a paper saying X on the basis of experiments he has done, even though X only appears in some particular circumstances, whereas not X appears in lots of other circumstances, then he's just as entitled to publish a paper saying not X as he is saying X. But it's X that he wants to support, because it supports some more general theory he likes, or it's more PC, so he publishes the former paper, not the latter.'

'It's the same in principle,' says Ken, 'as those researchers who do ten studies, and nine don't support X, but one does, so they publish that one.'

'The "bottom drawer effect",' says Halberd.

'And few people try to replicate these studies,' says Ken. 'No-one other than a few grad students starting our with some practise studies is much interested in replicating other people's work. Especially if you try one and it doesn't work. Then you just say, I'm not wasting my time trying to replicate someone else's work. As soon as you get a license to do your own studies, then you want to make a name for yourself with your own stuff.'

'And journals aren't very interested in publishing replications,' says Halberd. 'Especially negative ones. So X stays as the accepted wisdom.'

'Yeah, even if the author of the paper supporting X has sucked off the entire editorial board of *World Science* to get published,' says Ren.

'That's, ah, putting it rather more colourfully than I would have,' says Ken.

'All the section editors want to see their sort of stuff confirmed,' says Ren. 'They might get tough with the stats, and so on, but are they asking the really important questions, like, how robust is this result? Do you have data which doesn't support this conclusion?'

'And if so, why isn't that included in the overall data set?' says Ken.

'Does the supposed phenomena only appear if the circumstances are just right?' says Ren. 'We're not doing physics or chemistry. If you can show, say, that the gravitational effect doesn't hold in some circumstance, then that's big news, regardless of how circumscribed that circumstance is. But this is research designed to show that the human mind works, for the most part, in some particular way. If it often doesn't work in that way then your thesis is blown, or at least greatly weakened. Your conclusion may be something like "Men found to consistently undervalue woman's contributions", say, but really your conclusion should be something more like "In a certain limited, artificial set of circumstances, and only when they are suitably primed, men undervalued women's contributions. Assuming, that is, that our somewhat tendentious interpretation of the data is correct".'

'Well, all that sort of thing is a different issue to whether Lucius is faking his data,' says Ken. 'That's what we've got to concentrate on at the moment.'

'But all of what you've just told me means that your attempts at replication are a bit pointless. They're bound to fail, because even if Lucifer isn't faking anything, it's probably the case that you can't replicate his work because you don't know the exact right circumstances you need to have. These experimenters put an awful lot of time into finding just the right circumstances. You aren't likely to stumble across those first time. As you've just said, people who want to replicate these sorts of results need to be told the secret combination of circumstances for it to work. Whether to use one word, and not a similar one, for example. So these replications are likely to fail even if Lucius has been honest all along.'

'I see your point,' says Ken. 'You're right. But it's still worth doing them, it will help our case. If Lucius hasn't specified the circumstances sufficiently then that's his failing, not ours.'

'Well,' says Ren. 'Maybe it's worth finishing what you've started, but I wouldn't spend much more time on the replication side of things. It's the analysis that's more important.'

But he knows as he says it that Ken and Halberd will waste their time pointlessly trying to replicate Lucius's work. The replications are going to fail regardless of whether Lucius's data is made up or real.

2002-03
Semester 1

2002-03
Semester 1
Week 8
Friday

Months have gone by and Ken and Halberd have still not finished their analysis of Lucius's work. Ren spent August in bed with Wren and got nothing done, except for converting takeaways and alcohol into disseminate. Then Wren left to move to her new life in Manchester, and Ren thought he'd get something done then, but instead he stayed in bed, depressed, finding that he missed her. He was starting to think that maybe he'd made a big mistake in breaking up with her. But she was off to her exciting future, and wasn't go to stay in Grayvington, and he didn't blame her for that. Then the new term hit and the Lucius project got put onto the backburner, although Ken and Halberd sporadically worked on their attempted replications.

Ren has now decided it's time to move it on and get things wrapped up. He's worried that someone else will call out Lucius first, even though he's knows there's not really much chance of that. So he has gone around to Ken's flat on a Friday night to talk to the two grad students. He's bought them a bottle of fancy vodka, ostensibly to reward them for their hard work, although really he's bought it to loosen their tongues. If necessary he's going to kick them up their backsides. At the very least he's going to drink a lot of this vodka. The bottle is already half-gone.

'Another vodka and lemonade, fellas?'

'Another one?' says Halberd with a glazed look.

'Still going with this one,' says Ken.

'If you leave your gorgeous girlfriend all alone at a party then you can expect other men to move in,' says Ren as he pours some more of the vodka.

'Isn't that rather sexist?' says Ken.

'Is it feminist to ignore your girlfriend night after night, and then complain when you walk in on her getting licked out by an asshole bongo player with a goatee someone brought to the party?'

'That is a fucked-up metaphor in so many ways,' says Ken.

'I know. I mean, a fucking bongo player? Wouldn't you just kill yourself there and then? By the way, it wasn't a metaphor, it was an analogy. I can't believe they trust you psychologists with matters of import, Jesus, with the actual minds of human beings, when a simple distinction between a metaphor and an analogy is beyond you. By law you should be trusted with nothing more than frogs and gerbils. Now, another vodka for everyone?'

'Could I have one that hasn't got quite so much vodka in it?' says Ken.

'How about I just go to the kitchen, get out a knife, cut some lemons, and then come in and cut your fucking balls off as well? Or will they be too small to find?'

'You're too late,' says Halberd. 'His last girlfriend already cut them off.'

'Thanks mate,' says Ken.

'Well, at least I can trust a Dane not to cry when I put a healthy dash of vodka in his glass,' says Ren.

'You bet,' says Halberd. 'Could I have extra lemonade, though?'

Ren sighs and shakes his head. 'Do you have a note from Mummy that says you're allowed to drink, sonny? Is it a school night?'

Ren decides he should get down to brass tacks while things have loosened up, but before the evening starts spiralling out of control.

'Guys, an important question now. When are you thinking of plunging the knife?'

Ken recoils a little bit. 'That's not how I like to think

about it.'

'Pulling the lever?'

'Your metaphors are all very violent,' says Ken.

'Yes, because this is a nasty fucking business.'

'Well, maybe next summer. If we think we have a good enough case,' says Ken.

'I was thinking after we finish our doctorates, and have moved on with permanent jobs,' says Halberd. 'Next summer is too soon.'

'Too soon? Hells fucking bells, you call yourself young people? Young thrusting bucks with urgent big cocks?'

Ken and Halberd look at each other. 'I'm not sure that's how I'd fill out a self-description task,' says Ken.

'Then get busy and rub yourself a boner. This has to happen soon. Otherwise I'm going to go in flinging so much shit at Lucius, and your department, and Psychology in general that you'll be smelling it in your nostrils for decades to come. I don't give a fuck whether it pisses Grayvington off because it will make my life and career so much more fun that I'm itching to do it. I'm being Mr Nice Guy letting you social psychologists make out that you're policing yourself, even though it's obvious that someone hooked up the refuse pipe to the output pipe long ago, and you're all pretending not to notice the smell.'

'Are you just talking like this because you've drunk most of the vodka?' says Ken.

'No, I really will blow it open myself. We can't let this continue on for another year, another two years, that's just wrong.'

'Okay, okay, we'll talk to the Dean in a few months.'

'Don't take too long. Let Lucifer enjoy his Christmas, and then when the cold bleakness of January really bites you pull the trigger. Don't do it in summer when he might think that he can just go on holiday and do the Macarena and the whole thing will blow over. Do it when the frost bites at his soul.'

'Or his asshole,' says Halberd.

'A for effort, foreign-language person,' says Ren.

'I try.'

'You try your best, I know,' says Ren. 'That's the problem.'

'You were saying?' says Ken.

'Yes, expose this tertiary Philby in winter, when the weather is miserable, and he lies awake at night listening to the cold wind howling and starts to worry about being caught. And hit him hard. If you don't hit him good and proper first blow then he'll turn around and start ripping your limbs off, and then you'll wish to God you hadn't pulled your punches.'

'Aren't you supposed to be convincing us to go after him?' says Ken.

'When you wrestle the alligator onto the shore,' says Ren, not really listening to anything but his own drunken ramblings now, 'you fucking finish the cunt off. You don't let him slip back into the water again. Exenterate him and his figmental body of work. Fucking forget all this replication crap, it won't convince anybody. Just go for him and let him have to deal with the task of convincing everyone that all these amazing studies that no-one ever saw happen really did happen. Okay?'

'Er, okay,' says Ken.

'But let's hold back the train station info to start with.'

'I thought you said to hit him with everything straight up?'

'Sure, but let's keep that in reserve. If he manages to sew some confusion about whether he's faking and looks like getting the benefit of the doubt, then we finish him off with that. And even if he confesses straight away he'll try to make it seem not so bad. Just a few changed numbers here and there. Faking, but not the worst sort. He'll play for sympathy. A few bad decisions late at night. He's not a bad guy really, just a human being with weaknesses. Then the train station faking comes out and the scale of what he's been doing becomes clear, and then whatever credibility he's managed to hold onto collapses.'

There is silence for a few seconds.

'I'm not sure I really want to be a part of something that's going to be so horrible,' says Ken. 'This could destroy Lucius. Maybe he'll commit suicide.'

'He's hardly the type,' says Ren. 'Look, he's going down with or without you. If you pull out then it will still come out at some stage that you knew all about him, and you had the proof, but you chickened out of saying anything. So you can either take the credit you deserve, or you can go into the kitchen and get that knife, cut those lemons, and then cut your own balls off yourself. Or whatever's left of them. And cut your whole fucking dick off while you're at it.'

'I don't find this sort of drunken macho talk very helpful,' says Ken. 'These attitudes are behind a lot of the problems in modern academia. Even Lucius's behaviour, it all stems from an over-competitive and aggressive ultra-masculine culture. We have to stop talking and thinking like this.'

'A man who's thinking of chickening out on exposing a fraud is in no position to give a sermon,' says Ren. 'You're like a pacifist watching a battle criticising both sides for their participation in violence while your friends are being shot dead by Nazis. Take a stand for your fucking bullshit field. Get inspired by Joan of Arc instead. Or the suffragettes. Or whoever you approve of. But don't pretend that you looking the other way when a faker does his faking is about principle.'

Ken looks downcast. 'All right,' he finally says, before looking up with a gimcrack gimlet eye. 'Give me another vodka. A big one.'

'Certainly not,' says Ren. 'This stuff is terribly bad for your liver.'

2002-03
Winter break

2002-03
Winter break
Mid-January
Monday

Ren is in Robot's office discussing Lucius. Robot is temporary Dean of Humanities and Social Sciences while the usual Dean is on sabbatical, and as this is the Faculty that Psychology belongs to, Robot is currently the man in charge of deciding what to do about Lucius.

What Robot wants to do is to delay making any decision for as long as possible, until the regular Dean comes back, so he has to be the one to deal with the mess. Ren, Ken and Halberd went to see Robot a week ago and presented their analysis of his work, leaving out what they know about the train station study. It was, as Robot agreed, a damning analysis. They showed that there was a very large amount of results that were too good to be true. The Cronbach Alpha scores were very low. Whole rows of results in different studies were exactly the same, suggesting they'd been copied and pasted. There were many other statistical oddities. And many studies had supposedly taken place at high schools there was no record of. Lucius had thanked teachers who didn't exist. Enquiries within the Psychology department, made in a discreet manner that hopefully wouldn't raise any warning flags, had failed to find anyone who had ever collaborated with Lucius on doing data collection. He always insisted on doing it alone.

All of these things in isolation could possibly be explained. For instance, perhaps Lucius had disguised the names of the schools, and the teachers. Perhaps they wanted to remain anonymous. But taken all together, it pointed one way: a wholesale creation of data. Lucius has to be investigated, as well as being given the chance to defend himself. But Robot just wants to wait.

'Wait for what?' says Ren. He knows what Robot is thinking: wait for the regular Dean to come back. But Robot won't say that.

'Wait for, ah, wait for things to become clearer.'

'How are things going to become clearer?'

'Well, in time things might... over time things look...'

'If you don't act, then it's going to come out, and Grayvington, and you, are going to look bad because you knew what he was up to and you let it continue.'

'Going to come out? You all said you hadn't told anyone?'

'We haven't told anyone explicitly, but we've been making enquiries, as discreetly as we can of course, but there's a limit to how discreet you can be if you want information. Like me calling Lucius's old University recently to see if he really had done the research there that he said he had. I pretended it was me wanting to hire their rooms, and said that I'd heard on the grapevine that Lucius might have done so too. Which he hadn't. So I didn't ask them outright about Lucius, but they might be suspicious. Plus Ken and Halberd have been talking at conferences with other people about fraud in their field. Apparently some other grad students, from other Unis, have voiced their suspicions about Lucius, and they're probably getting these suspicions from their supervisors. Before too long someone's going to put two and two together.'

Ren suspects that a few people in Lucius's field have already put two and two together, but they've chosen not to say anything for political reasons.

'I wouldn't like to be the Dean in charge when somebody from another University discovers what Lucius's been doing, and Ken and Halberd and I will have to explain to the world that we told you all about it and you decided to do nothing.'

'I'm not deciding to do nothing,' says an irritated Robot.

He doesn't like having a junior lecturer talk to him like this, but he can hardly say that in this situation.

Robot sits silently, visibly churning.

'All right,' he says eventually.

'All right?' says Ren.

'I think we will have to act now.'

'Good. What are you going to do?'

'You'll have to leave that with me.'

'Okay. Well, you have the report we gave you.'

'Yes, thank you,' says Robot.

Yes, thank you Dr Christopher for getting me this shit sandwich from the Shittiest Ever Sandwich Company, and stuffing in into my mouth and making me eat it, is what Robot really means. Ren takes his leave.

2002-03
Winter break
Third week of January
Tuesday

Ren knocks on Robot's door.

'Sorry to bother you, Grant.'

'That's all right. Is it a question about the exam marking? Everything going all right with it?' asks Grant, with obvious insincerity.

'Same old. But it's not that. I was just wondering what's happening with the Lucius investigation.'

'I'm afraid I can't tell you anything about that.'

'What?'

'It's none of your business any more. It's out of your hands. I should also remind you to say nothing about it at the moment.'

'You're not still sitting on it, are you?'

'No. Look, it's started, so you need to let the process happen. I expect you'll be called in at some stage soon to say your piece. But apart from that it no longer involves you.'

'It does involve me, I'm the one who exposed him. Or should I say, I'm the one who exposed the possibility that there are issues with his data? But yes, I'll keep quiet for now.'

'Make sure you do.'

'What's he saying? Has he admitted it?'

'That's none of your business at this point.'

'All right, all right. Good luck with it.'

'Good luck? Nothing good will come of this, whether we have good luck or bad luck.'

'Clean the stables. Think of it that way.'

'Thank you for that. That's a nice viewpoint to have from

a distance, but you're not the one having to deal with all the ordure up close.'

'Well, you don't get the extra money as Dean for sitting on your arse all day just doing the usual. You get it for dealing with hard cases, and making difficult decisions.'

'Just go, Ren.'

'Back to the exam marking grind? Okay, but you may hear me bashing my head against the wall a few times this afternoon,' Ren says, closing the door before he can hear Robot getting really angry with him.

2002-03
Winter break
Fourth week of January
Thursday

Ren is trying to have a sleep-in, but all he's really doing is moping about Wren. How could he have let such a sensational young woman like that slip through his fingers? Why did it matter that she's only twenty-one? That summer will burn forever in his memory, not as a brilliant memory to cherish, but as a mocking image of what his life could have been like if only he hadn't been so stupid and proud. If only he hadn't assumed that someone else like Wren would be along within weeks. He misses talking and joking with her even more than he misses the bodily entrances and exits. Perhaps he should go back to moping about Lily instead.

The phone rings. It's Miles. Has he seen this morning's newspapers? No. Miles says that two of the papers today carry reports of a Lucius Birch, Professor of Psychology at Grayvington University, being suspended for possible academic fraud. The reports say that Grayvington University has refused to comment, and Lucius strongly denies the accusations. Lucius, it is said, is expected to make a public statement soon.

It's not surprising that the papers have now got the story. Ren heard from Miles a few days ago that Lucius, according to Lucius, has been rewarded by the University for his hard work and success by being given a sabbatical for the semester. Sabbaticals are never given out like that, and certainly not at such a late stage, with such little notice – Lucius was supposed to start teaching his usual Social Psychology class next week, and now someone else will have to do that at the last minute. Although there's been no official announcement about Lucius being suspended, and Robot is still saying nothing, it's clear to those in the know that it's a suspension, not a sabbatical.

Then rumours started up on the UK Psychology e-mail lists. First a rumour was passed on that a Psychology Professor has been sacked for faking data. Then the rumour changed to the Professor being suspended. Then someone posted some hints that those in the know could use to identify who it is. Then the list owners shut down the discussion, but too late to stop a lot of people from being able to work out who the person is.

Ren feels a little pang at hearing that the papers are now reporting the accusations against Lucius. He would have liked to have broken the story via an article somewhere himself, listing all of the claims against Lucius, but not only are his hands tied by the University, as an academic (and a sort-of colleague) he couldn't do that without giving Lucius a chance to explain himself. And what if it somehow turned out that Lucius hadn't faked anything?

Ren asks Miles to try calling his old girlfriend Tanja, who now works for the local rag *The Daily Gravy* (shortened from its original name, *The Daily Grayvington*), to find out what she's heard. Tanja started a couple of years ago as a freelancer contributing the occasional arts-based story, but now she's on staff, and she usually covers University-related stories. They still stay in touch, due to Tanja still having feelings, or rather loin-based desires for Miles.

Later on, when Ren is at his office searching the internet for Lucius-related stories, he gets another call from Miles. Tanja said that Lucius has called a press conference today. She wouldn't say where, though – she says it's press only. Miles thinks she's buddies with Lucius these days, through Tony Shaver. Miles knows that a lot of press conferences in town are held at the Royal Square Hotel, so he has just called them to ask what time the Lucius Birch press conference is, and they said 11:30. It's 11:15 now. Ren tells Miles to get in his car and pick him up outside the Terminal Building

ASAP.

When they get to the hotel, there's nowhere to park, so Miles drops Ren off and heads for a multi-story car park. By the time Ren has found the room, he can hear that the conference has started. He pauses outside the open door to listen.

'...victim of a right-wing conspiracy to de-legitimise my research, led by a right-wing academic called Ren Christopher.'

That's my cue, thinks Ren.

'Hi-de-hi campers!' he says loudly, entering the room. All the heads swivel towards him. 'It's right-wing conspirator Ren Christopher here. My ears were burning so I thought I'd pop into my Rupert Murdoch-funded teleporter and beam myself straight here.'

There's a dozen journalists, including Tanja, some photographers, and two camera crews in the room. A woman waits at the side of the room at the front. It's not Lenora Helminth, though – she and Lucius broke up last year. I wonder if Lenora got a whiff of what Lucius was up to, Ren thinks.

'What are you doing here?' demands Lucius, looking very angry. I hope he tries to punch me, thinks Ren.

'I've come to hear all these exciting tales you're telling about me to the press,' says Ren.

'You weren't invited.'

'Invited? Is this a private press conference? I thought this was all about making a public statement?'

'Get out.'

'Seeing as you're talking about me, I think I'll stay for a while, old chook.' Ren hopes this will prompt Lucius to rush over and try to punch him, or manhandle him.

'Dr Christopher, do you want to say anything about this issue?' asks one of the journalists.

'I may have something to say, but it's only fair to let Professor Birch have his full say first. It's his press conference.'

Lucius continues on, clearly flustered.

'I will say again that the accusations against me are false.'

'What are those accusations again, exactly?' says a journalist.

'I'd rather not give these baseless accusations further legs by specifying them,' says Lucius.

'But whatever they are, they're false?' says the journalist.

'Yes,' says Lucius.

'Can you explain why they're false?' asks another journalist.

'I'm not a liberty to do that either.'

'So what was the point of calling a press conference if you're not going to say anything?'

'To assert my innocence in public. Look, my hands are really tied here. The University has asked me to not to comment in public on anything specific. But my name has been dragged through the mud by your organs this morning, and I feel I am entitled to at least stand up in public and say that I am not guilty of...'

'Of academic fraud?'

'It is absurd to even use that phrase in connection with me.'

'But your University of accusing you of it?'

'No. No, they are not. Let me make this very clear. My University has not accused me of anything at all. It is Ren Christopher who is accusing me, an armchair philosopher who doesn't understand the practise of scientific research. The University is just looking into the situation. They are trying to work out who is the liar, him or me.'

'So you're calling this man here, Dr Christopher, a liar?'

'Yes I am,' says Lucius. Desudation is starting to drip from his brow. The journalists turn back to look at Ren. He's lying back comfortably in his seat, one arm draped over the next chair, not paying attention.

'Oh,' says Ren. 'Has he accused me again? Well. Naughty boy. You know I do feel for Dr Birch being named in the papers this morning. At the moment he is an innocent man, and he is entitled to say something publicly in view of that. But I never said anything publicly about him, and now he's saying in public that I'm a liar, when all I have done is provide the University with an analysis, performed by several people, not just me, pointing to... irregularities... in Professor Birch's research. Irregularities which I'm sure he can easily clear up. Just a pity the newspapers got involved, and a pity that Professor Birch resorted to public mud-slinging.'

'I am just...' begins Lucius.

'What was in that report, Dr Christopher?'

'Oh, well, that's not public at the moment. And this is Professor Birch's stage. I wouldn't want to rain on his parade. Perhaps he can clear everything up now for us, and close the case.'

'Professor Birch,' says a reporter, 'there are rumours online that no-one has seen you or any assistant do any data collection for your studies for years. Would you care to comments on those accusations?'

'They're not accusations. They're merely observations on my mode of working, which is to go out into the field to collect data, rather than do it all in the artificial environment of a University laboratory. There wouldn't be any issue about this at all were it not for the muck-raking of my political enemies.'

'Those enemies being Dr Christopher? Anyone else?'

'I don't know who's behind him, no.'

'You think he's being funded to do this? Who by?'

Ren is grinning at all this. He can see Lucius getting more and more nervous. It would have been so much easier for him to tell lies about Ren if Ren had not been here. Perhaps he should move on to blaming something more amorphous and less present, like the Jews.

A journalist turns to Ren. 'Perhaps you would like to reply to this, Dr Christopher?'

'He's not entitled to say anything,' yells Lucius. 'It's not his press conference.'

'Oh Lucius,' says Ren. 'I can easily invite these gentlemen and ladies to my own press conference in the corridor in five minutes time. But perhaps I can turn pressman myself, and ask you on behalf of my blog – yes, I too qualify as a reporter, of sorts – a question.'

'No, no questions from you,' says Lucius, as Ren gets out some pieces of paper from the inside pocket of his coat.

Lucius looks desperately at the woman at the front, as if he wants her to manhandle Ren out of the room.

'This is Professor Birch's celebrated "Dirt and Discrimination" paper that appeared all over the international media a few years ago. A study undertaken at Grayvington's own dear old train station. But look! Here is a signed letter from the General Manager at Grayvington train station, who swears that neither she nor any of her staff have any awareness of any such study taking place at that time in the train station.'

Lucius's face turns from very red to very white in an instant.

'Hey, that was a neat trick you did with your face colour then, Lucius' says Ren. 'It's like you've had an internal eboulement.'

'We did a, er... guerrilla study,' says Lucius.

Ren is tempted to say, 'You used gorillas to ask the questions? Is that why never needed help from grad students?' But he decides against it.

'I didn't get permission,' Lucius continues. 'I just went in and did it anyway. I thought if we asked they might say no.'

'So you're saying, then,' says Ren, 'that somehow you did all these tests at a train station, a train station with a foyer that isn't all that big, and none of the staff noticed? They didn't notice you getting lots of commuters to read stuff and fill in forms? And then somehow you single-handedly made the train station dirty, and swapped all the signs around, and none of the staff said, "Hey, why are you putting dirt and litter everywhere in our station?"'. And then you left it like that while you got more commuters to read stuff and fill in forms. And then you cleaned it up again, and put everything back to normal, and still none of the staff noticed?'

'Yes,' says Lucius firmly, his jaw twisted an an uncomfortable angle. 'That's the end of the conference. Thank you for coming.' Lucius turns to leave. The journalists besiege him, shouting questions at him. The photographers decide that this is a good time to take lots of snaps.

'Lucius!' shouts Ren. 'Lucius! Don't go doing anything silly, like going to the roof and jumping off.' Although he says that semi-seriously, he also hopes that Lucius will come over and try to punch him for saying it, right in front of the cameras.

Lucius escapes the pack with his female friend through the side door, which is then locked from that side, or else someone is holding the handle firmly. The press decide to lay siege to Ren instead.

'Have you got anything more to say, Dr Christopher?'

'Not really, it wouldn't be proper to do so while the investigation into Lucius is ongoing. I just wanted the chance to defend myself against accusations made against me in public. By the way, did anyone see that episode of Seinfeld last night? It's the one where Lloyd Braun is selling all those computers over the phone, and poor George can't sell any. Old Lloyd is racking up the sales, he's just relentless, it's too good to be true, he's leaving George in the dust. And then it turns out that Lloyd's phone isn't even connected. Very nice episode. I recommend you catch it sometime soon.'

2002-03
Winter break
End of January
Monday

The phone rings in Ren's office.

'You've really fucked things up now,' says Miles' voice.

'What?'

'The department are making me teach Social Psychology.'

'Oooh. Nasty. How's Lucius?'

'Gone.'

'Gone?'

'Completely gone. He's either been sacked or jumped. Nobody knows which at this point. But he is, in effect, no longer a member of the Psychology Department.

'Poor Lucius. If he'd only managed to avoid having his innovative methods being detected for another five or so years he would have been all right, because by then that sort of data-collecting methodology will be compulsory in Psychology.'

'And I wouldn't have to take his Social Psychology class, on top of everything else I have, with only a week to get ready for it. And guess what? I'm still marking fucking exams. And guess what? I have another one hundred and seventy exams to mark, coming in on Wednesday. How is doing all of this achievable?'

'At least your exams don't take as long as mine do to mark. We're in this impossible situation where you are supposed to properly read and re-read an exam in a ridiculously short time, and your classes start again the Monday after the last exam on Friday. You must get your exam marks in ASAP, by yesterday morning before nine, preferably the day before yesterday, but you must take care to mark each exam thoroughly and carefully. If I'd wanted an impossible job I would have gone down a fucking rabbit hole. You know how long it takes just to decipher the hand-writing in some cases?'

'You should see some of the hand-writing I have to deal with,' says Miles.

'And then you have to decipher whatever the fuck the student is on about. And essays are even worse because they're longer and more rambling and just when you think you have some time to do some research a big batch of them comes in and then you have to write long, insightful comments on every one. I must have done something bad in a previous life to have to spend so much time every term marking endless reams of undergraduate drivel.'

'You've done enough bad things in your current life to justify any amount of torture, mate.'

'You think you can't go on, it's 3am, and you look at your pile, and you've still got eighty left.'

'It does my head in after a while,' says Miles. 'After about four I need a lie-down in a dark room. Then I start wishing that I worked on a building site instead. Sunshine, sports talk, physical work, that's what I need.'

'I usually look at the classifieds during every marking period,' says Ren. 'But I'd only end up a high school teacher, which would be even worse.

'Or working for a funding body, which would be like a really crappy type of academic job, without the prestige.'

'Hang on,' says Ren. 'Lucius was suspended, or given a sabbatical, however you want to put it, a week or so ago. Shouldn't they have assigned someone to Social Psych at that point?'

'They should have, yes, but they're hopeless at making decisions. Wouldn't have made much difference, I've had to spend the whole week marking, and couldn't have prepared anyway.'

'So when are you going to prepare? When's the first

class?'

'Monday of next week.'

'Blimey. So you'll get like, Sunday evening to mug up on a whole field of Psychology?'

'Yeah. Mind you, it won't be hard will it, considering that the whole field seems to be based on nothing but the conviction that everyone's a racist, consciously or unconsciously. Seriously. I'm not joking. That does seem to be the underlying insight, insight in quote marks, of the whole field. We're all racists, and sexists, and our behaviour is driven by crude stereotypes. And there are so many influential papers in the field that look very dodgy to me. I wonder how many other Luciuses there are in Social Psychology? It's enough to turn me into you.'

'There are advantages to that, like the enormous cock, and the genius in varied fields that could be put to use one day, not to mention the fact that I've got a new hi-tech squash racquet. Are there any lecture notes, or overheads, from previous years that you can use?'

'No. And Lucius isn't going to give me anything now, is he?'

'So, any idea what's happened to Lucius?'

'Last person to talk to him says that Lucius claimed, in an unconvincing fashion, that he was innocent. He seemed very rattled, and shifty, apparently. And then said he was going off to take his sabbatical, yes, he was still talking about a sabbatical, in Wales with his new girlfriend for a few weeks to start with. He refused to say anything more.'

'But you said he's gone for good?'

'Yes, the Head told us a day after this happened that Lucius no longer works for the department. He wouldn't say anything more. I presume that also means he no longer works for the University in general, because I doubt they've offered him an alternative job in the kitchens. Of course, everyone in the department, everyone in British psychology, is talking about his work, and poring over it. Suddenly, it seems, it was always obvious that his data was fake, even though some of the people now saying this had previously acclaimed Lucius for his fantastic work. Has Robot spoken to you about...?'

'About the press conference esclandre? Yes, he was very pissed off with me, as usual, but I told him that I heard about the press conference at the last minute, and went for a listen. Then Lucius start libelling me in public, to the press, so I had to say something. He wasn't happy about me producing that train station letter, but I told him I got that recently, which I did. And the University hadn't seemed very interested in my help in the investigation anyway.'

'So are you in the clear? Is he just jealous because you got your picture in the papers?'

'Well, as I said, he's pissed off with me. He's always pissed off with me. I'm getting fucking sick of it, frankly. He walks around like he's got a mouthful of wasps. He disapproves of lots of other members of the department as well, of course, it's not just me, but it's like the sight of me pains him every time he sees me. I could respect that if he had some achievements to his name, and an admirable character, but he doesn't. He's an all-round nothing. So fuck him. There's not much he can do to me over this. It won't look good if they try to do anything to me after I've exposed Lucius.'

'How long do you think before the media works out that Lucius has been sacked, or quit?'

'If it gets discussed on the Psychology internet forums then not long.'

'Maybe they'll run another picture of you?'

'If they call me I'm going to say that most of the hard work was done by a couple of graduate students. I won't say who, though, because I don't think they want the attention, at least not at this stage when everything's feverish.'

2002-03
Semester 2

2002-03
Semester 2
Week 10
Friday

'Let's go outside,' says Ren.

'Foucault and Gramsci are kind of similar.'

'In what way?'

'But we just got here,' says Lily.

'Well, they both, like, try to explain power relations in terms of the, uh, complex mechanisms of society. And, like Gramsci, Foucault views power as a relation of force. A relation of force, right, that can be found only in terms of action.'

'I think it would be nicer outside,' says Ren. 'Better conversation.'

'But Gramsci sees power relations through the lens of binary oppositions.'

'What sort of oppositions?'

'You don't have to listen to conversations on other tables,' says Lily.

'Leaders and the led, the rulers and the ruled, and er... well, that sort of thing. But for Foucault though, power is diffused.'

'It's hard not to hear it.'

'But Gramsci and Foucault, they both make use of Machiavelli's idea of relations of force. Foucault's analyses are fundamentally, er...'

'Fuckdamentally?' says Ren.

'Fundamentally based on the notion of power, right? It's everywhere. Always being produced, all the time, every second.'

Ren pours some salt into his hand. 'Let's produce some

power,' he says.

'But Gramsci's different. For him power inheres in ideology.'

Ren throws salt in the general direction of Malcom's table.

'What the fuck was that?' says Malcom, rubbing his hair.

'Just some salt,' says Ren.

'Ren, what are you doing?' says Lily. 'Don't be a drunken arse again.'

'Just wanted to see if you shrivel up and die if you get salt on you,' says Ren, who decided a while ago that he if he has to behave like Lily expects then she'll just think him a wimp. And she's still going out with Jason anyway.

'Piss off,' says Malcom. He turns back to his friends. 'Where were we?'

'I was going to say that for Gramsci a social group can modify the aggregation of relations to create a hegemonic order,' says someone who looks like Malcom on beard-and-bullshit steroids.

Lily gives Ren a look.

'Just a bit of horseplay,' he says.

Lily thinks of telling Ren to slow down with the drinking, but then she thinks, why should I be the one to spoil the fun? If Ren misbehaves then he can suffer the consequences himself.

'The sun's coming out,' says Douglas. 'I'm making an executive decision to move outside.'

'You create power merely by being aware of the complex social network-hegemonic forces within which an individual is situated.'

'Douglas is creating power,' says Ren, 'by his acute awareness of complex social network-hegemonic forces.'

'And by his masterful decision-making,' says Lily.

'Get your coat, Douglas, you've scored,' says Ren. 'The complex mechanisms of society are yours tonight.'

'But this issue can't be resolved without a discussion of Gramsci's philosophy of praxis,' says Malcom.

'Quick,' hisses Ren. 'Move it.'

When they have found themselves a nice spot on the grass outside the bar, Miles says, 'Jesus, Malcom talks that sort of shit all the time. He never stops. That's why I couldn't do another year of TITE.'

'Are the Humanities and Social sciences already lost, then?' asks Douglas.

'Sociology is beyond repair,' says Ren. 'Then again, Sociology was always bad.'

'Sociology was like the Trojan Horse for this rubbish, wasn't it?' says Douglas.

'Some say English was the original Trojan Horse,' says Ren. 'Something so subjective was always bound to get taken over by those with agendas. And I don't just mean political agendas, I also mean those who wanted to increase the perceived prestige of the people who teach English. If English Lit is just a glorified bookclub, then as the leader of a bookclub group you don't have much status. But if you link the study of English Lit to the health of civilisation, you make yourself more important. And there's some justification for that sort of claim. Literature is important. But then the claims get bigger and bigger, and then you find that if you introduce heavy theory from the Continental philosophers that you get even more prestige. You don't even have to bother talking about novelists and their silly characters any more. Or poets and their boring imagery and rhymes and metre. You can talk about your pet political ideas, dressed up in fancy language, and suddenly you're like a modern priest. This is also what the Sociologists, and a lot of the Political Scientists, found.'

'And the Science and Technology Studies people,' says Douglas.

'And Film Studies,' says Miles.

'And Cultural Studies,' says Lily.

'And American and Canadian Studies, and all the languages, and any sort of field that looks at some geographical or cultural area,' says Ren. 'And Art History, of course, and even a lot of Theology these days.'

'And Geography,' says Douglas.

'Geography? Really?' says Miles.

'Oh yes,' says Douglas.

'And everything you say is unfalsifiable,' says Ren, 'but you're preaching to people who haven't foggiest notion of what that means. And neither do you.'

'Malcom and his gruesome Politics mates inside the bar definitely seem to have no notion of that,' says Douglas. 'I asked Malcom at a TITE class break once what post-structuralism means, because he'd been going on about it, and to explain it he just threw around a lot of other half-baked terms.'

'And if you asked him to explain those, it would be more of the same,' says Miles. 'You can't ever pin them down to anything concrete.'

'Speaking of the titty, have you all passed your probation now?' asks Ren.

'I have,' says Douglas.

'Me too,' says Lily.

'And me,' says Miles.

'You too, Miles?' says Ren. 'How did you pass it? You only did one year of TITE.'

'I got a letter the other day saying I had passed probation, but that the University expects me to finish the second year of the course at a later stage.'

'Hah! As if you're ever going to do that!' says Ren.

'Might be a good idea to do it,' says Lily. 'If Miles wants to get a job at another University they might want you to have a degree like TITE.'

'I think I'll take my chances,' says Miles. 'I'm not ever going back into that class again.'

'So did you not pass probation, Ren?' asks Lily. 'You don't look like you're going anywhere, though.'

'His bags are packed and in his office. He has to be off-campus by midnight tonight or security will throw him out,' says Miles.

'My letter said that I have passed probation, subject to me passing the first year of the TITE. Not the whole thing, any more, at least. But until I do a year of it I'm still on probation.

'So how is the University treating you now over Lucius?' says Lily.

'They still haven't decided whether I'm a hero or a villain. They're not kicking me out for not doing TITE. So I won that battle. Sort of. But they're not letting me off TITE either. I stay in probation limbo until I've done a year of it.'

'So are you going to do it?' says Lily.

'No.'

'But you don't want to stay on probation forever. You're more vulnerable to being sacked if you're still on probation. Even quasi-probation. You want to get made permanent.'

'I just need to get promoted. Then my probation will be removed.'

'Are you sure about that? Maybe they'll stop you being promoted until you've passed probation.'

'That's not what I've been told. There's nothing in the contract about that. I've been told that you can become Senior Lecturer even if you're still on probation, and if you're promoted then probation is considered to have been achieved.'

'Are you likely to get promoted soon?' says Douglas.

'A year or two. I'm publishing loads.'

'Still in philosophy of science?'

'Metaphysics and philosophy of science, as I have often told you.'

'Sorry, my mind just blocks the term "metaphysics" for some reason.'

'I've published more in three years than most philosophers publish in a lifetime. Not doing TITE has helped with that, it's given me more time. Although it's mostly to do with innate genius.'

'How have you managed to publish anything?' says

Douglas. 'You're always drunk.'

'I'm always drunk when I see you, because those are get-togethers for the express purpose of drinking. I'm not always drunk when I'm working in my office.'

'He's only drunk sometimes in his office,' says Miles.

'Are you one of those academics who pretend they do no work, who get publications without even trying, but secretly you're beavering away day and night to get things out?' says Douglas.

'I don't pretend I do no work,' says Ren. 'You're under an illusion about that because of the social circumstances you mostly see me in.'

'Yeah,' says Miles, 'Ren balances things nicely. One hour of working. Then one hour of drinking. Then one hour of working. Then another hour of drinking. And so on.'

'I think there are lots of the opposite type of academic,' says Lily.

'You mean one hour of drinking, and then one hour of working?' says Miles. 'That's more my style.'

'I mean the academic who makes out that they work a lot, but really they do very little.'

'I think Bill Porterfield in my department is like that,' says Ren. 'Every time I see him he says he's so busy, got so much on, so much admin, so many papers he's working on, but he never seems to do anything. And he has a light admin load.'

'How come you're publishing so much, Ren, when you claim that Philosophy is not even what you want to do in life?' asks Douglas. 'What's motivating you to put so much after-hours work in?'

'I figured that if I was going to be stuck in Philosophy for a while then I might as well put in a few years hard work and get myself onto the next salary band. Then I can coast in comfort while I work out how to get myself out.'

'Sounds to me like a recipe for getting yourself further entrapped,' says Lily.

'He's too lazy to work out what he really should be

doing,' says Miles.

'So you're saying I'm working hard because I'm lazy?' says Ren.

'Yes,' says Miles. 'It's also avoidance.'

'Avoidance of what?'

'Avoidance of a lot of things,' says Miles. 'Do you want me to list them?'

'Hey, there's Garrett from your department, Douglas,' says Ren.

'Just in time for your round, Garrett,' says Douglas.

'Bugger,' says Garrett, who goes off, and then comes back with more drinks.

'How's that twat of a head of your department going, Garrett?' says Miles.

'Beresford?' says Garrett. 'Still a twat.'

'Taking twatness to new places?' says Ren.

'He's a pioneer,' says Douglas. 'He discovers places that you didn't think anyone could be a twat in, and somehow he manages it.'

'Perhaps he's built a time machine, and he goes back in time to study his past behaviour,' says Ren. 'He observes himself being a twat, and he thinks, that was pretty good, but I could have been even more of twat had I done such-and-such. So he goes back again, replaces his former past self with a new past self, and does the such-and-such instead.'

'I think he's just a natural,' says Garrett.

'What have you been up to then, Garrett?' says Miles.

'I'm writing a book examining global warming from the perspective of a physicist. Not much in it, as far as I can see.'

'Really?' says Lily. 'Isn't global warming settled fact now?'

'It's nothing of the sort,' says Garrett. 'Nothing stands up to scrutiny. You should see the dodgy tree ring data. And the computer models that give you a hockey stick whatever data you enter. The constant manipulation of the temperature records. The refusal to release raw data so that other people can analyse it. It's about as solid as the Nazi's world ice theory.'

'You can't publish that,' says Miles. 'You'll be crucified.'

'Nonsense,' says Garrett. 'It'll be objective science. No scientist can object to that.'

'You're very wide-eyed,' says Ren. 'I admire you and I'm not saying don't do it, I'd like to see it published, but you don't know what you're getting yourself in for. It'll be the end of your career.'

'But I'm not a right-winger who's saying this because he wants unrestricted capitalism.'

'Oh, for fuck's sake,' says Ren.

'I've been a member of the Labour party all my life,' says Garrett, ignoring Ren, 'that's no secret, so I'm still on the right side. This will be about science, not politics.'

'The fact that you said "the right side" is the reason why you should be scared,' says Ren. 'Publish it because you're brave, great. But I hope you're not going to publish it because you're an innocent fawn.'

'You don't give working scientists enough credit, Ren. You spend too much time looking at all these weirdo scientists when you do your philosophy of science. The rest of us normal scientists can make decisions without politics getting in the way.'

'Global warming is mostly about politics, Garrett, rather than science. Why do you think it is that the global warming theory, which as you say evaporates under serious scrutiny, has become the mandatory opinion?'

'Well, we'll see. I'm not scared.'

'Nice knowing you,' says Ren, shaking Garrett's hand. 'Finally an Arts guy can say to a Science guy that you need to practise saying "Do you want fries with that?"'

'Can you get another round Garrett, before you lose all your money?' says Miles.

'No, if I'm to be poor, as you seem to think, then you can get the round in.'

A few rounds later on, the sun makes a surprise late

burst for record books, and even a blinking Malcom and his Politics stablemates come outside. A toast is made to the end of the teaching for the semester, and to the sun. A bet is held on whether Malcom will shrivel up and die as the rays of the sun hit him. Toasts are made to three of them getting through their probation. A toast is made to Ren for not getting sacked for not doing the TITE. A toast is made to Garrett and his book and his bravery/stupidity. A couple of nearby female Psych students with glowing faces try to lasso Miles with their halos. (This is metaphorical talk; they aren't wearing fancy-dress.) Gay Jay turns up for one drink, but the student bar isn't a place he wants to be once teaching has finished, so he doesn't stay long.

Then the cosmic architect spills some toner across the sky while changing the celestial laser printer's cartridge. One moment the sun was centre-stage, threatening a spring sunburn for anyone who didn't respect her, the next moment the electric light bulbs around the bar entrance seem very bright in the gloom.

Despite his incessant talking Ren starts to become abstracted from the scene. He feels himself being drawn back, watching the outside bar scene from a distance, and then his mind is gradually drawn upwards. He can see all of the academics and students of Grayvington at their end-of-term parties all over Baron Heights, and in the surrounding student suburbs, and in Tinfields in the inner city.

He goes higher still, and across the country he sees, lit up, all the University cities and towns. He sees all the University parties that are happening tonight across the land, all full of academics and students drinking and talking in the chipboard student bars and the uncleanable student houses and the soft-lit, tasteful academic homes. There's Deadly Hedley, the Beagle, trying to get a handsome young male graduate student away from the Longford Philosophy department's party. There's Jason at the LSE, boring a bunch of grad students by going on about EU economic policy. (Unfortunately for Ren the female grad student who was thinking of seducing Jason tonight has now changed her mind.) There's the Grayvington Radical Thinkers Society party, full of students doing nothing but admonishing one another for their wrongthought. There's Millicent, admonishing herself, as she fends off the advances of a lesbian colleague, for her failure to embrace more correct modes of being. And then admonishing herself some more for her thought that maybe if the colleague was better-looking she might be tempted. There's Ken and Halberd mingling as normal at a social psych party – they have had to renounce any association with Ren in order to be accepted back into their social psych milieu (their integrity only goes so far.) There's some cute female Psychology students in a corner at a student party talking and giggling about Miles's arse, and giving their ratings for the sexual attractiveness of the other male Psychology lecturers. There's Mika, one of Ren's old Oxford MCR sparring partners, hosting a party for some fellow thought-dodgers as they plan new ways to protest against the greatest threat to humanity in the modern world: Israel. There's Violet Wells, at home for the summer break, all alone, who's swapped staring at the dirty ceiling in her tiny college room for staring at the clean ceiling in her much larger bedroom at her parent's place. There's Fitzroy Donleavy, a vague young Philosophy lecturer who Ren knows from conferences, smoking dope and trying to make his ideas understood to his fellow smokers. There's the TV don Helena Bosquet in her SCR, having a little drinks party where right-thinking members of the TV industry are introduced to right-thinking members of the academy. There's Lucius Birch, no longer in academia – the story is that he's become a backroom boy for a mental health charity – drinking at home alone and plotting his revenge on Ren. There's the VC, Niall Raven, and his gorgeous but bored wife Dymphia, hosting a party at Cathradean Hall for some other VCs, and promising Pro-VCs, and New Labour politicians, and a few Conservatives who are more at home in this company than in their own party. Dymphia is wondering whether any of the guests are worth seducing – there are so many rooms there that Niall would never find her even if he got suspicious and went looking.

Ren wonders how many there are in those parties who are like him. And how many other Garretts are there, prepared to go against the grain on modern shibboleths like global warming? What will happen when Garrett's book comes out? What will Grayvington be revealed to be like, once the heretic self-exposes? Even in his four years here he can see that Grayvington is becoming even more left-wing. The leftism is of the corporate, progressive type, a smoothed-over type of Cultural Marxism, but it's still leftism, and dissent from the party line is being gradually squeezed out, like air bubbles trapped behind a sticker of the University being pushed towards the edges with a University purchase card. He gives it ten years – ten years, or maybe fifteen – until the cultural left gets a complete stranglehold on the Universities, as well as more of a grip on society, and individual political opinions are stamped upon. Conquest's Second Law of Politics has it that every institution that is not explicitly right-wing sooner or later becomes left-wing. That even seems to apply even to institutions that are explicitly right-wing, so left-leaning places like Universities have no chance. Especially Grayvington, with its ruthless New Labour Vice Chancellor, and its sixties expansion departments with their corridors of posters with fists and slogans on them, and its unhappy students who resent the fact that it's only Grayvington they get to complain about, rather than Oxford or Cambridge.

Until then, though, Ren is content to drift. He drifts through the air from imaginary party to imaginary party, listening in on the conversations, in the same way that the general direction of his life is drifting. For the time being he lets the imaginary astral winds blow him about however they will, while he absent-mindedly fondles the almost-conscious belief that this state of intoxicated pleasure can last for decades while his body and mind stay young and unchanging.

He remains in this trance-like state for an age, until his consciousness spreads out so far that it eventually becomes indistinguishable from unconsciousness, and the tenuous control it has over his body finally breaks. Miles and Douglas take his body – for all they know it may be his former body – via taxi, to Miles' place, where it is deposited on the floor while Miles and Douglas put on some music and drink whisky. Before they get so drunk that their minds follow Ren's path, they put a pillow under his head, and a bottle of water next to him, in readiness for his rude awakening tomorrow. For his scattered motes of consciousness will eventually regroup, and will eventually re-animate his creaking, reluctant corpse, and thrust him back into the fray.

For the latest updates on the author, visit:

www.hectordrummond.com

39126594R00230

Printed in Poland
by Amazon Fulfillment
Poland Sp. z o.o., Wrocław